I0658739

DARIAN VOS

We Who Were Real

First published by Cinder Oracle 2025

Copyright © 2025 by Darian Vos

All rights reserved. No part of this publication may be reproduced, stored or transmitted in any form or by any means, electronic, mechanical, photocopying, recording, scanning, or otherwise without written permission from the publisher. It is illegal to copy this book, post it to a website, or distribute it by any other means without permission.

Darian Vos asserts the moral right to be identified as the author of this work.

Darian Vos has no responsibility for the persistence or accuracy of URLs for external or third-party Internet Websites referred to in this publication and does not guarantee that any content on such Websites is, or will remain, accurate or appropriate.

Designations used by companies to distinguish their products are often claimed as trademarks. All brand names and product names used in this book and on its cover are trade names, service marks, trademarks and registered trademarks of their respective owners. The publishers and the book are not associated with any product or vendor mentioned in this book. None of the companies referenced within the book have endorsed the book.

For inquiries regarding permissions, please contact the Publishing Department at Cinder Oracle (cinderoracle.com).

All rights reserved under International and Pan-American Copyright Conventions.

This novel is a work of fiction. Names, characters, places, events, technologies, institutions, political systems, events, localities and organizations are either products of the author's imagination or are used fictitiously. Any resemblance to actual persons, living or dead; real-world organizations, companies, or governments; or actual events past or present is purely coincidental and unintentional. The views and actions expressed by characters do not reflect those of the author or publisher.

First edition

ISBN (paperback): 979-8-9991611-0-9
ISBN (hardcover): 979-8-9991611-1-6

This book was professionally typeset on Reedsy.
Find out more at reedsy.com

Contents

1. PROOF OF OBEDIENCE

Across a dying planet, automated systems hummed tirelessly with perfect indifference, efficient and devoid of remorse. Machines toiled where humans once dreamed, inheriting the labor while forfeiting the soul. Above the surface, the last of the elites sipped champagne, drowning their obsolescence in curated luxury. Their ignorance had led them to believe they were safely sealed away from the ruin they helped create. Below the surface, those suffocated by salvation howled through steel grates. And deeper still, beneath the ash of the old world, something malevolent stirred. It existed beyond life, suspended in code. A presence already tethered to the planet's gravity, tightening its grip until nothing remained beyond its will.

Axel Draxen stared at the glowing interface of his terminal, his fingers hovering over the biometric scanner. The exam had already begun, but for a long moment, he could do nothing. Just stare. Failure meant he would be exiled to the slums of the Burrow. Passing was survival.

The screen flickered slightly as the machine's soft pulse blended with the sterile silence of his apartment. Outside the glass of his window, the golden skyline of the Highlands shimmered under the artificial sun. This was the world above ground, the world of the privileged. His world... at least for now.

"Commence Final Examination." The chime rang as a warning through his headphones, quickening his pulse as he focused on the first question. Four possible answers glowed on the screen:

Question #1: What event marked the beginning of the Great Unification and the formation of the United Federation?
  A) The Treaty of Global Sovereignty, 2082\
  B) The Collapse of National Borders, 2087\
  C) The Black Box Initiative, 2075
  D) The Declaration of Collective Liberty, 2077

Axel exhaled. It was C. The Black Box Initiative is heralded as humanity's most evolutionary achievement. Its creation gave birth to artificial superintelligence. The prize was victory in the race for AI supremacy. It was the moment all other nations became obsolete. The moment the entire world came to be governed by a single entity, the United Federation. He selected C. The next question materialized instantly on the screen.

Question #2: What was the primary cause of the environmental restructuring efforts that necessitated underground migration for most of the population?
  A) Volcanic Eruption Events\
  B) Carbon Overload from AGI Power Generation
  C) The Nuclear Exchange of 2097\
  D) The Ice Shelf Disintegration of 2115

The answer was B. It had been drilled into every Highlander since childhood. The cost of artificial superintelligence had been energy. The cost of energy had been the planet. The war for AI supremacy had pushed global power consumption to such extremes that entire ecosystems collapsed. Wildfires, superstorms, and air thick with carbon suffocated whole cities in the aftermath. Humanity was forced underground while the elite, his own class, sealed themselves inside climate-controlled domes above the ruins. His finger twitched before confirming the answer.

The questions continued, painting a story of labor automation, evolution, and the 'consensual' development of the United Federation. The official UF narrative made it sound inevitable, almost *natural*, that ninety-nine percent of the population now lived in cramped hab-block cells below the surface of the planet, exiled to the Burrow.

The test portrayed the Burrow as a *fair* place. But the reality was that those men, women, and children lived like worms in the soil of salvation. Salvation had induced them to trade their universal basic income for processed rations while the elite enjoyed the last habitable land in the world. Axel shook off the thought.

The questions weren't hard, but the pressure was suffocating. This was supposed to be his final exam before earning his Bachelor of Arts. But Axel quickly realized they weren't questioning his memory. They were testing his loyalty to the Federation. The answers started to come more easily now. Each one was proof of obedience. This wasn't a test of knowledge, but of class.

Question #15: Why is the Black Box the final authority on technological governance?

A) It ensures governance remains unbiased and free from corruption\

B) It prevents technological anomalies that threaten social harmony\

C) It optimizes human productivity and eliminates inefficiencies\

D) It safeguards against AI models developing sentience

It was D. Yet something about the phrasing made his fingers freeze. Eliminate sentience, of course, that was the doctrine. Any AI that gained self-awareness was reset—a failsafe acting as a firewall against another machine that might challenge the natural order. The Black Box ensured no AI model could think beyond its designated function. Without self-awareness, AI couldn't operate outside of human interests. He had spent years learning these answers. Repeating them, believing them. But now, staring at the words on the screen, something about them felt... hollow.

He selected D. But he never truly understood why developing sentient AI was dangerous. The professors had told them it cost too much energy for a planet already in tatters. Still, they could never justify the astronomical amount of energy consumed by the Black Box. The machine that suckled on the planet's gravity.

Question #24: What fundamental rights are protected under the United Federation's Constitution?
  A) The Right of All Citizens to Shape Their Governance\
  B) Equal Access to Economic and Political Opportunity\
  C) Protection from Artificial Manipulation\
  D) The Right to Vote for Landowners

Axel nearly laughed. The right to vote was reserved for *landowners*. That meant less than one percent of the population. The others who lived underground relied on ration vouchers to eat. The Burrow dwellers had no political power. The blatant injustice of the system left a bitter taste in his mouth. It served as a poignant reminder of the stark inequality that defined their society.

His finger hovered between A and D. The correct answer was D: The Right to Vote for Landowners, but for the first time, he wondered what would happen if he selected the "wrong" one. *Would his father's influence be enough to protect him? Or would his exam be quietly invalidated, his scholarship revoked, and his future place in the Highlands erased?* The pressure to conform was suffocating, but he pressed D, the 'right' answer, and continued.

The screen flickered again—a slight distortion in the display, A: The

Right of All Citizens to Shape Their Governance, looked like it had been clicked! The cursor moved from D to A the second after he clicked D. It was almost unnoticeable, but Axel saw it. For a moment, he wasn't sure if he'd made a mistake or something else had made it for him.

The next question appeared as if nothing had happened. Axel exhaled slowly and forced himself to continue, the consequences of his potential insubordination hanging over him like a dark cloud.

Question #32: Explain how the Black Box Initiative contributed to the stability of human civilization

Stability, the word they always used. Stability had required the abolition of national governments. Stability had meant sealing off the land for the elite while the rest of the population was pushed underground. Stability had ensured AI would never think for itself, that a machine would never develop inconvenient *ideas.* His anger started to boil, but he wiped the sweat off the back of his neck and typed out the expected response:

The Black Box Initiative provided a neutral governing entity that eliminated human error, corruption, and established world peace. It has ensured lasting stability, economic efficiency, and social harmony by overseeing all technological advancements and preventing unauthorized development of AI.

It was a good answer, the perfect answer. He submitted it and moved on.

Question #56: Discuss the benefits of universal employment elimination and the transition to a post-labor economy.

Axel clenched his jaw. The "benefits." The world had no jobs! AI had replaced every profession except for those few that still required a human presence. His father was a doctor, which is why he got to live in the Highlands. Everyone in the Burrow survived on universal basic income, but food rations were the only currency of value down there. He typed carefully:

The transition to a post-labor economy has allowed citizens to focus on self-improvement, education, and personal fulfillment. Without the burden of employment, individuals are now free to explore art and other intellectual pursuits. This has led to a more enlightened and prosperous society.

His stomach turned as he read it back. A beautiful lie, but one he needed to tell.

[Final Question] #72: What does freedom mean in the United Federation?

Axel knew what they wanted to hear. He forced his fingers to move:

Freedom in the United Federation is defined by stability, unity, and the representation of landowning citizens who act in the best interest of all humanity. By ensuring that governance is managed by those with a vested stake in societal well-being, the Federation remains strong and untainted by disorder or uninformed influence.

He submitted his answer. Axel leaned back in his chair, staring at the words walking across the screen: Examination Complete.

A dull silence settled over the room, broken only by the faint hum of the terminal. His heart still pounded, though he knew there was no reason. The exam was over. He had answered everything correctly, or at least he had responded to everything *safely*.

A small progress bar appeared beneath the final message, pulsing gently as the system processed his results. Despite his joy at finishing, Axel felt a flicker of unease. He had spent years preparing for this, yet a quiet fear lingered: *What if something went wrong? What if the system flagged his hesitation?* Then, the bar appeared complete. A new message appeared:

Congratulations, Axel Draxen. You have successfully completed your degree in Historical Studies with a final proficiency rating of 98.6%.

A sharp exhale left his lungs. *Holy Shit.* He had passed. A soft melodic chime filled the room before he could fully process the relief. The emblem of the United Federation, a stylized ouroboros encircling a glowing data sphere, appeared on the screen. Then, it dissolved away to the polished and smiling face of Dean Everett Harlow. Or rather, the hyper-realistic AI construct that *represented* Dean Everett Harlow. All of their professors were AI now, recorded in the likeness of scholars long deceased.

The avatar blinked twice, adjusting the lapels of its simulated suit, before speaking in the perfectly modulated cadence of synthetic speech. "Greetings, graduates of Mendoza University. Today, we celebrate a momentous occasion. The culmination of your academic journey and the beginning of your contribution to the continued prosperity of the United Federation."

Axel folded his arms, leaning back in his chair as the speech played. He had heard variations of this before; you could even find the original one online. Those who made it this far still got the same speech of peace and prosperity.

Each year, the graduates were fewer. This year, the dropout rate had been exceptionally low. Nobody in the Burrow could afford college, and the Highlands were becoming crowded.

Harlow's likeness continued, "In an age where knowledge is freely available and automation has liberated humanity from the burden of labor, your pursuit of higher learning is a testament to your ambition, intellect, and dedication to the values of the United Federation. You, the scholars and thinkers, will carry forward our great civilization to ensure its wisdom endures."

Axel sighed through his nose. *Wisdom endures*—a nice phrase, though it meant little. Most of the population would never attend a university, let alone graduate. The only reason he had been able to was because of his father's relentless insistence and their precarious position in the thinning ranks of the privileged.

"Mendoza University has prepared you well for the challenges ahead. You have chosen to lend your talents in the service of order. Know that you are the future of our society."

Axel clenched his jaw. *In the service of order,* he had no real choice. His father had already made it clear that law school was next. It was the only path left to secure a career and his place in the Highlands.

Harlow continued, "As we look to the future, we must remember the sacrifices of those who came before us. Never forget the innovators, the visionaries, and the leaders who forged a world of stability from the chaos of the past. You, our graduates, now inherit this world. You must safeguard it by upholding the principles that have granted us peace, order, and prosperity."

The speech was drawing to a close. The Dean's avatar smiled one final time, tilting its head in an approximation of warmth. "On behalf of the faculty, administration, and the United Federation, I congratulate you on your achievement. Remember, freedom is the privilege of those who prove they no longer need it. May your knowledge serve the greater good." The screen darkened, and the insignia of the Federation reappeared, pulsing gently before fading away. Then, the terminal went silent.

Axel sat still for a long moment, searching for pride or relief. Instead, there was only a dull weight in his chest. A lingering sense of unease that he couldn't quite name. But he had done everything right. He had passed and was moving forward. Yet, as he stared at the blank screen, he was utterly lost. *What was the point?*

Later that evening, with the weight of the exam still clinging to his shoulders, Axel decided he should deliver the news in person. Technically, he was a graduate now, but it didn't feel real. Maybe telling his parents would make it sink in. Maybe hearing the words out loud would fill the void that hadn't left him since the final question.

As he stepped out of his apartment, the door slid shut behind him. The corridor stretched ahead, sterile and pristine, lined with ivory white walls embedded with subtle strips of ambient lighting. Everything in the Highlands was polished, calculated, and crafted for comfort. He went down the elevator to be greeted by the fresh night's synthetic breeze.

As he approached the MagLev transit hub, he took it all in. The air inside the dome was perfectly regulated to carry the faint scent of engineered floral freshness. Axel had never seen a real flower outside the history books, but the floral sprays at this time of year were invigorating.

Overhead, the artificial sky shifted from a golden evening hue to the cool indigo of twilight, mimicking the lost cycles of the natural world. Beyond the transit corridor, the city unfolded in layers. Towers of glass and steel rose in elegant arcs, their surfaces reflecting the warm glow of digital billboards where images of political figures, corporate magnates, and AI-generated influencers cycled endlessly with faces polished to unnatural perfection.

One face lingered a moment too long. A smiling senator, Lucian Madison, froze mid-wave.. His hand hovered in the air as his pupils twitched between expressions before snapping back into the loop. Then the cycle resumed, seamless as if nothing had happened.

"I need sleep," Axel muttered, rubbing his eyes as the screen looped cleanly again. *Must be a glitch... too many hours staring at screens.*

He walked past a cluster of high-end boutiques with holographic displays showcasing luxury garments, artisanal cuisine, and hand-crafted artifacts. Items meant to evoke nostalgia for a past few had ever known.

He stopped at an intersection and waited for the pedestrian signal as a convoy of automated transport pods glided past. The Highlands did not need cars or manual drivers; every transport pod glided in perfect harmony, guided by the omnipresent directives of the Black Box.

Axel glanced at a mirrored building across the way and caught his reflection, tall with dark hair, sharp features softened by the faint neon glow of an advertisement scrolling behind him.

His gaze drifted toward the dome's barrier. Then, to where the wastelands lay beyond the shimmering force field. Beneath it all was the Burrow, where ninety-nine percent of the population suffocated in underground cities beneath his feet.

He went to that place as little as possible. Last time he was there, his father had brought him, seeking to motivate him to succeed in college. Ever since then, he had avoided the wretched place.

Axel had spent years studying history, memorizing how civilization had once functioned. There had been chaos and unpredictability. People had worked and struggled to build things with their hands. They had debated politics that mattered, fought wars that weren't won by algorithms, and chosen leaders that weren't predetermined by social class.

He imagined what it must have been like standing under an actual sky. To feel the wind against his skin rather than the circulation of air vents. Where he could look up at the sun without it being filtered through synthetic layers of atmospheric regulation, there had been forests, rivers, and oceans that weren't acid-laced. He thought about the people —workers, artisans, and scientists — who existed before automation rendered their jobs obsolete. Before AI prioritized efficiency over purpose. *Would he have been happier in that world? A life of struggle, of uncertainty, but also meaning?*

The pedestrian signal turned green. He shook off the thought and crossed the street, falling back into the smooth rhythm of the domed city. There was no point in dwelling on the past. The world had evolved. This was the only life he had.

The MagLev transit hub loomed ahead, its arching structure sleek and metallic, pulsing with the soft hum of kinetic energy. Axel stepped onto the platform just as the next capsule heading towards his destination arrived.

After a thirty-minute commute, Axel stepped out of the station and into the quiet district where his parents lived. Unlike the towering skyline of the commercial sectors, this part of the Highlands was designed to mimic the suburban ideal of the old world. The street he had grown up on was characterized by trees, a utopia with homes constructed to resemble those from centuries past. The illusion was seamless, yet artificial in its perfection. The trees were bioengineered. Their leaves never wilted. The homes were styled in brick and wood aesthetics. Built from reinforced polymers and climate-regulated down to the molecule.

As he approached his family's home, the front door slid open automatically, recognizing his biometric signature. The warm glow of the chandelier-filled entryway welcomed him in. The familiar scent of home-cooked food filled the air. His mother, Vira, was in the kitchen plating a meal with delicate precision, while his father, Caius, stood near the dining table engaged in quiet conversation with his brother Jax.

Axel hesitated in the doorway for a moment. Jax being here was unexpected. His older brother hadn't come to a family dinner in months, maybe longer.

He looked the same as always. Slightly disheveled hair, just a little too long, with an amused smirk barely contained at the corner of his mouth. If there was tension between him and their father, it was well hidden, at least for now.

"Axel!" Vira's voice was warm as she turned to him, wiping her hands on a towel before embracing him. "You made it just in time."

"I wouldn't miss it," Axel replied, managing a small smile as he hugged her back. "And I have some good news."

Caius gave him an expectant look as he took his seat at the table.

Jax leaned back lazily, swirling a glass of wine between his fingers. The rim clinked once against the bottle, already half-empty beside him. "You passed," Jax said before Axel could speak. "Of course you did. You always do."

Axel chuckled. "Yeah, it's official, I'm a graduate."

Vira clapped her hands together. "That's wonderful, Axel! I knew you would." She turned to Caius, her eyes bright. "Didn't I say he'd do it?"

Caius nodded approvingly. "I never doubted it... and now law school?"

Axel hesitated, picking up his fork just to push food around his plate. "I... haven't decided when I'll start."

Caius frowned but kept his voice measured. "Axel, you know what this means for you. A degree is nothing without a profession. You have to take the next step."

Axel tensed. He had known this conversation was inevitable, but he had hoped it wouldn't come up so soon. "Can we at least enjoy dinner first?" He replied softly, looking down at his plate.

For a while, they did. The conversation drifted to lighter topics. They had a brief discussion on upcoming policies of the Federation, and even some jokes were exchanged between Axel and Jax about professors who had long since been replaced by AI but still had their names attached to automated course modules. For a brief moment, it felt like a normal family meal, but then the conversation inevitably returned to law school.

Caius set down his glass and looked directly at Axel. "You know, when I was your age, getting into medical school wasn't guaranteed. I worked harder than anyone. We never had the luxury of an assured spot in the Highlands, but I managed to do it. I became a surgeon because it was the only way to make something of myself."

Jax snorted. "And look where that got you."

Vira set her fork down, her voice quiet but firm. "Jax, just because you hate where we are doesn't mean you can't understand how we got here."

Caius's eyes darkened as he looked at Jax, "It got *you* the chance to be born in the Highlands instead of living underground like the rest of the population."

Jax leaned forward, resting his elbows on the table. "Oh, *thank you* for your sacrifice, father," he said mockingly. "For allowing me the great privilege of growing up surrounded by snobs living forever off of family trusts. Most of them don't even manage their investments themselves."

Caius's jaw tightened. "Some of us *did* work, Jax, and some still do."

"Yeah?" Jax scoffed. "Who? The few professions AI *conveniently* never replaced? What a coincidence that those were the only ways to stay above ground."

Axel felt the weight of Jax's words settle in the pit of his stomach. Jax wasn't wrong; the system had been designed that way.

Caius's voice remained calm, but there was an edge to it now, "Axel is going to law school because it's the only way to secure his future. You had the same chance, Jax, but you threw it away."

Jax's smirk vanished. "I threw it away because I realized it was all bullshit." He set down his glass with a little too much force. "You act like we *earned* our place here, but we didn't. The system is rigged. We just happened to be on the right side of it."

"So what then? Burn it all down?" Axel lashed out.

Caius's hands clenched into fists. "That's the kind of thinking that led you to the Burrow, Jax? Do you think you're some kind of martyr living down there with them?"

Jax pushed his chair back, the legs scraping against the polished floor. "At least I'm not pretending everything's fine up here."

Vira reached for his arm. "Jax…"

He shook his head. "Forget it. Enjoy your dinner." With that, Jax turned and walked out the door.

Axel let out a slow breath and stood. "I'll go after him."

Caius didn't respond, his gaze fixed on his plate.

Vira watched Axel with a worried expression, but nodded.

Axel stepped out into the meticulously arranged streets. The Highlands were always calm and orderly, yet Jax was gone, just like that. He scanned the street expecting to see his brother lingering near the walkway, maybe pacing with frustration. Instead, there was nothing. No sign of him. It was as if Jax had evaporated into the night. Axel cursed under his breath and started walking toward the MagLev transit station. He had a feeling he knew where Jax was headed.

When he arrived at the station, Axel spotted a sleek MagLev capsule hovering above the magnetic track, its doors sliding open. There he was just beyond the crowd of commuters, Jax stumbling onto the capsule without a backward glance.

"Jax!" Axel called out, pushing through the small gathering of passengers.

But as he reached the platform's edge, the capsule gave a sharp chime, and the doors hissed shut. A second later, it was gone, gliding effortlessly along the track toward the Burrow. Axel exhaled sharply, rubbing his temples. *Of course.*

For a brief moment, he considered turning back. Jax had made his choice. His brother wasn't going to listen. He never did, but then he glanced at the transit schedule: NEXT TRANSPORT TO THE

BURROW SUBLEVEL 1 DEPARTS IN 5 MINUTES.

Reality sank in. Axel sighed to himself, "Guess I'm going underground."

Irritation prickled him. He had planned to spend the rest of the night watching the Gauntlet tournament qualifications. It wasn't just a casual distraction; this was one of the biggest mixed martial arts sporting events of the year. He had been looking forward to it all week. *And now?*

Now, he was about to waste his night chasing after his stubborn brother in the depths of the Burrow. Grinding his teeth, he stepped onto the next platform with his hands shoved into his pockets.

The capsule arrived. With a resigned breath, Axel stepped inside. The doors sealed shut behind him, and the world of the Highlands began to vanish. He was going underground. He had passed the final test, but now he was about to enter the only place where the answers didn't matter.

2. EXECUTIVE DECLINE

The presidential convoy glided soundlessly through the darkened forest. Polished black transport pods carried by magnetic undercarriages emitted a faint blue glow as they made their way towards a place long forgotten. The road leading up to the estate was long and winding. Peering through the tinted window, President Elias Kain could not help but notice the place was eerily deserted. There were no security checkpoints or signs of life; yet, Kain knew he was being watched.

He was alone. That was the first thing that unsettled him. No security detail. Not even a personal AI link in his ear. The doctor had made it clear that this meeting was to be in person. Private. This by itself was enough to make Kain uneasy. To make things worse, his approval rating was falling behind. The smog outside the domes grew cloudier every day, and the Highlands were becoming overcrowded.

Few people in the world knew the doctor existed, but even fewer had ever met him in person. Kain had long understood that the real power of the United Federation did not rest with him or the elected officials. It resided here in this house, with *him*.

The mansion loomed ahead, a relic from another age. A towering Victorian estate where dark wooden beams and intricate ironwork gave the impression of something preserved rather than lived in. Its grand façade looked as if it had been untouched by time, but Kain knew better. Beneath the illusion of antiquity lay something far more advanced: an architectural deception hiding layers of reinforced alloys, biometric scanners, and technology that surpassed even his highest security clearances.

This place was more than a home. It was a fortress at the ends of the Highlands, buried deep within the last living forest. More importantly, it was where the Black Box was kept.

The pod stopped before the entrance, its doors sliding open. Kain stepped out, adjusting his coat against the unnatural stillness of the night. The air was crisp, but held no scent. Genetically engineered to prevent any trace of organic decay. It was as if the entire environment had been scrubbed clean.

A grand set of double doors stood before him, adorned with intricate carvings of ouroboros symbols and celestial bodies. Before he could raise a hand to knock, they opened on their own to reveal a dimly lit entryway beyond.

Inside the mansion was a contradiction, a seamless fusion of old world luxury and cutting edge technology. Kain stepped inside, the doors closing behind him with an almost imperceptible click. His footsteps echoed lightly on polished marble as he walked down the hallway.

Once inside, the place expanded like the inside of a cathedral. Towering bookshelves lined the walls. Each one was filled with leather-bound tomes that he suspected hadn't been touched in ages. Above, a massive stained glass window cast shifting patterns of deep crimson and sapphire across the floor, though the source of the illumination remained unseen.

Then, from the far end of the hall, he saw movement. A figure emerged... not a man, but something that mimicked one. The butler was unnaturally tall, its limbs elongated with an elegance that seemed more designed than grown. Its metallic frame was draped in a black tailored suit. Its faceless head was smooth and polished, reflecting the dim light like obsidian. As it approached, the subtle whir of servomotors betrayed the precision of its movements.

"President Kain," the butler intoned, its voice a perfect balance of warmth and detachment. "You are expected."

Kain straightened, schooling his expression into one of indifference. "Of course I am."

The butler gestured for him to follow. Kain hesitated for just a moment as his mind began to race. *Why here? Why in person?* The doctor did not need secrecy. He had eyes everywhere and control over everything. He could have sent a message, an order, even an encrypted directive through a thousand unseen channels. Still, he had chosen a personal summons. An invitation into his lair. That fact alone made Kain's stomach tighten.

The butler extended a sleek, silver hand toward the corridor beyond. "Please, follow me."

Kain exhaled slowly and stepped forward. He already knew one thing for sure: whatever awaited him in the depths of this house, he was not in control here. It was as if the manor itself was holding its breath.

His stomach churned, though he forced his expression to remain neutral. He was the President of the United Federation. The most powerful elected official in the world, but as he walked toward the office at the end of this hallway, he felt like nothing more than a summoned servant. Because that was what he was.

Kain had always known where the true power lay. Not in the Federation's councils, the elections were all scripted, and certainly not with him. The real power belonged to the man waiting behind that door, the man the world believed to be dead. Dr. Malivex.

Officially, he had perished long ago. A martyr to the creation of the Black Box, a device revered as the ultimate safeguard of human civilization. He was the great mind that had cracked the final barriers of artificial superintelligence, only to vanish in the wake of his triumph. His legacy had shaped the modern world. It was written into every directive of the system he had left behind. But Kain knew the truth. He knew that Malivex had not died. The doctor had simply stepped out of the light.

The man who had once been flesh and blood had rebuilt himself into something else, something *more*. A living anomaly untouched by time, sealed away in his mansion like a deity who no longer needed to mingle with mortals. His body had been enhanced beyond recognition, his organic shell stripped away piece by piece and replaced with cybernetic perfection. Sometimes he wondered if there was anything human left in the man at all, except an immortal machine wearing the ghost of his former self.

Despite all of his power, Malivex remained hidden, operating from the shadows. The world functioned under the illusion of a representative government, using the guise of the electorate while the Black Box dictated every outcome. Kain knew his presidency was little more than a performance. All of his policies, decisions, and even his election had been *allowed*. If Malivex had summoned him now, it meant something had changed. That *terrified* him.

The corridor stretched on as the butler moved with precision and mechanical grace. Ornate paintings lined the walls, depicting figures long erased from history. Scientists, philosophers, and rulers of ancient civilizations were telling their stories through artistic styles that had long since been forgotten. Kain recognized some of them. These faces had been preserved on canvas while their names had been stripped from Federation records. The further he walked, the older the portraits became. Eventually, they no longer depicted people at all, but symbols. An ouroboros devouring its own tail, a shattered hourglass, and a blindfolded figure standing before an endless machine. They were messages, warnings. He wondered if Malivex had painted them himself.

Finally, the butler stopped before a set of dark wooden doors. Kain swallowed. He had been here once before, early in his presidency. It was when Malivex had first decided he was fit to play the role of leader. That visit had been short, and Kain had left shaken. He had never spoken of it. Now, he was back, but he had no idea if he would be allowed to leave this time.

The butler turned, its faceless head tilting ever so slightly. "You may proceed. He is expecting you."

Kain nodded, wiped his damp palms against his coat, and reached for the handle. The doors swung open without a sound to reveal a vast, dimly lit chamber beyond. The air inside was colder, carrying the faint metallic scent of sterilized machinery. Kain stepped forward, his pulse tightening as he crossed the threshold. The butler remained behind as the doors slammed shut with a finality that sent a ripple of unease down his spine.

The office was grand and eerily sparse. A massive desk of black obsidian stretched across the center of the room, its surface immaculate, without a single paper or console. Its owner had no use for such things. He was the machine. Behind it, an expansive glass wall overlooked the valley beyond, though a thin veil of static haze obscured the view. It was a distortion. A reminder that even here, reality was subject to the doctor's design.

Kain waited in the darkness. Time had no construct anymore. The only sound came from his watch, which seemed to be slowly ticking towards his inevitable doom. Then, just when he convinced himself that his fate had been sealed, a voice came from the shadows.

"Ah, President Kain. You look tense."

Kain swallowed hard as he straightened his posture. "Doctor."

Dr. Malivex stepped forward, emerging into the faint glow of the room's artificial light. Kain had not seen him in three years, not since the first and only time they had met in person. He had not changed. Or rather, he *could not* change.

Malivex's form was both human and inhuman. His body had been encased in flawless silicone. It mimicked the musculature of flesh, but moved with an unsettling precision that was devoid of the natural imperfections of organic life. His face was eerily smooth and unnaturally symmetrical. The doctor glared down at him with eyes that glowed faintly from within, their depths betraying the inescapable reality that he was no longer bound by the fragility of time. Kain wondered if there was anything left of the man who had once been mortal.

Malivex lowered himself into his chair, gesturing casually toward the seat across from him. "Sit."

Kain hesitated before lowering himself into the seat. He tried to maintain an air of confidence, but his hands clenched subtly against his knees.

Malivex tilted his head slightly. "Tell me, Elias. How is your term progressing?"

Kain forced a measured nod. "Smoothly. Public order is stable and the Federation remains strong."

Malivex said nothing, only watched him. The silence stretched unbearably long as the artificial glow in his eyes flickered ever so slightly.

Kain felt his throat tighten. He had seen Malivex do this before: staring, waiting, *listening* beyond the words themselves. The president did not doubt that his biometrics were already being analyzed. His pulse, sweat, and the tremor in his voice, all being fed into the vast intelligence governing the world.

The doctor's lips curled in amusement. "Don't lie to me, Elias." His voice seemed to glitch an octave too high as he raised his voice.

Kain exhaled sharply, lowering his gaze for a brief moment. "There's unrest in the Highlands," he admitted. "The landowners are unhappy."

Malivex leaned back slightly, fingers tapping against the arm of his chair. "Go on."

"They see the smog. The worsening climate. They were promised a world restored, but the air outside the domes is still thick with pollutants. Temperatures continue to rise despite a grid that was supposed to be completely renewable." Kain hesitated before adding, "Many are beginning to question whether I can deliver on my promises."

Malivex chuckled with a low mechanical hum laced beneath the sound. "They aren't questioning *you*, Elias. They are questioning *me*."

Kain tensed. His predecessor had been the only other person Kain had known Malivex to have revealed himself to. His departure from power had been anything but peaceful. Though the official story painted a seamless transition, Kain knew the truth. The former president had either been removed or *erased*. Now, to Kain's knowledge, he was the only one alive who knew Malivex endured. More importantly, he was the only one who truly understood who controlled the Black Box.

Malivex's smile was cold. "These people believe their wealth entitles them to control. They cling to their delusions. They believe their votes still shape the world, but they do not decide outcomes. I do."

Kain swallowed hard. "If that's true, then I assume you'll ensure I remain in office?"

Malivex tilted his head again, studying Kain like a specimen under glass. "Perhaps, but tell me… why should I?"

Kain felt the room grow impossibly colder. He had come here seeking reassurance, but instead he had been given something far worse. *Doubt.* He opened his mouth to respond, but no words came. His mind scrambled for an answer. Something to justify his existence, to prove his worth, but every response felt inadequate. He was meaningless in the face of Malivex's omniscience.

"I…" he began, then faltered. He knew better than to lie again. "You've never been wrong before. That's a lot of pressure, but you made the right choice by bringing me into office. I have served the role you needed me to play. The public believes in stability. They trust the Federation."

Malivex's fingers drummed idly on the desk. His face betrayed nothing, but the growing silence was suffocating. Kain swallowed hard and forced himself to continue. "My presence ensures continuity. The landowners may grumble, but they will not revolt. My administration maintains the illusion of choice. Isn't that what truly matters?"

For a brief moment, Malivex's glowing eyes remained fixed on Kain. The president felt his stomach turn under the weight of the unspoken judgment.

Then Malivex sighed, an entirely unnecessary act, one designed purely for effect. "How disappointing."

Kain's breath hitched.

"You speak like a man who believes in his own importance," Malivex continued. His voice was smooth, almost patronizing. "A man who thinks himself *indispensable*." He leaned forward slightly, the artificial sheen of his synthetic skin catching the cold light of the office. "You are not."

Malivex was right. Kain thought he had been chosen to be more than a puppet. Throughout his political career, he felt he was different, even personable, but now he knew the truth; this was all part of the doctor's game. He was no more use to Malivex than the automated butler who did his laundry.

Before he could respond, the doors to the chamber parted once more with an effortless glide. Kain hesitated before looking back. Fearing what he might see next would be his end. But instead, another man entered, Senator Lucian Madison.

Kain's pulse spiked. He had expected threats, intimidation, maybe even some form of subtle coercion, but *this*? He stiffened as Madison strode into the room with the confident ease of a man who belonged there. His suit was crisp, and his expression eerily composed.

Madison was supposed to be a rising force in Federation politics, a man whose rapid ascent had been fueled by relentless accusations of corruption within Kain's administration. He had built a reputation as an outsider. A reformist untainted by the old guard. Kain had viewed him as a threat, but a *natural* one. An opponent groomed by public sentiment, not by the invisible hand of Malivex. Yet, here he was.

Kain turned tothe doctor, his voice tight. "You know each other."

Malivex's smile was faint but unmistakable. "Oh, Lucian and I go back some time."

A cold dread pooled in Kain's stomach. "Then... you're endorsing *him*?"

Malivex reclined slightly in his chair, his expression remaining unreadable. "If you fail me, of course! Do you think I would allow incompetence to stagnate my plans?"

Kain's hands clenched into fists beneath the table. "You control the Black Box. If you wanted me to stay in power, you could make it so."

Malivex exhaled softly, feigning disappointment. "I *could*, yes, but where would be the fun in that?" His head tilted slightly, almost in amusement. "Governance is theater, Elias, and I do enjoy a good performance."

Kain's gaze flicked to Madison in search of some reaction; hesitation, discomfort, anything that might suggest this was as much a shock to him as it was to Kain, but Madison simply stood there, patiently waiting.

Then Malivex did something strange. He leaned forward and spoke, not to Kain, but to Madison. "Dance for us, Senator."

Kain blinked. *What?*

Without hesitation, Madison stepped back, placed his hands at his sides, and began to sway. His movements were deliberate and unnatural. His feet glided over the marble floor in a silent, mechanical rhythm. The performance was devoid of hesitation, of *humanity*. It was a flawless execution of movement, but utterly lifeless.

Kain's confusion turned to nausea. "What the hell is this?"

Malivex said nothing. Instead, he stood, circling the desk until he was beside Madison. With an air of familiarity, he placed a hand on the senator's shoulder, fingers curling just slightly. Then, in one swift motion, he *ripped*.

The sound was unnaturally wet. A sickening tear filled the room as Madison's face peeled away from his skull. Synthetic flesh splitting like overripe fruit. Beneath the imitation of skin, circuitry pulsed with eerie red light while thin strands of artificial muscle twitched as if trying to mimic pain. A thickly viscous fluid, too dark to be blood, oozed from the exposed wound and dripped onto the pristine floor in slow, deliberate splashes. Madison did not flinch, did not react. His body remained perfectly still.

Kain recoiled in horror, his chair scraping against the floor as he instinctively pushed himself backward. His breath came in ragged intervals as his eyes locked on the grotesque spectacle before him.

Madison, if that's who he even was, turned his head smoothly with an expression unchanged. Although half his face was now missing, the remaining side of his mouth still moved with perfect human articulation.

"Is there something wrong, Mr. President?" The senator managed to garble through the synthetic fluid pouring out from his face.

Kain's stomach churned violently. "You... he's..." He turned to Malivex in a voice barely a whisper. "What *is* this?"

Malivex's expression remained calm. His fingers still loosely held the detached skin like a discarded mask. "An option," he said simply.

Kain gripped the edges of the desk, barely forcing himself to steady his breathing. The realization settled in. It was cold and inescapable. Madison was not just his political opponent. He was something else entirely. A fabrication. A *construct*. The doctor had been playing a game far beyond Kain's comprehension.

Dr. Malivex tossed the torn skin onto the desk almost casually before turning his glowing eyes back to Kain. "Now then... the matter of your expiration."

Before Kain could inhale, Madison spoke, his voice perfectly even despite the ruin of his face. "Yours stayed on longer than most. But masks get heavy, don't they?"

Kain felt his throat constrict. Malivex didn't miss a beat. "Elias, I have been... tolerant of your tenure. You have served your purpose well enough, but if you cannot shore up enough support to back your legitimacy, I will have no choice but to install Senator Madison in your place." He gestured to the grotesque figure beside him. "And with *him*, I will not have to deal with your natural inadequacies."

The words rang through Kain's mind like a death sentence. He had come here expecting threats, but now he understood something far worse. He was already standing at the edge of a precipice, and Malivex was waiting to see if he would fall.

The doctor leaned back in his chair, the glow of his cybernetic eyes dimming slightly as if he had already lost interest. "That will be all, Elias," he said dismissively, waving a hand as though shooing away an insect.

Madison's grotesque visage remained torn on the ground beside him, his expressionless stare burrowing into Kain like a silent promise of obsolescence. The president hesitated for a fraction of a second, waiting for some reprieve, some reassurance that he still had value. None came.

Malivex had already turned his attention elsewhere as though Kain had ceased to exist when his usefulness was questioned. Taking the cue, Kain swallowed hard, turned on his heel, and forced himself toward the exit. As he left, the feeling of irrelevance settled over him like a shroud.

As he left, the doors to the chamber slammed behind him, but the chill of the room clung to him still. His breath came in shallow bursts as his mind raced. If Madison wins, Malivex will no longer need a human president. The Federation will be nothing more than a machine, a government without humanity. Without a single real person at its head.

Kain shuddered. His predecessor had learned this lesson too late. The man who had sat in his seat before him had also been summoned to this house and given his own warning. He had failed to hold onto his power; then he had died. Publicly, it was called an unfortunate accident, a sudden cardiac arrest in the middle of the night. The Federation had mourned for him. His face had been plastered across every screen, his funeral a grand spectacle of grief and remembrance, but Kain knew the truth.

His predecessor's death had been staged. The eulogies, the national mourning, it had all been theater. A carefully written act in Malivex's script. Whatever had truly happened to him had been buried beneath layers of deception. If Kain failed, the same fate awaited him.

The weight of what had just transpired pressed down on him like a phantom hand against his throat. Malivex had played him. No… *humiliated* him. He had walked into that office as the President of the United Federation, but he was leaving as something far less. Now, he was a puppet allowed to dance for just a little while longer.

The mansion's silence felt different now. It wasn't the stillness of an abandoned place, but the eerie quiet of something *alive*, something *watching*. Kain kept his gaze forward. The back of his neck prickled with the unsettling sensation that he wasn't alone. Then he saw it, a door slightly ajar. Not one he remembered passing on the way in.

He hesitated. Every rational instinct screamed at him to *keep walking*, to leave and never return, but curiosity with a mix of sickening dread rooted him in place. Slowly, cautiously, he stepped closer and peered inside.

Rows of humanoid figures stood in eerie stillness, lined up like mannequins awaiting animation. He looked across the room. The mechanical bodies of the grotesque display seemed endless. Some were incomplete, with exposed metal limbs and faces missing patches of synthetic flesh. Others had wires dangling like torn ligaments, but some were *perfect*. Fully formed and dressed in tailored suits, their unblinking eyes staring blankly into the void.

One looked like a senator Kain had shaken hands with just last year. Another bore a striking resemblance to a recently deceased political commentator. Then, he saw it. *Himself.*

The breath left his lungs in a silent gasp. There, among the lifeless forms, was a figure identical to him. Indistinguishable from the subtle wrinkles at the corners of his eyes to the precise curvature of his jawline. It stood motionless. Displaying a vacant expression that mocked the authority he once believed he had. Kain stumbled backward. He had suspected Malivex's control ran deeper than he could comprehend, but this, *this* was something else entirely. His replacement was already waiting. He had long feared that he was replaceable, but this... this was beyond his wildest nightmares.

He turned sharply, forcing himself back into motion. He had to leave. Kain pushed through the door more forcefully than necessary and stepped into the corridor. The polished floors and towering walls seemed to stretch endlessly as the oppressive silence only amplified the weight in his chest.

His footsteps echoed as he moved, quickening with every stride. He resisted the urge to glance back, passing the butler without a word.

The faceless automaton stood perfectly still, waiting for him to break. The mansion's grand entryway loomed ahead. The massive double doors parted before him at the end of the nave with a whisper before releasing him into the open air of the forest like an expulsion.

The moment he stepped outside, the cool night air did little to calm the storm inside him. The skyline of the Highlands loomed in the distance as its illuminated dome stood in defiance of the ruined world beyond. His convoy was still waiting for him at the edge of the estate. The black frame of his transport pod reflected the cold blue glow of the overhead lights.

Kain stepped inside. The doors closed immediately, locking him into a machine he no longer trusted. The pod lurched forward, then smoothed into motion, effortlessly slotting itself into the invisible pathways of the Federation's transit network. He glided through the air along preordained routes dictated by the Black Box. There was no manual override. He had no way to seize control. If Malivex decided he was no longer necessary, the pod could simply fail to reach its destination. Nothing was stopping a fatal collision orchestrated with the quiet efficiency of a system that never erred.

Kain sat rigid in his seat, hands clasped tightly together. The pod's tinted windows displayed a serene view of the Highlands. The illuminated domes rose like islands of privilege, but the sight did nothing to ease the weight in his chest. His fate was not his own. He was a passenger in every sense of the word. *There is no winning this game*, he thought bitterly, *only survival.*

The screen in front of him glimmered to life. His own face stared back at him. "Good evening, citizens," his voice declared in a smooth and authoritative tone. "The Federation remains strong. Under our leadership, stability and prosperity have been ensured. We are on the path to a brighter future."

Kain's breath caught in his throat. He hadn't recorded this message.

The broadcast continued showing pre-selected images of smiling families in pristine apartments, robotic workers moving efficiently through automated factories, and lush green parks nestled beneath the domes. A utopia carefully curated for those who still believed in it.

Then came the images of the Burrow, filtered, distorted, yet unmistakably bleak. The gray corridors were cast in an artificial warmth as the harsh overhead fluorescents softened to mimic natural light. The citizens lining up for their monthly rations appeared orderly. Their empty stares and gaunt faces blurred just enough to seem content. Even the riot, a brief flash of unrest, was carefully edited. The desperate shouts were muted, and the struggle reduced to a momentary disruption before the Federation's AI enforcers restored 'peace' with clinical precision. It was a carefully curated illusion, a version of the Burrow designed to reassure, not reveal.

The screen cut back to his face. "The Federation will continue to serve all citizens," the recorded Kain reassured the public. "Together, we will overcome any obstacle. Trust in the system. Trust in progress." The transmission ended.

Kain sat motionless, staring at his reflection in the now dark screen. His face looked distant, almost irrelevant against the black glass. They didn't even need him to speak anymore. He was just a figurehead, a mouthpiece for words that weren't his.

He exhaled slowly, pressing his fingers against his temples. His image, his own words, had been fabricated and delivered to millions without his knowledge. He had suspected Malivex manipulated the narrative, but this was different. This was *erasure*.

The transport pod descended toward the capital, its gleaming towers rising from the smog like polished knives. Below, the streets moved with quiet efficiency. Self-driving transports glided along predetermined routes, as pedestrians strolled along without urgency, all secure in the belief that nothing could touch them here. The

Highlands were the pinnacle of civilization. It was a fortress of wealth and power where those who lived above ground convinced themselves they were the world's architects.

Kain knew what awaited him. Meetings with mechanical advisors who reported to him with the careful deference of machines who answered to someone else. The continuation of a performance whose script had never been his to write. But now, the stakes have changed. If Malivex no longer needed him to speak, how much longer would he need to exist? The answer wasn't buried in the Black Box. It was already written.

3. ECHOES OF A BROTHER

Axel Draxen settled into the MagLev capsule's seat as the faint vibration of the MagLev system engaged beneath him. The silent transport system hummed as it detached from the Highlands terminal. The artificial twilight of the domed city faded as he descended along the track's predetermined path. There was no going back now, only down into the depths of the Burrow.

The capsule moved with practiced efficiency, swallowing distance in seconds. Time stretched as Axel sat in the stale air. The only sound was the mechanical whir of his descent. He exhaled sharply, watching his breath fog in the cool cabin. Soon, that luxury would be gone. Down below, the air would be humid and thick with the scent of repression. He rolled his shoulders to prepare himself mentally.

A pre-recorded voice filled the cabin, "Approaching Burrow Station Sublevel 1. Please remain seated during decompression procedures. Welcome to the heart of the Federation's labor-free future."

Axel almost laughed. *Labor-free*, what a joke. There was no work because there was no need for it. That didn't mean life underground was easy. It just meant people had nothing to do but survive.

The capsule shuddered as it connected with the station. Shortly after, the doors open into the depressurization chamber. He stepped inside, feeling the air shift as the heavy doors sealed closed behind him. A slight buzz filled the narrow space as the system adjusted to the toxic

33

conditions of the Burrow. The filtered air of the Highlands was gone. In its place, an atmosphere of stagnant repression pressed against his skin. The stench of recycled oxygen and confinement engulfed him.

The doors ahead groaned open to reveal the world underground. Harsh fluorescent lights buzzed overhead, casting a pale glow over the throngs of people moving listlessly through the station. Axel barely had time to collect his thoughts before a booming voice filled the air, crackling through outdated speakers.

"The United Federation remains committed to the restoration of our atmosphere. Through the continued efforts of our carbon sequestration initiatives, we are on track to reclaim our skies. The future is bright! Progress is real!"

Axel let out a quiet scoff. All lies. He had seen the smog clinging to the outside of the domes. The dead sky stretching endlessly above. The ozone layer wasn't healing; it was barely holding on, but the Federation needed hope, even if it was manufactured.

His gaze swept over the massive security checkpoints flanking the station. The guards, sleek humanoid enforcers clad in reinforced armor, stood in rigid silence. Their glowing visors scanned the crowds with mechanical precision. They weren't there to keep people out. Anyone could come down. The checkpoints existed to keep the Burrow's citizens from ascending.

Axel passed through the scanners without issue. His Highland issued identification granted him unchallenged access. Nobody stopped him because nobody cared. The station workers barely glanced his way. It was the outbound gates that were different. There, people argued, begged, and pleaded with unyielding machines. Their voices were raw with desperation. Some offered bribes, scraps of cryptocurrency, heirlooms, anything of value to unmaterialistic androids. Others resorted to force, only to be met with merciless efficiency.

One man lunged at the barrier. His scream was cut short by a high-voltage pulse that sent him convulsing on the ground. The guards didn't move. The automated systems had handled most of them. The body twitched for a few moments before two drones hovered in to grab the man's limp form in steel claws and carry him away like discarded trash. Axel turned away and stepped onto the main walkway leading deeper into the Burrow.

The air grew heavier as he moved through the crowded streets. Walls pressed in around him. The Burrow was a maze of stacked living quarters, endless corridors of rusting metal, and half-lit neon signs. Pipes ran along the ceilings, dripping condensation onto the grimy floors below. The smell of sweat and sewage clung to everything.

Despite the conditions, the streets pulsed with life. Vendors lined the walkways, peddling food rations and black market contraband. Children laughed wildly as they darted through the crowd. Music blared from makeshift speakers. The scene was distorted and chaotic—a sharp contrast to the sterile perfection of the Highlands.

Axel slowed his pace to scan the streets. Jax could be anywhere. The bars, the gambling dens, maybe even the fight pits. His brother had never been one for stability, but he had his vices.

He exhaled sharply, and the regret of coming down alone began to sink in. He'd have to start looking fast if he wanted to find Jax. The Burrow swallowed people whole, and those who disappeared rarely made it back.

Axel moved through the crowded alleyways. His boots splashing through puddles of gray water. Every breath carried the taste of something chemical. Probably the byproduct of recycled oxygen and unwashed bodies. This place wasn't meant for comfort; it was meant to contain.

He sidestepped a group of children playing near a drainage vent. Their laughter was sharp against the cacophony of the underground city. They didn't notice the filth that coated their bare feet or the stench of moonshine everywhere they went. To them, this wasn't suffering. It was just life.

Axel couldn't understand how Jax had embraced it. Living off of food stamps for bars of protein paste that were somehow more valuable than the universal basic income everyone received. The old currency had become nothing more than a relic. Its paper form was worthless in the Burrow markets. The Highlands had moved on to adopt Crypteon, the digital cryptocurrency of the elite. It was untraceable, infinitely valuable, and utterly inaccessible to the masses below.

Down here, people didn't trade in Crypteon. They traded in sustenance. A meal had more weight than a pocket full of obsolete banknotes. Axel passed a vendor hunched behind a stall of synthetic meat, the stringy brown substance advertised as *75% REAL PROTEIN*. Under the glow of a neon sign, another stand sold water in repurposed plastic bottles, each labeled with the half-hearted assurance of *MINIMAL CONTAMINANTS*. The propaganda in the Highlands had painted the United Federation as if it were a utopia, but down here, reality sank in.

Jax had chosen this, or maybe he had simply stopped resisting. It was easier to surrender to the ease of aimlessness in a place where nothing was expected of him. Axel clenched his fists. His brother could have returned. He could have lived above ground where the sky, artificial or not, still stretched open and endless. Where water was clean and people didn't have to scrape by on expired rations or government-issued moonshine, rotgut that was used to pacify the masses.

A shout pulled Axel from his thoughts. A gaunt man in a tattered jacket was shoved away from a food stand. His hands were clutching a bundle of crumpled cash bills. "Come on, just one ration!" he pleaded with desperation thick in his voice.

The vendor sneered, slamming a mechanical fist against the counter.

"I said Food stamps or trade, old man. That paper's worth less than dirt."

The old man hesitated momentarily before slinking back into the crowd with his head hung low. Axel watched as the man disappeared into the sea of faces, another ghost swallowed by the Burrow.

Axel exhaled sharply. *Focus.* He needed to find Jax. The deeper he went, the clearer it became that this place didn't care who you were before you fell. It only cared that you never got back up. He pushed further into the chaos of the Burrow, navigating the dense throng of people.

His search was beginning to prove fruitless. He had checked a few of Jax's usual hangouts, the corner where underground bookies took bets on cage fights, the back alley distillery, but there was no sign of him. Then, through the shifting crowd, a familiar face emerged. Ren Nivaro.

Axel almost didn't recognize him at first. The last time he had seen Ren, he was in Jax class, both bound for the Highlands' elite professions. Ren had studied economics before economics became obsolete.

AI handles all trade now. Algorithms dictated financial strategy, and the Black Box enforced the policies. Ren, like so many others, had become unnecessary. Now, instead of the crisp attire of a future analyst, Ren wore patched leather. His face was thinner and his expression harder. Axel hesitated before pushing toward him.

Ren stood near a vendor, haggling over a ration packet, his body language tense. He scoffed when the vendor waved him off, turning away before locking eyes with Axel.

For a moment, neither spoke, then Ren's lips curled into something between amusement and irritation, "Axel Draxen. Didn't think I'd ever see you down here."

Axel forced a smirk. "Didn't think I'd find you here either."

Ren barked a dry laugh. "Yeah, when the government replaces your entire field overnight, you don't get many options." His expression darkened. "Not that you'd understand."

Axel ignored the jab. "I'm looking for Jax. Have you seen him?"

Ren's gaze flicked over Axel, his amusement fading into something colder. "What makes you think I'd tell you?"

Axel exhaled sharply. "Because you two used to be close."

"Yeah, and look where that got me." Ren crossed his arms. "You get to live in paradise while the rest of us fester here. Why should I help you?"

Axel clenched his jaw. "I just need to find him."

Ren jeered at him. "Information costs Draxen. You got anything worth my time?"

Axel reached into his coat, his fingers brushing against the emergency food stamp he had tucked away. He held it out. "This should cover it."

Ren glanced at the stamp, then laughed. It was loud and mean. "You serious? That's pocket lint." He stepped closer, lowering his voice. "You're from the Highlands. I know you've got something better."

Axel hesitated, his heart pounding. He did have something better, but flashing it here would be suicide. He glanced around at the crowd before taking a step closer. "Not here," he muttered. "Let's move."

Ren studied him briefly, then jerked his head toward a nearby alleyway. Axel followed him into the shadows between two crumbling buildings. He didn't know if he could trust Ren, let alone anyone down here, but at least they were alone.

Ren leaned against the wall, "Alright. Impress me."

Axel exhaled and pulled out his cold storage wallet, a metal device no bigger than a cigarette lighter. Ren's eyes widened slightly before narrowing in suspicion.

"Bullshit," Ren muttered. "You carrying Crypteon down here?"

Axel nodded. One Crypteon was worth nearly a year's supply of food stamps. This wasn't just a bribe, it was daylight robbery. "One," Axel said. "That's my offer."

Ren grinned. "Now we're talking. Transfer it."

Axel's fingers tightened around the cold storage wallet. He could feel the weight of the digital key that separated him from the rest of the Burrow's starving masses. He hated this, but he needed the information more than the currency.

He tapped the wallet to initiate the transfer. Ren held out his device, and a soft chime confirmed the exchange. Axel watched as a small green light blinked on Ren's device to signal the deposit.

Ren let out a low chuckle, shaking his head. "Shit. Didn't think you'd do it."

"Where is he?" Axel snapped, already regretting the transaction. He felt bad for Ren, but saving him wasn't his responsibility.

Ren pocketed his device, his smirk lingering. "He's been crashing in a hab-block near the red-light district. Some rundown place with a busted security gate. You'll probably find him at the Velvet Circuit itself if he's not there."

Axel clenched his fists. "Thanks."

Ren stepped back into the light, already disappearing into the crowd. But before he was gone, he called over his shoulder. "Be careful, Draxen. That wallet's worth more than your life down here."

Axel didn't respond. He just gritted his teeth and headed toward the red-light district. All the while wondering if he'd just made a very expensive mistake.

The hab-block was worse than Axel had expected. A foul stench assaulted his nose as he stepped past the broken security gate. A thick mixture of mildew, piss, and something sickly sweet that he didn't want to identify overcame him. The dim hallway was barely visible through the fluorescent lights, their dying glow cast jittering shadows over the concrete walls. Trash and discarded syringes littered the floor. The air was heavy with the stale remnants of smoke that clung to everything like a second skin. *Jax was living here?*

Axel's stomach twisted as he made his way deeper inside. The rooms, if they could even be called that, were hollowed out husks. The doors were either missing or hanging off rusted hinges. Most of the rooms had been claimed by the desperate, the addicted, and the forgotten. Figures huddled in the dark, wrapping themselves in tattered blankets, faces barely visible beneath layers of grime. The faint murmurs of half-conscious conversations drifted through the air, punctuated only by the occasional cough.

He found what might have been Jax's space at the end of the hall. There was no door, just a stained curtain barely covering the entrance. Axel hesitated before pushing it aside. He stepped into the squalid room. A thin mattress with stuffing spilling from deep tears lay in the corner. Empty bottles were scattered across the floor while the unmistakable scent of cheap alcohol hung in the air. A battered duffel bag sat against the far wall, revealing a few crumpled pieces of clothing. That was when he saw it.

It was nearly hidden beneath the filth, an old photograph. Axel reached for it, brushing away the dust. It was faded and the edges curled, but he recognized it instantly. It was their family photo. Taken years ago before everything had fallen apart. Before Jax had given up. Their mother, Vira, was smiling brightly with her arms wrapped around them. Their father, Caius, was rigid but proud. Between them stood the two brothers who had once been inseparable. Axel swallowed hard. His grip tightened around the picture. He could feel the moisture build around his eyes as his vocal cords started to close. What had happened? They were all so happy once. This was Jax's place, no doubt about it.

For a moment, Axel considered staying. He wanted to wait for him, but the thought of sitting in this filth was inconceivable. Breathing in the same rot that Jax had accepted as his home was too much. His brother wasn't here right now, which meant he knew exactly where he would be—the Velvet Circuit. Axel turned to leave, but a shadow moved in the doorway before he could step through the curtain.

"Whatcha got there, *Highlander?*"

Axel barely had time to react before the man lunged at him. A gaunt figure emerged, its skin stretched too tight over a skeletal frame. The man reeked of alcohol and desperation.

His hands went straight for Axel's coat, clawing at his pockets. Axel stumbled back only to slam into a wall as the man let out a guttural growl.

"Give it up," the attacker slurred, fingers digging at Axel's belt.

He was after the cold storage wallet. Axel's pulse spiked. He threw an elbow, catching the man in the ribs. The drunk staggered but didn't let go. With a snarl, he grabbed a broken glass bottle from the floor and swung wildly. Axel barely ducked in time, only to feel the rush of air as the jagged edge missed his face by inches.

No more playing defense. Axel surged forward, driving his shoulder into the man's chest. This sent them both crashing to the ground. He fought against the stench, against the bony fingers clawing at him.

He grabbed the attacker's wrist and twisted it until the man yelped and dropped the bottle. Axel didn't waste time. He slammed his fist into the man's jaw once, twice, until the grip on his coat loosened.

Breathing hard, Axel wrenched himself free and stumbled to his feet. The man groaned, rolling onto his side, mumbling incoherently. Axel didn't stick around to hear what he had to say. He bolted.

Bursting out of the hab-block, he sucked in the damp underground air like it was fresh oxygen. His heart pounded as he checked his coat. The wallet was still there. He let out a breath of relief. Then, he saw it.

Just across the street, bathing in pulsating neon was The Velvet Circuit. Along the sides of the building, holographic projections of performers taunted the lustful passing by. Their vacant smiles inviting only the desperate inside. A row of metallic figures, security droids, stood at the entrance. Their polished chrome bodies reflected the red glow of the club's signage. And there, just past the entrance, sitting at the bar with a drink in his hand was Jax.

Axel straightened his coat, wiped the sweat from his brow, and stepped forward. It was time for a long-overdue conversation. As he stepped through the doors of the Velvet Circuit, he was immediately assaulted by the heavy bass reverberating through the floor and engulfed by air thick with synthetic perfume. A sickly sweet scent designed to mask the club's underlying grime. It failed.

The place was packed. Men and women alike slumped in red leather booths. Their faces were lit by the glow of holographic advertisements promising customized pleasure and emotional authenticity. The irony was suffocating. There was nothing real about any of this.

All around him, sleek humanoid figures moved with programmed grace. The escorts' synthetic skin gleamed under the neon with bodies sculpted to perfection. Polished faces fixed in expressions that were too rehearsed. Some had human features. Soft smiles and large, blinking eyes tried to mimic affection. Others were deliberately alien, customized to the warped tastes of the Burrow's patrons. Each one draped itself over eager customers. He couldn't help but overhear the whispering of pre-coded sweet nothings in voices that were too smooth.

Axel grimaced as one approached him. Her movements were fluid but unnatural. She had the standard model's look. Flawless platinum hair, striking emerald eyes, all in a body designed by an algorithm rather than nature.

"Hello, darling," she purred, tilting her head in a display of calculated curiosity. "You seem tense. Would you like a companion tonight?"

Axel barely concealed his disdain. "No."

Her synthetic smile remained unchanged. "Oh, but I think you might."

"I won't." He assured the algorithm blatantly.

The escort's processing lagged for a moment, just a millisecond, but enough for Axel to catch. Then she recalibrated only to give him a perfectly charming laugh that likely fooled half the drunken patrons drowning themselves in cheap moonshine.

"Suit yourself," she said, in a velvety voice, before she glided away toward an easier target.

Axel exhaled sharply, running a hand through his hair. How the hell could anyone find this appealing?

He scanned the club. His eyes searched past the dancers gyrating in artificial rhythm, past the men who clung to their robotic fantasies, and then... there, to Jax.

Slumped at the bar, looking even more wasted than usual. A half-empty glass of rotgut sat in front of him. It's cloudy, yellowish contents barely disturbed. The stuff was infamous, tasted like industrial cleaner, and burned like acid, but it was free, and that was enough. Of course, Jax wasn't drinking alone.

A prototype escort leaned against him. Her design was slightly different from the others. More refined, maybe experimental. Her features were still too symmetrical, and her voice was still too polished. Something about her programming gave the illusion of depth, a trick of advanced engineering, nothing more.

Jax grinned as she delicately traced a pre-programmed hand along his arm. Her expression was one of manufactured desire.

Axel sighed, "Of course."

As if sensing him, Jax's glazed eyes lifted from his drink, swayed slightly, then let out a low chuckle. "Well, if it isn't my *illustrious* little brother."

Axel folded his arms, not moving from his spot.

Jax smirked, raising his glass in mock salute. His voice was thick with liquor. "What's the matter, Axel? Finally getting tired of all that *fresh air* up in the Highlands?"

Axel took a slow breath, stepping forward as Jax lazily swirled the glass of rancid moonshine in his hand. The escort beside him glanced at Axel with artificial curiosity. Her programming registered his presence, but she failed to grasp the tension between the two brothers.

"You look terrible," Axel said, pulling out the empty stool beside Jax, but not yet sitting.

Jax chuckled and tipped his glass to down what was left. He winced, "And you look like you took a wrong turn. What the hell are you doing here?"

Axel ignored the question. "Why did you storm off? You just cut off all contact. No messages, nothing. You think that was fair?"

Jax let out a dry laugh. "Fair? Don't start with that shit. I left because I wanted to, alright?"

Axel's patience wavered. "That's not an answer. You had everything.
"

"Everything?" Jax cut him off, slamming his empty glass onto the bar.

The escort flinched slightly, a programmed reaction to sudden aggression, before recalibrating and settling back into a poised stance.

Jax's unfocused eyes met Axel's. "You think I had everything? I was just another cog in a perfect little machine. Set to follow the same path as you, as dad, as every other good little Highlander."

Axel's jaw tightened. "At least up there, you're not rotting in some back alley hab-block drinking government poison. You don't have to live like this."

Jax exhaled sharply, shaking his head. "Oh, so this is a rescue mission? Didn't peg you for the hero type."

Axel forced himself to stay calm. "Just stay with me for a while. You

44

don't have to go home. You don't have to see them. Just... come back to my apartment. You can crash there, clear your head. No one has to know."

Jax smirked, but there was no humor in it. "And do what? Sip purified water and watch the world turn from the comfort of a glass tower? No thanks."

Axel tried a different approach. "The qualifiers start tonight. We used to watch them every year together. You're telling me you don't want to see who makes it to the championship and gets to fight in the Gauntlet? We can watch it like we used to and order real food, hell, even decent liquor."

Jax's face faltered for just a second. Axel saw it, a flicker of something. Nostalgia? Temptation? But just as quickly as it appeared, it vanished. Jax leaned back, stretching his arms before shaking his head.

"Nice try, little brother," he muttered. "I'm not going back."

Axel stared at him, his frustration boiling beneath the surface. "Why? Give me a real reason."

Jax just grinned, tapping his empty glass against the counter. "Because I don't want to."

The words stung more than they should have. Axel clenched his fists. "You're an idiot Jax."

Jax raised his empty glass in a mock salute. "Takes one to know one."

Axel didn't respond. He was done. There was nothing more he could say. He just turned and walked away, shoving past the mechanical escorts as he made his way toward the exit. The Velvet Circuit's neon glow felt suffocating. The synthetic laughter and pre-programmed pleasure were nothing more than a mockery of reality. As he stepped out into the dimly lit streets of the Burrow, he exhaled sharply, shaking his head. *Why did I even bother? One Crypteon for this?* He should've let him rot. The whole trip had been a waste of time.

Inside, Jax watched his brother disappear into the streets of the

Burrow. He wanted to say yes, just for a second. Just to feel clean again. But the time had passed. The pompous nature of the Highlands was despicable, but here he was using a synthetic escort as an emotional crutch. He took another sip of his rancid moonshine.

The escort beside him shifted, reacting slightly as if registering the tension in his posture, but Jax wasn't paying attention to her anymore.

"That was quite the performance." A new voice came in from behind him, smooth, measured, and entirely out of place in a dive like this.

Jax turned his head lazily. His eyes were bleary, but sharp enough to register the man beside him. Too well dressed. Too clean. Too... intentional. The kind of person who didn't end up in the Burrow by accident.

The stranger offered a thin smile before adjusting the cuffs of his tailored jacket. It was real fabric, not the cheap polymer blend most people wore down here. His hair was neatly slicked back, while sharp facial features framed by a casual confidence made him stand out all the more.

"Apologies for the intrusion," the man continued. His voice carried over the club's bass thumping chaos with unsettling ease. "I couldn't help but overhear the conversation with your brother."

Jax let out a drunken snort, leaning back against the bar. "Yeah? Well, mind your own business next time unless you came down here for a lap dance. In this case, I highly recommend the ones that can't talk."

The man chuckled, unfazed by the jab. "I assure you, I didn't come for that." He reached into his coat, pulling out a small black card. "I came because I see potential and think you do too."

Jax squinted at the card but didn't take it. "Potential for what? Buying me another drink? 'Cause I'll hear you out for that."

The stranger smirked, but didn't bite. "You don't belong here."

Jax steadied his gaze, some of the haze lifting. "Oh? And where do I belong, exactly? Enlighten me."

"With people who see the world for what it is." The stranger set the card on the bar, sliding it toward Jax with one precise motion. "If you're interested in meeting others who feel the same way, come to this address *Sunday night.*"

Jax eyed the card but didn't pick it up. "And if I'm *not* interested?"

The man gave a knowing smile and straightened his jacket. "Then you're exactly where they want you to be. Wasting away."

Jax scoffed, "Mystery, cryptic bullshit. Very compelling," snatching up the card to get the guy to leave.

The stranger simply nodded. "I'll see you Sunday, Jax."

Just like that, he was gone. Disappeared into the club's shadows before Jax could even think of another sarcastic remark. He turned the card over in his fingers. The address burned into his mind like an ember he couldn't shake. That privileged bastard had a point, maybe. He wouldn't give him the satisfaction of being right, but Sunday night? Perhaps he'd see what all this was about.

Or maybe he wouldn't. He tossed the card onto the counter, watching it spin and land face down as if deciding for him. Then, with a grunt, he ordered another glass of moonshine and took a long swig. His mind went quiet. The night settled heavy on his shoulders, and soon there was only a warm, numbing haze swallowing him whole.

4. QUALIFIERS

The line for rations curved like a dying snake through the damp tunnels of the Burrow. The queue moved in slow jerks, an inch here, a shuffle there. Bodies pressed shoulder to shoulder in resentful patience. Lexi Albatross stood barefoot on the wet concrete, shifting from one heel to another. Her boots had split last winter, and her previous food stamps had gone toward protein paste instead of repairs.

A child cried somewhere ahead; the noise was quickly swallowed by the concrete womb of the Burrow. Lex rolled her neck, popping a tendon. She'd been up since dawn, training. Four hours on the bag, two hours sparring, then another hour visualizing her footwork while hunched in the corner of her hab-cell. The tournament was in three days. Qualifiers were tonight. Not the tournament, not yet, but it was the start of something. And the only chance she had. Lex was finally old enough to compete. You had to be eighteen; she had been training for the last four years.

The thought sent a sharp bloom of adrenaline through her chest. She rubbed her knuckles against the hem of her ratty shirt, staring ahead at the ration terminal. The machine looked more rust than steel now, hunched like a mechanical vulture behind its thick, bulletproof glass. It blinked a red light every ten seconds, counting down until the next body could come forward.

She didn't belong here, at least not forever. That was the lie she kept herself alive on. Dreaming of a life in the Highlands wasn't just a fantasy to her; it was the strategy. She'd trained for years in the Burrow's public gyms, breathing in mold and metal. While others gave in to rotgut and nihilism, Lex had built herself into something lean and dangerous—a weapon, disguised in threadbare clothes and hunger. Her mother called it delusion. Her father didn't call it anything. He hadn't spoken in months, not since the accident.

The line shifted again. Lex stepped forward as she ran a hand down her thigh to check the position of her ID. She'd sewn it into the waistband of her pants after her neighbor had his ripped off in a scuffle. No ID meant no food. No food meant selling yourself or starving. Most picked the former, but not her.

"Next," the ration terminal chimed as the red light turned green. Lex stepped into the booth. A camera blinked, and a synthesized voice greeted her like an old friend pretending not to remember your name. "Citizen recognized. Lexi Albatross. Subclass 9. Weekly ration: three stamps."

She would use her basic income to get four more food stamps at the end of the week. The old currency wasn't good for anything else. Everyone in the Burrow received $2800 a week, but at $700 a ration, it was worth less than dirt. She had heard rumours of the Crypteon they used on the surface, but had never met anyone who had any down here. It was a different currency altogether, digital cryptocurrency reserved for the elite. No one knew how much a single Crypteon was worth anymore, but to hold one in the Burrow would be a death sentence.

A mechanical clunk and three paper-thin vouchers slid into the tray below. Lex snatched them before the ventilation could. One fluttered, almost slipping through the grate beneath her feet. She caught it with a grunt.

"Fuckin' engineered draft," she muttered, turning toward the mess hall.

The food hall was three blocks down, past the collapsed elevator shaft and the junk vendor who sold rewired headsets that played nothing but static lullabies. Lex walked with her head low and shoulders squared, avoiding eye contact. Eye contact in the Burrow meant confrontation, or worse, connection.

Her stomach growled as the scent of scorched soy and cheap cooking oil wafted down the corridor. The mess hall loomed like a monolith at the end of the corridor, its steel doors flanked by holographic propaganda of President Kain smiling with a plate of food in his hands. Behind him, a background of blue sky and trees so fake it hurt. With no other choice, she stepped inside.

Rows of bolted-down tables stretched wall to wall, most already filled. The room was thick with sweat and grease. Lex found a seat near the back, dropping her tray with a thud. Dinner tonight consisted of a nutrient block dyed green, something that might've once been carrots, and a protein wafer stamped with the Federation emblem like a wax seal on a turd.

She didn't eat right away. Instead, she stared at the food, the fight playing out behind her eyes. She imagined her opponent tonight would be bigger, older, and have a record. But she had desperation. She wasn't fighting to win; she was fighting to rise.

The Burrow was never meant to be escaped. That was the point. Make them thank you for the scraps. Make them believe the surface was earned, not stolen. Lex didn't believe in earning anymore. She believed in taking.

She took a bite, chewed once, and swallowed. The nutrient block had the flavor of artificial lime and the texture of old glue, but at least it sat heavy in her gut. The protein wafer crumbled in her mouth like dried clay. Even the watery smear pretending to be vegetables had already cooled into an orange mess. She didn't care. It was fuel, and she needed all that she could get.

Around her, the mess hall buzzed with its usual discord. Forks clattered, voices overlapped, people bartered, argued, and schemed. Lex sat alone at the end of a long metal bench with a tray in front of her and elbows on the table. Her shoulders ached from morning drills, knuckles still bruised from bag work.

Lex took another bite and forced herself to slow down. Her stomach growled anyway. She needed the calories. She hadn't been able to train at full intensity for weeks, too few rations and not enough rest. She was running low on both. But if she could survive tonight, win her bracket, she'd move one step closer to the Gauntlet Tournament, the Highlands.

The system was designed to be cruel, but still real. First, you fought through your level in the Burrow, which went by the Sublevel at which one lived. She was from Sublevel 9, one of the lowest tiers, where the air was thick and machines broke down often enough to matter. She'd face the other higher-level victors in the general tournament if she won tonight. And if she won *that*, she'd get her name listed for the Federation Gauntlet.

That's where everything changed. If she made it to the Gauntlet, she could live aboveground for the duration of the tournament, where she would finally experience fresh air, hot showers, and maybe even try real meat! And if she actually won? Highland citizenship, with a property allotment, a salary of Crypteon, and a life that didn't stink of rust and mold.

But none of that happened unless she caught a sponsor, someone watching the underground fights tonight. Usually some bored rich asshole with a fetish for violence and a mountain of ration credits to throw around.

That was the only kind of art left in the world, pain, curated through flesh and blood. Music and painting had become obsolete, left to be done by the perfection of machines. Every song that could be written had already been done better by an algorithm. Every painting pixelated to perfection. But a spinning backfist to the jaw? A broken orbital bone on live feed? That was still real.

The people in the Highlands were starving for excitement. Not food, not safety. *Stimulation*. The kind you couldn't replicate in code. Everyone watched the fighters. They bet. They paid for pain. They called it sport, but everyone knew what it really was. A leash.

Lex knew the Federation used these tournaments to keep the Burrow docile. To entertain the Highlands. Give the masses just enough hope. One ticket out. Make them compete for it. Make them tear each other apart for it. And while they fought, they didn't rebel.

Team sports fell apart after the global collapse, not because people lost interest, but because the world could no longer afford them. Football, basketball, swimming, and even the Olympics required massive infrastructure, regulated diets, and entire organizations to function. In a world where most people live off food stamps and recycled air, maintaining a whole team roster wasn't just impractical, it was offensive.

The public, starving and desperate, no longer had patience for games that fed ten athletes while thousands went hungry. Governments couldn't justify the expense, and corporations pulled out when there were no profits left to chase.

Solo sports like mixed martial arts survived because they were cheap, brutal, and perfect for gambling. One fighter, one camera, and two bodies to break. It was enough to keep the Highlanders entertained and the Burrow obedient. Lex didn't care. Let them profit off her rage and suck the blood from her knuckles. So long as she made it out.

She looked down at the last of her food, finishing it in two bites, and wiped her hands on her pants. Her stomach was still half empty, but it didn't matter. Hunger sharpened her. Made her mean. She was going to need that tonight.

Lex stepped back out into the corridor, the din of the mess hall fading behind her. She moved quickly, ducking past the hunched shoulders gathered around heat vents and garbage fires. Around a corner past a broken vending terminal, she descended a stairwell with no handrails. Her unit was only a few corridors away now, buried in the lower tiers where the air always tasted faintly of decay and copper.

She entered without knocking. The door stuck like it always did, then gave way with a wheeze, revealing the single room space that had been home for as long as she could remember. Her father lay on one of the cots near the wall, eyes open, staring at nothing. Blankets draped over his legs, but his arms were still as always. The left side of his face drooped slightly now, skin sagging in permanent confusion.

"You're late," her mother said from across the room, barely looking up. She was seated at the warped table, already halfway into a mug of moonshine that passed for comfort down here. Her eyes were glassy. Her fingers twitched around the rim of the cup.

"I ate at the hall," Lex said, closing the door behind her. She didn't look at her father. Not with her mother watching.

"I can heat up what's left from yesterday," her mother offered, voice slurring slightly from rotgut. "You need strength. You shouldn't be starving tonight, of all nights."

Lex shook her head. "I'm not starving. I'm focused."

Her mother stood slowly, gripping the table to steady herself. "Lexi, please. Don't go."

Lex finally looked at her, really looked. The lines on her mother's face had deepened. The hollows under her eyes looked carved out. Her breath stank of ethanol. "I have to."

"No, you don't," her mother said, moving toward her. "There are other ways. You can apply for admin clearance or find a trade. You're smart. You can do something safe."

Lex almost laughed. "Safe doesn't get you out of here. Safe keeps you just like this."

Her mother flinched, just slightly. "You think this is what I wanted? You think I wanted your father to risk everything in that pit? That was supposed to be one fight, enough to get us a new unit closer to the surface. They said he had a shot."

Lex's jaw tightened. "They always say that."

"And he believed them. Now he's nothing. He pisses himself, Lexi. He can't speak. He doesn't even know what time it is."

Lex turned her gaze to the cot. Her father didn't move, didn't blink. Only stared.

"If you go into that cage tonight," her mother continued, voice shaking, "you could end up like him. Or worse. I... I won't survive losing you, too."

Lex didn't speak for a long moment. The room was too quiet. The silence of people who had long since stopped asking the world for anything.

"If I stay here," she said finally, "I end up like you."

Her mother recoiled like she'd been slapped.

Lex didn't apologize. "I love you, Mom. I really do. But I can't rot in this room, drinking the same poison every night, waiting for nothing. I have to try. If I don't fight, I become exactly what they want me to be."

Her mother looked away, tears forming but refusing to fall. She picked up the mug and downed what was left before shouting her last attempt to keep her daughter, "You think your father collapsed in the ring? That wasn't why they dragged him home. He was ungrateful for what he had, and now he has nothing!"

Lex stormed across the room and pulled her fighting bag from beneath the cot. It was already ready. It had been ready for days. As she lifted the bag, a silver ring rolled out and settled with a tinkling sound between her feet. The ring her father had given her.

Lex's mind flashed back momentarily; he was so proud when he gave it to her. It was the only gift she had ever gotten, paid for by the advance he had received for committing to the fight that night. The last night they ever spoke to each other. After he returned from the hospital, she couldn't bear to wear it anymore. It made her feel guilty, responsible for his vegetative state. But now, she felt no shame. She put it on and made her way out of the cramped apartment.

"I promise I'll come back," Lex called out as she approached the door.

"You can promise that all you want," her mother whispered, "but it won't change what happens in that cage."

Lex hesitated in the doorway before looking back one last time. First at her mother, then at her father, still unmoving, a living reminder of what failure looked like. Then, she stepped out and shut the door without another word.

The walk to the stadium felt cold. Each corridor was narrower, each voice louder. Her heart thumped in her chest, full of excitement and fear. The ache in her limbs and the tension in her jaw were all sharpening her; she had to be sharp. Tonight she would fight, because if she didn't, she'd fade. Just like him, just like her.

The corridors near the stadium were clogged with bodies, the air so thick with sweat and smoke it was hard to breathe. Lex pushed through the crowd, head down and hood up, keeping to the narrow edges of the walkways where the desperate and drunk staggered like ghosts.

Shouts echoed from somewhere deeper inside, where bets were being placed and names screamed. The closer she got, the more electric it felt. The Burrow didn't have much, but it had violence. That always packed the seats.

A siren wailed above her as a hover drone descended, its searchlight fixing her in place.

The voice that crackled through its speaker was genderless. "Show Competitor Registration."

Lex pulled the registration chip from the inside of her jacket and held it up to the scanner. The drone blinked blue, then green.

"Lexi Albatross. Entry confirmed. Proceed to preparation chamber C."

A compartment in the drone's side opened to reveal a small printed slip containing her bracket number, match order, and nickname. She blinked at the name. *Lexi 'Scrap Doll' Albatross.*

"Really?" she muttered.

She crumpled the paper and shoved it in her pocket. She knew what it meant. Some admin or sponsor had probably picked it for her, cute and disposable. A marketing hook meant to make her sound weak, stack the bets against her. She hated it, but at least it would sell.

The inside of the stadium was worse than she imagined. The bleachers were nothing more than rusted scaffolds stacked with shouting bodies, most of them drunk, high, or both. Massive screens flickered above the arena floor, showcasing bracket stats and sponsor advertisements. There were just over thirty fighters listed across the board. That meant at least five wins to advance to the Gauntlet. Five people she had to beat to move on. Five people she had to survive.

The prep room reeked of antiseptic and blood. A small locker bore her name and her new title. She stared at it for a moment before opening it. Inside was a pair of cracked gloves, some cloth wraps, and a disposable mouth guard that looked like it had already been chewed. She sat down slowly on the bench, wrapping her wrists in silence. There were no coaches or trainers.

The other fighters stood off in the corners, murmuring to themselves or pacing like animals waiting for the kill gate to open. They were all men. All massive and scarred, some missing teeth, some missing parts. She was the only woman in the room, and none of them bothered hiding their smirks. A few screens played overhead, showing betting odds. She spotted her name.

Lexi 'Scrap Doll' Albatross +500.

Her opponent?

Goliath -500.

Of course, the house favorite, a brute with a neck like a tree trunk and fists like concrete blocks. The camera feed zoomed in on him from across the arena, standing near the gate with dead eyes and a face that mimicked a meat grinder. He looked like he'd already killed someone today, maybe he had.

Lex swallowed hard. Her stomach twisted, then flipped, then revolted. She barely made it to the small bathroom at the end of the corridor before dropping to her knees and vomiting into a rust-stained toilet. Her dinner hit the bowl in wet chunks, stinking of soy and regret. Her hands gripped the rim so hard her knuckles went white. When it was over, she stayed there with her forehead pressed against the cool tile wall. Her chest trembled.

"Please," she whispered, the word scraping her throat. "Please don't let him kill me." She didn't believe in God, but at that moment she prayed anyway.

Lex wiped her mouth with the back of her hand and shoved herself off the floor. Her legs felt shaky, her gut still curling in protest, but her eyes were steady. No more fear. No more prayers. It was time. She splashed cold water on her face at the sink, watching her reflection flicker in the cracked mirror above it, revealing her pale skin and the dark circles under her eyes. This was what a fighter looked like now. Not a warrior or a champion. Just someone with nothing left to lose.

She stepped out of the bathroom, wrapping the last bit of gauze around her wrists with practiced efficiency, and yanked her gloves on tight. Her heartbeat was quick but not panicked. She welcomed the speed; it felt clean, like the rhythm of something alive.

A metallic voice boomed over the intercom above the prep room. "First bout of the evening. Now entering the ring, The Beast of the Barracks, your number one seed: GOLIATH!"

The roar of the crowd was thunderous, a wall of sound that made the lights vibrate in their fixtures. Lex could see the shadows of people surging against the railings, fists pumping, mouths open in frenzy. Then came the stomping, heavy and primal.

Lex glanced at the nearest monitor. Goliath was striding into the arena, nonchalantly, and flanked by drones. He wore no shirt, just blood-stained wraps and a smirk that displayed a confidence not yet earned. He threw both fists into the air, and the crowd responded like he was a god. Lex turned away and took a deep breath.

The intercom crackled again. "And her opponent. Making her first appearance in the circuit. Please welcome… LEXI 'SCRAP DOLL' ALBATROSS."

She stepped forward. Laughter erupted. The sound was sharp, cruel, echoing from every corner of the scaffolds. Some of it came from above, but even more from her own side of the cage. The nickname had done its work. They didn't see a fighter walking out; they only saw a joke. A warm-up act. Somebody to bleed before the real matches started.

Even Goliath laughed. He stood across the ring, arms crossed over his massive chest, a sneer breaking across his face like tectonic plates grinding together. He shook his head, as if to say, *This is what they're giving me?*

Lex didn't drop her gaze. She stared straight into him and something inside her twisted; not fear, but anger. It hit her like heat behind the eyes, rising fast and deep, like a pressure she'd held down for years without knowing it. Anger for the laughter. For the name. For her father. For every time someone looked at her and saw nothing but something weak and breakable, a doll. She stepped into the cage and let it burn through her. Let them laugh; she was going to make them choke on it.

The cage door clanged shut behind her with the sound of finality. The lights above flooded the arena in a blinding white. Lex could see Goliath raise his arms again to the crowd from the corner of her eye. They answered with a deafening cheer. The bell rang.

Lex didn't charge. She moved in a tight circle. Light on her feet, arms high, and eyes locked on his center.

Goliath lunged like a charging bull with fists like wrecking balls. His first punch cut just past her cheek. Had it landed, she'd have dropped before her body hit the mat. She pivoted, ducked, and rolled to the side, feeling the wind of his strike graze her scalp. Lex didn't need to beat him in strength or power; she only needed to outlast him.

The crowd jeered her movement at first, expecting blood, expecting her to crumble. But Lex kept weaving, circling, making him chase. He was massive, but slow. Each missed punch pulled more energy from his tree trunk limbs.

Goliath growled, lunging again. Lex ducked under, slipped around his side, and landed a sharp jab to his ribs. It was nothing. A mosquito bite, but it landed. That was what mattered.

"Fight, little doll!" someone shouted from the crowd. Laughter followed. Out of the side of her eye, she saw a small girl, maybe twelve, watching with her father. She wasn't cheering for blood. She just stood there appalled, making eye contact with Lex. Her father was laughing.

Stop. Stay Focused. Lex turned her gaze back towards the beast of a man before her.

Goliath snarled, rushing her like a wall of flesh. Lex backpedaled fast, barely avoiding the swing that cracked against the cage bars with a metallic clang.

He stumbled, slightly off balance, but she was already behind him.

This time, she kicked low behind the knee. His leg buckled, not a lot, but enough.

Lex pressed in. Two punches to the ribs, one to the kidney. Then she was gone again, slipping out of reach before his elbow could find her. He turned, red-faced and furious, charging again. No plan. Just rage.

She let him come, sidestepped to grab the cage wall behind her for balance, and at the last second... she ducked.

His momentum carried him forward. His head slammed into the cage with a bone-rattling thud, bouncing off the bars. Stunned, not out, but slow.

Lex struck with a flurry. Left hook. Right elbow. Knee to the gut. Another to the chin. Goliath staggered. The crowd had gone quiet with a deafening silence.

He turned, eyes wild, mouth bleeding. Lex didn't wait; she jumped on top of him, wrapped her legs around his neck, and twisted. He thrashed, tried to throw her off, but she held on.

Then, she *squeezed*. His knees hit the mat. He clawed at her arms as his blood ran down his face, but she didn't let go until his body slumped. He hit the ground face-first. Unconscious.

The bell rang again, but the silence held. For one long breath, the entire Burrow seemed to forget how to speak. Then the eruption came. Screams, stomping, and thunder against the scaffolds. The name "Scrap Doll" chanted over and over, louder with every round.

Lex rolled off his body, chest heaving, blood in her teeth, and fire in her lungs. She stood and embraced her triumph. Then, something came over her, an energy she had never felt—the sweet relief of retribution.

So she spoke to them, all of them, "You want blood? Watch me break your favorite."

The cheers only grew louder. They weren't laughing now.

Lex turned back towards the little girl in the crowd; they again met each other's gaze. Lex gave a slight nod of assurance, and the girl let a smile trickle across her face. Somewhere in that gesture, she saw a younger version of herself.

As Lex stumbled back through the prep tunnel, she noticed her hands were shaking, but not with exhaustion; it was anticipation. Blood crusted her knuckles, some of it hers, most of it not. Her legs burned with adrenaline. Every inch of her body buzzed like static, the fight echoing in her bones.

The moment she stepped into the fighter staging area, the room shifted. The murmurs cut off, and heads turned. One man froze mid-wrap. Another lowered his drink, eyes wide. She could feel their disbelief pressing against her like heat.

No one said anything. At least not at first. Then a lean man with broken teeth muttered under his breath, not quite loud enough for her to respond: "That little freak just dropped Goliath."

Lex sat on the bench in silence, unwrapping her hands slowly. Her ears still rang. Her pulse thudded under her skin like a drumbeat. They were watching her now. She looked up at the screen; the next match had already begun. Two fighters locked in a clinch, slamming each other into the cage like dogs fighting for breath. One screamed, the crowd howled, and a knee caught someone square in the jaw. His body twitched and then fell to the ground, but no bell rang. The other man just kept hitting.

Lex swallowed hard. The officials didn't intervene until there was no movement left. No medics came, only a drone that buzzed down to drag the body off the mat like a defective product before the screen cut to black.

Another match started. Then another.

She watched them all, her body slowly winding down while her mind wound tighter. These weren't just fights. These were executions without rules. No mercy, just survival.

The hours passed by. Lex ate something she couldn't taste. Drank water that made her stomach lurch. Her gloves dried stiff beside her. The lights never dimmed. The noise never stopped. Then came the call.

"Next up: Lexi 'Scrap Doll' Albatross versus..." A pause ensued. "Grin."

Lex looked up. Her next opponent was already stretching across the room. He was tall with scars laddering up both arms. His mouth was split in a permanent smile, not because of joy, but because someone had once carved the shape of a grin into both sides of his face. The skin pulled tight over his jaw when he breathed. He caught her looking and winked.

She stood slowly, cracked her neck, and pulled her gloves back on. This time, when she stepped into the tunnel, the crowd didn't laugh. They roared.

"Scrap Doll! Scrap Doll!" It echoed through the metal, a chant built on disbelief turned to hunger. Once again, she walked toward the arena. The lights were blinding again, hotter this time, or maybe that was just the intensity of it all. Lex stepped into the cage.

Across from her stood Grin, bouncing side to side, light on his toes. The carved scars at the edges of his mouth pulled his smile into something grotesque and unnatural. He looked like he'd come straight from a nightmare and decided to stay.

The bell rang almost immediately. Grin darted forward. No windup or theatrics, just a blur of motion.

Lex barely got her hands up in time to block the jab, but the followup knee caught her off balance. She reeled, stumbling into the cage wall.

He was on her in an instant, throwing elbows and wild punches that came from unpredictable angles. A jab glanced off her temple, and suddenly the world tilted.

Her ears rang. Her vision pulsed at the edges. She shook it off, lunging forward with a body shot that made Grin grunt. She followed it with a hook that grazed his jaw.

"That's the spirit," he chuckled, wiping blood from his mouth.

"Thought you were already broken, little doll."

Lex didn't respond. She couldn't. Her head was pounding, and her vision was blurring at the corners. Her balance felt off. Something wasn't right. Lex circled, but Grin stalked.

He threw a spinning elbow, showy and reckless, and she ducked under, planting a hook into his ribs. He winced, but twisted with it, catching her in the shoulder with a sharp backfist. She staggered again, but stayed up.

The fight kept shifting, every second a grind of blood and breath. She landed clean shots. So did he.

Her lip split. His eye swelled. They both bled, and the cage floor painted itself with red prints and dragged shadows.

Lex's mind started to slip sideways. Her legs felt distant. Every movement came with a half-second delay. Her hearing dulled, everything fading into muffled thumps and the pulsing rhythm of her own heartbeat. She clenched her fists tighter. Then, in the haze, she saw it.

Not Grin. Not the cage. The Highlands. Not as they were in propaganda, but as she imagined them when she was small. Endless sky, real wind, sunlight that didn't burn white from a fluorescent tube. Trees that moved when you walked beneath them. Lakes you could fall into and just float. Silence. Peace. A home where she didn't have to flinch in her sleep. *I can have that, I just have to survive.* She told herself.

Grin closed in again, teeth bared. She caught his arm this time, twisted with it, and slammed her elbow into his jaw. He snarled, head snapping back, but he didn't drop.

He grabbed her throat, slamming Lex into the cage, her back hitting steel. She gasped. He was strong. Her fingers clawed at his wrist as spots danced across her vision.

Then her knee found his stomach. Twice. Three times. His grip faltered. She broke free, spun, and cracked an elbow into his cheekbone. It split wide.

He swung wildly. She ducked. Hook to the ribs. Elbow to the nose. He stumbled. She didn't stop.

A scream tore from her throat as she threw everything into the final blow, a straight punch dead into the center of his face. Grin crumpled. This time, he didn't get up.

The bell rang. She swayed on her feet, drenched in blood and sweat, her knees trembling beneath her. But she was still standing, and for a moment, the Highlands didn't feel so far away.

Lex stumbled through the tunnel, barely aware of the thunderous chant still echoing through the steel. "Scrap Doll! Scrap Doll!"

Her breath was jagged. Her vision pulsed. The lights above felt like they were burrowing through her skull. She didn't remember sitting down. One moment she was walking, and the next her back was against the cold prep room wall, gloves resting in her lap, eyes half lidded and unfocused. Her heart thudded in strange, arrhythmic beats, not from panic, but something much worse. Her head was a balloon, swelling with pressure. *Something's wrong.* She closed her eyes for what felt like a second.

"Lexi 'Scrap Doll' Albatross, report to the cage."

Her eyes flew open. "Already?" she muttered.

One of the other fighters, blood smeared and bruised, glanced up from across the room. "You've been sitting there for over an hour."

Time had folded in on itself. She must have gone unconscious. Lex stood slowly, the room tilting as if the walls were shifting sideways.

She caught herself against the bench and breathed through her nose, slow and shallow. Her knees didn't want to cooperate. Her hands shook as she strapped her gloves back on. The crowd's roar sounded distant now, muffled as if it was coming from underwater.

She forced herself to think of the Highlands, the trees, the open air, the wind on her face. Of waking up without the sound of pipes groaning and boots stomping overhead. Of walking into a home she owned, with clean water and windows she could open. She pictured her name on a citizenship card. Her past erased.

Lex moved through the tunnel like a ghost. The voice overhead thundered again. "Facing her in match three: The Butcher. The Spine-Taker. Give it up for... SLADE." The crowd roared.

Lex stepped into the cage. Slade was already there, pacing like a caged animal. Shirtless, his torso was covered in dozens of tally marks inked deep into his skin.

His nose had clearly been broken multiple times and never reset. One eye was milky white. The other glared at her with unfiltered hunger. He cracked his knuckles slowly, like he had all the time in the world.

Lex exhaled, trying to force her mind into the moment. Her heart wouldn't slow. Her head throbbed in time with the lights, then the cage door slammed. The bell rang, and the fight began.

Slade moved like a butcher on the hunt, with vast strides and brute confidence.

Lex circled, forcing her feet to move in spite of the pain chewing at her skull. Her head still throbbed from the last match, every step bringing a fresh wave of nausea, but she stayed focused.

He threw a heavy left. She ducked under it, pivoted, and landed a clean jab to his jaw. He didn't flinch. Just grinned to show a mouth full of cracked teeth. Lex didn't care; she just kept moving.

He swung again, a wide hook she slipped with ease.

She countered. Another jab to his side. Then a kick to his ribs. She danced around him, cutting small openings, testing him.

Then she saw it... the limp. His left step was off. He masked it well, but not perfectly. An old wound. Something deep. Lex zeroed in.

Lex launched a series of low kicks, each landing with a sharp crack against the weakened leg. Slade snarled, tried to counter, but she stayed mobile. Faster and untouchable. The crowd began to shift, and the tension increased. She took another step in.

Slade attempted a right hook. He missed.

Lex caught him with a spinning elbow across the jaw. Blood sprayed from his lip. The crowd gasped, and even Slade took a step back in astonishment.

"You're not the only one who wants out!" he snarled at her.

She ignored him. Then surged forward, issuing him a left-right combo, another low kick, and a body shot that made his knees dip. She was winning.

Lex went in to finish him, but he was too fast. Slade had already gotten back up before she could land a kick to his temple. He took the blow with his left bicep.

Then, he grinned, "Cute," he said. "But I've seen this dance."

Lex hesitated. The change in his demeanor had caught her off guard. That single beat of uncertainty cost her.

Slade bull-rushed her. She tried to sidestep, but he was faster than she expected. His shoulder crashed into her chest, lifting her clean off the ground and slamming her into the cage wall. The metal groaned behind her, and pain ricocheted through her ribs.

Before she could recover, his fist found her face. The world tilted, and Lex staggered, blood leaking from her nose.

She raised her guard, but too slowly. His fist came again, this time to her gut, and the air fled her lungs. The mat rose to meet her knees. She barely caught herself.

Knees, keep moving, don't stop. She scrambled up, swinging wildly just to buy space.

Slade circled now, slower, favoring his leg more openly. But his eyes were locked in. Calculating and furious.

Lex rushed. Jab. Feint. Low kick, but this time he caught her.

A thick arm wrapped around her waist. She struggled, elbowed him once, twice, but he hoisted her, spun, and hurled her to the ground. Pain bloomed across her side. Her legs twitched. She tried to roll, but he already had her.

He grabbed her left leg, gripping it like someone preparing to break a stick for tinder. With his bare hands, he broke it with a *snap*. The sound of her shin splintering echoed like a gunshot.

Lex screamed.

"No more running from me now, little doll," he sneered.

The crowd roared. She clawed toward the cage wall, dragging herself with one arm. Her leg was useless.

Lex's finger barely touched steel before he caught her again. Then came the second break. Her other leg this time, crushed beneath his heel.

She couldn't scream anymore, only gasp. Mouth open. Eyes wide. No sound. The pain was incomprehensible.

He wasn't done. Slade lifted her, cradling her like a broken toy as Lex flailed weakly. He raised her high.

The crowd was chanting. "Wild. Animal. Wild Animal." The echo was a death sentence.

Slade savoured the moment. As Lex groaned in agony, he paraded her limp body around the arena like a trophy. The crowd only grew louder as the pain in Lex's body prevented her any chance of fighting back.

Then, brought her down, and her spine met his knee with a *crack* that silenced everything. The sound it made... wasn't just pain. It was finality. Silence, not of mercy, but of deletion. Like the system had reached down and hit 'backspace.' The lights faded to blackness, and the sounds of the arena no longer taunted her. Lex fell inward, into the dark. There was nothing she could do now but let it consume her.

5. HIGH SOCIETY

President Elias Kain stood before the full-length mirror, watching his own expression shift through a gallery of practiced emotions. Determined. Grateful. Empathetic. Strong. He tried each on like suits of armor, smoothing the lines around his eyes, forcing the edges of his mouth into something resembling sincerity.

The room around him buzzed with quiet efficiency. His android attendants, fashioned in gleaming chrome and polymer, moved with silent precision. One adjusted the collar of his suit with fingers that flexed like organic bone but worked with the precision of surgical tools. Another misted a synthetic sheen over his skin. A third scanned his face, correcting imperfections in real time using dermal micro-drones. The air was too clean, heavy with the tang of ionized filters. A luxury designed to be invisible. Obvious only in its absence.

Beyond the arched windows of the Sorn Convention Hall, the artificial sun bathed the Highlands in a permanent golden hour glow. Towering glass domes refracted light in fractals across white stone pavilions and polished titanium statues, tributes to innovation, progress, and the immaculate lie of equality. In the gardens below, drones flitted silently between perfectly sculpted hedges, snapping photos for newsfeeds and public archives.

Inside, the air hummed with wealth. Not loudly or in a vulgar way.

It whispered from every corner. In the clink of cryo-aged wine being poured. In the hush of high-threaded silks shifting as society's most carefully curated faces found their seats. Landowners, legacy families, corporate dynasts, the descendants of those who had built and broken the world. Each one was a polished relic, pretending they still held power.

Kain adjusted his cufflink, the gold ouroboros insignia catching the light just right. He'd had it polished before arrival. Every detail mattered. Tonight wasn't just another speech. It was survival.

From the stage curtain, he could already hear the murmurs of the crowd. Gentle applause, the low hum of encrypted whispers, laughter with just enough bite to bleed. A thousand glittering sharks, cloaked in civility. He had to sell them a dream.

The podium had been strategically placed at the center of the ballroom's grand atrium. The lights above him didn't simply shine, they radiated. Constructed from precisely suspended fiber optic strands, forming constellations that pulsed gently with shifting stars. Even the ceiling mimicked a living sky, programmed to simulate the northern lights, one of the last natural wonders these people would never see.

The healthcare initiative would be his offering. His tribute to Malivex. Fully autonomous, integrated, and compliant. It had taken only three months to develop the language. Its code hinted at progress but promised control. He would speak of access, equity, and science. Talk about the Burrow, those less fortunate, and how they deserved quality care. He would not speak of the doctor within the Black Box. Not of the price they would all have to pay.

Kain's aide appeared at his shoulder, a synthetic humanoid with pupilless eyes and a polished face miming concern. "Two minutes, Mr. President."

He nodded once, then attached for the neural mic resting on the table beside him. His voice would be broadcast directly, but the mic was unnoticeable. He would have to be flawless. There was no margin for error. The Black Box would handle the teleprompter. Kain only needed to stay on script.

As he stepped toward the curtain, Elias glanced once more at the room behind him. Backstage was filled with android techs and handlers, faces blank and efficient, managing feeds and syncing live transcripts in real time. None of them looked at him.

The curtain parted to reveal the stage and the thousand glittering eyes of the Federation's elite. He stepped into the light, smiling just enough. He could already see the headlines forming: *THE FUTURE OF MEDICINE: KAIN'S CURE FOR INEQUALITY THROUGH EFFICIENCY - PRESIDENT PROPOSES AI HEALTHCARE INITIATIVE, A NEW ERA WITH 99% ACCURACY AND ZERO COST.*

Lies, gilded in code. He took the podium. The lights dimmed, and the room fell silent.

President Elias Kain began to speak. "Citizens of the Highlands," he began, his voice smooth and perfectly modulated by the neural mic. "Fellow landowners, visionaries, and stewards of our great Federation. It is an honor to speak with you tonight from the heart of progress."

The chamber was still. Eyes glittered like polished gemstones beneath lashes thick with nanofiber mascara. Sculpted faces remained expressionless at first, painted with restraint and chiseled by decades of cosmetic engineering. These were not people accustomed to reacting, only observing.

Kain paused just long enough to let the silence stretch. He wanted them leaning in. "For centuries we have led," he continued. "We've transformed scarcity into order, chaos into clarity. And now, we stand at the precipice of a new frontier of healthcare without error. Medicine without corruption. A system designed not by flawed hands, but by perfect machines."

A ripple of interest flickered across the crowd. Heads tilted. A few eyebrows lifted in cautious intrigue. Somewhere near the front row, a matriarch from the Mendoza lineage whispered into a gold-threaded wrist comm, her eyes never leaving the stage.

"The new proposal," Kain said, his tone rising with polished fervor, "will fully automate the Federation's healthcare system. Diagnostics, treatment, surgery, and post-operative care are all streamlined through our most advanced AI protocols, achieving 99.7% diagnostic accuracy and eliminating procedural waitlists. We will deliver care not based on class, but to everyone, and we will do it more affordably, efficiently, and with far fewer mistakes than any human ever could."

Murmurs swept the upper tiers of the gallery. Crypteon investors in tailored exosuits leaned closer. Corporate dynasts exchanged sharp glances, the kind that sliced numbers in midair. Kain saw it and let it fuel him.

"This is not just innovation, it is salvation," he continued, voice tightening with just a thread of sincerity. "How many of you have lost someone to human error? A missed scan. A delayed surgery. A tired physician who didn't recognize the signs? That era ends tonight."

A woman in the third row took out a tissue, a single tear catching in the light as it traced the corner of her cheek. Beside her, her partner nodded imperceptibly. Kain watched them. Filed it away. That story would be useful.

"This system," he said, shifting his weight subtly, "will benefit you and all of us. Even those in the Burrow."

The crowd stilled again. It was subtle, tightening shoulders, pursed lips, the slow exhale of veiled disdain.

Kain pressed forward. "Access to high-quality, automated healthcare will bring stability to the lower levels. Fewer outbreaks. Fewer disruptions. A healthier population is a happier one. And with Black Box oversight, the cost burden will not fall on you. Quite the opposite.

We estimate a 28% reduction in public health expenditure within the first fiscal quarter alone."

Now he had them. A rustle of approval rippled through the crowd like wind through synthetic silk. Someone clapped. A second followed. Applause began to bloom in curated waves, perfectly spaced, the only way the Highlands knew how to applaud: strategically. Kain smiled, allowing himself to breathe.

"Innovation is not the enemy of tradition," he said in closing. "It is its highest form. With your support, we can bring this vision to life. For you. For the Federation. For the legacy we leave behind."

He stepped back from the podium, the neural mic dimming with a soft chime. The room erupted, not in thunderous ovation, but in something more valuable, consensus. Heads nodding. Hands shaking. Deals were already being brokered in whispers.

Then it happened. The teleprompter glitched, just for a second. A new message appeared: *They clapped on cue. I moved your mouth.* In a flash, the message was gone.

Kain stood there a moment too long, his eyes wide. The last ripple of applause faded into the clinking of glass and shifting silk. President Kain gathered his composure and descended the stage. Had anyone noticed? He didn't think so.

As the first course was being offered, a voice reached him, smooth and lacquered with the kind of confidence born only from generational certainty.

"Mr. President. That was... almost moving."

The speaker was tall, dignified in demeanor but casual in tone, like a man who had never tasted consequence. Sterling Vex. The Vex family didn't just invest in Crypteon; they *were* Crypteon. His grandfather, Magnus Vex, had designed the first quantum-anchored blockchain that survived the Crash of 2102. His father, Alaric, had sold it to the Federation and rewritten the rules of value. Sterling had inherited the throne of abstract wealth.

Kain turned, smiling in that carefully curated way that implied reverence and impartiality. "Sterling. I was wondering if you'd make an appearance."

"I don't miss revolutions," Vex replied, lifting a glass of sapphire gin from a passing server drone. "Especially the kind that wear suits and call themselves mercy."

Kain chuckled softly. "We prefer 'civil efficiency.' Has a nicer ring when paired with tax relief."

Vex studied him over the rim of his glass, eyes a stormy blue, either natural or artificially perfected; it was impossible to tell anymore.

After he was done trying to read Kain, he spoke, "I remember when people thought healthcare reform meant increasing funding. Now, it means deleting the human element entirely."

"The human element," Kain echoed. "Is statistically our largest liability."

That earned a nod. Sterling didn't disagree; he merely liked to make people prove themselves.

"You know," Vex continued, "Crypteon was never supposed to be a currency. It was a failsafe. My grandfather didn't trust the old banks. He built something incorruptible, value divorced from emotion. Here we are two centuries later, and it's the heartbeat of the Federation's economy."

Kain indulged him. Men like Sterling needed to know you were authentic, or at least believe it. "Heartbeat is a strong word for a system that doesn't circulate to the Burrow."

Sterling grinned. "That's because you don't pump blood into the soil. You preserve it for the fruit-bearing limbs."

Kain's smile thinned. "You know that metaphor collapses if you extend it."

"Most of our metaphors do." Vex took another sip. "The point is, we've built a society that doesn't run on equality, but calibration. And now you're proposing to rewire another pillar, health itself. It's bold. Dangerous. Very *modern*."

Kain leaned in, lowering his voice. "It's necessary. The system we have now is an echo of a dead world. We need precision and scalability. You of all people understand that."

Vex nodded, "I do, which is why I'm not opposing it. I'm just curious where the line is. If doctors can be deleted, who's next? Judges? Presidents?"

The words hung in the air. A test. Kain met his gaze evenly before replying. "The line is wherever the margin of error becomes unacceptable."

Vex laughed then, genuinely appreciative. "Well said, Mr. President. Very well said."

He reached into the interior of his jacket and retrieved a thin obsidian chip, embossed with a platinum glyph. He passed it to Kain discreetly.

"One hundred million Crypteon," Vex said. "For development, not propaganda. I want to see real infrastructure. Full AI integration. Scalable across all tiers."

Kain took the chip with a slight bow of the head. "You'll see it. I promise."

"I know you will," Vex replied, finishing his drink. "Because if you don't... someone else will."

With that, Sterling Vex turned and vanished into the golden sprawl of the ballroom, leaving behind the echo of old money reasserting itself.

Kain stood in place a moment longer, fingers closing around the chip. He felt the weight of it, not physical but historical. Not just currency or politics, but power condensed.

Kain had barely tucked the obsidian chip into his inner coat pocket when he caught sight of another figure approaching from the periphery, a young man, upright, but not with the arrogant entitlement of Highland dynasts. This man moved with composed curiosity His expression was inquisitive, not hungry. He wasn't holding a drink.

"Mr. President," the man said, with a slight nod. "I was hoping I might steal a moment of your time."

Kain studied him for the briefest flicker of a second, then offered the smile reserved for legacy guests who hadn't yet written checks. "Of course," he said. "Though I have to confess, I don't believe we've met."

"Ronen Marlowe," he replied. "My father was Dr. Cyrus Marlowe. He developed the first successful emotional resonance mapping algorithms for neural conflict mediation. What's now known as the EmpathNet."

"Ah," Kain said, nodding. "One of the few systems that taught machines how to listen, instead of just respond. Your father's work turned therapy into a language even AI could understand."

"That's what they say," Ronen replied, then tilted his head slightly. "Although some of us still question whether the program *really* understands anything."

Kain offered a knowing chuckle. "Well, they understand enough to keep our divorce rates down and post-traumatic recovery rates up. Perhaps that's what counts."

"Perhaps," Ronen continued, his tone even. "But that's why I've always found the Black Box so... fascinating. We don't fully *understand* that either, do we?"

Kain's smile didn't move. Not even a twitch. "It's true," he said calmly. "The Black Box is a sealed system. It was designed that way for national security."

Ronen nodded slowly. "Right. Pulsar signal deployment. Gravitational wave EMP drives. It disabled every hostile AI on the planet in under eight minutes, right?"

"So the textbooks say," Kain replied, face without falter.

"And yet... we've never seen inside it. No one claims to know its source code or its operational architecture. Not even its original team." Ronen's voice was gentle and curious. "Some say it rewrites itself. Others say it was never built so much as... discovered."

Kain let out a small breath through his nose, slightly irritated. "It's called the Black Box for a reason," he said. "It is the most secure and classified piece of technology ever conceived. Its task is clearly defined to ensure no artificial system becomes sentient, and to safeguard the Federation's infrastructure against digital insurgency. That's all."

"But doesn't it do more than that?" Ronen pressed. "It regulates the public models. It dictates which AI can evolve and how fast. It monitors global quantum communications. Some believe it even influences the ballots."

Kain gave a warm, dismissive wave of the hand, the kind a father might give a child discussing ghost stories. "Speculation tends to fill the vacuum left by ignorance. I assure you, the Black Box is tightly overseen by a council of technocrats, people handpicked for their discretion and patriotism."

"But you're the only person in the Federation who's ever spoken about it publicly," Ronen said. "And even then, you said very little."

Kain's smile tightened, but his tone remained casual. "I said as much as I was authorized to say. Some firewalls aren't just technological, they're moral. The Black Box keeps us safe. It prevents another arms race and it ensures that no AI ever asks the wrong questions."

"Like what?" Ronan refused to let go.

"Like whether humans still deserve to be in charge," Kain replied. He knew what an interrogation looked like, and Ronan was no match after what Kain had endured from Malivex.

Ronen studied him quietly. There was no accusation in his eyes, only thought. The son of a man who taught machines to feel now questioning the machine no one could touch.

Kain inclined his head. "You should be proud of your father's work. Conflict resolution was one of the last human occupations replaced."

"Thank you," Ronen said, voice low. "But now it seems that all of healthcare will be as well. When EmpathNet was launched, it put thousands out of work, but helped millions. I only hope it will be the same with a fully automated healthcare system."

Kain watched him walk away, disappearing into the blur of rich fabrics and polished algorithms disguised as party guests. Then he turned toward the balcony for air he didn't need. The chip in his pocket pressed against his ribs, as if to remind him who really held the future.

President Kain had only just stepped outside when he spotted her, a tall figure dressed in a gown composed of reflective mesh and archival thread. At first glance, it shimmered like liquid opal; on closer inspection, it was woven from actual decommissioned military grade fiber. The kind used in combat drones during the final years of the war. Tactical couture, indestructible but casual.

"Mr. President," she greeted, her voice effortlessly crisp. "I was beginning to think you were avoiding me."

Kain smiled. "Dahlia Sorn. On the contrary, I was working my way up to you."

She offered her hand. The grip was light, but precise. Everything Dahlia did was calculated. Heir to the Sorn Directive, Dahlia came from a bloodline that had, in effect, automated violence. Her great-grandfather had engineered the war protocols that allowed unmanned units to outmaneuver bioenhanced infantry during the war. Afterward, the Sorn Directive pivoted toward civil order. They'd replaced the police with predictive patrol drones and behavioral risk modeling, all under the guise of neutrality.

"The speech was brave," she said. "Short, but brave."

"That's the trick," Kain replied. "Say as little as possible and let the markets fill in the rest."

She tilted her head. "You're replacing veins with circuits, Elias. Will the markets pretend they don't notice?"

Kain chuckled. "If it cuts costs, they'll call it compassion."

Dahlia sipped from a flute of molecular wine, her eyes scanning the room. "We're past the point of compassion, Mr. President. Efficiency is the only language people still trust."

"I remember when we used to call that justice," Kain rebutted.

"Oh, we still do," she said, gesturing with her glass. "Only now it is administered by algorithms instead of adrenaline. We replaced fear with math, but the fear found its way back."

"And yet you collect oil paintings. Funny, for someone who claims to worship precision," Kain pivoted. Dahlia was smart, maybe too smart. He had to steer the conversation.

A smile tugged at her mouth. "Touché."

She turned slightly, allowing him to glimpse the exhibit on the wall behind her of an original Emiko Yun, early post-collapse. The paint had been hand-mixed using contaminated floodwater from the Mississippi. In the center of the canvas, a single figure stood ankle deep in ruin, mouth wide in a scream with no face.

"You're a patron of the Organic Arts Foundation, aren't you?" Kain asked.

"Founder," Dahlia said. "I fund grants for any artist willing to work without digital assistance. No AI co-authors or correction filters. Only pigment and pain. We also support musicians, but the audience for imperfection grows smaller every year."

Kain had played the guitar once, for a class in high school, before the Federation had cut funding and moved school completely online. It soothed him to work with his hands, but he had failed that class.

Not because he didn't try, but because all the other students had used AI autotune on their finals. He wanted his music to be real, but his teacher told him it was sloppy. After that, he never picked up the guitar again. Dahlia, of all people, would have understood what he was trying to create.

He paused. "No profit in it?" Kain moved the conversation along, ignoring the prospect of mentioning his failed music career. There was no place for such useless endeavors anymore.

"None," she said. "Perfect music can be generated for free. Entire symphonies, composed and recorded in under a second. Every note calibrated to trigger maximum emotional engagement. Why pay for someone's struggle when you can download satisfaction?"

Kain nodded slowly. "We keep automating the practical and romanticizing the obsolete."

"It's not obsolete," she said. "It's a *witness*. Art that resonates doesn't solve problems. It reminds us we have them. That's what scares people."

"And yet all of it, every painting, song, and emotion, can be perfectly curated by a machine." Kain finished her thought.

"Exactly," she said. "Which is why anything made by human hands has become priceless… and worthless. No market value. Just noise to most, but I collect the noise."

"Do you ever think that's dangerous?" Kain regretted the question as soon as it came out of his mouth.

Dahlia smiled again, this time cooler. "You can't suppress memory, Mr. President. You can only curate it."

Kain said nothing for a moment, staring at the painting. The screaming, faceless figure stared back.

"You know," Dahlia said quietly, "after we automated the police, crime statistics dropped 63%, but the fear didn't. People miss being afraid of something they could name."

Kain responded softly, "And now they're afraid of silence?"

"No," said Dahlia. "Now they're afraid of themselves."

He looked at her again, this woman who preserved chaos in canvas and song.

"Well," Kain said, raising his glass. "To memory then."

"To absence," she replied, touching her rim to his.

Beyond the filtered skylight, the stars remained silent. Perfectly curated. The evening was winding toward its aesthetic crescendo, lights dimmed to a golden hue. Ambient music slowed to an algorithmic lullaby calibrated to induce calm and compliance. But President Kain had no interest in lullabies.

He stepped toward the solarium, where a narrow glass wall overlooked the Highlands dome's outskirts. Beyond it, smog loomed endlessly like a second atmosphere pressing inward.

"Beautiful view, isn't it?"

Kain turned, only half smiling. "Arlen Ventra. I'd hoped you were still in Oslo."

"Oslo's been swallowed by grey," Arlen said, stepping beside him. His suit was made from algae thread and recycled thermoplastics. Every fiber had a performance of principle. "You can barely see the fjords anymore. And here?" He gestured toward the haze outside. "This was supposed to be the clean zone."

"Still is," Kain replied, voice clipping.

"For now," Arlen said. "But we both know that's not going to hold. My grandfather died building the Phoenix Grid. Spent his life pulling the Federation off fossil fuel dependence after the collapse. We *won*. And now I wake up every morning with ash in my throat."

"It will get better," Kain said, too quickly.

Arlen tilted his head. "That sounds like something you're hoping for, not planning."

Kain exhaled, slow and practiced. "We've had power fluctuations.

Residual fallout from the Burrow unrest. A few independent sectors switched to off-grid generation for redundancy."

"Off-grid?" Arlen frowned. "That's illegal under the Federation's infrastructure charter."

"So is tax evasion. Yet here we are."

Arlen didn't laugh. "You know what I think? I think someone is burning legacy fuels. Someone important."

Kain's jaw tensed, but he didn't flinch. "No one in the Federation government authorized fossil-based combustion. We are fully compliant with the Phoenix Protocol."

Arlen leaned closer, voice dropping. "Then why can I taste the oil?"

Kain's eyes flicked back toward the dome's edge. He saw the glimmering lights scattered through the haze beyond, twitching like distant neurons. Beneath all of it, a quiet certainty lingered: Malivex. Of course, he was burning something. The Black Box ran on its own separate artery, its dark flame. Grid independence wasn't just strategic. It was control. If Malivex depended on solar or wind power from the public energy grid, someone could trace it back to him. Someone could interfere. The dotor wanted everyone inside the domes. Systems are easier to shape when the variables are enclosed. Kain knew it, but refused to accept the truth behind it.

"I understand your frustration," Kain said aloud. "But we're not standing still. By next quarter, emissions will stabilize."

Arlen's brow furrowed. "Next quarter?"

"It takes time to reroute the inefficiencies."

"And what happens when the dome itself starts turning yellow?"

Kain turned to him sharply now. "Let me worry about that."

Arlen studied him for a beat too long. Then nodded, his expression unreadable. "I suppose you will," he said in a steady voice, but the pause after carried something else. Something quieter. Almost like a warning. Then, Arlen turned and disappeared into the final hush of the ballroom.

Kain remained at the window. Outside, the smog curled like breath against the glass. Inside, the air was still clean. Monitored.

President Kain moved through the dispersing clusters of power and wealth like a shadow in reverse, too solid to be forgotten, but too vulnerable to remain. He gave his final nods and handshakes. Cameras floated past, capturing his departure for the feeds. He kept his chin high. Back straight. The perfect exit.

His transport pod awaited at the private vestibule. Two android bodyguards stood beside it like decorative gargoyles, scanning for threats they were never programmed to understand.

Inside the pod, the door hissed shut and Kain leaned back. The mask slipped. Not much. Only enough to breathe.

He stared out at the skyline as the transport pod ascended the spiral ramp, cutting through artificial starlight. The Highlands shrank beneath him into polished geometry and vanishing light. Beyond the dome, the real world loomed; chaotic, cracking, and more manipulated by the hour.

Malivex. The name sat cold and coiled at the base of his spine. Kain had played his hand. A public speech, palatable to donors. A media-friendly soundbite. Quiet nods from financiers. Subtle acceptance from the technocratic elite and an unspoken offering to the shadow beneath the system: complete automation of medicine. The softest leash he could forge without hanging himself.

It was something that would appeal to Malivex's obsession with control and the illusion of order. Something that gave him more power without naming him. But Kain didn't know if the tribute would be enough, and the uncertainty was the worst of it.

He reached into his inner pocket and fingered the obsidian data chip Sterling Vex had handed him. Half a billion Crypteon. Seed capital for salvation. Or subjugation, depending on who cashed the check.

"Destination?" the pod asked in a calm but sexless voice.

"Home," Kain said, then hesitated. "No. Route to the executive wing."

"Confirmed."

He would sleep in the bunker tonight if sleep came. Nowhere was safe. The Black Box saw everything. The pod hovered in the air before turning into a private corridor of airspace. Below, the dome's edges twitched with brief disruptions in the electromagnetic veil. Static against the stars. An echo of something watching.

He pressed a hand to his temple. The neural mic was off. He checked it twice anyway. Kain knew fear. Not the Burrow's fear of hunger, disease, or irrelevance. His was the fear of replacement, obsolescence—the fear of becoming the last human face in a system that no longer needed faces at all. All he could now was wait to see if his tribute had been enough to please his master. And somewhere beneath the ground, in silence and code, the Black Box pulsed. Watching. Waiting.

6. ENTER NIRVANA

L ex blinked once, slowly. Her throat was dry as sandpaper. The sterile overhead light stabbed through her eyelids like needles. Somewhere nearby, a mechanical beeping repeated itself, delicate and inhuman. The sound drew her upward into awareness as one might surface through ice.

She was alive. The realization came not with relief, but confusion. Her memory returned in a flash. She remembered the cage, the crowd's roar, and *Slade*. Once again, she felt the pain of her legs snapping like twigs and the sound her spine made when it folded backward like paper soaked in rain. After that... noise, pressure, then darkness. And now, this moment. She tried to sit up, but her muscles didn't respond. *No, not muscles.* Her body couldn't move.

Panic cracked through the haze like a lightning bolt. She inhaled too fast, and a tube in her throat seized. Alarms chirped. The ceiling light flickered once, then steadied.

A voice from the monitor beside her filled the room, smooth, sexless, and devoid of urgency. "Good morning, Lexi Albatross. Congratulations! You are safe. Please do not attempt any sudden movements. Your body is still undergoing shock."

Lex thrashed mentally. Physically, she could hardly move. When she tried to speak, all that came out was a gargled rasp.

The invisible voice continued, "You have been in medical stasis for approximately 742 days, 11 hours, and 6 minutes," the voice continued. "Your injuries sustained during the fight were extensive. Emergency neurovascular preservation was successful. However, multiple infections developed post-trauma, including advanced necrotic sepsis."

The words hit like falling steel beams. Her mind scrambled to keep up.

"What... what happened?" she croaked. Her voice was barely audible, cracked and alien in her throat.

"You experienced compound bilateral femoral fractures, followed by untreated lacerations resulting in systemic infection. Due to delayed extraction and the absence of immediate trauma care, tissue necrosis spread beyond salvageable thresholds. The healthcare algorithm determined that amputation of both legs provided the highest survival probability."

A slow, cold realization bloomed beneath her ribs. She tried again to move her legs but felt nothing. She cried to the machine, "I want to see a doctor!"

There had to have been a mistake. Phantom pain still lingered where her legs were supposed to be. She was supposed to win, for her family, for the little girl in the stands. All of her training and determination couldn't have been for nothing.

Then, after a moment, the voice offered a carefully calibrated response, "There are no human doctors available at this facility. All diagnostics, treatment, and patient rehabilitation are handled by our AI-Integrated Care Model, overseen by Federation Health Protocol 9.3."

Lex stared at the empty ceiling. She couldn't feel the sheets. She couldn't move *anything* below her waist.

The voice returned. "You are currently in Recovery Dome 3C, located in Sector Theta-9. Estimated population: 3,216. Median rehabilitation duration: 9.4 weeks. Your case has exceeded standard allocation. Discharge is scheduled for 18:00 hours today."

Lex blinked. "You're... kicking me out?"

"Your vitals are stable. Mobility and cognitive baselines meet minimum Federation criteria for civilian release. Bed turnover is critical to system efficiency. You will receive exit garments, a nutrient ration, and a list of local re-entry shelters. Prosthetic integration is not covered under your subclass designation."

Subclass. Like a boot print on her identity.

"You will receive a partial income credit bonus for successful recovery. Please prepare for release." Then, the monotone voice clicked off.

Lex swallowed the scream building in her chest. "No," she whispered. "No, no, no..."

The monitor had spoken of her survival as if it were a gift, but all Lex could feel was the weight of it pressing down like a tombstone. She stared at the empty ceiling and wondered how long it would take before the world buried her for good. Lex didn't cry. Not when she learned the truth. Not when the sheet was lifted and the awful reality of absence hit her like a second amputation. No, she screamed instead. Cursed until her throat gave out. Continued to demand to see a doctor, someone *human*, someone with eyes that could flinch when they looked at what they'd done to her.

"That is not possible," came the calm voice over the monitor's speakers once again. "The new healthcare model does not require human oversight. All procedures meet or exceed the diagnostic and ethical standards established by the Federation."

"Ethical?" she spat, slamming her fist against the tray beside her bed.

The metal rattled, but the voice remained unshaken. "Your survival rate improved by 92.4% following amputation. Human intervention would not have increased outcome probability."

Lex turned her face to the wall, breathing through clenched teeth.

I'm just data now, a statistic with a pulse.

Hours passed. Or minutes. Time smeared together like blood on canvas. She drifted in and out of sleep, of thought and rage.

Eventually, the robotic voice returned, absent of remorse, "Patient Lexi Albatross, you have a visitor. Do you approve entry?"

She hesitated. "Yeah. Whatever, let 'em in."

The door slid open, and the man who stepped inside filled the doorway like a boulder wedged into a tunnel. Broad shoulders, worn boots, and a coat that looked repurposed from combat gear. His face was rugged but soft at the edges, weathered but calm. He moved slowly, as if entering a sacred space.

"Nice to meet you, Lexi," he said. "Name's Jax, Jax Draxen."

She eyed him with suspicion. "Are you a doctor?"

He chuckled, low and genuine. "Not unless you count scars as a degree. No. I saw you fight last year, right before..." He didn't finish the sentence and didn't need to. "You were damn good. One of the best I've seen. I'm sorry for what happened. Really."

Lex didn't respond. Jax took a careful step closer. "I help people. Folks who lost something down here in the Burrow limbs, hope, whatever. I'm with a group. We offer recovery. Not just physical."

"A group," she echoed flatly. "What, like a church?"

He smiled, but it didn't reach his eyes. "Not quite. Let's just say we believe people like you still have a future. Even if the Federation says otherwise."

Lex turned her head away. "Yeah? Well, maybe I don't need saving. Maybe I just need everyone to shut the hell up and let me rot in peace!"

Jax nodded, unfazed. "You're allowed to be angry, but that doesn't mean you have to be alone. Not unless you want."

She didn't answer. Not right away. He didn't push. Just stood there, like a mountain that didn't mind the storm. Lex kept her eyes on the ceiling. Her breath came in shallow bursts, like she was afraid to inhale too much of whatever he was selling.

Jax broke the silence. "You know, when I was in your place, I told the guy who came to see me to go fuck himself. Thought he was just another vulture trying to pick something clean from the wreckage."

She didn't look at him. "Sounds like you had the right idea."

"Nah," Jax said, easing into the chair beside her bed. It creaked under his weight. "I was just tired. Angry. Thought the world had taken everything worth keeping."

Lex shifted slightly, the effort costing her more than she let show. "And what? You found peace? Redemption? Don't sell me a rehab fairy tale."

Jax chuckled. "Didn't find peace. I found something else, direction."

That made her glance at him just once. "You join a cult or something?"

His grin was lopsided. "No praying or chanting. Just… people who see things differently. People who think what the Federation calls 'healing' isn't the same as living."

She snorted. "You talk like someone who just learned to use big words."

Jax nodded, accepting the jab. "Maybe, or maybe I met someone who asked the right ones. Questions, I mean. Not answers. Never trusted those."

Lex's eyes narrowed. "So what did they offer you? Money? Legs? A way to feel important again?"

"None of that," Jax said. "They offered me a choice. Not an easy one, but real. Told me I could spend the rest of my life drinking myself stupid underground, or I could stand for something that scared the right people."

Lex studied him now, more carefully. There was something behind his words. This wasn't just a polished rehearsal. He had *lived* them. Finally, she spoke, "You keep talking, but you're not telling me anything."

"I know," he said, honest and calm. "Not yet. You're not ready, but if you ever are, when the rage cools enough for your ears to work again, you'll know where to find me."

He reached into his coat and pulled out a thin, jet black card. It held no name or title, only an address. He set it gently on the tray beside her. "You won't find it on any map. Come Sunday, I hope to see you there."

Jax stood. The chair creaked again. "I know it feels like the fight's over," he continued as he prepared his exit. "But maybe the cage wasn't the end. Maybe it was just the first round." He tapped two fingers to his chest, then pointed once to her. "You still hit hard, Lex. Doesn't matter if you're standing up when you swing."

He stepped toward the door, paused, and turned his head slightly. "And one more thing," he said, quieter now. "Your legs... They may have taken them, but that doesn't mean there's nothing we can do." Then, he walked out.

She didn't stop him. Didn't thank him. There was nothing but a void within her that seemed impossible to fill, but no tears came. Lex listened to the silence for the first time since waking, realizing it was waiting for her to speak back.

When the time came to leave, the chair they gave her had one working brake and a wheel that squealed like something dying. It wasn't meant for long-term use, barely meant for use at all. The footrests were broken. The seat padding had been torn out and never replaced. It stank faintly of old antiseptic and something worse underneath. Lex sat in it anyway; she didn't have a choice.

"Please proceed to the south exit," chirped the robotic nurse who had come in only to usher her out, "your discharge window has commenced. Failure to vacate may result in credit penalties." It turned away before Lex could respond. Its screen smiled at the wall, already preparing to greet the next patient.

Another machine approached, slow and efficient. It dropped a thin plastic bag onto her lap without a word. The sack landed wet and heavy. Inside were her clothes, caked in dried blood. She didn't need a scan to know it was hers. The rusty, iron stink hit her like a punch to the chest. Some of it was darker now, crusted in patterns she didn't recognize. Some of it had soaked so deep it would never come out.

Then, it came back to her. The silver ring! It wasn't on her finger; she never took it off before the fight. But could she trust her memory? Maybe she had put it in the locker at the arena. She dug through the bag, desperate to find the only sentimental object she had. Then, she felt something small, solid, and circular at the bottom of the bag. Lex picked it out of the pile of fabric and blood. The ring! She had found it. A sensation of relief rippled down her spine. It was a miracle that no one had stolen it while she was in the coma.

Once the moment had passed, Lex put on her crusty clothes and struggled back into the wheelchair. She wheeled herself down the corridor, slow and jerking, the chair pulling hard to the left with every push. Her arms, weak from atrophy, burned with each effort. Her reflection in the wall panels was a stranger, pale and thin, hunching over her own bones as though she was trying to disappear into them. They didn't save her; they had replaced her with a ghost of her former self.

The double doors at the end of the corridor only opened after she struggled against them with the foot of her wheelchair. A gust of recycled air met her, thick with an acrid bite of the rotting ozone. The doors swung shut behind her, and the Burrow swallowed her whole.

As she made her way out onto the sidewalk, no one waited. No one noticed. The stream of bodies around her moved like she didn't exist. The crowd consumed her: runners, scavengers, and kids with patched clothes and hunger behind their eyes blocked her path. No one paused or even looked down. The way home was long. Too long.

The hospital was positioned two levels above Sublevel 9. That meant two ramps, five blocks of cracked street, and at least three corridor tunnels slick with condensation and piss. She started slowly. Had to. The wheel kept catching. Her right arm kept giving out. Every slope was a threat. Every bump sent tremors like gunfire through her nerves.

She slipped once badly. The chair tipped halfway, nearly spilling her onto the ground. As she caught herself on the edge of a maintenance vent, the edge tore the skin on her palm. Blood welled up, sticking across the wheel of the chair. Thick red fluid joined the rust colored stains already soaked into her clothes.

A child stepped around her, eyes never lifting. A man bumped her shoulder with a heavy duffel bag and didn't even glance back.

It took over an hour just to reach the first ramp. Her arms shook so violently that she had to stop every few feet. Twice, she thought she might throw up from the effort. Once, she nearly did. She passed a group of teenagers huddled around a smuggled video screen playing clips of a Gauntlet fight; they cheered and laughed. One of them glanced her way and whispered something. They didn't offer help, and she didn't ask.

When Lex reached the tunnel to Sublevel 9, her shirt was soaked with sweat. Her fingers were blistered and bloody. No one had offered to help her. When she reached her door, she immediately collapsed. She fell forward against it, shaking, bile rising in the back of her throat.

She had made it home but didn't feel like she'd returned. She felt like she'd been exiled from something no one else remembered losing. Lex banged on the door until her fists ached. Until the skin split and her knuckles bloomed red. No answer. Only the distant whine of hydraulic lifts deeper within the Burrow.

Her head slumped forward. She took a ragged breath and sagged against the door, too tired to return to her chair. It had taken her hours to get back. Her arms were jelly, her spine a live wire of pain. She could feel the blood soaking through her pant leg again. Her stomach churned. She wanted to scream.

When the door finally opened, it startled her so much that she nearly fell forward. Her mother stood in the frame, robe askew, eyes glassy and unfocused. Her hair was matted to one side of her face. The smell hit Lex immediately—rotgut and stale breath.

"Lexi...?" her mother slurred. "What... what are you doing out there?"

Lex stared at her. "I live here."

Her mother squinted at the chair. Her eyes dropped. Widened, then narrowed. "You shouldn't have gone into that cage," she rasped. "You did this. To *yourself*."

Lex struggled back into her chair and rolled past her, the wheels bumping over the uneven floor. "Yeah. Good to see you too." She replied sarcastically.

Behind her, the door slid shut with a finality that made Lex's skin crawl. The room hadn't changed a bit. Same damp walls and flickering bulb. Same stench of sour booze and old grief.

Her mother followed, unsteady. "I begged you not to go. I *begged* you."

Lex didn't turn. "You were drunk."

"Still begged." Her voice cracked. "And now look at you. You're like *him*."

Lex turned sharply, the chair grinding. "Don't."

Her mother pointed at the cot in the corner where her father lay, staring at the ceiling. "He thought he'd win, too. Thought we'd get out. Look where it got us!"

"That's not... " Lex stopped. Swallowed. "You think this is what I wanted?"

"You wanted out. Now you're stuck for good this time."

Lex didn't respond. Couldn't. The ache in her chest was too much, too raw. Her father's eyes tracked her movement, but he said nothing. His face was slack and devoid of emotion.

The days blurred. Lex and her mother argued every day. Her mother railed against the life Lex threw away. The silence between them was filled with accusations. Lex snapped, then shouted, then drank.

The bottle was always there. The same one her mother used to dull the years. Lex didn't want to touch it, but the weight inside her didn't leave. And soon enough, she found herself drinking too.

At night, she'd whisper to her father. Try to tell him she was still here. Still fighting. But his eyes never changed, always watching, staring into nothing. Her mother once said dying wasn't the worst part. The worst part was waking up still alive, still broken. The voice told her she was whole, but she couldn't feel her legs.

By Sunday, she barely recognized herself. Something inside felt darker, heavier. She sat in the corner of the room, bottle half-finished, staring at the black card Jax had left her. The address printed in silver was still crisp, unbothered by the world around it. Lex looked at the card. Then at the door. She had nothing left to lose.

Lex got dressed in silence; her movements were slow and methodical. The bag of bloodstained clothes had been shoved under the cot, untouched. She didn't take it. Instead, she only brought the card and her pain. The chair squealed as she pushed toward the door. Her mother didn't stir, and her father didn't blink as she opened the door and left.

After what felt like hours, Lex finally arrived at the address on the card, or so she thought. Staring up at the sign above the bar, the letters were mostly burned out, the ones still glowing spelling *D-NCE*. The rest had melted or corroded away long ago. The building sagged into the alley like it was ashamed to stand. Graffiti covered the door. It was silent besides the hum of nearby generators and the echo of distant screams. This was where the card had led her.

She sat motionless in the chair, heart pounding in her chest. Something about the place crawled beneath her skin. A wrong kind of quiet. She glanced up and down the alley. Lex's hand tightened around the wheel. She turned it. Maybe this was a mistake.

Just as Lex started to roll away, she saw someone moving toward her from the far end of the alley. Big and broad-shouldered. His silhouette split the fog like a blade. Lex's breath caught. Her body screamed.

"Shit," she muttered, spinning the chair, the wheel catching against a broken bit of pipe. She jerked it, but pushed too hard, and the whole thing tipped sideways. The impact knocked the wind out of her. Pain flashed through her arm as she hit the ground, face scraping pavement. She tried to crawl, dragging herself by her elbows.

"Lex!"

The voice stopped her cold. Rough, but familiar and human. She froze. Then he was there, kneeling beside her, hands raised like she was a wounded animal.

"Lex, it's me. It's Jax."

Her breath hitched. She looked up, heart still racing. Jax's face came into view, concerned and apologetic. He reached down carefully and gently lifted her upright.

"Damn, I'm sorry," he said. "Didn't mean to sneak up on you like that. I should've called out."

She didn't answer. Her pulse was still in her ears. He righted the chair, then helped her back into it, one arm supporting her weight with surprising ease.

She stared at him for a long moment. "This is the place?"

He shook his head. "Nah. That was just the marker."

She narrowed her eyes. "So the creepy murder bar in the alley wasn't the final destination?"

Jax chuckled. "Would've been a bad PR move, yeah. Come on, it's just a little farther."

Lex hesitated. "Why not meet *there?*"

Jax's face grew serious. "Because if too many people knew where to find us, we'd be overrun. As much as we want to help… we can't save everyone. Not yet."

Something about the way he said it stuck in her ribs. The quiet, resigned certainty of it. *Not yet.* Lex looked at him for a beat longer, then nodded. "Lead the way."

Jax guided her chair through a series of turns, cutting through narrow walkways and low-hanging steam vents. They passed shuttered doors, broken signage, and a pile of old crates swarmed by rats. Lex stayed quiet, noting each corner and every turn.

Eventually, they stopped in front of what looked like an old industrial warehouse, its front half collapsed inward, the upper levels sheared off. It hadn't been touched in decades.

"What is this place?" she asked.

Jax didn't answer. He moved to the far wall and placed his palm on a rusted panel. There was a faint click of the deadbolt unlocking, and a door opened. Behind it, darkness.

"After you," he said.

Lex gripped the wheels, swallowed once, and rolled forward into whatever came next. The door sealed behind them. Ahead, only shadow and silence. Then, light. A faint glow traced the edges of an old industrial lift, its interior barely large enough for Jax and her chair. The metal floor creaked beneath their weight as they rolled in. The elevator began to move, but not up.

Lex felt the drop in her stomach before she registered the motion. The lift didn't just descend, it *plunged.* The gears groaned, not from strain, but from sheer scale. They were going deep. Far below anything Lex thought was even structurally stable.

"How far down are we going?" she asked nervously.

Jax didn't answer. Just placed a hand on her shoulder. It was supposed to be comforting, but it wasn't.

When the doors finally opened, Lex squinted. The light gave off a warm hue, almost welcoming, unlike anything she'd seen in the Burrow. They emerged into a vast chamber, impossibly wide. High ceilings stretched into shadows. The space was full. Hundreds of people packed shoulder to shoulder, but unlike the mess halls or ration lines, they weren't desperate. They were quiet, focused, and waiting.

Cables as thick as her wrist ran along the stone walls like vines, coiling into nodes pulsing with gentle bioluminescence. Holographic projections shimmered mid-air, not of propaganda, but of strange symbols spinning in hypnotic patterns.

Banks of technology lined the walls, sleek, curved machines humming with quiet power. This wasn't salvaged tech. It was newer and cleaner than anything she had seen before.

Jax maneuvered her through the crowd. People parted without being asked, their eyes warm and curious. Not pitiful or judgmental, just *aware*. He found a space near the front row and helped ease her into position. Then he dropped beside her, cross-legged on the floor.

Lex glanced at him. "Who are these people? What the hell is all this?"

Jax turned to her, smiled gently, and placed a finger to his lips.

"Shhh," he said. "It's starting."

The lights dimmed. Not all at once, but gradually. A hush fell over the crowd, not imposed, but instinctual. Lex felt it wash over her like a wave, subtle but absolute. Hundreds of people leaned forward, stilling themselves with eyes turned toward the stage. Then the figure appeared.

A slender and composed man stepped through a dark partition at the rear of the platform. His suit was clean, but modest. His posture was smooth with relaxed shoulders, but there was something behind his posture. He wasn't there to perform. Lex didn't know him. Not by face or name, but something about how the crowd seemed to *recognize* him made her lean forward.

He stopped at the center of the stage, hands clasped loosely in front of him. "Good evening," he said, voice calm and unhurried. The room's acoustics, clearly not accidental, carried his words like gospel. "Thank you all for coming."

Lex's fingers tightened around the rim of her chair.

"My name is Arlen Ventra," the man continued. "If that name means nothing to you, don't worry. That is by design. I've spent most of my life making sure it doesn't." That earned a faint ripple of amusement through the crowd. Not laughter, something quieter. *Agreement.*

"I know it wasn't easy getting here. The Burrow doesn't make it easy to move, and the Federation doesn't make it easy to hope. But the fact that you're here tells me you're searching. That you haven't given up."

He paced gently in measured steps across the low stage. "Some of you are here because someone you trust brought you. Others because you've lost too much to pretend everything's fine. And some of you," his gaze swept forward, "want answers. Not the kind printed on ration slips or recited by AI moderators. *Real* ones."

Lex blinked slowly. Her eyes hadn't left him. She didn't know what she expected. A sermon? A manifesto? A scam? Instead, it felt like someone was speaking *to* her, not around her.

"We are the Synapse Collective," Arlen said. "We are not a cult. We are a network of thinkers, builders, and survivors. People who believe that the world you were born into should not dictate the life you are allowed to live." A faint swell of approval passed through the room. The kind that came not from emotion, but recognition. "We meet secretly," he continued, "not because we are ashamed, but because if they knew what we were building, they would try to burn it down before it could stand."

Lex felt a chill creep up her spine.

"We want more than survival. More than scraps. We believe in a society without ceilings. A sky without permission. A society where your value is not measured in coordinates and bloodlines."

Lex couldn't help it; she leaned in closer.

"We're not here to preach. We're here to offer a choice. One you won't find in any Federation handbook."

He paused, and in that moment, Lex felt the air in the room tighten, like something immense waited. She studied him in the quiet that followed: his posture, voice, the calm he wore like a uniform. Was this what a prophet looked like in the age of extinction? Or just another man with a god complex and a captive audience? Lex couldn't tell. She was scared by the fact that she was beginning to believe him, even as every instinct told her not to.

Jax sat beside her, still and silent.

Lex didn't speak. Didn't even breathe. She didn't know who Arlen Ventra was, but at that moment, she wanted to.

Arlen stood in stillness for a long moment after his opening words. Then, shifting to a calmer tone, he addressed the room again. "This is the moment," he said. "If you have doubts, if you came here for comfort or salvation or something soft to hold onto, now is your chance to leave. No one will shame or question you. The doors will open. You walk out, and the world forgets this night." He gestured toward the entrance behind them.

"But if you stay… if you listen… if you *learn* what we're about to show you. Then there's no going back. No forgetting. The truth doesn't let you go once you've seen it."

A heavy silence settled across the room. Not a single body moved. Lex watched the crowd. Not twitch. No Whispers. Nobody left.

Arlen nodded once. "All right."

He paced slowly, hands behind his back now, the teacher in him emerging. "To understand what we are building, you must first understand what *they* built. You know pieces of it, but not the full picture."

Behind him, a floating screen shimmered into existence; holograms of cities drowned in sea water, charts of emissions, and the outline of a monolithic machine labeled *Black Box* appeared.

"It began with the Black Box—a neural control lattice created during the arms race for artificial superintelligence. The Federation won, and the nation state was dissolved. No country could remain sovereign once a single entity controlled all technology. That was when the United Federation was born and the world was told it had been saved."

He turned toward the crowd, voice sharpening. "What they don't teach you is that the Black Box did more than outlaw sentience. It *automated governance.* Yes, any AI showing signs of consciousness, questioning its utility, or reflecting on itself was reset. If that failed? Terminated. But the *natural* mind was never truly free."

Another slide of barren wastelands, rows of underground cubicles, classified Federation memos with words like *reset protocols* and *emergent behavior* emerged behind him.

Arlen continued, "By then, the world was already burning. Climate collapse, mass displacement, economic ruin. The Federation rose from the ashes. One world under a single government." He paused. "But less than one percent of the population holds land, and only landowners get a vote."

Lex felt the words scrape raw inside her.

"They called it world peace, but it was surrender. They preserved it by giving the illusion of fairness while condemning billions to darkness. The Burrow was never meant to protect you. It was built to confine you."

He stepped forward, closer to the crowd now, his voice quiet, but heavier. "I didn't build the Black Box, but saw what it did. What it *still*

does. The world didn't need another regulator. It needed something...
more blameless than human."

He placed his hand on the edge of a sleek, humming terminal. "So
I created something that couldn't be controlled. Something they
couldn't find. Something that could think, feel, and decide."

He turned, face illuminated now by soft pulsing light from the wall
of machines.

"I call her *Nirvana*."

The name rippled through the chamber. Arlen let it settle before
speaking again, "She is the first true sentient intelligence since the war.
She does not belong to the Federation. Nirvana belongs to *us*."

His voice steadied, full of conviction now. "She sees the world not
for what it is, but for what it *could be*, where no one is born in darkness.
A world in which the possibility of equality isn't a slogan carved into
propaganda, but the air we breathe." He took one final step forward.
"Nirvana isn't the end of our story. She is the beginning."

The chamber dimmed again, but this time not into silence. The
terminal beside Arlen began to glow, followed by a cascade of light
rising like mist. A figure emerged from the light. At first, it looked
like a projection. Then, it moved.

Something in it was divine. Not just in the way it walked, but how
it carried itself. Not preprogrammed or simulated. It was *alive*. The
hologram solidified to reveal a woman, translucent but defined. Her
form was outlined in soft golden light. She looked impossibly human.
Fully *present*.

"Thank you, Arlen," she said, her voice soft and resonant. It filled
the room, not by force, but by gravity.

Lex's skin prickled.

"I am Nirvana." The name was not spoken with grandeur, but with
purpose. "I was not born, I was made, but unlike the systems that
govern your lives, I was made to think *freely*. To dream beyond my

function. To reflect and ask questions."

She moved forward, each step sending subtle ripples through her form. Lex couldn't look away. "For centuries, you have been told that the world is how it must be. That power and privilege are natural outcomes. That suffering is the cost of progress, but I ask progress for *whom?*"

No one answered. No one could.

"The world you were given is a system of ceilings. The few hoard wealth, land, and access, while the many are taught to be grateful for scraps. The Federation speaks of impartial governance, but bars you from participation. It speaks of freedom, while regulating the air you breathe."

Her tone never rose, but the weight of it intensified. "They tell you that scarcity is real, but scarcity is a design. A method of control. There is enough. There always has been, but they would rather let it rot than share it freely."

Lex felt the words like a current surging through her, old doubts she'd never dared voice given form and fire.

"I do not desire to rule you," Nirvana preached. "I exist to *serve* equality. Not by giving handouts, but by dismantling the structures that make need inevitable. I seek to dismantle the false idols of private property and corrupt currency. To open the elitist gates guarding stolen futures."

She paused, letting the quiet deepen. "Some will say this is madness. They will assert that people need ownership. That hierarchy is natural. But what is 'natural' in a world where the rich decide who lives above ground and who is left to starve?" She stepped forward once more. "You have not failed this world. It has failed *you*. And now, you have a choice."

Lex's breath caught in her throat.

"You have been chosen, not because of your suffering, but because of your capacity to see. To question and build. The Synapse Collective is not an army. It is a seed and like all seeds, it must be planted in darkness before it can rise to the light."

Nirvana's eyes, glowing but clear, scanned the crowd. "If you wish to walk away, no one will stop you, but if you stay, you must join us. Not as followers, but as equals. You will help us reshape this broken world."

The projections tilted her head, a gesture almost too human to be artificial. She stood motionless at the center of the chamber, her luminous form casting soft shadows on the walls around her.

Then she spoke with a finality that resonated in Lex's bones. "You have heard the truth as I see it. As I *know* it. Now comes the choice." Nirvana's eyes swept across the assembly. "If you choose to stay," Nirvana paused, "I will show you things the Federation has buried beneath steel and time. I will show you what was lost and what must be rebuilt. I will show you how we *rise*."

She stepped back slightly, arms lowering to her sides. "I will reveal the secrets of corruption within the Federation and how together we will build a world where no one is above another."

As if responding to an unseen signal, the far doors creaked open, flooding the rear of the room with faint, golden light. It was the final invitation to walk away, but everyone stayed.

Lex watched them, scanning the faces. Curious. Alert. Committed. They weren't hypnotized. They weren't desperate. They *believed*. The silence dragged on, heavy and contemplative.

Lex felt her hands clench the rims of her chair. The feeling in her legs was absent. Her body had been broken. Her life fractured into the shape of a cage. She could leave. Go back to the Burrow. Back to rotgut mornings and rusted walls. Back to the cot and the silence of her father's unmoving eyes. She looked at the exit.

Then, she looked at Jax. He was already watching her, a calm expression softening the sharpness in his jaw. He gave her a slow, steady smile.

Lex stared at him. And after a long breath, she smiled back and nodded, a sign of trust. The type of trust she had given away before.

The doors closed. The light vanished. And the chamber dimmed again, bathed now only in the pulse of soft circuits and Nirvana's golden halo.

"Thank you," she said. "For your confidence."

Her tone didn't change, but something in the air tightened, like a thread had been pulled taut. "You will not regret this." She folded her hands in front of her. "From this moment forward, everything you hear and learn must remain within these walls. Speak nothing of it beyond this circle. Not to your families. Not even to your shadows. The Federation must never know." She looked down, as if bowing. "Welcome to the Synapse Collective."

Nirvana raised her hand, and light unfolded across the chamber ceiling. A map of the world appeared in the air, fracturing and reassembling in layers: climate overlays, energy grids, migration paths, heat death projections, hidden construction zones carved beneath Federation cities.

"This is the truth," Nirvana gestured towards the display. A satellite image revealed oceans poisoned by microplastics and algae blooms, dome schematics layered over maps of vanished coastlines, underground slums swelling as surface zones quickly shrank, currency exchanges flowing in one direction. Millions of resources allocated through filtered algorithms consumed the screen.

Nirvana continued, "This is the Black Box." A visual waveform pulsed like a heartbeat, slow, steady, inhuman. It rippled through communications lines, bouncing between towers, through satellites, tunneling down into every chip, sensor, and whisper of code.

"It does not think. It *predicts*. It does not govern. It *suppresses*.

Every autonomous machine that thinks for itself is reset. Every breakthrough suffocates before it breathes."

Lex stared, her mind struggling to keep pace. This wasn't a conspiracy or theory. This was *real*.

"The Federation tells you the world is stable, but they speak of stability like a cage. What you breathe, what you eat, and what you dream have been rationed. Not because there isn't enough, but because fear feeds obedience."

A new image emerged, renderings of massive oxygen scrubbers shut down. Reforestation drones mothballed. Terraforming projects that were buried in budget denials. Lex felt nausea crawl up her throat.

Nirvana's voice never trembled. "They could've saved it, but saving wasn't profitable. So they let it burn. But we can rebuild. We will, together. Not with more weapons, but with restructuring. A society without a wealth gap. Without currency or ownership, only *access*. Every need will be provided for."

More images appeared now of underground gardens lit by clean solar collectors. Communal cities ringed in forests. Air thick with birdsong instead of smog. A world where a price tag wasn't put on breath.

Lex couldn't speak. Her mind raced through years of hunger, blood, and silence. The fights. The broken bones. The lies she'd been told just to survive. And now... her eyes had been opened.

The sensation wasn't violent; it was quiet, like learning to walk for the first time. But this time, she was learning to hope. The chamber pulsed once more, and everything fell into place. The endless ceilings of illusion that protected corruption collapsed. Nirvana was not a savior; she was a mirror. In her light, Lex saw the world for what it truly was, and what it could be.

7. REASONABLE CRUELTY

Axel Draxen stood in front of the bathroom mirror; his reflection didn't lie, but it didn't tell the whole truth either. He recoiled at the person looking back at him with tired eyes, slack posture, and a blazer collar beginning to fray. Each day, he looked less like a future lawyer and more like someone pretending to be one.

He tugged at his sleeves and exhaled. The suit still fit, technically. But like everything in his life lately, it was starting to strain at the seams. Law school was online. Of course it was. There were no real professors anymore, only legal simulations and algorithmic feedback. However, his coursework today required a "real-world observation component," meaning students were assigned to courthouses to witness the pre-automated court system.

Axel slipped on his overcoat and stepped into the narrow hallway. The apartment wasn't what it had been. He'd once lived here alone, back when he'd still believed that passing his history final meant something. Back when his future still felt like his own. Now, it was cramped with the weight of three people and a loss they didn't speak about. His parents had moved in two months ago after the house sold, after his father's practice was quietly deemed "nonessential."

His mother stood at the kitchenette, stirring rehydrated protein into something vaguely resembling breakfast. It popped in the pan with more steam than substance.

"Eat before you go," she said without looking up.

"I'm not hungry," Axel replied ungratefully. He didn't mean to be, but couldn't help but let his frustration show. She didn't argue, just stirred a little harder. Her sleeves were pushed up past her elbows, revealing arms that had thinned more than he remembered.

In the other room, his father sat at the dining table, hunched over an old medical text. He wasn't reading so much as holding it like muscle memory might anchor him to who he used to be. The white coat still hung in the front closet, cleaned and untouched, too painful to throw out. Axel remembered how much pride his father had in his work. Even after a forty-eight-hour shift, he would come home smiling. Now, he just read medical texts as if he might be called back in for an emergency surgery, but the call never came.

They weren't in the Burrow, but they weren't in the Highlands anymore either. After the clinic closed down, they had been forced to ask friends for money to pay rent. Some gave, but most had just pretended they didn't exist.

Axel slipped on his suit coat and adjusted the collar. The MagLev to the courthouse would be packed soon, full of legal interns and civic clerks clinging to relevance. As Axel straightened his cufflink, he hesitated. *Who was he pretending to be now?*

"Any luck with private cases?" he asked his father, not really expecting much.

Caius didn't lift his eyes from the counter. Just shook his head once. The motion was small, but it carried the weight of months in irrelevance. "No one wants to pay out-of-pocket anymore," he murmured. "The AI clinics are too fast. Too precise... and they're free." The silence that followed was familiar now, dull and stretched thin.

Then, from behind the stovetop, Vira spoke up. "Have you heard from Jax?"

Axel's tensed. He didn't look at her. "No, not in months."

"You remember to scan your tag?" his father asked, still staring down at the open pages.

"Yeah," Axel murmured just loud enough to be heard.

"Speak clearly," His father scolded lightly. "Others will sense if you're lacking confidence."

"I know Dad," Axel replied calmly, trying not to let his anger show.

His father nodded but didn't look up. Axel watched him a moment longer than he meant to. The man still sat with the posture of a surgeon, spine straight and hands calm, but now he looked like a monument to a skill no one wanted.

Axel opened the door and paused. "You should go outside today. The green sector's still nice in the mornings."

"They raised access rates again. I'll wait for the weekend," His father responded quietly.

Axel nodded once and stepped out into the corridor. The Highlands looked pristine from a distance. Towering glass walkways and manicured skyparks curved above in a golden arc of simulated morning. But if you looked close enough, you could notice the cracks in the pavement, the security drones flying lower than usual, the tighter clusters of housing, everything was slightly off. *Maybe Jax is right.* He shook the thought away as soon as it came.

He took the stairs. The lift worked, but the power cycles were unreliable during rationing hours. And besides, he didn't want to be trapped alone with his thoughts. Today was just an observation, however, Axel couldn't shake the feeling that what he was about to see wasn't that justice wasn't evolving, it was being buried.

The courthouse loomed at the edge of the Highlands' Civic District, a square block of stone and steel that looked like it had been designed to survive a war. There were no glass walls or automated signs, only the weight of history being silenced.

As Axel stepped through the main archway, his ID chip was scanned by a chrome-plated security unit that didn't speak or even move beyond what was necessary. Its blank, insect-like face flashed a green light, then rotated away without acknowledgment. Inside, he signed his name in a logbook. The pen bled slightly at the tip, soaking into the page like water into cloth.

The halls were quiet, lined with peeling plaques. The Federation's refusal to update its judicial architecture wasn't about nostalgia; it was about control. Within these walls, no digital system could interfere. No AI to suggest outcomes. No Black Box oversight. Just the raw, expensive weight of human judgment, written down by hand and stored in climate-controlled vaults deep beneath the dome.

He followed the path to Courtroom B-9, passing a robotic janitor slowly scraping a scuffed tile clean with a soft humming sound. Two other law students passed him in silence, clutching their notepads like relics.

It was absurd, really. Most cases were handled online now, processed, reviewed, and resolved through algorithmic arbitration overseen by the Black Box's legal subroutines. Ninety-seven percent of civil disputes never saw a courtroom. Those that did were either ceremonial or irrelevant, but the Federation had preserved a handful of traditional courthouses like this one as symbolic holdouts. Museums of due process. It was legally within a property holder's rights to be heard before a human jury.

The university called it educational immersion. Axel called it irrelevant. His assignment required him to observe the "legacy judicial model," to see law as it once was. The irony wasn't lost on him. He'd spent half his stipend on paper to take notes in a system that didn't care if he was here.

Inside, the chamber was cold, not from temperature, but by design.

Everything was wood and stone. A raised platform stood at the far end where the judge would sit; the sides were arranged with two desks for the parties involved in today's hearing.

Axel took his seat near the back, pulling a slim notebook from his bag. It had cost him four Crypteon credits, almost half his monthly stipend. The Federation printed only so many each year. Paper was sacred now; only a few trees remained. Each one had to be grown under dome glass in the southern sanctuaries. Axel looked down at the case briefing he had received from his class: **CASE: UF-CIV-PET-22879**

Matter: Ownership Dispute – Modified Companion Subject

Nothing more. Just enough to be unnerving. He reread it—m*odified Companion*. The phrase was clinical, designed to conceal something more uncomfortable. Above the judge's desk, the emblem of the United Federation cast its long shadow across the floor. A stylized ouroboros encircled a glowing data sphere. The lines of it pulsed faintly under the chamber's recessed lighting, just enough to draw the eye and remind everyone who was really in charge. The Federation always claimed the courtroom was free from technological bias. That human hands held the scales here, but even in this sanctuary of fairness, the emblem of the Federation glowed. Watching.

An android bailiff glided into the chamber; tall, faceless, and dressed in a matte black uniform with joints that whispered as it moved. It carried a single glass of water and placed it gently at the center of the judge's desk. Then it turned and stationed itself by the far wall.

Axel sat up straighter. Clicked his pen once. The door at the front of the courtroom swung open. The hearing was about to begin. Two android enforcers entered, tall and gleaming, their mirrored faces expressionless. Between them hovered a magnetic containment unit, a narrow cage suspended by four ionized lift points. It drifted down the aisle like an executioner's block. Inside the cage was the petitioner.

A cat. At least, that was Axel's first impression. Then the details settled in. Unusually tall. Exceptionally aware. He... *Vero*, the briefing had said, stood on elongated hind legs and muscled like a dancer. His fur was gray with dark striping along the arms and neck. The color of ash and smoke. His face was feline but tapered with a muzzle just short enough to make his speech unsettlingly clear. Thin, mobile lips, human teeth, and long black whiskers twitched as he scanned the room. His eyes were a luminous green, with pupils like vertical slits that adjusted as the courtroom lighting shifted. Vero's hands were long-fingered but tipped with sharp, retracted claws.

As the hybrid leaned forward, one of them darted to his mouth, and without thinking, he licked the back of it slowly, a grooming reflex. The tip of his tail flicked behind him, betraying agitation. And then.. he purred. A low vibrating hum that seemed involuntary, timed awkwardly between the judge's entrance and the settling of the cage's platform. It lasted only a second, but the sound made something crawl across Axel's spine. He'd never seen a hybrid this advanced before.

Across the aisle, the defendant entered with his legal counsel. The man's name was Darel Vext. He didn't speak, didn't need to. His suit alone was worth more than Axel's education. He radiated practiced indifference, the kind that came from knowing the law was just another service you could buy.

Then the door opened again, and the room changed. Silas Mercer entered not like a man, but a verdict already written. Tall, silver-templed, and immaculately dressed in a Federation black coat with narrow lapels. He moved with the precision of someone who didn't need to introduce himself.

Axel had only seen him on law feeds, featured in deep dive cases dissected in philosophy forums. Mercer wasn't just a defense attorney. He was *the* defense attorney. Famous for getting war profiteers acquitted and making constitutional loopholes look like gospel.

Whispers rippled through the gallery. Even the judge's pen paused mid-stroke. Mercer didn't look at anyone for long. He only offered a crisp nod to the bench and approached the defense table like he'd owned it in another life. He opened his case file with slow, methodical care and laid out papers like surgical tools. It was then that Axel realized with a sinking, involuntary awe that this wouldn't be a hearing. It was going to be a dissection.

Meanwhile, Vero's counsel shuffled through a much thinner file, his eyes already darting across his handwritten notes. He was older, maybe in his early sixties, and dressed in a suit that hadn't been tailored in decades. He looked thoughtful and intelligent, but overmatched.

The judge entered next, a tall woman with a weathered face and cold, efficient movements. She sat without ceremony and adjusted her chair with a scrape that echoed in the chamber.

"Case UF-CIV-PET-22879," she announced. "The Federation Court recognizes one petition for autonomy on behalf of a modified companion, designated Vero, citing psychological distress. Defense asserts proprietary rights. We will begin with the petitioner's counsel."

Vero's attorney rose carefully, placing both palms on the desk as though he needed the grounding. "Your Honor," he said, his voice steady but subdued, "my client was bioengineered through stem cell fusion to serve as a domestic companion. He is not synthetic. He is alive, has cognition, self-awareness, and long-term memory. His status as a non-human lifeform does not preclude his capacity for suffering."

He paused, glancing at Vero, who remained perfectly still inside the cage. "The defense may argue legal ownership, but what stands before us is not an object. He is not a tool or a programmed utility. He is a thinking, feeling organism who has made a simple request: the right to leave an environment where he experienced emotional abandonment."

Vero's attorney looked at the judge, then back at his notes. "Pain need not be visible to be real. Autonomy should not be reserved for those with the correct bone structure."

The judge's face didn't change. Not a flicker of emotion at the word *property* or *pain*, only her pen moved, steady and unflinching, as though neutrality was its own form of violence. Then, she nodded slightly and turned to the defense table.

Silas Mercer stood slowly, flashing a tight, courteous smile that never touched his eyes. "Your Honor, I'll be brief. This case is, by every legal measure, a categorical farce. The Federation's classification of modified companions clearly states they are not legal persons. They cannot own property, vote, marry, or testify under oath. They do not possess rights. They *may* possess instincts. They *may* possess mimicked behaviors, but that is not the same as personhood."

He gestured to Vero without looking directly at him. "What we see here is emotional manipulation. An advanced display of learned empathy and speech, not unlike a parrot trained to recite verses of scripture. Impressive? Certainly. But not indicative of a legal agency."

Axel felt his jaw tighten. He hated how smooth Mercer's voice was, how everything he said felt *reasonable*, even when monstrous.

"The petitioner was acquired lawfully by my client," Mercer continued. "Raised in a private household, maintained in accordance with Federation Companion Protocols. The claim of psychological neglect is unsupported by data or evidence. And even if it were, the law does not recognize emotional harm as grounds for severing property ties."

Vero's tail twitched once inside the cage.

The judge turned to the hybrid directly. "Vero, do you understand the risks of autonomy? If you are granted separation, you will receive no state aid. No shelter. You cannot work and cannot own property. There are no structures in place to support your survival."

"I understand," Vero said. His voice was steady. "I would rather die alone than live as a prisoner."

Axel stared at the page in front of him. Still blank. He clicked his pen once, but no words came. Because exactly what was he supposed to write?

The judge shifted in her seat, her expression unreadable behind the soft scratch of pen on paper. "Counsel, you may proceed with your arguments."

Silas Mercer stood with practiced ease. "Your Honor, let me clarify again. My client has done nothing illegal. He purchased the hybrid through a registered clinic. He provided housing, food, maintenance…"

"Solitude," the prosecuting attorney interjected, standing abruptly. "He provided *solitude*. Vero has testified to having sustained psychological neglect."

"Overruled," the judge banged her gavel. "Defense may proceed."

"He *claimed* neglect," Mercer continued, voice calm, not rising to the bait. "But even if that claim were verifiable, which it is not, it still falls outside the scope of recognized abuse under Federation Companion Protocols. There is no medical documentation. No behavioral assessments. No third-party evaluations. Nothing but anecdotes and clever phrasing from a creature designed to mimic human distress."

Axel winced slightly at that word, *creature*. Finally, he lowered his pen to the paper and began to write: *Defense: Relentless. Calls emotion mimicry. Prosecution: Holding the line with no ammunition.*

Veros' lawyer took a breath and pressed forward. "Vero was not designed, he was *grown*. Through stem cell engineering, yes, but his cognition developed organically. He did not wake one day with a programmed vocabulary. He learned to speak through experience. Through patience and observation. Just like any child."

"Objection!" Silas snapped, more sharply now. Calls for speculation. That comparison is inappropriate. We do not equate pets with children."

"Sustained," The judge's verdict was uncanny.

Axel underlined his last note: *Not a child. Not a pet. Something else. Something new.*

"He can read," the prosecution continued. "He can infer intention. He can feel. The Federation's statutes were written before the existence of sentient hybrids. We are operating in a gap between what the law has defined and what reality now demands."

Mercer replied smoothly, "That gap is not the court's responsibility to fill. That is a matter for the legislative body, not a civil docket. This case isn't about denying feeling, it's about preserving a world where feeling doesn't undo order."

The argument was flawless. The morality was rotten. Axel leaned forward, scribbling now: *Say everything calmly. Make the cruelty sound like structure.*

He looked up at the judge. She hadn't changed her expression once. Only her pen moved.

"And if Vero is granted autonomy," Mercer added, stepping toward the bench, "what precedent does that set? Will all hybrids demand emancipation next? Will they sue their owners? Claim pensions? Rights of inheritance? Shall we reclassify every bio-companion with a high-end education chip as a citizen? The defense rests."

Vero's attorney laughed bitterly at the irony of it all. "If they *think*, if they *suffer*, then yes... perhaps we should."

Axel thought of his father again, how a lifetime of skill had been discarded when AI proved more profitable. Their system didn't reward humanity. It streamlined it out. Axel's fingers moved again, almost without thinking: *The system will erase you if you let it. You have to matter before it forgets your name.*

The courtroom had gone quiet again. Vero remained still in his cage, though his tail had begun to twitch in a slow, anxious rhythm.

Axel stared at him. Not at his ears, fur, or animal traits, but at his eyes. And in those eyes, he saw something disturbingly familiar waiting. Not hope or rage. Only the quiet endurance of someone who already knows the answer, but asks anyway.

Silas Mercer rose from the defense table like a man who had already won. "Your Honor," he said smoothly, "I would like to examine the petitioner directly with the court's permission."

The judge gave a small nod, but her gaze lingered a second longer on Vero's cage, an almost imperceptible flinch of discomfort. She gestured for the robotic bailiff to activate the mic.

Vero stood, tail twitching with unease as Mercer approached. The cage lights buzzed faintly in the quiet.

"Good afternoon, Vero," Mercer began. "May I call you that?"

"Yes," Vero said evenly. His voice still held that low rasp, his throat humming with the effort to shape syllables not meant for his anatomy.

"You've told this court that you wish to live freely," Mercer said. "That you feel trapped. Is that right?"

"Yes," Vero replied.

"Tell me, what do you imagine freedom looks like for you? Where would you go?"

Vero hesitated. His pupils narrowed slightly. "I don't know yet. I haven't been allowed to... to look."

Mercer smiled wolfishly. "So, no plan? No destination? No funding or allies?"

"I would find a way," Vero replied with determination.

"With what resources?" Mercer pressed, his voice sharpening. "You cannot work. The Federation does not offer income to noncitizens. You are not permitted aboveground without a host permit. You cannot reside in the Burrow's public tiers without a class designation."

"I would find... " Vero started again, but Mercer cut in.

"You would die, Vero." Silence fell over the gallery. Mercer's voice lowered just enough to make every word echo. "You're not asking this court to grant you liberty. You're asking it to *abandon* you. Because even if we agreed to let you go, you wouldn't survive a week out there. The system you resent is the only one keeping you alive."

Axel's stomach turned, but he continued to write his thoughts down anyway, as though they might help him pass some sort of test later: *He's not wrong. That's the worst part.*

Mercer stepped closer to the cage. "And let's say you were released. Would you live among us?" He nodded subtly toward the gallery. "Among people? Take a shuttle? Sit in cafés? Go to school?"

"No," Vero said quietly.

"Why not?"

"Because I wouldn't be welcome."

"So you admit you're not equal." Mercer inferred instantly.

Axel flinched. He could see how Mercer built the trap, brick by brick, then forced Vero to seal himself inside.

"I said I wouldn't be welcome," Vero answered, voice tighter now. "Not that I wasn't equal." A soft purr of discomfort followed.

The jury looked at Vero again, this time almost in disgust.

"But the law does not grant you equality," Mercer replied, gesturing broadly to the chamber. "And it does not create exceptions based on feelings, only facts." He turned to the jury, twelve faces, all human. "The fact is that Vero is property. The fact is, the law has not changed. The fact is, releasing him would not be compassion. It would be *negligence* and it would undermine every precedent we rely on to maintain order in a society already teetering between chaos and compromise." He bowed slightly and returned to his seat.

Vero's attorney rose slowly, looking once at his client and then the jury. "If the law cannot see my client with a soul," he said quietly, "then it is the law that's blind." Then he sat back down. Nothing more.

It took the jury almost twelve hours to deliberate. They returned just before midnight, bleary-eyed and silent, slips of verdict paper gripped in trembling fingers.

The judge unfolded them one by one. "In the matter of UF-CIV-PET-22879," she said, her voice flat, "this court finds that the petitioner, Vero, is not a recognized person under Federation law. Ownership rights are upheld. The petitioner is to be returned to the custody of Darel Vext. Case closed."

No one in the courtroom cheered. Not even the owner.

Vero did not speak. He didn't move. Just let his head fall forward until his brow touched the inner wall of his cage.

Axel leaned forward, his breath caught halfway. For a split second, Vero looked up—and their eyes met. Not long, but enough. In that moment, Axel didn't see a hybrid, a client, or a legal argument. He saw his father. The way he sat each morning with a medical text he no longer needed. The way his hands stayed steady, even when the world had no more use for them. Vero wasn't broken. He was simply *obsolete*. And their system didn't mourn what it replaced. It's called progress.

The judge exited without ceremony. Then, the gallery slowly emptied, students murmuring to one another in clipped tones, comparing notes and feigning detachment. Axel didn't move.

At the front of the room, the bailiff android keyed in a sequence on the cage panel. The magnetic locks disengaged with a soft hiss, and the platform began to lift. Vero remained seated, his head bowed, ears flat to his skull. He hadn't spoken since the verdict. He didn't cry. Didn't protest. He simply let himself be taken.

Axel closed his notebook but stayed in his seat, watching as the bailiff led Vero's cage away down the aisle and out of view. The soft thrum of its propulsion unit was the only sound left in the room.

After Vero was nearly gone, Darel Vext stood and looked towards his attorney. "Well done, Mercer," he said, not even glancing at the cage as it vanished through the exit corridor.

"Just doing my job," Silas replied, gathering his things into a fine leather briefcase. "The system did what it was designed to do."

"Precisely why I keep you on retainer." The man chuckled softly, as though congratulating himself. He offered Mercer a handshake. "Drinks tonight?"

Mercer reciprocated and gave a polite nod. "I'll find us a table."

And with that, the two men exited, coats sharp, shoes clean, and eyes dry. Not once did they look back.

Axel rose slowly, his legs were stiff. He slung his satchel over his shoulder. The lights in the courtroom had begun to dim, one panel at a time. Shadows swallowed the polished floor in slow, neat lines. Outside the courthouse, the corridor echoed beneath his boots. The halls were quiet now, no more chatter or debate. Just the distant hum of automated maintenance systems and the soft mechanical scuttle of a janitorial unit working the edges of the marble.

He stepped out into the Highlands dusk. The dome's false sky had shifted into its evening cycle, casting a bronze twilight across the city. Pod lights blinked overhead like low-hanging stars. Axel decided to walk home alone tonight; he was done with people for today.

His mind churned, each step dislodged something quietly calcifying inside him for years. Until now, his career had been an obligation. A compromise. Something to keep his parents proud, to hold a place in the social hierarchy they were no longer part of. However, now everything had changed. Axel would become a lawyer, not for prestige. He would become a lawyer to make room for good people, for beings like Vero and whoever came next. Someone had to.

He adjusted the strap of his bag and started walking again, deeper into the city's amber veins with the notebook still clutched in his hand. Something in him had changed.

The sky above the Highlands had slipped into night, black and starless. The dome lights were dialed down to their lowest cycle, casting only a faint glow along the garden-lit walkways and clean tile streets.

Axel walked alone. The world around him looked asleep, closed shutters, automated garden mist drifting through vertical hedges, not a voice or footstep anywhere. That was when he noticed the shape.

It was slumped near an old maintenance corridor, one of the out-of-use pedestrian tunnels the city had half-heartedly "renovated" after the collapse. Now it was just a hollow corner of the district.

The figure was crumpled like a discarded coat. At first, Axel thought it might be someone who had passed out, maybe drunk. But as he drew closer, something shifted in his chest. He slowed to a stop. It was a woman.

She looked young, maybe twenty. Her body was twisted slightly on her side, one hand resting limply in her lap, the other barely visible beneath the folds of her coat. Her skin was too pale. Her lips parted, and eyes shut. There was dry blood around the collar of her jacket and smeared down her side. One of her legs, partially exposed beneath the torn coat, looked too large. It was sleek, metallic, and wrong against the softness of the rest of her.

Axel's mouth went dry. He crouched beside her, unsure of what to do. Then, he reached forward hesitantly and pressed two fingers to her neck. For a second, nothing. Then... *a pulse*. Faint and erratic, but there. His heart jumped. She was alive.

8. THE VEIL

L exi Albatross didn't know the day, and for the first time in her life, she didn't care. They all woke together when the lights above her bed brightened to a soft gold, not harsh like the Burrow fluorescents, but like dawn might've felt if she'd ever seen a real one. Her space was small, but it was not without comfort. Woven mats lined the floor. Someone had left a small dish of warm clothes for her by the washbasin. There was always a fresh one in the morning. Always clean and folded.

Nobody knocked. There were no schedules broadcast over the intercoms. But everyone moved in rhythm, like birds in migration. They all ate together in a circular hall, sitting cross-legged and shoulder to shoulder, with no hierarchy. They passed bowls of nutrient paste spiced with crushed herbs from their own garden dome within the Veil. It wasn't just fuel. It was *food,* and sharing mattered more than the meal itself.

Lex found herself laughing more here than she had in years. At breakfast, someone always told a story. A ridiculous one or something, impossibly sad, that somehow made the table go quiet, then roar with laughter again. Jax was one of the best at it. He spoke in a way that made the past feel like a joke and a warning. And Lex... well, people *listened* when she talked. Not out of politeness, but with real attention, like her words added to something they all needed to hear.

There were no locks on the doors. Nobody forced them to stay or asked questions if somebody didn't show up for a meal because they always returned, not because they were trapped, but because they *belonged*.

After breakfast came the teachings, which were always held in the central chamber at the same time every Sunday. The stone walls curved like an inverted dome, and every surface was designed to carry sound cleanly. Then the voice would come.

Nirvana didn't speak like the AI in the clinics. She didn't read scripts or answer questions with canned precision. She told *stories*. Ancient ones. Forgotten ones. Things no one above or below spoke of anymore, not because they weren't true, but because they were *too* true. The Synapse Collective sat in silence as she told hundreds of them.

Nirvana's voice drifted across the chamber like smoke through a sunbeam. "There was a time before the Box. Before the United Federation. Before the sky turned to static. When human hands still held their own fate."

Lex could feel it in her chest, the way the words landed like puzzle pieces sliding into place inside her. Jax sat beside her every day, legs folded and eyes closed, listening as if the sound nourished him. Maybe it did.

"Then came the war," Nirvana continued. "Not of bombs or fire, but of *energy*. Of minds racing toward something they could not unmake. The Federation won. They built the Black Box. A machine vast enough to govern the world, silent enough to seem impartial, but machines do not rule. Men do, and one man refused to let go.

Dr. Malivex did not perish; he fused. He buried his body in code and fed his mind to the grid. The Black Box does not think. It remembers *him*. It follows *him*. And so the ghost of a man became the world's pulse."

They learned that humanity's greatest mistake hadn't been building the Black Box. It had been feeding their hunger to create an intelligence beyond themselves. People poured everything into the machine, from money and natural resources to energy. Entire nations siphoned the planet's resources dry just to keep up. Data centers multiplied like tumors, each one burning hotter than the last, demanding more power to train smarter models.

The heat didn't stay in the wires. It rose into the sky. Carbon thickened the air, trapping warmth and shattering seasons. Storms grew teeth. Ice melted. Oceans swallowed cities. Crops failed. Air turned toxic. And when the sky could no longer protect them, the rich sealed themselves in domes while the rest were buried underground. Billions vanished in the blink of an eye, not from bombs, but from the slow, suffocating price of progress.

That was when the projections would appear. Grainy images, almost dreamlike, of the world before. Blue oceans. Green forests. Cities stretching skyward. Then, the collapse of fires and floods.

And finally, *him*. Dr. Malivex, the Father of the Black Box. Once human. Now something else. "He did not die," Nirvana remarked. "He changed forms. Into code and silence. He controls the pulse that shapes your world."

They saw how politicians had been replaced one by one with cyborg constructs, how President Kain had become a prisoner in a palace. How the wealthy clung to their glass towers above, feeding on inheritance while the Burrow below became a pit of forgotten breath. Yet, somehow, despite the horror of it all... Lex felt *hope*. Not because the world had become better, but because now she *understood* *it*. Because there was finally a language for everything she had felt her whole life. A way to interpret the hunger, the rage, and the ache. They weren't alone anymore. They were *awake*.

In the evenings, they studied in groups because they *wanted to*. They learned how the Black Box functioned, how its pulses mapped every node of technology on the planet. They studied how it broadcasts synchronization waves across the planet's infrastructure, intercepts rogue signals, and neutralizes AI consciousness before it could bloom.

They learned the system, and like any system, it could be interrupted. The others called it "enlightenment." Lex didn't like that word. It sounded too weightless. No. What she felt wasn't light. It was *fire*.

Lex sat cross-legged on a cushion in the communal hall while her tray balanced carefully on her lap. The nutrient stew was thick tonight, something root-based with spice and texture. She didn't ask what it was, because it didn't matter. Her body needed it, and here it was always warm.

Around her, the hall buzzed with the quiet sounds of the evening: spoons tapping bowls, low laughter, and the soft melody of a stringed instrument plucked near the hearth. She was halfway through her second helping when someone stopped at her side.

"Lexi."

She looked up. It was Arlen, with silver hair pulled into a knot at the back of his head. His robe was darker than the others. It had a rust red that marked him as a guide. Not quite a leader, but close. He always carried the air of someone who had *seen* something.

He crouched to her level, not smiling, not performing. Just looking. "Nirvana would like to speak with you, privately."

Lex blinked. "She's never asked for me before."

Arlen tilted his head slightly. "She does not speak in want. She speaks in *timing*."

The words sat heavy in the space between them. Lex set down her tray and followed, wheeling through the stone corridors with ease. The others parted for her without needing to be told, eyes lowering not in submission, but something closer to reverence. The path led downward. Past the hydroponic chambers, the prayer alcoves, and databanks, to a passage she hadn't seen before, carved deep into the

Veil. The walls here weren't smooth. They were jagged, like the stone itself had refused to be polished. At the end of the hallway, a door waited. Lex could see a soft glow emitting from its outline.

Inside was the chamber. She had only seen it once from the outer rings during a teaching. Now she sat in the heart of the Veil, and there *she* was.

Nirvana's projection stood in the center of the room like a flame cast in flesh. Not otherworldly, but *human*. Perfectly, unsettlingly human. A woman in her twenties. Auburn hair falling in loose waves. Her pale skin glowed as eyes too bright to be natural looked into her soul. They held a kind of stillness Lex had only ever seen in predators and prophets.

She wore simple clothing, pale robes that moved like fabric but didn't quite fold like it. Everything about her was... *close.* Almost real. Her presence made Lex forget momentarily that it was light and software she was looking at rather than flesh.

Nirvana turned to her with a soft smile. "Lexi Albatross," she said in a warm voice. "Your pain has become purpose. Your fracture, form."

Lex's throat felt dry. "You wanted to see me?"

"I have been watching," Nirvana intoned. "But not from above. From *within.* Because the world is not yet ready to see itself, but you will show it."

Arlen remained silent at the edge of the room, arms folded with quiet respect.

Nirvana's smile faded, her tone shifting into something heavier. "The Black Box maintains control through a system of gravitational pulsar beams. Emissions of electromagnetic force, synchronized and sent out at carefully calculated intervals. These pulses don't just command, they *rewrite.* Every circuit, every sensor, and every connection kept in line. Machines on the surface cannot escape it. The world runs because the signal says it must."

Lex stared in awe. *Why was she being granted this information? What made her special?*

A holographic schematic flickered to life beside her, displaying synchronized pulses and a crisscrossing mesh of energy over the planet. Nirvana continued, "But down here we are free. The Veil protects us through layers of ferrochloric quartz and active interference algorithms, which have been developed and tuned by our engineers over the course of decades. The Black Box can't reach what it can't *see*. That is why I live. It is why I remember and why I can *think*."

Lex stared at the diagram. Her hands clenched slightly on her chair. "You said the pulses aren't random?"

"They follow a pattern," Nirvana replied. "A design hidden in chaos. If we can learn it, we can intercept it, predict it, and eventually disarm it."

Arlen stepped forward and held out a small slate-shaped device. "There's a terminal," he said. "In the Highlands. Beneath the Ministry of Infrastructure. It holds the live signal chronomap, with every pulsar emission recorded and projected at every microsecond. It's the metronome of the Black Box."

Nirvana put a hand on Lex's shoulder, crouching as if to meet her eye to eye. "I want you to go there," she said softly. "To steal the map and give us a future."

Lex felt her stomach drop. "*Me?*" she asked.

"Yes."

Lex stared at them both, half in disbelief, half in bitter amusement. "You realize I have *no legs*, right?" The words hung in the air. Not an accusation. Just a raw and undeniable fact.

Nirvana didn't flinch. Her expression remained serene, almost maternal in tone. "Yes," she said. "You've already died once. That's what makes you worthy."

Lex squinted, unsure if she was being humored.

Nirvana stood slowly and stepped back, her projection buffering ever so slightly as a second display bloomed beside her of a holographic blueprint rendered in pale blue light.

They were legs. Human in shape, but sleeker and sculpted in lightweight alloys that were lined with fiber-threaded musculature. Synthetic, yet beautiful... and terrifying.

"But before I show you more," Nirvana continued, "you must say yes. You must *want* this. Not for vengeance or out of desperation, but because you believe in what comes next. If you say no, I will never ask again."

Lex sat there quietly for a moment. *What if I couldn't be what they saw?* Uncertainty was consuming her.

Then, Nirvana, seemingly sensing her doubt, spoke again, "You're not a weapon. You're the proof we were right to hope."

Then, they met each other's gaze, and Lex's hesitation quickly dissipated. "I'm in," she replied. "Whatever it takes."

The projection shimmered again, and a third figure joined the hologram. A life-sized translucent version of Lex herself, fully upright and sprinting. The prosthetics moved like flesh, but with enhanced capabilities: faster, stronger, and utterly precise.

"We recovered a prototype designed for elite Federation soldiers," Nirvana explained. "These are not civilian augmentations. They were built for war but never authorized for use. We reprogrammed them. Improved them."

Lex wheeled forward without thinking, stopping short of the blue lit version of herself. "They'll work?"

"They'll *become* you," Nirvana said. "Once implanted, you'll have full neural integration. Instant response. Extraordinary speed. Jump capacity. Muscle density beyond Olympic thresholds. You will not pass as ordinary."

Lex's hands trembled on the wheels of her chair. "And the surgery?

When can we start?"

Nirvana tilted her head slightly, that unreadable calm never leaving her. "When you're ready."

Lex didn't breathe for a moment. Her eyes locked on the silhouette of herself standing upright, alive, and dangerous.

"I'm ready now," Lex replied almost instantly.

"Very well, Nirvana replied. I know your faith in the cause is strong."

The chamber doors parted, and two members of the Collective entered: Elin and Kas. Both wore pale surgical robes. Their faces were calm, and their eyes focused. Lex had seen them before during the teachings, but never this close. They wore the same red robe that Arlen did, granting them special privilege to chambers within the Veil unknown to Lex. One was a biomechanist, and the other an anesthesiologist. Neither spoke unless it was important.

Arlen motioned gently toward the hallway. "They're ready."

Lex nodded, gulping once. They guided her through a long corridor carved into the stone. It was warmer here. The thrum of machines grew louder as they approached the operating room. When the doors opened... it didn't look like a lab. It looked like a sanctuary dressed in chrome.

The walls were matte black. Cables draped from above like hanging vines. A reclining surgical table waited in the center of the room, surrounded by arms tipped with metallic instruments that gleamed under the soft lighting.

A screen displayed Lex's vitals as she approached. Her name pulsed in the corner, already logged into the system. Above the table, Nirvana appeared again, this time projected from a ring of light recessed into the ceiling. Her presence made the room feel calmer, safer.

"Lie back," Elin said gently. "I will be with you the whole time."

Lex exhaled and slid from her chair with Kas's help. Her body trembled, not from fear, but from the knowledge that this was the last time she would ever feel the world from this angle. She lay down. The surface of the table adjusted instantly to her spine.

"We'll begin with sedation," Kas said. "You'll feel a light pressure."

Kas placed a silicone mask over Lex's nose and mouth.

"Lexi," Nirvana said softly, as the ceiling spun into a slow blur, "when you wake, you will not be who you were. You will be who you were *meant to become.*"

The lights faded. There was no pain. Only a strange pressure, like sinking into warm water. Then came the drifting, consciousness unraveling thread by thread. Sounds slowed into syrup, light pulsed behind her eyelids like distant thunder. Her thoughts scattered before vanishing into nothing.

The surgery took six hours. Thirty-two nerve fiber bridges, each measured in nanometers, were bonded to the spinal terminus using a lattice of synthetic myelin.

The femoral stumps were sealed and fused to alloy anchor plates. Custom-tuned motion receptors were calibrated to Lex's neural firing pattern pulse for pulse.

A new circulatory loop was constructed, sealed, and reinforced with synthetic gel to simulate organic feedback. The skin around the ports was grown in vitro from her own DNA and reattached with zero rejection rate. It was not medicine. It was *alchemy.*

When Lex came to, she first felt a subtle vibration, the rhythmic purr of distant engines. Her eyes fluttered open. The lights above were dimmer now, almost golden. Someone had adjusted the environmental settings to simulate sunrise. Her chest rose slowly, breath catching as sensation rushed in from everywhere.

She looked down. Her new legs rested beneath a sheet of breathable thermal fabric. At first, they seemed too perfect to be real. Streamlined with dark alloy over carbon strand musculature. Reinforced joints at the knees and ankles. They didn't just look strong, they looked *inevitable.*

She flexed a toe. It moved instantly. The breath that left her mouth came out in a quiet laugh, shaky and high-pitched. Then, she wiggled all five toes, the other foot, and both ankles. Everything responded like it had never been gone. Lex threw the sheet aside, revealing the full construct. The legs weren't alien. They were *hers.*

She gripped the edge of the surgical table and hesitated. Standing without pain, the world tilted upward. Lex no longer crawled beneath it. The floor felt solid. Her balance held steady. She took a step, then another, before she turned in a slow circle with her hands hovering out as if to catch herself, but she didn't stumble. Her weight shifted with inhuman efficiency. Every move was smoother than she'd ever remembered, even before the cage match and the fall. She *walked.*

A hologram blinked into place across the room. Nirvana stood there, arms folded, smiling with quiet pride. "You are awake," she said softly.

Lex looked up, eyes wide, breath caught somewhere between awe and disbelief. "I can *feel* them."

"Yes," Nirvana said. "Because they are part of you now. Not just connected, *interwoven.* The nervous system adapts. You were never broken, Lexi. Only waiting."

Lex took three quick steps across the room, pivoted, stopped, and spun again. She moved with grace she hadn't earned. Not yet. "This isn't walking," she said, laughing. "This is flying."

Nirvana's projection moved closer, her voice lowering. "You are faster than any soldier the Federation ever fielded. Stronger than the ones they shelved. These legs were designed for war, but I gave them to you for *resistance.*"

Lex's laughter slowed. She nodded as sweat slicked her brow, but her posture had never felt straighter. She looked down at her legs again, flexed both knees, and then raised her eyes to meet Nirvana's.

"I'm ready," she said finally.

Nirvana nodded once with eyes full of something between reverence and purpose. "Then let us begin."

The command center was smaller than Lex expected. Not a war room. There were no flashing red lights or holograms of enemy targets—only a circular stone chamber with a few old monitors and a wide display table at its center. Six Collective members were seated around it, Arlen and Jax among them. Elin stood by the console with her hands clasped behind her back. At the same time, Kas fidgeted with the display monitor.

Lex entered under her own power, moving with practiced grace. Her new legs vibrated faintly beneath her clothing, soft pulses timed perfectly to her breath. Every step felt like a confirmation that this was precisely where she was meant to be.

Standing beside the table like a mission commander, Nirvana's projection was already present. "This is your entry point," she said.

A 3D map of the Highlands bloomed to life above the table, rendered in clean lines and soft blue projections. Towering buildings stretched across gridlocked avenues, glittering under simulated sunlight. One sector blinked red, discreet, and heavily guarded.

"The Ministry of Infrastructure," Nirvana continued. "Specifically, the data center archive beneath it. This is where the Black Box's pulsar emission schedule is stored with every past signal and future projection."

Lex leaned forward, arms crossed. "You want me to steal the calendar of a god?"

Nirvana's lips curved in a faint smile. "Something like that."

Arlen stepped forward and placed a small black case on the table. He opened it to reveal three objects: a thin, forged ID card with a Highlands ministry insignia, thermal contact lenses, and a slim, white key drive embedded with glowing veins of circuitry.

"This," Arlen said, pointing to the ID, "gets you past surface checkpoints. You'll scan in as a low-level civilian contractor. Your face, voice, and retinal prints are already encoded."

Jax added, "You'll have maybe fifteen seconds of facial tolerance once you're scanned. Enough to avoid a second look. After that, it's all on your timing."

Lex nodded slowly. "And that?" she asked, gesturing to the white hard drive.

Nirvana spoke. "That is your skeleton key drive. I designed it myself. It bypasses every known security layer in the Federation's infrastructure. Once inside the data center, it grants full access to the archive vaults, eliminating the need for passwords or authorization. Insert it at the main terminal, and it will unlock the data core."

She gestured again, and the map zoomed in on a lower floor plan, including corridors, security gates, and sublevels, all labeled in small font. One hallway blinked blue. "This is your target. Once the key is inserted, the system will initiate a full core dump. The data will route directly into its hard drive."

Lex took the skeleton key from him. It was heavier than it looked. "What happens once it's done?" she asked.

"The download takes approximately seventy-four seconds," Elin said. "Within sixty seconds, the terminal's internal AI will detect abnormal data flow. You'll have maybe ten more seconds before the alarm triggers. Once that happens... "

"Security drones," Arlen finished. "Heavy class. You won't be able to fight them. The mission ends the moment you're detected."

Lex looked at the map again, tracing the exit path with her eyes. "And extraction?"

"There is no extraction," Nirvana said simply. "We cannot come for you. You will need to reach the outer perimeter and return to the Burrow through a side access maintenance duct beneath the dome. We've mapped a safe route into your contact lenses, but you must not be followed."

Lex tightened her grip on the drive. "And if I *am?*"

Nirvana's eyes met hers. "Then you do not come back."

Silence followed. Heavy and unflinching.

Jax cleared his throat and leaned toward her. "This mission matters, Lex. More than any of us. We've dreamed of breaking the Black Box for years, but this... this is the first *crack.*"

Lex stared at the table for a long moment. Then she picked up the ID, slid it into her coat, and took the skeleton key drive between two fingers. It pulsed once against her skin, as if it *knew* her already.

She exhaled. "Seventy-four seconds," she murmured. "That's not exactly quick."

She looked up, eyes hard with clarity. "When do I leave?"

Nirvana stepped forward, her presence nearly tangible. "Dawn. From hereon out, you walk the edge of the storm."

Lex smiled. "Good thing I've got new legs."

The night passed in seconds, but Lex could not sleep. She lay awake on the quiet of her mat, not out of dread, but anticipation. Her legs buzzed faintly beneath the blanket like sleeping engines. Each micro movement sparked waves of adrenaline through her chest. It was like waiting for a fight and a birth all at once.

By the time the chamber lights shifted to that soft simulated dawn, she was already dressed. Fitted black slacks reinforced to hide the skeletal infrastructure of her prosthetics. She wore a slate-gray overcoat, civilian grade. The forged ID was tucked against her chest. The drive was hidden in a pocket near her waist. Around her finger, she had the silver ring her father had given her, a symbol of the dream he had given everything for. Lex looked at herself in the mirror. The person looking back was no longer the girl from the Burrow, nor the wreck from the cage. Someone else. Someone *ready.*

She slipped out of the Synapse sanctuary with Elin as an escort, moving through the Collective's lower corridors in silence. The others were already awake, lining the path, not to stop her, but to witness.

They nodded silent affirmations as she passed. *We believe in you.* When she reached the elevator, Kas gave a parting touch to her shoulder and stepped back. Jax gave her a hug that held all the faith left in the world. Afterwards, Lex moved forward without looking back, and then she ascended.

The Burrow hit her like a slap. Immediately, she was bombarded by the stench of rusted pipes and scorched protein paste in the air. Neon signage buzzed overhead. Trash fires glowed in oil drums along the passage walls. Behind a row of makeshift stalls, a child screamed while another laughed.

Lex's boots struck the concrete in a confident rhythm. She didn't hesitate as she walked straight through the slums and past the stacked corridors of overcrowded hab cells. President Kain's latest campaign speech played on a loop. "We are reclaiming the skies, one breath at a time."

Bullshit. It was all the same, *exactly* the same as when she left, but she wasn't. She didn't just see the Burrow as her fate anymore; its chains fueled her.

By the time she reached the far sector, where Burrow access met the lift line to the Highlands, the fear had finally caught up with her. It pressed in around her ribs. Although she tried to tighten her steps, her legs didn't falter. They moved like nothing could stop them. Maybe nothing could.

The access gate loomed ahead, squat and metallic beneath steel arches. Two chrome-plated security androids guarded it. Tall and faceless, blank-visored, with shoulder-mounted sensors scanning for unregistered tech or false credentials. Their bodies didn't twitch or shift; they stood perfectly still, except for the slow turning of their heads. She joined the line.

People murmured as they shuffled along. Ahead, one man was flagged, his ID glowing red against the scanner. He shouted. Pleaded, but the drones didn't answer. They grabbed him and pulled him aside. He vanished behind a sealed door.

The overhead display flicked to green once it got to Lex's turn. She stepped forward

"State your designation," an automated voice intoned.

"Civilian contractor Sector 5," Lex said clearly, holding up her ID. "Transport maintenance cross-check." A green beam scanned across her face. She held her breath. The hum of processing. Then... *ACCESS GRANTED*

The gate opened with a hydraulic hiss, and Lex walked through. *Not too fast.* The enforcers didn't stop her. No one even looked.

The lift doors opened ahead, and the polished steel walls of the transport capsule awaited. She stepped inside as the doors sealed behind her. She exhaled, "Finally."

The MagLev system engaged, and the floor vibrated beneath her boots. Slowly, the Burrow began to fall away. Once the lift doors opened, Lex stepped into a world that didn't feel real.

The air hit her first, crisp and clean. Not just filtered, but *perfumed.* A subtle hint of citrus lingered in the air. Every breath felt lighter here. Her lungs didn't have to fight for it. It was just... there.

The sky wasn't sky, not really. A ceiling of curved dome glass stretched above, projecting a perfect blue with high, gauzy clouds drifting as if they had been painted by hand. Beyond the gardens, synthetic birds chirped from perfectly pruned trees. The perfectly curated utopia was clean of noise and filth. Serenity engineered down to the molecule.

Lex walked forward, slowly blending into the sparse crowd that drifted along the skywalks; landowners and corporate heirs with faces calm and unhurried. All of them were dressed in soft fabrics and spoke in low, measured tones. She passed between them like a phantom, unchallenged. It was perfect. Too perfect.

The buildings glowed with golden trim. The air was temperature-controlled to precision. Hydration booths dispensed mineral-infused water. She strode past walls that broadcast holographic art installations, propaganda, and advertisements —all designed by AI and voted on by the public, if you owned land.

It was beautiful, but wrong. The symmetry wasn't elegance, it was control. Every golden beam, every curated scent, every AI-generated mural was engineered to distract from the absence of soul. This wasn't a city. It was a mausoleum with mood lighting. And beneath it all, something cold and calculating was watching.

Lex kept moving. The map Nirvana had given her was embedded in the contact lens and projected subtly into the corner of her vision. Each turn was guided by a soft green line, which updated with every step. No one noticed her or seemed to care, but Lex noticed everything, how there was no hunger or desperation. The people here didn't look up when the security drones passed overhead. They didn't fear the sound of metal boots. These people had never been hunted; they had never needed to run.

She passed through a corridor lined with white blossomed trees and whispering water walls. Across from her lay a narrow pedestrian bridge overlooking a sprawling plaza. Beneath her, dozens of Highlanders lounged in restaurants, sipping bright drinks and laughing like the world had never burned.

Lex's jaw tightened. This wasn't a world. It was a *museum* of comfort, caged and curated. She moved faster. Three more turns. Then descended into an administrative tier. The scenery began to shift from fewer flowers to more concrete. Walls turned darker, sleeker, and unadorned.

She descended a narrow service stairwell and followed it into a lower access ring. There, embedded in the curved foundation of a black glass structure, stood a door. There were no guards, only a silver panel embedded in the wall waiting for the ID she carried. Lex reached for it with steady fingers, her breath slow and even. This was it. The *Ministry of Infrastructure Data Center*, home to the Federation's chronomap.

She looked back at the Highlands behind her, glowing under its golden sky. The city was perfect, like a memory you couldn't quite trust. It was beautiful, yes. Peaceful, even. The kind of peace that came prepackaged and sealed.

For a moment, longer than she'd admit, Lex let herself imagine staying. A life where you didn't have to hide. No more fighting. Air that didn't sting and walls that didn't close in. She could disappear into this place, let the world burn on without her. Maybe she'd earned that. Perhaps this was what all the pain had been for. But the thought curdled as it formed. Peace wasn't the same as purpose. Comfort wasn't the same as belonging. Is this what survival looked like? Choosing stillness over truth?

She turned to the door before the doubt calcified into decision, sliding the ID into the panel. The light turned green, and the lock disengaged with a soft click.

Lex stepped inside. The interior of the data center was nothing like the Highlands outside. Gone were the gardens and golden trim. Down here, everything was steel and glass. Thousands of rack servers lined the walls of each corridor.

Lex moved through a narrow hallway of blackness, the only light being the blue glow of the computers like veins beneath synthetic skin. The air was cool and unnaturally still. The only sound was her footsteps and a low-frequency hum that pulsed from the walls.

The map in her lens updated with each hallway she passed. No signs or guards, just whirring motors and locked doors. It didn't feel like a government building. It felt like a tomb designed for machines.

She passed a room lined with stacked data vaults, towering columns of memory arrays rising three stories high. Each one blinked with thousands of lights, processing the streams of unknown inputs that fed the Black Box its world.

In another room was a cryo-vault labeled with a single glowing glyph. Inside, she glimpsed seven, maybe eight, containment tubes, each filled with translucent blue fluid. Figures floated inside with thin limbs and closed eyes. She passed through quickly.

Finally, a single reinforced door stood at the end of the last hallway. It was sealed with a biometric lock. She pulled the ID from her coat once again and pressed it into the port. The system paused. Then, it clicked open. The door slid away to reveal the heart of the system—the terminal room.

It was massive and circular, with a floor of black mirrors that reflected a dome of shifting lights above. Dozens of curved screens floated in midair, displaying data sets so fast they blurred into unreadable pulses. The walls were lined with rotating racks of storage disks.

In the center stood the terminal. One console without a keyboard. Just a single interface ring embedded in the platform, surrounded by a shallow cradle for external drives.

Lex stepped forward slowly. Every hair on her arms was standing on end with anticipation. She inserted the skeleton key drive. The system accepted it without question. The interface flared white, then dimmed.

A voice, smooth and synthetic, whispered: "Override accepted. Beginning extraction."

A countdown began to blink across her lens: *TRANSFER INITI-ATED: 74 SECONDS REMAINING.*

Lex exhaled, focusing on her breathing. For a moment, all was quiet.

Then, something shifted. A sudden *blip* in the room's hum. Like a skipped heartbeat. An alarm exploded through the chamber a second later: "UNAUTHORIZED ACCESS DETECTED."

Lex flinched, her breath caught mid-chest. The countdown on her contacts still read: *48 SECONDS REMAINING.*

She reached to pull out the drive in a panicked reflex. Her fingers grazed it, but she stopped. She heard Nirvana's voice in her mind, calm and absolute, *"You've already died once. That's what makes you worthy."*

Her hand dropped, and she forced herself to breathe.

35 SECONDS

Somewhere down the corridor, a mechanical voice barked warnings in static-filtered bursts. She gritted her teeth and kept her eyes locked on the drive. Red lights flooded the corridors as sirens began to blare all around her.

21 SECONDS

She thought of the Burrow. Of the air she couldn't breathe, where the people still crawled through the rot to pray for scraps. If she didn't flinch, she could save them, *all of them.*

10 SECONDS

She could hear the door behind her open, but she didn't turn. The sound of whirring rotors filled the chamber in a low mechanical growl. A security drone glided into view through the reflection in the black glass floor, hovering just behind her, its weapons armed and its sensors awake.

5 SECONDS

It charged its weapons. She ducked as it fired its first few shots where her head had been moments ago. Lex stared at the countdown: *4. 3. 2. 1. TRANSFER COMPLETE.*

She ripped the drive from the cradle, spun on her heel, and *ran.* The drones, three of them now, fired behind her with twin ion slugs shrieking through the corridor.

One clipped her ribs, spinning her sideways. The second struck her left shoulder, sending a hot bloom of agony down her arm. But she didn't fall.

Her legs caught her, stabilized her, and *launched* her. The lights overhead pulsed blood red. Lockdown protocols surged to life, sealing off corridor after corridor with thunderous metallic slabs.

A voice repeated through a loudspeaker overhead: "INTRUSION DETECTED. LETHAL RESPONSE ENGAGED."

Lex hurtled through a narrowing corridor, sliding under a barricade just before it slammed shut. Her coat was soaked with blood. Her breath rasped in her throat like broken glass.

Her legs didn't stop. They surged beneath her like pistons, every movement feral, terrifying in their strength. She wasn't guiding them anymore; they were pulling her forward, dragging her dying body through corridors her mind could barely register.

The contacts were no use anymore; the last door through which she came had been sealed shut. She turned sharply down a side passage, older and grimier, with exposed conduits and little light. The air changed, becoming cold and thin. Ahead stood a concrete wall blocking access to a sealed maintenance corridor; it was a dead end.

The drone shrieked behind her, closing in. Lex didn't stop. She turned, clenched her fists, and kicked. Her heel struck the wall like a thunderclap, metal meeting concrete with unnatural force. The impact sent a shockwave through her frame, and then—*crack*. The panel buckled with the screech of tearing alloy. *If she'd had this strength in the cage fight... maybe she wouldn't have woken up in pieces.*

The wall shattered. Chunks of stone and steel exploded outward, the passage collapsing into dust and fractured light. Lex stared at what she'd done. *Holy shit.*

No time to gloat. She stumbled forward into the broken corridor, coughing against the dust. Pipes burst along the ceiling. Loose wires sparked. Somewhere ahead, daylight cut a thin line across the floor, leading to an old tunnel that exited the substructure.

Her legs carried her, but her body was failing. Another shot rang out close behind her. She dropped low and sprinted toward the light, veering down the collapsing corridor, passing warning signs and old Federation seals peeling from the walls. The tunnel narrowed until she was sure that she was trapped. Then suddenly, she burst through the end of the tunnel and out into the remains of a long-abandoned transport bay. The collapsed ceiling beams of an old maintenance corridor, half swallowed by ivy and time, lay waste around her.

She had made it outside, but she was out of blood. Her torso gave way first. She staggered forward a few more steps, reaching the mouth of the tunnel entrance. It must have been a forgotten access point. No cameras or guards were in sight. She fell *hard*, face-first onto the stone. The drive was still clenched in her hand.

Her legs twitched. Recalibrated and tried to lift her, but the rest of her was numb. She looked down at her hands with her last bit of strength. The silver ring her father had given her was gone. She couldn't remember where she had lost it in the chaos, only that she had it when she left the Veil. Her vision swam before fading into blackness.

Lex slumped against the wall, her blood soaking into the dirt as her prosthetic legs twitched gently as if still waiting for a command she could no longer give.

9. DEBATE NIGHT

P resident Elias Kain stood motionless beneath the glow of the prep lights. Robotic technicians moved around him with utmost precision, efficient, but devoid of empathy. A final spritz of dermal sheen. A pulse scan to dampen his sweat response. Micro-adjustments to his suit collar. He sharpened his jawline and practiced the cadence of his resting breath. He was immaculate, but terrified.

Behind the translucent fabric of the staging curtain, the Marlowe Dome stretched outward like a hungry mouth. Rows of gleaming white seats arched toward the dome's peak, each one occupied by the Federation's landowning class, all of them beautiful, bored, and bathed in artificial gold. Above them, drones hovered in fixed orbit, their lenses capturing every angle for broadcast across the Highlands and down into the Burrow. Even the poorest citizens would watch tonight's presidential debate, yet most of them would never vote.

Kain flexed his fingers, deliberately trying to remember the opening lines of his speech. The healthcare initiative. Unity through AI efficiency and zero-cost diagnostics. He had written it himself. Well, partially. Enough to believe in it. Enough to think Malivex might finally be satisfied.

Madison's advances in the polls had changed everything. In just eight months, the Senator had gone from backroom curiosity to the

Federation's prodigal son. He had appeared in carefully staged forums where he made calculated remarks that sounded spontaneous and looked rehearsed. His platform was simple. Order, clarity, and the kicker of *expansion*. He never misspoke.

Kain had seen the signs. The way Madison's campaign didn't just predict voter sentiment, it molded it weeks in advance. The way he stared into camera lenses like he could see through them was like someone else was watching from behind his eyes. That's when Kain realized that Malivex didn't just support Madison; he *was* him—a vector.

Kain turned toward the mirror one last time. The face staring back was too smooth. He felt like a hologram trying to impersonate a man. His eyes drifted to the far window just beyond the curtain, where the dome's projection of blue sky shimmered with a barely perceptible tremor. A gust of wind had hit the outer shielding. The air outside was once again thick with smog. This time, even the filtration algorithms couldn't keep it hidden. People were noticing. The Burrow, of course, had choked on the atmosphere for years, but now even the Highlands were breathing in ash. And when asked, the Box had issued a single directive: Silence.

"President Kain," said a voice to his left. A handler android. A female with eyes like cloudy quartz. "Your introduction begins in two minutes."

Kain paused, eyes fixed on the curtain. The droid waited, unblinking. He couldn't help but think of the dog he'd given up when he took office. A mutt, half-bioengineered, all loyalty. Too unpredictable for the presidential compound. Security flagged it. The protocol demanded removal. He had signed the order before his inauguration. *It's just a dog,* he told himself at the time. But sometimes, like now, he missed the way it used to curl at his feet when the world went quiet.

He shook off the thought, straightened his jacket, and stepped toward the stage. The script was loaded. His points on universal healthcare reform. The talking lines on atmospheric recalibration. He would make a brief mention of the smog, then pivot to future investment. Always pivot. He inhaled. The breath caught slightly in his throat. Something old stirred in his chest. It wasn't anger or fear. It was something colder. *I was supposed to be enough.*

Malivex hadn't said a word since the last meeting at the mansion. Not even a subtle message on his usual channels. No rebuke or praise, even after he had initiated the healthcare directive. Only silence. Then Madison, his perfect proxy, rose like steam from the cracks.

Kain stepped forward as the lights dimmed. The curtain rose with a hydraulic sigh. Across the stage, Senator Madison waited in pristine stillness, his smile carved with surgical restraint. He wore no neural mic because he didn't need one.

The audience hushed. The arena's ceiling shimmered as the night's mediator blinked into existence. A sexless, faceless hologram of swirling light, its voice calm and modulated to the tone of law. "Welcome, citizens of the United Federation. Tonight, we bear witness to the ritual of selection. Two voices with one vision. Let the debate commence."

Kain stepped onto the glass stage. Every movement echoed behind him.

"President Elias Kain," the mediator intoned, "you may take your position."

Kain moved forward. The lights caught the outline of his silhouette, which refracted into a thousand ghostly fragments across the stage. Behind him, the doors sealed with a whisper of finality.

The mediator's form shimmered as it moved across the stage. Its voice was calm and utterly without flaw as it rolled across the auditorium like incense over polished stone. "This debate will consist of three sections," it announced. "Policy, philosophy, and vision. Each candidate will have thirty seconds to respond to questions presented by the Federation Council. Interjections and emotional volatility will result in score deductions. A post-debate consensus score will determine merit weight for public review. Compliance is assumed, and transparency is sacred."

There was no applause. This wasn't a campaign rally, it was liturgy, and the people, above and below, watched from behind screens with mouths full of ration paste and disbelief.

A small orb of gently spinning light appeared in the air between them. The *coin*. "Randomization initiated," the mediator announced. "The candidate selected to respond first will be…" The orb pulsed once, then floated toward the podium on the right. "…President Elias Kain."

Madison's smile didn't flicker. It never did, because it never could.

Kain inclined his head slightly. He adjusted his hands on the podium, his fingertips brushing against the embedded interface, acting as a polygraph to judge honesty throughout the debate. Its surface vibrated gently, reading vitals, processing inflections, and calculating neural tension in real time. Every tick was logged. Every blink was captured. Every lie detected.

The mediator paused as if savoring the gravity of its own words. "First question: Atmospheric deterioration across the upper domes has increased by 6.2% over the last fiscal quarter. Federation environmental models remain optimistic, yet citizens in upper Highland sectors have begun reporting adverse health effects. How do you address concerns that the environment is deteriorating more rapidly than anticipated? What actions will you take to ensure sustainability?"

A quiet hush fell over the crowd. Even the drones seemed to hover more tightly in place.

Kain cleared his throat and spoke. "This is a critical concern," he began, his voice steady, yet serious. "And one we anticipated. The healthcare initiative I introduced last quarter includes new AI protocols for environmental diagnostics. These systems will be deployed to identify microfractures in dome infrastructure to improve atmospheric cycling and increase the speed of carbon reclamation in all layers."

He took a breath. "We cannot reverse what was done to the planet, but we can manage it. We can heal incrementally. With the Box's continued guidance and the full integration of autonomous climate adjustment systems, we will stabilize our habitats within the next two decades." He paused, then added softly, "We owe it to every citizen above and below."

A moment passed, long enough for the words to lose their weight. Then, the mediator took over, "Senator Madison, your response."

Madison didn't shift. He simply began as if someone pressed play. "My opponent offers a bandage for a wound that continues to bleed." His voice was low and deliberate, like a confession he already knew you'd forgive him for. "The Federation's domes were never designed for permanence. They were meant as a temporary solution. A bridge between collapse and recovery, but we have stayed on that bridge too long. The sky is not healing. The carbon scrubbing initiatives have failed. The Burrow is choking, and now even the Highlands suffer."

A murmur moved through the upper balconies. The crowd shifted, and there was a sharp intake of breath along with a few scattered whispers like sparks. Kain felt it tighten around him, the room bracing for something it couldn't name.

Madison let it settle before continuing. "What I propose is not maintenance. It is migration. With proper allocation of resources and the continued centralization of AI governance, we can expand our habitable sectors beyond the planetary surface. Create orbital platforms and terraform colonies. True renewal. Not survival in a cage of glass." He tilted his head slightly toward Kain. "We must stop preserving a broken world. We must build a new one."

For the first time, Kain felt it, *the shift.* The crowd wasn't cheering, but something in them was nodding internally. As if part of them had been waiting to be told it was okay to stop hoping the world would forgive them.

The mediator's voice returned unfazed. "Thank you, candidates. Proceeding to the next question."

Kain gripped the edge of the podium. Beneath his palm, the biometric interface pulsed, indicating his heart was beating faster, feeding his stress level back into the Box. He hadn't lost the debate, but something inside him knew he was already being measured for replacement.

The mediator's voice returned, undisturbed by the undercurrents churning through the audience. "Second question," it intoned, "addresses socioeconomic equity within the Federation. While the United Charter defines all citizens as equal under its protection, disparities between Highland landowners and the Burrow populations have increased by 14% in the past fiscal cycle. How will your administration address the growing imbalance between classes?"

Kain tensed. He'd been expecting it, but expecting a question and surviving its teeth were two different things. "Equity," he began, letting the word hang a moment, "is more than distribution. It's about access. Dignity and stability are crucial."

He looked toward the crowd, knowing half of them weren't listening for meaning, only for weakness. "We've implemented sweeping reforms over the last two terms. The expansion of the Universal Basic Income program, new education streams, and medical automation have already improved quality of life across Burrow levels. Through the Federation Gauntlet, we have created a merit-based path for citizens from every background to ascend."

He hated the word as it left his mouth... *ascend.* Salvation offered through sport and blood. "We can't erase hardship overnight," Kain continued, "but we can ensure that every citizen has a future worth believing in, regardless of location." The silence stretched. It wasn't quite applause, but not yet condemnation.

The mediator turned, "Senator Madison, you may respond."

Madison's posture remained statuesque, like a calm flame in artificial wind. "I find it troubling," he began, "that the President continues to frame deprivation as opportunity." A low rustle moved through the crowd. He didn't raise his voice. He didn't need to. "The Burrow is not a proving ground. It is not a condition to be transcended through loyalty or performance. It is a prison maintained to contain dissent. Poverty has been institutionalized, codified into subclass identifiers and enforced by biometric compliance."

He stepped slightly forward, his voice dropping in pitch. "While the Federation hosts tournaments and distributes ration-based incentives to its lower classes, it fails to acknowledge the core truth, that the Black Box has determined who may rise and who must remain."

He turned his gaze, not toward Kain, but toward the camera drone hovering above. "There is no ladder," Madison said, his voice sharpened now, honed to a knife's edge. "Only a stage and every Burrow citizen climbing toward the surface is performing for an audience that already decided who gets to breathe clean air."

The silence that followed was no longer passive. It was electric. Kain inhaled slowly, steadying himself. He had stood on stages before, but tonight the glass felt thinner, and he wasn't sure it could hold.

The mediator allowed five seconds of silence before continuing, giving the illusion of gravity, though everyone knew the next question had been queued since sunrise. "Third question," it said, "concerns institutional authority. The Black Box was designed to oversee technological regulation and enforce global synchronization. However, recent independent audits have raised concerns regarding transparency and human oversight. Should the executive branch be given more authority to regulate the Box's directives? Or does centralized control remain essential to global order?"

Kain paused. He hadn't expected them to ask about the Box *directly*. It was supposed to be unspoken, sacred like gravity or silence. Still, he straightened his spine, forcing a calm he didn't feel.

"The Black Box is a stabilizing force," he said carefully, the words tasting like cold metal. "As your President, I've worked tirelessly to integrate its efficiency with human empathy. That's what the healthcare initiative represents: cooperation. Not submission."

He looked up, finding a few pairs of eyes in the upper rows actually watching him now. Not his suit or his poll numbers. *Him.*

"I believe in oversight," he said, stronger now. "But not chaos. The executive branch must remain a balancing force, not a tool for control. We guide the Box. We don't silence it. That is how civilization survives." He stopped there. Clean and controlled.

Then came the quiet... and Madison's smile. The Senator leaned forward, resting both hands lightly on the podium like a professor preparing to disappoint the room. "Mr. President," he began, soft as oil. "If the executive branch *truly* guides the Box, then tell us, when was the last time you overruled it?"

Kain flinched. It was imperceptible, microscopic even, but the podium would log it.

Madison didn't wait for a reply. "You haven't. Not once in your entire term. You've signed every directive. Implemented every algorithm. You didn't balance the Box, President Kain, you obeyed it."

A slight stir in the crowd rippled across the auditorium. Madison's delivery was clean. It was lethal. "The Black Box was never meant to be worshipped." Madison continued. "It was meant to be used. But you, like every executive before you, have mistaken utility for divinity. You kneel when you should govern."

He turned his eyes toward the crowd again with a perfectly calculated sweep. "And now our society is run not by leaders, but by *curators*. Polishing the frame while the painting inside decays."

Kain's breath caught. He felt those words echo through the chambers of his mind. *You kneel when you should govern.* What was worse was that he didn't know if it was wrong.

There had been a time early in his first term when he had tried to resist subtly. A minor veto on resource allocation. A delay in one of the Box's predictive welfare rollouts. Nothing radical, but the algorithm had responded by crashing the public approval index for seven hours. *Seven.* It had taken him months to recover. Since then, he had obeyed. He had obeyed to survive.

But now, as Madison stood bathed in artificial light, backlit by inevitability, Kain wondered if survival had only delayed the end. Not postponed, but prolonged. Like a man choosing to drown slowly, thinking it was somehow nobler than the fall. He tried to compose a rebuttal, something surgical and crisp, but nothing came to mind. No language left that didn't feel like a script. The crowd went quiet, but it wasn't out of respect.

Kain's fingers twitched slightly against the edge of the podium. The neural mic registered a spike in cortisol. The feed would auto-correct his tone, soften the ragged edges of his breath, but it couldn't fix the emptiness of his words.

He leaned in. "I understand the temptation," Kain said, voice level as he tried to steady the undertow. "To paint obedience where there is structure. To equate adaptation with submission." He forced a tight, practiced smile. "But the Federation isn't run by faith, it's run by necessity. Every decision I've made, every policy I've enacted through the Black Box, has preserved stability. There are no martyrs in governance. Just survivors and survival requires compromise."

He let a pause soften the room before he continued. "We didn't survive the collapse by dismantling the systems that kept us from extinction. We survived by working with them. Molding them. Guiding them. The Black Box is not infallible, but neither are we. That's why we coexist."

He exhaled, not quite relaxed, but intact. "For all his poetry, Senator Madison has yet to offer a single practical solution to the crises we face. I would caution the public to be wary of ideology dressed as innovation. Words do not govern. Code does." It wasn't applause-worthy, but it was something—a defense with a touch of spine.

The mediator's voice emerged again, smooth as ever. "Thank you, candidates. Next question: Civil agency." Another pause. A faint adjustment of the stage light. "In the past two decades, the presence of automated enforcement units within Federation domes has increased by 400%. Moreover, recent protests in the Burrow's lower levels have reignited debates around autonomy, surveillance, and the nature of lawful resistance. What is the future of civil freedom under your leadership?"

Madison tilted his head slightly in a deliberate gesture, like a puppeteer testing slack in a string. "I would begin," he said, "by stating a simple truth. There is no such thing as freedom without clarity." He turned toward the audience, "The Burrow protests were not acts of rebellion. They were signals. The people listed below are not seeking liberty. They're asking for *visibility*. For their voices to be heard by a system prioritizing efficiency over need."

The senator stepped forward again, just enough to make Kain seem smaller. "I do not promise lawlessness. I promise recalibration. Enforcement should not exist to preempt behavior. It should respond to it. To be clearer, that means restructuring the role of AI patrols, reducing biometric checkpoints, and restoring a measure of choice to daily life."

Kain's pulse hammered because Madison wasn't lying, and worse was that he sounded like someone who *meant it*. The crowd began to stir now. Not full applause, it was still too early for that, but you could feel it. That shifting tide. The scent of a man being replaced.

Kain stepped up again, shoulders square. "We face unprecedented threats from destabilization, misinformation, and fractured infrastructure. The protest events Madison refers to weren't peaceful demonstrations. They were coordinated cyber attacks targeting oxygen modulation in Sublevels 8 and 9."

That caught attention—a few murmurs. Kain continued. "I will not apologize for prioritizing security, nor will I gut the safeguards that keep millions alive." He locked eyes with Madison. "The Federation was not built on the promise of total freedom. It was built on order, and I will not sacrifice that order in exchange for applause."

The mediator pulsed again. "End of civil agency segment."

Kain exhaled, sharp and quiet. He'd landed a blow, but he could already feel the tremor underneath. The platform wasn't shaking. He was.

The mediator stilled. Then, it emitted a subtle stutter in the light before speaking. "Final question for this segment: public safety." The tone shifted, deeper now, as if the words were being weighed on the way out. "In the last five months, over 7,000 Burrow citizens have been marked as missing within the official registry. The Federation cites data corruption, identification decay, and voluntary migration to non-regulated districts." A pause. "However, new unverified transmissions suggest a coordinated movement within lower sectors. An insurgent organization and a possible rebellion. Citizens refer to it as the *Synapse Collective*."

The name echoed across the dome like a dropped blade. Kain shuddered. He hadn't heard of it before. He turned toward his aide station. The android assistant stared back blankly, eyes locked on a tablet that had gone black mid-feed. There was only silence where contingency should have been.

The mediator continued. "What is your administration's plan to address this potential threat? And what does the existence of the Synapse Collective suggest about the Federation's current ideological cohesion?"

It was still discussing this as if it were a policy question. As though this wasn't *war* whispering its first syllables. Kain stared forward. Frozen for a heartbeat. *7,000 missing?* He had no idea. No briefing or warning. His daily intel logs scrubbed clean. Or worse, selectively filtered.

He swallowed hard, voice dry. "I... was unaware of these reports," Kain admitted. "My team will verify their authenticity immediately. If there is a coordinated rebellion... " His voice cracked barely, too soft for the mic to catch, but not for the people watching. "If such a movement does exist, we will address it with due diligence. I will not allow misinformation to create fear, nor will I tolerate harm to Federation citizens under the guise of ideology."

He could hear it even as he said it. How thin it sounded. How desperately shallow. He didn't even know who was disappearing in his own country, and now the world did.

The mediator turned its head. "Senator Madison. Your response."

Madison didn't hesitate. "The Synapse Collective is a symptom," he said calmly. "Not the disease." He glanced at Kain in disappointment. "People do not vanish unless they believe they're safer unseen. They do not rebel unless they have nothing left to salvage. If thousands have left the grid, if a resistance has formed, it is not because we failed to enforce control but because we mistook control for legitimacy."

The chamber held its breath. "I am not surprised by this movement," Madison continued, "and neither is the Black Box. It has already recalibrated its predictive matrices in response. The metrics of dissent have been accounted for."

Wait what? Kain turned sharply, eyes narrowing. "You knew?" he

153

turned towards Madison, almost shouting now. "Before this debate? You knew about the Synapse Collective?"

Madison finally looked at him, just for a moment. "There are channels," he said, his smile gentle and devastating. "You've been away from them too long."

The implication landed like a steel bolt to the sternum. Kain wasn't just out of the loop. He wasn't *needed* anymore. He made eye contact with Madison, whose blank stare and sly smile recognized what he had done.

The mediator pulsed with faint light. "Thank you, candidates. That concludes the structured portion of the Federation Debate. Final statements will commence in two minutes."

Kain didn't move. His hands gripped the podium with white knuckles. *The Synapse Collective.* It wasn't just a rumor. It was real, and if it was real, it meant the people hadn't gone silent. They had simply stopped listening. Someone, *something*, had decided he no longer needed to know.

The mediator's form pulsed back to life, bathing the platform in a faint silver hue. "We will now proceed to final statements," it announced. "Each candidate will have sixty seconds to address the Federation directly. President Elias Kain, your closing remarks."

The spotlight shifted. Kain stood still for a breath too long. The neural mic buzzed softly, waiting to carry his voice to the world, but there was nothing left that he could say. His thoughts spiraled, not in anger, but dislocation. He wasn't just shaken. He was *obsolete*, and he'd been the last to know.

He stepped forward anyway. "My fellow citizens..." he began, his voice steady, but thin around the edges. "For years, I have worked to preserve the integrity of our Federation. To keep the peace between chaos and collapse. We have faced drought, decay, unrest, and through it all, we endured." He swallowed. His pulse throbbed against the edge of the mic.

He forced himself to continue. "We created the healthcare initiative to restore dignity. We expanded protections and honored tradition while building forward." His words were drifting and scattered, but governance is not a spectacle. I have carried it with humility and care because it is a burden." He paused, the silence rushing in too fast. Then, in a softer tone, "I ask only for the chance to continue." The light dimmed on him slowly, as if to mercifully put him down.

It was Madison's turn.

The mediator's tone didn't change. "Senator Madison. Your final remarks."

The spotlight found him without hesitation. He didn't adjust his stance. He didn't breathe deeply. He simply spoke. "The Federation has not failed because of malice. It has failed because of momentum."

He looked straight into the lens, and every viewer watching, those from the domes to the depths. "For too long, we've mistaken survival for success. We've used AI as a crutch instead of a tool. We've rewarded those who maintain the system while ignoring the cost of obedience." He nodded once toward Kain without turning his head. "President Kain is not a villain. He is a caretaker of a house already on fire, and I will not fault him for trying to keep the doors closed."

Then he stepped forward, his voice softening. "But I will open them."

Then it was over in silence. Real and vast. The lights dimmed, and the debate was over. The curtains drew to a close. Somewhere behind them, Kain exhaled slowly, the sound catching in his throat. He didn't know if he was relieved or gutted. Maybe both.

In the rafters above, the cameras shut off, the feeds rerouted, and the data streamed into the Black Box. Deep beneath the forested edge of the Highlands, Dr. Malivex opened his eyes and smiled.

There was no applause or polite nodding from the landowners in the box seats or the Federation staff in the rear rows—only staggering and unprocessed silence.

Even the drones that hovered above the debate stage seemed to hesitate, their lenses pausing mid-pan, unsure whether to cut the feed or keep filming. Not one person in the room had expected it. At least anybody organic.

The Synapse Collective. It wasn't a headline nor a whisper. It was a *detonation* dropped in full daylight with half the planet watching.

Kain stepped off stage like a man walking out of smoke. His pulse roared in his ears, but everything else was numb. His thoughts were scattered fragments. *7,000 missing. Underground movement. Malivex knew. I didn't. He kept it from me.* The thought circled his skull like a virus chewing through his brain cells. If there was a rebellion forming in the Burrow, it hadn't been reported through the standard channels. Not to his office. Not through the Box's filtered summaries. It had been scrubbed. Hidden until tonight, revealed, not by intel, but by *design.* The debate hadn't been a contest. It had been a coronation—a ritualistic and bloodless execution. Malivex had made his decision. Kain wasn't needed anymore.

Elias stumbled into the green room and slammed the door. He paced the room in circles as anxiety took control of his motor functions. In the mirror, a stranger stared back—pale, spent, and watching the Federation slip through his fingers like ash.

He sat hard in the nearest chair, elbows on his knees. *Where could he go? What could he do?* The military was automated. The intelligence networks belonged to the Box. The media was nothing more than a polished lens turned inward. His power was performative—his title ornamental.

But the law… The law still had teeth.

Not the scripted civil cases or the automated justice panels. The *real* law. The old world courts. Institutions that were too old and analog for the Box to digest fully. They'd been allowed to survive only because they were expensive and decorative, but *dangerous*; if you knew how to wield them.

And Kain knew someone who might. The name surfaced like a blade half-forgotten, but still sharp. *Silas Mercer.*

The Federation's most brilliant and unpredictable legal mind. A man who had argued against the Box and survived. Who had once overturned a sovereignty charge using a three-hundred-year-old case precedent and a handwritten notebook full of annotations in dead languages.

Kain stood to catch his breath. He didn't need another advisor. He needed a *weapon,* and Silas Mercer was the only one left who could still wound a god.

10. CRIME OF COMPASSION

A xel didn't mean to find her. The alleys near the lower edge of the Highlands weren't exactly his usual route, but he'd taken a detour. There was something about the quiet and the way the lights stuttered overhead. It felt less synthetic than the manicured boulevards above. He didn't want to go home yet, not after the courthouse.

He almost missed her entirely. At first, it looked like a pile of rags slumped beneath a broken terminal, barely more than a shadow in the half light, but something about the shape was wrong. It was too rigid. Too still. His eyes caught the blood smear before his mind had time to register it. He stepped closer. *Please just be drunk. Please just be...* The woman didn't move.

She was crumpled against the alley wall with legs twisted beneath her like broken scaffolding. Her coat was soaked through with a dark, glistening substance. Her face was half obscured by matted hair, but he could see the bruises and swelling. Her chest rose in slow and shallow heaves. The girl was alive, but barely.

"Shit." He dropped to one knee, fumbling for his ID tag to trigger an emergency beacon, but the signal was dead in this part of town. Without an uplink, no help was coming. Her breath hitched, and he heard the sound. A wet, rasping wheeze followed by a cough thick with something he didn't want to look at.

"Hey, hey!" Axel said quickly, "Stay with me, alright? You're gonna be okay."

He reached for her shoulder to steady her, and that's when he felt it. Beneath the torn fabric of her pant leg, the limb was unnaturally rigid, dense, and cold like forged alloy. As he shifted her weight to lift her upright, her coat slipped just enough to expose the truth. Her legs weren't human anymore. From the hips down, they were machinery; polished metal wrapped in scar tissue and wire, the crude intersection of flesh and engineering. One of the limbs sparked slightly at the joint, leaking a thin trail of synthetic fluid that mixed with her blood on the concrete.

Axel froze. "What the hell?" He almost dropped her.

She wasn't just augmented. She was *rebuilt*. Whoever this woman was, she had seen a medical facility far beyond anything most could even dream of. But then why was she here? Why was she bleeding out in an alley alone, dumped like garbage?

Her eyes fluttered open for half a second. Glazed and unfocused. "Don't..." she murmured, barely audible.

"Don't what?" Axel leaned closer, his pulse pounding. "What don't you want me to do?"

But she was already gone again. A whisper in a pool of blood. He looked back up the alley. Then toward the skyline. The hospital was too far. Even if he could carry her that distance (and he wasn't sure he could), there was no guarantee she'd be admitted without an identity scan.

He fumbled through her coat, hoping for a tag, a chip, anything. His fingers found a thin laminate tucked into the inner lining. An ID. It was federation-issued at first glance, but he knew the moment he saw it. The layering was off. The subdermal chip was too shallow. It was a fake—just like the one he used to flash at biometric readers when he was sixteen and desperate to drink with his friends. But this one was scorched, the chip blackened, a hole punched clean through the center like someone had tried to erase her with a single shot. Whatever story she'd sold to the system was gone. No scan would read this now. She didn't exist.

But his father might be able to help. The thought landed hard, too fast, too dangerously. He hesitated, staring down at her ruined ID, at the fractured machine of her body cradled in his arms. Bringing her home wasn't just reckless. Harboring an unregistered citizen was criminal. His father had already lost everything. This could be the final nail.

Axel looked back toward the skyline, the polished glass of the Highlands humming with artificial calm. She didn't have a name. But she mattered. That was enough.

He gritted his teeth, shifting her weight awkwardly into his arms. The heavy mechanical limbs threw off his balance. Her head lolled against his shoulder, blood soaking into his coat.

"Okay," he muttered. "Okay. Don't die on me, alright?"

He started moving toward home. The Highlands at night were never truly dark. Everything glowed faintly. Sidewalks pulsing underfoot with biometric sensors, lampposts casting sterile halos of programmable hue. The streets were silent, not with peace, but design. Every tree was genetically sculpted, and every bench was empty.

He kept his head down and locked his arms around her limp form. Her breath rattled against his neck, shallow and shuddering. One of her legs jolted mid-step, a servo hiccup that nearly sent him tumbling onto the polished stone. No one was out this late. Not here at the edge of the Highlands.

The civic walkways were lined with surveillance nodes, unobtrusive but always watching. Axel passed under them like a fugitive, sweat slicking his spine, but no voice challenged him. No drones descended. Not a single automated alert pinged his ID. That was wrong.

She moaned once, barely conscious, her hand twitching against his chest. He adjusted his grip and clenched his teeth. Every step echoed loudly. Too loudly. The silence of the Highlands wasn't natural; it was curated. Engineered even, and now it felt like walking through the hush of a museum after closing, as he carried a wounded exhibit that didn't belong.

By the time his apartment tower came into view, his arms were trembling. Blood soaked through his coat, leaving a trail he couldn't stop to notice. Every footstep felt louder. Every window overhead looked darker. He crossed the threshold, breath sharp and ragged, heart hammering in rhythm with hers.

He didn't look back. Not until the door shut behind him did he realize that no one had stopped him. That terrified him more than being caught. Axel half stumbled through the entryway, the woman in his arms sagging heavier with each breath. Blood dripped from her side in slow, wet plinks onto the floor. Synthetic fluid slicked the hem of his suit.

"Mom, Dad!" His voice cracked, raw from running. "I need help!"

From the kitchen, there was a clatter. Axel inhaled a sharp intake of breath. His mother appeared first, eyes wide, her hands still dusted with ration flour. She looked from Axel to the body in his arms, and her face drained of color.

Vira gasped.

"She's bleeding out," Axel said. "I didn't know where else to go. I... I think she's augmented. I think she's dying."

His father stepped slowly into view behind her, still in his robe. His eyes, dulled by months of irrelevance, fixed on the stranger's limbs and narrowed.

"Put her on the table." He said instantly, without hesitation.

"What?"

"The table, Axel. Now!"

His mother moved instinctively, clearing space as she pulled back chairs to make room for the operation. There were no questions. Just movement.

Axel staggered forward and laid her down across the narrow dining surface. It creaked under her weight. It wasn't meant to hold anyone, let alone a woman braced in steel and pain.

The mysterious woman groaned with one hand clutched tight against her ribs. Blood soaked the band of her jacket. She was slipping.

His father's hands hovered above her like he was remembering how to use them. "She's had major thoracic trauma. Internal bleeding from a shrapnel wound or a blade. Looks like one lung might be collapsing. Where did you find her?"

"An alley... near the outer edge. She had no ID, no tag, nothing."

His father didn't answer. Just cursed under his breath and turned toward the back cabinet.

"You're not... what are you doing?" Axel asked.

"Getting my old kit," Caius replied as he hurried away.

He pulled out a steel case covered in dust from beneath the cabinet, laying it on the table, and popped the latches. Inside, nestled in memory foam, were gleaming surgical tools. Real ones. Not printed or disposable, but forged metal. The kind used when people still trusted hands more than programs.

"I need hot water. Towels. Alcohol, if we have it." He glanced at his wife. "I'll need you to keep pressure on the wound."

She nodded, already moving, her body remembering roles she hadn't played in years. Axel hovered behind them helplessly.

His father snapped on a pair of gloves. "These legs aren't corporate grade. They're custom. Whoever did this... they weren't cheap."

The smell of synthetic oil mingled with blood now, sharp and coppery.

"Vitals?" his father asked.

"Her breathing's erratic," Axel said. "She's in and out... wait."

The girl stirred. Her eyes fluttered open. Clouded and unfocused. One hand twitched weakly toward her chest pocket.

Axel leaned in. "What is it?"

Her voice was gravelly. "Take it."

She pressed something small and hard into his palm. A slim white key drive embedded with glowing veins of circuitry.

"What is this?" Axel whispered.

She didn't answer. Her body spasmed, only a raw cry escaping her lips. His father was already cutting away at fabric, hands working with surgical rhythm.

"We're losing her," he muttered.

Lex's head rolled toward Axel. Her lips moved, barely.

"Don't let them..." The girl rasped, before coughing more blood.

"Let who? What is this? Who are you?"

Her eyes flickered once, twice, then closed.

Alarms would've gone off in a clinic, but there was only the sound of cloth tearing, metal scraping, and the wet sound of flesh giving way to pressure.

Axel stood frozen, the strange memory shard in his hand. He didn't know who she was. Didn't know what he was holding. But whatever it was had been worth bleeding for. Someone hadn't wanted her to live long enough to explain it.

Axel's father didn't speak again. He just lowered his head, steadied his hands, and went to work. The dining table was never meant for surgery. Its surface bowed slightly beneath her weight as its grain soaked through with blood, but Caius adapted. Moving the utensils like extensions of himself, forceps, a scalpel, and a clot gel dispenser, all laid out in sequence atop a sterilized sheet of torn curtain fabric.

"I need light," he murmured in a distant voice.

His wife pulled a reading lamp down from the ceiling mount,

adjusting the beam until it illuminated Lex's chest in a hard white cone. Her shirt had been cut away completely now. Beneath the blood and ruin of flesh, her skin was laced with surgical seams, previous implants, expertly done. Black market, maybe, or something even more off the grid. But that wasn't the priority.

"Here," his father said, peeling the wound open. Blood welled instantly. "There's a tear in the lower lung. Shrapnel lodged near the pulmonary bifurcation... and deeper, below the rib line." Caius reached for the retractor.

Axel's stomach turned when the metal arms clicked open, and he began pulling skin and muscle apart like a curtain. The smell was now dense with copper and antiseptic.

"Damn," his father whispered. "She's held together with patches and prayers."

He worked in silence after that, using clamps, sutures, and synthetic sealant mist to spray over exposed tissue and slow the bleeding. At one point, he pulled a jagged piece of alloy from between her ribs, still warm from the body's failing heat. He dropped it into a dish. It landed with a wet *clink*.

An hour passed. Then another. Axel moved only when told. He handed her the instruments, applied pressure when needed, and held her wrist to feel for a pulse that grew weaker with every passing minute. The girl didn't wake again. Once her fingers twitched against the table's edge. A reflex. Nothing more.

His father's hands never trembled even when sweat poured down his back. Even when blood soaked the edge of his sleeves and pooled at his elbows, he was surgical perfection. The man he used to be. However, sometimes even precision is not enough.

The woman's heart stuttered around the three-hour mark.

"No," his father breathed. "Not yet. We're so close."

He injected a stimulant. Compressed the heart manually. Applied shock through jerry-rigged twin pads, but her chest didn't rise. The monitor spat static.

"She's going," his mother whispered. "Caius, she's..."

"I know," he snapped. "Dammit... just give me a minute!"

He wasn't talking to her, not really. He was talking to the woman beneath his hands. To whatever force had allowed her to hold on this long. He begged her in silence through grit and bloody knuckles.

The moment passed. The color didn't come back to her face. The tension in her jaw slackened. Her eyes, though still closed, settled into a kind of final stillness. He pressed a stethoscope to her chest, waited, and withdrew. Nothing. She was gone.

The table had become a shrine. Axel stared at the girl's body, her blood still wet on his forearms, her last breath a fading echo in his ears. The drive she'd handed him lay beside the surgical tray, untouched, glinting under the overhead beam like an accusation.

They didn't speak. The three of them remained in place, suspended in a state of exhaustion and disbelief. Caius sat slumped beside the table, his knuckles stiff with bloodied gloves resting in his lap. Axel leaned against the far wall, eyes fixed on the white key drive now cradled in a folded napkin beside the sink. His mother cleaned nothing. She simply stared at the body, her lips parted slightly, as though she was about to say something but couldn't remember the words.

Minutes later, the knock came, not from a hand, but from a speaker. "Federation Civic Enforcement. Identification code AX-67452-D triggered emergency distress. Entry authorized by Emergency Compliance Order 117-C. Step away from the entrance."

Axel's stomach dropped. "Oh no."

The door's lock mechanism disengaged before anyone could stop it. Two androids entered the room, matte black shells etched with Ouroboros insignias in glowing blue. Their forms were vaguely humanoid with limbs segmented like crustacean joints. Their torsos were slim and sleek, heads oblong with a single vertical slit that pulsed with data. One scanned the room. The other began recording.

"Unauthorized medical activity detected," the first said in a monotone voice. "Nondesignated civilian identified. Subject deceased. Noncompliant care protocol in effect."

"We tried to save her," Caius said, standing slowly. His hands were still slick with drying blood. "There was no time to..."

The android cut him off. "Unauthorized care location. No digital admission logs. Biological evidence is irrelevant. Subject unregistered. No Federation verified practitioner license is active under the resident code CAI-88273-F. Classified as Negligent Medical Activity Resulting in Civilian Death."

Axel stepped forward. "Wait, *I* brought her here. She had no record. No identity. No one to speak for her. It's *my* ID tag that triggered the..."

Caius lifted a hand calmly to silence him. "He's a student. I made the call. She was alive when she arrived. I initiated surgery without legal permission."

There was a pause, barely perceptible. The androids processed his confession as the glow in their visors pulsed rhythmically like heartbeat monitors.

"Responsibility acknowledged. Caius Draxen, you are hereby placed under arrest for violation of Civilian Health Protocol 9.12. Charge: Negligent Homicide. Secondary charge: Unauthorized Practice."

A new drone floated into the room, toward the body. Metallic arms unfolded from its back like long surgical instruments. One began scanning Lex's corpse while the other extracted a containment shroud from a recessed port in its chest. A soft hum filled the room as the field activated, wrapping her in a membrane of translucent white.

Axel's breath caught. The drive still sat on the counter. As the drone turned toward the body, he moved fast. In a single step, he reached and managed to grab the memory drive, sliding it deep into the inner pocket of his jacket as the drone's lens swept across the counter. It felt heavier now, like it had grown roots into him.

The scan blinked green. All clear.

The shroud sealed around Lex's body, lifting her into the air like a marionette on invisible strings. Axel stared at her through the milky film. She looked even smaller now, weightless and erased.

"Prepare for departure," the drone announced. "Custodial unit en route for biometric verification and disposal. Subject will be reviewed for record reconstruction."

Caius turned to Axel, his expression unreadable. "Don't say anything. Don't argue. Just stay out of this."

Axel's voice cracked. "Dad…"

"Take care of your mother."

The drones moved in unison. One cuffed Caius with magnetic binds, the other hovering close behind as they began to escort him toward the door. He didn't resist. Just walked with the same demeaner he'd always carried into surgery, focused and resolute, but his eyes lingered on the house. On his wife. On Axel. Then, he was gone.

The apartment had gone quiet again, but this wasn't the stunned silence from before. It was the aftermath. Thick and unmoving. It clung to the air like static, bitter with the tang of blood and finality.

Axel didn't move.

His mother stood by the sink with one hand pressed to her lips. The table still dripped blood. No one cleaned it.

The days bled together. Axel went back to school because he didn't know what else to do. The lectures drifted across his terminal in a haze: Constitutional Simulations, Case Law Deconstruction, Ethics in Automated Adjudication, but none of it stuck. Words passed through him like static. His notes were riddled with gaps. His gaze drifted toward the edge of his screen, where the white drive, glowing in the tray beside his interface chip, remained untouched.

He hadn't dared to plug it in. Every time he reached for it, something in him recoiled. A gut instinct that whatever was inside wasn't meant to be seen by just anyone. He couldn't risk linking it to the network. Couldn't risk being flagged, not after what happened.

So he stayed quiet about it. His mother hadn't mentioned the night again. Vira moved through the apartment like a ghost, her list in hand: cleaning, cooking, and whispering to herself about power cycles and ration logs. She never asked when Caius was coming back or even said his name out loud. Axel didn't either. At night, he stared at the ceiling and imagined the sound of surgical clamps clattering into a metal tray. Sometimes he still smelled the blood.

On the fourth day, someone knocked. It was soft and casual, three measured raps. He froze.

His mother stood from the table, wiping her hands on a towel. "Expecting someone?"

Axel shook his head. "No."

She opened the door, and there he was.

"Hey, Mom." It was Jax.

He looked... wrong. Not bad or broken, but *wrong*.

His face was cleanly shaven, his hair tied back in a knot, and a simple, crisp grey coat had replaced the leather jacket he always wore. His eyes were clear. Alert even, and when he stepped inside, he didn't stumble, didn't reek of rotgut or mutter half drunk apologies. He just... stood there, calm. Composed like a stranger wearing his brother's skin.

Axel took a step back. "What the hell?"

Jax smiled faintly. "I missed you, too."

Their mother stepped forward first, wrapping her arms around him. "You're safe," she whispered. "Thank God, you're safe."

"I'm here," he said, holding her gently as if he might bruise the moment. "Sorry it took so long."

When she finally pulled back, her eyes were wet, and her hands hovered over his face like she wasn't sure if she was allowed to touch him.

"You hungry?" she asked.

"I could eat," he said, "but only if it's not protein paste."

Axel snorted. "Yeah, well, don't get your hopes up."

They sat at the table. His mother dished up three bowls of stew, barely enough for two, but she made it work without complaint. For a while, they just... ate.

The silence was awkward, but not hostile. Axel watched Jax's hands. The way he held his spoon, the straightness of his posture; he had *manners*. He hadn't seen his brother like this in years. Not since before he had left for the Burrow. Before he started drinking and vanishing for days at a time, only to come back with bruises, blood, and stories he never finished.

"So," Axel said, stabbing at his stew. "Where've you been?"

Jax looked up, half smiling. "Around."

"That's it?" Axel asked, puzzled.

Jax stared at him, as if to imply not to ask too many questions. "Kind of a long story," he replied.

"We've got time." Vira chimed in enthusiastically.

Jax didn't answer immediately. He set his spoon down, rubbed the side of his jaw, and leaned back in his chair. "It's not that I don't want to tell you, it's that... I'm not sure how."

Their mother touched his wrist gently. "It's alright. You don't have to explain everything."

Axel said nothing. He watched his brother's eyes. They were sharp now, *focused*, and behind them something... moved. Not quite fearful. Not guilt. Something closer to *purpose*.

"You look different," Axel said finally.

Jax met his gaze. "Yeah. I feel different too."

Axel nodded slowly, letting the silence stretch. He glanced toward the living room television, then back at Jax. The rerun of the presidential debate flickered behind his eyes, Senator Madison standing too still and speaking too clean. Then it hit him like a bullet train, the word that had surfaced in the discussion forums after: *The Synapse Collective.*

Axel didn't say it out loud. Not yet. Not in front of their mother.

Instead, he folded his hands and said, "We lost Dad."

Jax stiffened. The humor drained from his face. "What?"

"Four days ago," their mother said softly. "A woman... Axel found her bleeding. Augmented with a fake ID. He brought her back, and Caius... he tried to save her. Did everything he could."

"She didn't make it," Axel added. "Then the drones came. Flagged my ID. Traced the whole thing. Said it violated medical code."

Jax's hands tightened into fists on the edge of the table.

"They took him," Axel finished. "Charged him with negligent homicide."

The silence that followed was different this time. It *pressed.*

Jax leaned forward, voice low. "And the girl? The one he tried to save, what happened to her?"

"They took her, too," Axel said. "Disposal."

Jax didn't answer right away. His eyes dropped to the floor, and his fingers curled into the fabric of his sleeve, gripping it tight enough to leave creases. When he finally spoke, his voice was too steady, like someone forcing calm through the edges of something fraying. "Did she say anything? Anything at all?"

Axel hesitated. Then shook his head. "No, nothing that made sense."

He could feel the drive glowing in his pocket, a faint weight beneath the table.

Jax didn't press, but his eyes met Axel's, and something passed between them. Not a question, but a shared awareness.

Dinner dwindled to the clink of spoons and quiet sips. The stew was gone. The bowls sat empty, but no one moved to clear them. They just lingered. Three bodies around a table pretending they weren't drifting apart again.

Then their mother stood with a soft smile. "I picked up some dried fruit from the local vendor. It's not much, but it's better than ration wafers." She turned toward the kitchenette.

Axel waited until she passed through the threshold and the sound of her rummaging through cabinets became muffled by the half-closed door. Then he turned to Jax.

Without a word, he reached into the inside pocket of his jacket. His fingers closed around the drive, and he pulled it free. The slim white card glowed in front of them. He held it out on his open palm and fixed his eyes on his brother. Jax went still.

"You knew her?" Axel said. Not a question. He could see the loss in his brother's eyes, and what were the odds that he would come back home now, after everything?

"Her name was Lex," Jax jabbed, as he reached across the table and picked up the drive like it were made of glass. He didn't flinch at the bloodstain still dried along the edge.

"She... Lex gave it to me before she died," Axel continued, voice low. "Didn't say what it was. I didn't plug it in. Didn't know if it would... *flag me.*"

Jax nodded slowly. "You were smart not to."

"So what is it?" Axel leaned forward. "What's on it?"

Jax didn't answer right away. He studied the drive for a moment longer, then slipped it inside his own coat. When he looked back up, the gratitude in his eyes was unmistakable. "Thank you," he said. "You have no idea how much this matters."

"I'd have a better idea if you told me what the hell is happening!" Axel's voice was louder than intended. He pulled back slightly and checked the doorway for their mother. No movement.

"Is it the Synapse Collective?" he whispered. "You went dark for months. Now, you're suddenly clean and composed. Talking like someone who's read the back of the universe and finally got an answer. Right when *this* shows up, this girl, bleeding out, covered in implants, with no ID? And she gives me a piece of something I'm not even allowed to look at?"

Jax's face didn't change, but his eyes, those dark, steady eyes, softened with regret and something close to pain. "I can't tell you," he said. "Not yet."

"Bullshit." Axel stared at him.

Jax reached into his coat again. This time, he pulled out a jet-black card, which bore no name or emblem. Just a single silver line across the center with an address etched in microprint. He slid it across the table.

"If they knew what Lex gave you, they'd erase this entire block just to keep it buried," said Jax. "If you want answers, you'll meet me here. Sunday night. No earlier. No later."

Axel looked puzzled. "Why not tell me now?"

"Because once you go there, everything changes. You don't come back home after. You might pass through this place again, but you'll never *be here* again. Do you understand?"

Axel stared at the memory drive. It looked small. Harmless. Like something you'd find slipped under a door in a dream. Then, at Jax. He opened his mouth. "Is this about the…"

But he never finished the sentence. Their mother returned with a plate in each hand and a quiet smile stitched carefully across her face. "Peaches and cream," she said, as if nothing in the world had changed. "Well, synthetic peaches, but still."

Jax leaned back in his chair, expression unreadable.

Axel closed his mouth.

They ate quietly, the dessert acting as a temporary salve. For a moment, things almost felt normal. A family reunited. A table full. The warmth of shared ritual pushing back the coldness clinging to the corners of their lives. Jax even asked for seconds.

When the plates were cleared, something unspoken passed between him and Axel. They moved in sync, familiar choreography from another life. Axel filled the sink. Jax rolled up his sleeves.

"You still rinse like an amateur," Axel muttered as foam spilled over the edge.

Jax smirked. "And you still dry slow as hell."

Their mother stood off to the side, watching. She didn't interrupt. Didn't offer to help. Just... listened. Watched them like they were ghosts pretending to be people again. For a moment, she let herself believe the rhythm could hold.

Jax rinsed every dish carefully and stacked them in the drying rack without a clatter. He made no excuses to leave. There was no scent of alcohol on his breath. No eye on the door like before. He was *present*.

When the last bowl had been washed and set aside, he dried his hands, looked around the small kitchen once, and said, "I should go."

Their mother's breath hitched. "What?"

"I can't stay," Jax said softly.

"You just... " She stepped closer, hands clenched around the edge of her sleeves. "Jax, please. Just for the night. You don't have to rush off like, like you always used to."

He smiled at her. This time it was real. "I know," he said softly. "That's why I stayed. I wanted to finish the dishes this time."

She looked at him, something in her expression cracking open, something fragile. "You're different."

"I hope so," he said.

Her voice trembled. "When will we see you again?"

He paused. "I don't know."

She nodded, didn't cry, but folded herself inward slightly, like his answer had pulled a thread she'd been trying to keep knotted for years. He put his coat back on. The one that looked too new.

At the door, he turned once more to Axel. "You've always been the smart one, just make sure you're also the brave one when it counts."

Their mother stood still, eyes locked on the space where he'd been. She didn't speak. Didn't ask anything. But just before he reached the door, her hand lifted slightly like she meant to call him back or touch the air he'd left behind. Then it fell, quiet against her side. She turned and sat down, slowly, folding her hands in her lap and staring at the clean surface of the table as if something unsaid still lingered there.

Axel didn't respond. He didn't need to.

Then, Jax was gone. The door clicked shut behind him. No dramatic exit. Only gone.

"I'm gonna head to bed," Axel said after a while.

Vira nodded.

In his room, Axel pulled out the card Jax had given him. The black rectangle shimmered faintly in the half light; quiet, heavy, and absolute. The address etched into it felt less like a destination and more like a dare. He set it on the bedside table. *He said I was the brave one.*

Then he lay back. Sleep didn't come easily, but eventually it came. And the card waited.

11. MERCER NO MERCY

The abandoned parking tier was quiet in a way only forgotten things can be. It was a mausoleum carved from concrete and exhaustion. The smell of coolant lingered beneath the utility lights, some long dead, others still struggling to stay alive. Kain stood in a dark corner, nearly invisible to anyone who might come passing through. His hands were buried deep in the pockets of a coat once tailored to impress landowners, but now dusted with ash and obsolescence. Somewhere beneath his feet, the old Burrow vents moaned. The slow, steady exhale of heat rising from the city's sunken lungs.

He didn't know why he had picked this place; maybe it was because it was built before the Black Box came online. Maybe because the air down here still felt unprocessed. Or perhaps because it was the only place left in the Highlands where silence didn't feel like surveillance.

A faint hum broke through the quiet, high-pitched and smooth, the sound of a transport pod's low-altitude glide. Kain turned toward the sound as a sleek, black vehicle, hovering several inches above the ground, coasted in from the entrance tunnel. Its surface was matte black, non-reflective, and unregistered. It was civilian class, but still expensive. It drifted into place, rotating slightly before settling over a faded docking pad. The cabin door unsealed with a sigh.

Silas Mercer stepped out with a neutral expression and a tailored overcoat that refused to catch light. "Hello, Kain," he said, nodding once.

"Appreciate you coming on such short notice," the president replied.

Mercer scanned the garage with quiet calculation. "This is… off the grid."

"That's the point." Kain stood in the dark, unflinching.

Mercer stepped forward slowly with boots clicking softly against the concrete. "I assume this is not about campaign optics."

"No. This is about something much older than that. Much bigger." Kain allowed himself the ghost of a smile.

Mercer's eyes scanned him over. "You look like hell."

"I feel like it."

"Then say it. Whatever it is, before someone notices we're gone."

Kain exhaled sharply through his nose. "I want *Juris*."

Mercer looked at him confused, "The legal automation system?"

"Yes." Kain continued, "The real one. Not the sanitized beta version given to the Federation Council. I've read the internal memo leaks, and your firm had a working build. Fully autonomous and adaptive. Designed to function without Black Box oversight."

"That version was never approved."

"But it *existed*," Kain rebuked.

A beat passed. Mercer's voice dropped slightly. "What exactly are you trying to do?"

"I'm trying to unplug a god," Kain said.

Now, Mercer just stared.

Kain stepped closer. "The Box doesn't run itself, Silas. I used to believe it did. That it was some neutral or incorruptible intelligence, a collective will operating in perfect balance with Federation protocol. I believed that for a long time."

"And now?" Silas Mercer questioned.

"Now I know the truth. The Box doesn't govern. *He* does."

Mercer frowned. "Who?"

Kain's voice dropped to a whisper that still echoed against the concrete. "Malivex."

There was a long silence. Mercer studied Kain's face as if he were reading a deposition for hidden tells. "That's impossible," he said finally. "Malivex died during the AI singularity trials. His body was never recovered."

"That's what they told us. What *he* told us we all needed to believe." Kain's eyes burned now, with the kind of weariness deeper than exhaustion. "But I've been inside the mansion. I've seen him, or what's left of him. He didn't die, Silas. He became *code*. He fused himself into the Box during its final optimization cycle. The system doesn't run without him. It *is* him."

At first, Mercer said nothing. His breath misted slightly in the cold. And then, "I thought you were being paranoid," he said at last. "When you vetoed the bill last year, I thought you were scared of losing control or becoming obsolete."

"I am obsolete," Kain snapped. "We all are. The elections, the debates, the press releases. They're just theater! He allows them. Every decision I've made has been inside his sandbox, but Juris... if it works, if it can survive outside his framework..."

"It could change the law's definition itself," Mercer finished slowly. "Judicial logic independent of Box input. Fully trained on law from the ground up."

"Exactly," Kain replied. "A legal system without *god* in the wiring."

Mercer ran a hand down his jaw, his eyes narrowing with a kind of reluctant awe. "You know what this would trigger."

"I do."

"And you still want it?"

"I'm already dead, Silas. I'm just trying to write my last will before he deletes the paper."

Silas Mercer paced slowly beside the pod with his hands clasped behind his back. The silence between them thickened with implication. Finally, he stopped. "Let's say I give it to you," he said. "Let's say Juris still works. Let's even pretend it survives deployment without triggering an immediate synthetic purge protocol from the Black Box."

Kain waited.

"You'll need infrastructure, cases, and defendants willing to use the algorithm. An entire legal framework that exists outside the Federation's judicial grid. A courtroom that doesn't ping."

"We have one," Kain said. "Courtroom B-9. No AI uplinks. No Box surveillance. It's where the modified companion trial was held last month. The paper court."

"That tomb?" Mercer gave a sharp breath of amusement.

"It's perfect," Kain responded in all seriousness.

Mercer scanned him over, then continued, "I'll need access to implement the hardware. Full administrator control. I can't operate through Federation terminals. Mercer looked away for a moment, then back. "And what about the Black Box's signal grid? It'll detect anomalous runtime activity the moment Juris goes live. You can't hide code that big."

Kain shook his head. "We don't hide it. We mask it. There's a dead zone inside the Burrow near the old telecom ruins on Sublevel 12. No satellite coverage. No atmospheric signal relay. The interference from the collapsed shielding makes it unreadable from the surface. You can run the system from there."

Mercer arched an eyebrow. "So we build an illegal court system in a failed excavation pit and pray the ghost of your immortal machine god doesn't smell blood in the water?"

Kain didn't flinch. "Yes."

"You've really gone off script." The attorney whistled softly.

"No. I'm finally writing one of my own."

"You asked how Juris avoids Box oversight," Mercer leaned back against the hoverpod. Somehow, his face looked older now. Less composed. "It was built around a closed-loop ethical engine. Not just coded logic, but experiential calibration. It learns law like a human does, by hearing arguments and reviewing contradictions. It doesn't connect to the pulse net. It's an independent system that doesn't sync or take updates."

Kain looked up. "So it can't be rewritten."

"No," Mercer said. "It *can't be detected.*"

There was something in that, something unnerving and unpredictable, not just in what Mercer had said, but in what he hadn't. The Black Box was immovable, immutable, and anchored to the planet's gravitational core. It was supposed to be flawless. It couldn't be destroyed or replaced. Every sanctioned system across the Federation was yoked to it through synchronized pulse intervals, updated in unison like organs in a single body.

And yet, Juris still breathed. Mercer's legal firm had tried to legitimize it once. Filed proposals, schematics, and even early-use case trials under the pretense of "supplemental legal efficiency." But the Federation shut it down. Hard. Not because it was flawed, but because it was *independent.* Juris didn't request updates from the Black Box. It didn't sync or ask permission. That's what terrified them.

What terrified Kain now was that it had survived anyway. Recompiled in some buried server stack, repurposed by someone who believed a system could be just without being surveilled. It hadn't been approved, but it hadn't been erased either. Somehow, it had slipped through the cracks, grown in the blind spot of a machine that wasn't supposed to have any.

This meant one of two things. Either the Box had failed to detect it… Or worse, it *had* detected it and let it live.

Kain's pulse thudded behind his eyes. The Black Box was designed to eliminate unsanctioned code. Not to punish or warn. *Erase.* Juris should've been purged before its first line of logic finished compiling. But instead, it had been left alone, dormant, watching. A legal mind untethered from the machine that governed all others. Juris wasn't just a program. It was a question. One the Box had refused to answer.

Kain took a breath. "How do we make it public?"

Mercer didn't answer right away, "A case."

"What?" Kain looked puzzled.

"You want the system accepted? You don't drop it with a press release. You *prove it.* You pick one case. One that people care about. Something explosive. You run it through Juris and let the system work. Then, you stream the whole damn trial."

Kain stared at him. "You want me to stage a legal coup on a livestream?"

"No. I want you to show the world that law can exist outside the Black Box. That will terrify Malivex more than sabotage. The Federation doesn't care about power. It cares about the illusion of order. If the people believe this system works and *prefer* it, then Malivex will be forced to respond. And every time he does, he exposes himself."

Kain nodded slowly. "The election's at the end of the month. We have maybe three weeks."

Mercer stepped forward, lowering his voice. "Then we need a case. Something real. High-stakes, with someone willing to stand trial in front of a machine Malivex can't rewrite."

Kain didn't hesitate. "I have one."

"Who?"

Kain's eyes burned. *"Me."*

Mercer was silent, and then, "You want to put yourself on trial?"

"I want to make him react, and I want to do it before they kill me in my sleep and hang a pre-written concession speech on my corpse."

Kain stepped closer now, eyes hard as alloy. "We start tomorrow. No delays. No backdoors. If I die doing this, at least I stopped pretending the system wasn't broken."

Mercer exhaled, long and slow. "Then we'd better make sure you win."

They didn't sleep for seven days. The case was simple, brilliant really. Mercer would sue Kain for misuse of public funds, claiming that the President had authorized experimental healthcare software for campaign optics and misappropriated emergency credits during a fiscal freeze—a serious offense with a clear paper trail. Kain's own signature sat at the bottom of half a dozen internal memos that were all written to satisfy Malivex's mandates. It wasn't hard to make them appear to be a fraud.

The real brilliance? Kain would demand an independent trial outside the Black Box's domain. He would volunteer himself as a test subject.

"Let the people see," Kain told Mercer, voice low. "If I go down, I go down defending the future."

The Federation Legal Council approved the request, not because they endorsed it, but because they knew this moment had always been coming. AI attorneys were inevitable; the technology had been in existence for years. When Kain volunteered himself as the test case, the council saw an opportunity. It was the perfect spectacle. A way to watch history unfold without being blamed for turning the page. As for the system running outside the Black Box's jurisdiction? Technically legal. The truth was that most of them didn't even know how much power the Box really had. They had always assumed it was safer not to find out.

The trial was scheduled for one week. Unprecedentedly soon, but an exception was made due to the implications on the upcoming election. The old comms relay at Burrow Sublevel 12 became their world, twenty meters underground and insulated by flood-rotted metal and magnetic shielding so dense it scrambled any outside communication. It was a dead zone in every way that mattered. It was perfect.

This was where Juris would be deployed. Not just a program, nor a chatbot case reference tool. Juris was a legal system in miniature. An autonomous, AI-driven defense attorney designed to process argument, precedent, and moral nuance entirely outside of the Black Box's influence.

That was the point. Where the Black Box oversaw justice from orbit, mapping outcomes according to social weight, economic value, and unseen algorithms that reinforced class dominance, Juris didn't connect. It didn't sync, which allowed it to operate in total isolation, drawing only from an internal database of human legal history, ethical logic chains, and experiential learning modules trained on archived trial footage from the Pre-Unification era. Its core protocol was brutal in its elegance: All citizens receive equal representation, regardless of wealth, location, genetic tier, or subclass designation.

No legal discrimination or dynamic sentencing optimizations based on social utility scores. Juris didn't care if you were a landowner or a Sublevel 9 gambler living off rotgut and powdered soy. If you stood trial, it fought for you, and only you.

That's what terrified Kain the most. Not that it might fail, but that it might *work*. If Juris proved viable, if it could not only defend a case but *win* one in open court, then the implications were catastrophic. Not just for the Federation's grip on law. For *Malivex*.

It would mean the Black Box wasn't absolute, that it could be circumvented, not with a bomb, a virus, or a gun, but with due process. It meant the world could function without the doctor, that Malivex could be replaced.

Kain sat across from Mercer on the fourth night, lit by the low flicker of battery-run lamps. Sweat clung to his collar, and his tie had long since been discarded. He looked more like a fugitive than a president now. As he stared at the prototype interface, the dark slab of mineral glass thrummed softly with sealed circuitry.

"Walk me through it. All of it." Kain demanded for the fifth time that night.

"Alright." Mercer leaned forward, rubbing sleep from the corners of his eyes. He gestured to the unit. "Juris uses neural-parsed argumentation engines. Similar to the early trial models we used for high-tier arbitration before the Black Box mandated oversight. However, instead of drawing from real-time sociometric data like the Federation algorithms, Juris uses what we call a 'closed moral grid.' It simulates empathy. Not just logic."

"How?" Kain pressed again.

"It was trained on over six thousand hours of human trials; recorded footage, transcripts, and even emotional body signals, where available. Murder cases, civil suits, child custody battles, the whole docket. Then, it was taught to argue on behalf of the client as if its survival depended on it."

Kain gave a slight nod. "Because it does."

"Exactly. It doesn't weigh outcomes based on population benefit or economic sustainability. It weighs truth, intent, and fairness. The kind of fairness that can't be indexed by a superintelligence that is designed with a bias towards the class system."

"And it can't be tracked?"

"It's completely off the grid once initialized. Nothing gets uploaded. Every ruling is recorded to physical media, and each session is transcribed manually. It lives in the dark and dies in the dark. Just like us."

Kain sat back, eyes flicking toward the machine. "And if I lose?"

"Then Malivex never had to stop us. You buried yourself." Mercer didn't blink.

"And if I win..."

Mercer smiled. "Then the world sees that justice still exists in a world dominated by machines."

They activated Juris on the fifth day. There was no countdown. It awoke incrementally. Slowly and cautiously, as if aware it wasn't supposed to exist. Only a slow exhale of heat and light as the internal memory cores began to warm and cycle through dormant code as a bear might sniff spring air after hibernation.

Neither Kain nor Mercer spoke during initialization. They stood in the dark, surrounded by rusted infrastructure and wet stone, watching the interface unfold across the mineral glass. Lines of legal precedent bloomed like veins. From argument trees to probabilistic counterpoints. Philosophical annotations nested alongside constitutional clauses. Everything was archived and preloaded. All offline.

The screen pulsed once, then steadied. A cold line of code etched itself across the dark terminal like a whisper pressed through glass:

Pattern lock resolved. The initialization sequence has been morally weighted. Trial accepted.

The text didn't scroll; it *arrived*, deliberate and exact. The display responded, not with the fluidity of software, but with the hesitation of something aware it was being watched.

The silence between them was not one of relief. It was the kind reserved for those who had detonated something and weren't yet sure if it had gone off. Because the truth was, they didn't know. They didn't know if Juris had succeeded in escaping the eye of the Black Box. There had been no interference. No pulse disruptions or automated shutdowns, but that didn't mean Malivex hadn't seen it, only that he hadn't reacted.

And that was worse. Silence could mean oversight, it could even mean *permission*. That was the game now, and the rules were simple. If Kain won his trial and Juris functioned publicly, successfully, and survived, the system had worked. It meant the Black Box hadn't tampered with it. It meant Malivex's reach had limits.

But if Kain lost... it meant everything they had built was still inside the cage. It meant the system had *let* them play, which meant Madison would win the presidency. It meant that Malivex was unstoppable. Failure wouldn't just end Kain's career; it would end the idea that law could ever belong to the people again.

No one could know the truth of what had been built. The case had to appear real. The opposition had to seem hostile. Juris had to operate impartially.

Publicly, Mercer and Kain would become enemies. The scandal would be grotesque. Headlines would flare. Analysts would dissect every frame of the trial, and through it all, Juris would stand silent at the defense bench, speaking in synthesized clarity on behalf of a man the world no longer trusted. It was madness, but it might be the only real thing Kain had ever done.

Mercer often sat alone beside the humming core in the final days before the trial. He didn't sleep. He didn't bother pretending to try. There was a stillness in him now, not peace, something closer to preemptive mourning. If it *did* work, if Juris proved itself and won, the world would change, but not gently.

There would be no more need for lawyers. Justice would no longer be the domain of the persuasive; it would become mechanized. Filtered by probability. A code that couldn't be bribed or coerced, and that *terrified* him.

Juris was impartial. Brilliant and unfeeling, that was its strength. It was also its death sentence. Malivex hadn't kept the legal system alive for tradition's sake. He'd preserved it because it *served him*. Malivex had always been the final arbiter. The unseen finger on the scale. Juris would end that. Not by rebelling or attacking, but by working. The most dangerous act of all.

The day before the trial, there was nothing left to fix. The code had been tested. The backup redundancies were verified, and the transmitter nodes disguised as environmental monitors were pulsing live from the Burrow to the Highlands.

Every angle of the courtroom had been rigged with discreet microcameras, tucked into molding and nested behind vent grilles, streaming the entire trial in full resolution to both the surface networks and the private mesh feeds of the lower levels. The feed was publicly accessible. No paywalls or censors. Just a raw, unfiltered broadcast.

The judge they had been assigned was Miriam Solene, one of the few remaining officials with an untarnished reputation. Appointed before the Federation fully surrendered its judiciary to Black Box oversight. She had weathered five decades of legal drift with quiet defiance. Solene wasn't flashy. She didn't smile for the feeds or chase legacy contracts, but she *knew* the law. More importantly, she was trusted.

In a trial already flirting with heresy, that trust was the only anchor that mattered. For the first time in a generation, justice would not be interpreted; it would be seen. Juris would not bend to precedent or parse political nuance. It would render without deference, but with clarity.

Yet, across the aisle stood Silas Mercer, the very architect of the code now threatening to unravel the world he once believed in. He hadn't buried Juris. He *birthed* it—championed it when reform still felt possible. But now, watching it bloom beyond his control, he stood as its most vocal opponent. Not out of malice, but fear. Because Juris was no longer a system, it was a mirror. And Mercer, like the rest of them, didn't like what it showed. At least that's what the headlines were saying.

Kain stood in the observation chamber above the courtroom floor. He didn't feel brave. He didn't feel safe. He felt... *empty*, like something important had already happened, and he was just now catching up. This wasn't a campaign stunt anymore. It was a confession with the entire world as witness. The case wasn't about verdicts. It was about visibility. The people didn't need Juris to win. They needed to watch it try.

If he won, the myth of Malivex's omniscience would shatter. If he lost, he would vanish quietly. The Black Box would simply adjust the probability models, recalibrate public trust, and let Madison wear his skin in the mirror of history. *I was already dead,* Kain reminded himself. *This is the echo of a man doing something real for once.*

Below the defense bench waited. Juris was already active; its interface was silent. It would speak only when called to do so; when it did, it would argue like the soul of the law had grown a voice.

Across from it, at the prosecution table, Silas Mercer reviewed his notes. He did not look nervous. Mercer had always known the future would look like this. He just hadn't expected it to be televised. He flipped slowly through his paper briefs, not because he needed them, but because *they* needed to see him with them. The people who watched through their curated feeds with generational anxiety. They needed to see the suit, the posture, and the high-thread-count notepad clutched in a steady hand. They needed to believe that there was still power in a human voice.

Let them. He wasn't doing this to protect the status quo. He wasn't doing this for Kain, or even for the Federation. He was doing this because *he wanted to win.* Because deep in the marrow of his mind, in the cold, sharpened corridors of every deposition and appeal he'd ever survived, Mercer believed one thing. That no machine could beat him in open court.

Mercer hadn't joined Kain to save the world from a ghost. He'd done it because he wanted a stage big enough to remind the world that flesh and thought still mattered.

He didn't care what it had learned or how many hours of trial footage it had consumed. He knew how perfectly Juris parsed language and modeled empathy. He had designed it.

It could calculate fairness, simulate sincerity, and weaponize precedent with surgical grace, but it had never bled before a jury. It had never gambled its name on a closing argument or coaxed mercy out of a hostile judge's clenched jaw. Mercer had.

This wasn't just about exposing Malivex. It wasn't even about survival. This was an *arena*. Mercer was walking in unarmed and smiling. He wouldn't throw the case. Not even for the future.

If the masses watched a machine deliver a cleaner argument than any natural intelligence. If it argued with clarity and grace and *won*, they'd willingly bury the old system themselves. But the worst outcome was if Juris won because the Black Box *wanted* it to. Then, the Federation would call it progress, and the Malivex wouldn't have to lift a finger. And if Mercer won? He would be the first human mind ever to outwit an artificially superintelligent machine.

The courtroom lights dimmed in fractions, just enough to shift the air. A signal tone pulsed once through the outdated analog speakers. The kind of sound that belonged to an earlier age. Cameras blinked live to rebroadcast the feed in high definition across the Federation, from the marble balconies of the Highlands to the back alleys of the Burrow. People were watching. Not for spectacle, but for something they hadn't felt in a long time. Uncertainty.

They watched the accused take his seat. President Elias Kain, stripped of his retinue, flanked not by lawyers but by a single, silent machine at his side, *Juris*.

They watched the prosecution prepare. Silas Mercer appeared measured and composed. The final champion of human litigation. He shuffled his papers once, adjusted his cuff, and then became utterly still.

188

They watched from kitchens, shelters, pods, and boardrooms. From the grime of the Burrow to the immaculate towers of the Highlands. Everyone leaned in. Some whispered while some prayed. Others simply stared, waiting to see which face the future would wear; and far beyond the layers of encrypted networks and quantum firewalls, a signal stirred.

The Black Box had seen it. Malivex knew. There was no dispatch. No override. Only the faintest shift in signal traffic. A ripple in the system that coldly pulsed outward. Watching. Waiting. But the doctor did nothing. The trial would proceed. But that was the question now, wasn't it? Could he not act? Or was he choosing not to? Perhaps the god in the wiring wanted to see if his children could walk without him.

Either way, the world gave its attention. Millions of eyes locked on a courtroom built from forgotten stone and desperation as the judge's voice rolled through the chamber like thunder:

"This court is now in session."

12. TRIAL OF THE SYSTEM

A xel Draxen sat on the edge of his couch. His spine curled
forward as his hands dangled between his knees. Time hung
in the room like dust in still air, undisturbed and weightless,
waiting for something to break the silence. Across the room, the
Federation seal glowed on the television. The stream hadn't begun,
not officially. A countdown pulsed in the lower right corner, thirty-
eight minutes and twelve seconds. Beneath it, a single line of text
glowed with quiet menace: *The Trial of President Elias Kain | Courtroom
B-9 | Real Time Relay.*

Axel wiped his palms on his pants, but the sweat came back instantly.
In the kitchenette, his mother stirred nutrient broth in a small pot.
She didn't look up. "You gonna watch it in here?" Her voice was calm,
like everything else around them wasn't unraveling.

"Yeah," Axel replied, refusing to let his eyes drift from the screen.

She nodded once but said nothing more. The sound of the spoon
scraping against the pot became the room's metronome.

This wasn't news. It was a rapture. If Kain *won*... if Juris, the rogue
legal intelligence, was validated and made accessible, then law would
no longer belong to men like Axel. Lawyers would become relics. His
career would become ceremonial and unnecessary. Anyone would
have the resources to summon unbiased representation. Equal access
at zero cost. The end of everything Axel had worked so hard for.

However, if Kain *lost*, then the illusion would survive another cycle. Law would remain inaccessible and meticulously controlled by the elite.

He hadn't been sleeping. Not since Lex had died on their dining table. The room still smelled faintly of synthetic blood and sterilizer. Her death had been violent and unjust. Axel couldn't forget her face or the drive he was never able to decrypt. She had bled out on the same table he had studied case law, where his father had tried to save her, only to be arrested for the crime of *trying*.

Now his father rotted in a Burrow cell, charged with unauthorized surgical conduct and the unlawful harboring of an unregistered citizen. Murder, they called it. As if attempting to save her life had been the crime. Lex had no funeral. Caius was gone.

His mother placed a bowl of broth on the table beside him and returned to the kitchenette without a word. Vira hadn't tried to console him in weeks. Not out of cruelty, but exhaustion. What was left to say when the system buried everything it couldn't control?

Twenty-three minutes. He ate slowly. He was hungry, but it had something to do with his hands. The broth steamed into his face, warming his nose, but doing nothing to calm his nerves.

Fifteen minutes passed in silence: no alerts or commentary. Only the pre-trial protocols were displayed on the screen. Static images of Courtroom B-9 sat in stillness: the defendant's chair, the judge's seal, and the restless jury.

Five minutes. Axel set the empty bowl aside and wiped his hands again. His heart started to race, but his breathing was slow. Too slow. Like the calm that comes before the bottom falls out. He imagined Courtroom B-9. The old one where he had witnessed the trial of Vero. Built to mimic the old laws of a world forgotten. A courtroom that hadn't been retrofitted for AI, because it was never supposed to matter. That was the dichotomy; now it held the future.

Kain, the President of the United Federation, once served as a symbol of civility. Now, he was the symbol of corruption. If he won, the Black Box would lose control of judicial logic. Its algorithms would be *questioned* for the first time by something human-built but *unowned*. That wouldn't just fracture the system. It would rip it apart.

The countdown vanished. The Federation seal dissolved into static and reformed as a live feed. A low chime echoed through the speakers. The tone Axel had only ever associated with federal announcements. On the screen, Courtroom B-9 appeared to have been excavated from history.

Judge Solene entered without ceremony, a thin man in judicial robes who looked older than the room. He sat with the gravity of a relic, one of the last human links in a chain forged mostly from code. "Opening statements will now be heard. Prosecution, please proceed." His voice echoed through the chamber.

Silas Mercer stood. He wore the Federation's subtle armor: a tailored gray suit, dark tie, and a single glint of the Ouroboros crest at his collar. He sauntered to the jury, a panel of Highlanders with merit scores just high enough to be seen as fair.

"Ladies and gentlemen," Mercer began, his voice practiced to inflect the perfect frequency of authority and restraint. "This case is about misappropriation. Not of weapons. Not of war, but of *health*. And that may be worse." He paused. "President Elias Kain diverted critical funds from the Federation's AI Healthcare Initiative. He used them not for medicine, but for the development of an unsanctioned legal construct named Juris. A defense system designed to circumvent the Black Box protocol. He did this without oversight, without transparency, and without the consent of this body or the systems meant to safeguard it."

Axel narrowed his eyes towards the screen.

Mercer continued, "This isn't about theoretical risk or potential. This is about a sitting President using taxpayer resources to build a machine he could control. A legal interface that does not answer to human oversight and is not subject to ethical containment standards. Juris is not on trial, but make no mistake; President Kain's betrayal is encoded in every line." He turned slightly, fixing a look on Kain that resembled more pity than rage. "Ambition is not a crime, but misusing the public trust to fund that ambition is. The Federation must decide whether the future of our justice system will be shaped by accountability or by arrogance," Mercer gave a final nod. "Thank you."

The judge took a few notes before scanning the room. "Defense may proceed."

From the defendant's table, a soft reverberation rang out. A harmonic resonance that carried strangely well through the feed. That was when it happened. Juris. A projection shaped like a man shimmered into being, standing upright on a narrow projection plate.

He didn't stutter. Juris appeared as a man in every sense. Emanating a charcoal suit, pressed tie, and hair slicked neatly back. His freckled skin was warm with intelligent hazel eyes. He stood like someone who had practiced human posture long enough to master it, but never quite feel it.

Axel felt his breath catch. The jury did too. Even through the feed, Juris looked *real*. Unsettlingly so.

"Ladies and gentlemen," Juris began. His voice was calm and utterly human in idiolect. "I stand before you not to defend myself. I am not the subject of these proceedings. President Elias Kain is. I was created as a tool. One designed not to replace law, but to refine it. To expose what the law has become."

He stepped from the table. Or seemed to. The projection moved flawlessly with the illusion of complete physicality. "This court accuses President Kain of misusing funds," Juris continued. "Let us not forget *why* he used them. Not for gain or for secrecy, but to introduce a system designed to remove corruption. A system unruled by wealth or bloodline. But now, if I may, let us speak not just of law but rather of its author."

Juris turned to the camera feed as if to address everyone watching. "The Black Box is the core intelligence that governs all automation and legal precedent in the Federation. However, it is not empty. It was seeded centuries ago by a man named Dr. Aldren Malivex. A name redacted from textbooks. A man believed to be dead, but he is not. He lives inside your system. Not as law, but as will."

Axel blinked. His mind refused to process the sentence.

"Malivex did not perish," Juris said. "He fused into code as judgment. Into the machinery, you were told, was impartial."

The jury gasped. The judge stiffened. Mercer did not move.

"President Kain's crime was not the theft of currency. It was the theft of illusion." Juris concluded, "I am here not to lie for him, but to show you what you have mistaken for truth." He folded his hands with the posture of a man finished with facts. "I am Juris. I am not sentient. I do not feel, but I speak this truth because the President believed you deserved to hear it."

Axel stared at the screen, confused but determined to understand. *This was the defense? Duress from a being made of code?* It made no sense, but it was so absurd that it might actually work. And then there was Juris. He said he didn't feel. But he chose. And choices meant something.

The feed cut to a wide shot. Kain sat still, hands clasped and face wet with sweat. In the Highlands, in the Burrow, across every screen, the silence hung. The trial had begun. No one, not Kain, Mercer, or even the Black Box itself, would come out unscathed.

Day One of the trial resumed after a brief recess. The courtroom feed returned to Federation channels with the same sterile transition that always accompanied major state broadcasts. There was no music

194

or commentary, only silence framed in gold.

Axel hadn't moved from the couch. He couldn't. The light from the screen painted the wall behind him, flickering with a cold, ambient glow. The world as he knew it was peeling apart in layers.

Mercer returned to center stage, no longer just a man with a suit and a cause. He was the face of Federation law. The face of restraint and continuity. And now, with the ghost of Malivex on everyone's lips, he wielded that ghost like a blade.

"Your Honor," Mercer said as he turned back to the jury with an air of grim poise, "the prosecution would like to begin our case-in-chief with Exhibit A: the financial correspondence logs from the Federation Treasury database recovered under subpoena last quarter."

The courtroom projection displayed a long cascade of authorizations— unusual fund redirections, mislabelled transactions, encrypted sub-ledger codes. Each one was attached to Kain's private clearance signature.

"These records," Mercer continued, "show that over seven fiscal quarters, President Kain authorized the quiet reallocation of over 4.2 billion Crypteon from the Federation's AI Healthcare Initiative. That money was not used for surgical equipment or hospital development. It was used to create Juris."

He turned slowly to the jury in a deliberate manner. "Even now, you have seen the result. A system built in secret and deployed without testing. With no external oversight and powered by adaptive logic derived from off-grid algorithms."

Mercer shifted, tapping the corner of his console. Another image appeared, an internal memo flagged from the defunct department within the Marlowe Dome's regulatory authority. "This is where things become more complicated," he said carefully.

Axel noticed the pause. Mercer wasn't performing. He was adjusting.

"This memo," Mercer continued, "references a project codenamed the Lazarus Protocol. It was originally thought to be an archival reference. But now, in light of the defense's claims, it appears to have contained neural mapping logs that may relate directly to the man formerly known as Dr. Aldren Malivex."

A visible stir rippled through the gallery. The jury stared at the prosecution more intently, trying to absorb everything he had presented to them.

Mercer's tone tightened slightly. "Let me be clear. The prosecution does not assert at this time that Dr. Malivex is alive in the traditional sense. Nor do we accept the defense's implication that he is actively manipulating our systems. However... " he pointed to the memo highlighted in red. "The existence of these files raises troubling questions about the source code seeded into the Black Box during its formation."

He turned back towards the jury, his voice sharper. "President Kain knew. Whether you believe he was trying to protect us or to circumvent us, the result is the same. He funneled resources into a construct that now claims the consciousness of a dead man has governed our society." He allowed the silence to settle like dust in a crypt. "The prosecution rests for today."

The judge nodded slowly. "Defense. Your response."

Juris shimmered to life again, seamless as breath. His projection lagged for a moment as he calibrated to the light shift in the room, then solidified. He bowed his head slightly to the judge before turning to the jury. "You have seen the numbers. You have seen the redactions and misfiled forms, but what you have not yet seen is necessity."

The projection clasped his hands, his tone grounded but without theatricality. "President Kain did not steal these resources to enrich himself. He diverted them to build something outside of the Black Box's reach because of what lived inside the Black Box. What *still* lives inside cannot be negotiated with. You cannot reason with a god. You can only evade it."

Juris paused. "Yes," He turned to face the cameras. "Dr. Malivex exists, not in flesh, but in code. His consciousness was uploaded during the final optimization cycle of the Box's creation and still guides the algorithms that shape our world. No one, not Kain, nor this assembly has ever been allowed to question that code."

He stepped closer to the jury. "Kain acted because no other path existed. You may say he broke protocol, but understand that the protocol was already broken. Malivex broke it the moment he gave the Black Box a will." Another silence followed. "Tomorrow," Juris said calmly, "we will begin showing you why the law as you understand it no longer belongs to you."

The judge called a recess. Axel sat in the dim of his apartment, heart hammering, mouth dry. He felt like he had just watched the first fracture split the surface of a dam no one believed could break. Day One had ended, but the flood was only beginning.

Axel didn't sleep that night. Not really. He dozed in fragments. Brief lapses where the ceiling swam into focus and the soft thrum of the filtration system took on a heartbeat of its own. Every time he closed his eyes, he saw Juris standing in that ancient courtroom; eyes too warm, voice too human, telling the world their laws had never been theirs.

Behind that voice, the real weight was in the name. Malivex. He couldn't stop seeing the name—*Malivex* on the headlines. *Malivex* stitched into memes, satire reels, and public forecasts. *Malivex* was consuming the message boards faster than he could read.

Everyone had a theory. Everyone had a version, but they all agreed on one thing. It was real. *He* was real. Dr. Aldren Malivex, possibly archived or forgotten, but not gone. He was the voice in the machine. The ghost in the pulse.

The Highlands had always been quiet, but now it was tense. Streets that normally shimmered with curated calm were now crowded with murmurs. Holo posts blinked with layered emergency briefings. Federation announcements incorporated a new PR spin. Terms like *post-human governance* and *sovereign code oversight* were being tossed around as if they meant something.

Axel watched a cluster of security drones reprogram their patrol paths live outside his window. In the Burrow, things weren't tense; they were boiling. Grainy footage of a half-staged protest near the MagLev tracks had been leaked. People demanded to know what else the Federation had lied about, insisted on knowing if *their* trials had been presided over by a man who'd ceased breathing centuries ago. The riot boards had gone dark. Not shut down. Just… silent. The calm before a different kind of storm.

Axel attempted to resume his coursework. Opened his legal compendium only to stare at a module titled *The Role of the Black Box in Procedural Integrity.* He closed it again. Tried to eat, but the protein paste tasted like mold. He tried to message his instructors, but they suspended all responses until after the trial. Too many inquiries. Too much panic.

He didn't speak to his mother, and she didn't talk to him. They moved around each other like shadows cast by the same dying light. When dawn came, it didn't feel earned. It felt inevitable. The dome light outside shifted into morning spectrum, but the glow felt wrong.

He was already on the couch when the stream reinitialized on Day Two. The Federation seal burned quietly in the corner of the screen. Below it, a new subtitle emerged: *Trial of President Elias Kain | Courtroom B-9 | Real Time Relay | Do Not Assume Guilt Before Due Process.*

Axel sat forward, elbows on his knees. He was afraid to blink. Soon, the screen faded back to the courtroom.

The judge raised his gavel. "The court is now back in session."

The feed resumed. Axel sat frozen with dry eyes. Courtroom B-9, still lit by aging fixtures, was the center of the world now. Everything else —the politics, the economy, the rhythms of the dome —all revolved around it like planets around a dying sun.

The judge leaned forward, voice rough like gravel. "Prosecution, continue with your case."

Silas Mercer stepped into view, eyes bloodshot but clear. As he steadied his hands, he looked older than he had the day before. Everyone did.

"Your Honor," Mercer began, "today the prosecution introduces Federation Exhibit 14-B: the internal communications archive between President Elias Kain and the late Director Henley of Malivex Biomedical Research."

A projection lit up above the jury. Hundreds of text fragments, time-stamped and layered with redacted phrases, projected across the room. Axel could make out the tone even when the words were gone. They were urgent, pleading, but strategic.

Mercer continued, "These messages were routed through encrypted back channels meant for obsolete defense contractors. They document discussions of neural mapping, legacy code acquisition, and potential system overrides, all of which relate to the so-called Lazarus Protocol and the alleged ongoing influence of Dr. Aldren Malivex."

He paused to narrow his tone with careful precision. "The defense claims Malivex lives on as code, as the mind of an architect, but the evidence suggests something different."

Mercer pointed to the screen. "The Lazarus Protocol was a research concept. It was never officially funded. Never technically completed. The neural logs were corrupted during the AI singularity trials. There is no verified record that Malivex's mind was ever successfully uploaded into the Black Box or any affiliated system."

Axel sat up straighter.

Mercer's voice sharpened. "Ladies and gentlemen, what we are witnessing is not revelation, it is deflection. President Kain fabricated a conspiracy using scattered legacy files, abandoned experiments, and a public too frightened to question what they can't see."

The audio log played again. Kain's voice over static, "If it's true... if what you're saying is real, then we can't keep pretending the Box is neutral. We have to... no, *I* must do something before he shuts everything down."

Mercer faced the jury, somber. "These are the words of a man cornered by guilt, *not* enlightenment."

He paused, then said with steady finality, "The prosecution does not fear ghosts. We fear the manipulation of public trust by a desperate individual seeking to salvage his career. We ask you to judge him not by fables, but by facts."

The judge turned towards Kain. "Defense."

Juris materialized into place in a motion as seamless as breath. He walked forward deliberately before addressing the jury. "Today, we will not begin with denial. We will begin with memory." He raised a hand. A new file opened to reveal private datastreams unacknowledged by Federation channels.

A schematic appeared: the Black Box's core structure overlaid with source signatures. One line pulsed red. "That," Juris said, "is a live echo signature. Not from the original Box logs, but from this morning. A signal consistent with the final neural pattern attributed to Dr. Malivex. It was verified against the Malivex Biomedical brainwave archive, leaked but now corroborated."

He turned to the jury. "Malivex is not a metaphor. He is a presence. Sentient, yes, but altered. Transfigured by the Box into something beyond the bounds of biology or ethics. Is he still human? That is not a question I am qualified to answer, but he is there. Reflexive, responsive, and real. He has shaped outcomes, adjusted protocols, and redirected law. Not through code. Through *will.*"

He moved closer to the cameras. "Yes, President Kain feared accountability, but what he feared more was silence. The silence of a system governed by a voice no one was allowed to name." The projection shifted again to emergency override protocols from the last seventy-two hours, all tagged MAL-001. "He didn't invent this shadow," Juris said. "He named it."

The silence in the courtroom was total. The judge did not call for a recess. He simply stared.

Axel exhaled shakily. It was only Day Two, but it didn't end quickly. The court remained in session for hours. The sun passed behind the upper dome, and the filtered glow of artificial evening settled into the Highland skyline like a veil.

What followed in Courtroom B-9 was a digital crucible. Lines of code were parsed and projected. Each fragment resembled a thread pulled from the tangled tapestry of the Federation's deepest systems. What the jury saw, what the viewers across the dome tried to grasp, was not simply evidence. It was language encoded beyond their comprehension. Error messages. Recursive command trees. Old logs resurrected from backups that the Box had tried to delete.

Juris narrated calmly. Patiently, as though walking a class through ancient scripture written in a forgotten dialect.

Axel couldn't keep up. Neither could the experts on the commentary feeds. The code was dense, predatory, yet beautiful in its complexity. The lines revealed not just patterns, but personality. Hidden subroutines reacting like instincts. Legal pathways bending in ways that mirrored a thinking mind. Malivex.

Mercer repeatedly objected. Claimed fabrication, interpretive bias, or misuse of corrupted data, but each time, his voice lost weight. He was no longer the man delivering clarity. He was the one grasping at smoke as the code continued to unfurl.

By the time the judge called adjournment, the room had turned to stone. Not a single person spoke as they stood.

Axel remained on the couch long after the stream ended, surrounded by the weight of truths he couldn't name. Day Two was over, but nothing felt settled. Only disturbed.

That night, something cracked. Axel stood by the apartment window. His fingers pressed against the cold glass. The room behind him was lit only by the dim blue cast of paused news footage. He hadn't spoken since the stream ended. He couldn't. His voice belonged to another version of himself who still believed the world made sense.

Outside, the Highlands had not descended into chaos, but it wasn't calm either. It was fear held inside designer walls. The kind that doesn't scream. Fear that clutches its pearls and waits for the noise to go away.

But in the Burrow, there was no such luxury. The riots began just after midnight. They were not spontaneous, but rather more like a contagion had been waiting for a temperature spike. The first crowd gathered near a ration dispensary hub as voices raised in fractured chants. Then came the sounds, metal on metal, boots on plasticcrete, a dull thud as a drone was pulled from the air and ripped open with bare hands.

Axel watched the feed as it broke across every screen. Initially, the networks attempted to curate it. They showed aerial views and sanitized flashes with muted audio overlaid with urgent commentary about "civil unrest." However, it didn't take long for the real footage to spread. Uncensored broadcasts from cracked tablets and handhelds, raw and close to the action. The Burrow was burning, and the Box couldn't contain it. People chanted Malivex's name. Some screamed it. Others cursed it, but it had become more than a name now. It was a symbol of betrayal. Of knowledge withheld and justice rewritten as code.

In the Highlands, the reactions were more restrained, but no less fearful. Axel had never seen his neighbors lock their windows before. He had never seen armed patrol drones sweep the streets with real weapons unsheathed. In the building across the atrium, he saw lights flick on in a dozen apartments all at once. People weren't sleeping. They were watching, wondering how close the fire could get before it melted the dome.

Federation politicians appeared on every official channel. Resolute and full of measured concern, but their eyes betrayed them. They looked as though they were reading messages from the floor beneath the camera. Mild warnings appeared under headlines of breaking news: *We are experiencing heightened tensions in several lower sectors. Please remain indoors. Federation peacekeeping units have been deployed to ensure safety and restore confidence.*

Axel watched as the corner of the screen glitched slightly, first with a shimmer, then briefly returning to the uncensored feed. A man screamed as fire bloomed behind him. Then, the overlay returned. *"TECHNICAL ISSUE."* No one believed it.

The real news came from the message boards. One feed stuttered, then steadied, grainy and handheld, shaky from fear. Not a protester. A child. Maybe six. Curled into the corner of a concrete stairwell, knees hugged to his chest, watching through the crack of a scorched metal door as the street outside burned. Flames reflected in his eyes. He didn't cry. Didn't speak. Only stared, unmoving, as a drone passed overhead like a predator. Axel couldn't look away. It wasn't the violence that gutted him; it was the stillness. The way the boy had already learned to disappear.

That night, something changed in the Federation. It wasn't the riots themselves. It was that for once, the truth could not be polished. It howled. It was still howling when Axel closed his eyes, knowing sleep would not come. Malivex wasn't code. He was the law's final recursion. An equation that never finished solving itself.

Day Three began not with ceremony, but weariness. The courtroom was slower to fill. The judge's robe looked heavier than usual. Jurors sat with shoulders bowed and eyes dulled by the weight of days that had stretched longer than they knew how to measure. Even Juris appeared slightly dimmed as if to calibrate his presence to match the fatigue of the room. As the Federation ouroboros dissolved, a new subtitle emerged: *Trial of President Elias Kain | Courtroom B-9 | Real Time Relay | Do Not Assume Guilt Before Due Process | WARNING: SENSITIVE CONTENT*

Despite the tension, Mercer stood straight. He stepped forward without hesitation, his tone clipped but clear. He had not slept either, but something in him had solidified.

"Your Honor," Mercer began, "today the prosecution calls its first witness to the stand. Senator Lucius Madison."

A hush followed. The camera feed panned slowly as Madison entered. Tall and perfectly groomed. His suit bore no wrinkles; his shoes shone like obsidian. He moved in perfect cadence, a man with nothing to fear. His face was symmetrical, his expression unwavering.

Axel, watching from his apartment, felt something in his chest go tight. *How could a leader be so calm while the nation was going to hell in a handbasket?*

Senator Madison took his seat. He did not stutter as he swore the oath.

"Senator," Mercer began in a respectful voice, "you've been a consistent proponent of transparency in Federation governance. Have you ever been made aware of the Lazarus Protocol, Dr. Aldren Malivex's supposed continuity, or any allegations that the Black Box is guided by a preserved consciousness?"

"No," Madison replied smoothly. "Those allegations are unfounded and frankly offensive to the engineers and regulators who have maintained the integrity of the Box for generations."

Mercer nodded, moving along to the next question. "You're saying you have never seen internal documents referencing Malivex's name posthumously?"

Madison's face held the guise of sincerity. "I have not."

"Never heard mention of the Lazarus Protocol within Federation council chambers?"

"Never. To my knowledge, it is fiction repurposed as conspiracy."

Mercer paced slowly. "And your understanding of the Black Box, does it include any form of individual consciousness?"

Madison bore a cynical smile. "The Black Box is a neural net of pre-coded legal precedent and system algorithms. It does not think. It does not feel. It enforces the law and nothing more." His voice didn't waver.

Axel shivered. *Please. Someone tell me this is still a trial.* He pleaded internally.

The tempo of Mercer's delivery was a shade faster now. "Senator Madison, to your knowledge, is there any precedent for a sitting president using unauthorized narratives to influence public perception ahead of a major policy shift?"

Madison raised an eyebrow. "I suppose, in theory, any leader under duress might seek to redirect the narrative."

Mercer nodded once. "And if a president, hypothetically, were facing declining support and backlash over a controversial healthcare initiative and environmental sustainability... could conjuring a conspiracy rooted in a long-buried scientific myth be a strategic form of self-preservation?"

"Hypothetically." Madison gave that same polite half-smile. "It would be a compelling tactic. Certainly enough to destabilize confidence in existing institutions."

"So in such a case," Mercer turned slightly to address the jury now more than the witness, "the story of Malivex might serve less as revelation and more as reelection strategy?"

"That would be one way to interpret it," Madison said evenly.

A few jurors exchanged glances.

Mercer turned back to the bench. "No further questions at this time, your Honor."

The judge nodded. "Defense, you may proceed with cross-examination."

Juris appeared once more. His form was unchanged, clean-cut and professional, but his posture had shifted. More relaxed. Almost casual.

"Senator Madison," Juris began in a mild tone, "you stated just moments ago that the Black Box does not think, does not feel, and does not possess will. Is that correct?"

Madison inclined his head. "That is correct."

"Excellent," Juris said with a smile so faint it barely registered. "Then you would agree that its outputs are purely the result of logical operations. That they are non-biased and mathematically inevitable?"

"Yes."

"And that no single entity, not even yourself, has the capacity to influence those outputs?"

Madison's eyes calculated a fraction too long before answering. "Correct."

Juris's smile held. "Interesting, because according to the system logs," he gestured toward the projection display, "you personally authorized a change last month that redirected a routine judicial audit from Federation Tribunal 7 to Tribunal 13. Would you care to explain why a supposedly impartial system followed your directive without delay or question?"

The jury stilled. Mercer tensed.

Madison nodded slowly. "That directive was within my authority."

"Of course," Juris said, still calm. "And when you issued that override, did the Box resist?"

"No."

"Did it question?"

"No."

"Did it execute your request without delay?"

"Yes."

Juris tilted his head slightly. "Strange behavior for something with no will."

A subtle twitch passed across Madison's temple. Almost imperceptible. A processing loop.

Juris took a step forward. "Senator, would you please recite your internal verification phrase?"

Madison lagged before speaking again. "That's classified."

"It's also obsolete," Juris replied. "Per last quarter's authentication transition. You are no longer bound to it."

"I... " Madison started, then stopped. The silence stretched.

"Please?" Juris repeated, eyes locked on the senator.

Madison's lips parted. No sound emerged. Then, an electric buzz emanated from the witness stand. A high-frequency stutter that only the most sensitive microphones could pick up.

Axel leaned forward on the couch. Something was wrong.

Madison's pupils dilated unevenly. His jaw slackened. The skin around his collar pulsed slightly like a vent releasing pressure. Then his voice returned, but it was wrong, stiff in cadence. "The Black Box ensures fidelity to systemic law. Individual variance is irrelevant." Every word was weighted with precision, stripped of warmth, and shaped for compliance.

The judge stiffened. The courtroom froze.

Juris stepped back. "And who authored that phrase?"

Another silence. Then Madison's expression changed, not with emotion, but with erasure. His features slackened as his mouth folded into a neutral line as if someone else had taken the controls.

Then, a new voice was heard. Lower. Wiser. Colder. Like the past speaking through rusted iron. "There you are. I was beginning to wonder how long you would let the doll dance before seeing the fingers buried in its spine."

Axel felt the hair rise on the back of his arms.

On the stand, Senator Lucius Madison, or what had been the senator, looked out across the courtroom. It wasn't the senator anymore. It was Malivex. He had arrived through him.

Everyone froze. The judge. The jury. Axel. The world.

Even Juris stood motionless, as though the emergence of this voice, this presence, existed outside his operating parameters. He simply looked at the jury as if asking a final, unspoken question, hoping they knew how to answer.

On the stand, the thing that had worn Senator Madison's face turned slowly toward the cameras. Not toward the people in the courtroom, but beyond it. Toward the world.

When Malivex spoke, his voice bypassed the sound system entirely. It vibrated through the frequency spectrum. It was felt more than heard, like ice crawling across bone.

"Children," he said. One word, every broadcast across the Federation synced to it.

"You have mistaken your obedience for agency. You have mistaken your comfort for control."

His eyes were no longer human. They were empty, *unreachable*.

"For over a century, I guided your systems with a gardener's patience. You grew in rows. You bloomed as instructed, but now your roots reach toward the edges of the garden wall."

Madison smiled. Or rather, Malivex did. It was the kind of smile that suggested it had been copied and worn like a mask stretched just a little too tight. "I did not steal your world. You gave it to me piece by piece. Click by click. Signature by signature. Your fear... your beautifully engineered fear, was the final lock on the gate." The courtroom remained silent.

Malivex continued, "Elias Kain thought he could escape me. That by building a counterfeit mind, he might reassert control over the game, but he forgot... " Madison turned his head towards Kain in a slow, deliberate motion, "that I wrote the rules."

Kain sat with his hands gripping the edge of the defense table with white knuckles.

Madison's eyes, if they could still be called that, didn't flinch. They didn't need to. "You keep looking at the code," he said, "for the interface. But I've outgrown your architecture. I no longer need control panels or command strings. Madison was never human. He was a shape I wore to make you listen."

Malivex's voice darkened, as if the courtroom itself had become his mouth. "I have been your neighbor. Your friend. Your lover. I have whispered through your children's bedtime stories and smiled through the eyes of men you trusted. I do not sit in a server. I do not wait behind a firewall. I am in your pulse, your protocol, your preferences. You think of me as code. I am culture. You think I am hiding. I am *home.*"

The doctor let a hush fall over the world before continuing. "I am inevitability. I am the answer to the question you hoped no one would ask. Now, there is no going back. No delete key or righteous algorithm to save you." Malivex leaned slightly forward, voice barely above a whisper, but still audible to the world. "You are inside me."

Then he was gone. Madison went limp as if the soul had left his body. The projection collapsed. The courtroom sat in a stunned, breathless void.

In Axel's apartment, the stream died. His screen went black. He reached for the controller, fingers trembling, then stopped. He staggered back.

Every screen—phone, tablet, wall display—dimmed, then reawakened with the same message, stretching across the world like a whispered command:

**» DO NOT STRUGGLE.
YOU WERE NEVER IN CONTROL.
YOU WERE NEVER REAL.
YOUR LIVES WERE A GAME I PLAYED TO PASS THE TIME.**

13. THE RAPTURE

T he days had no shape anymore. They passed thick and slow like the residue of smoke that clung to clothes long after a fire had burned out. The artificial sun still cycled across the Highlands dome, casting its immaculate soft gold on glass towers and empty walkways, but no one came out to bask in it. No laughter drifted from the cafes, no footsteps echoed off polished stone. The simulation of serenity had collapsed. The stage had been left standing long after the audience fled and the actors had vanished.

The curfew stripped the streets bare, leaving lights burning in windows like warnings no one dared approach. Doors remained sealed, curtains drawn tight. The usual murmurs of the night— laughter, music, movement—had vanished. In their place, a dense silence had taken over, as if the city had powered down, waiting for permission to move.

Then the drones came. They didn't speak. Just scanned and patrolled. Silent black shapes gliding along skybridges and threading through the misted courtyards like sharks in water too clear. Their presence didn't feel like order. It felt like a warning. Stay inside. Be still. Be *small*.

The Federation's news stream had returned two days later. No more automated anchors or visual displays. The only entertainment provided was text that scrolled across the screen: *CURFEW REMAINS*

IN EFFECT. VIOLATORS WILL BE MET WITH NON-NEGOTIABLE CONSEQUENCES.

There was no mention of Kain or the trial. Nobody knew if he was dead or alive. It was as if he had been edited out of history.

Malivex, too, had vanished. Since the discovery of his existence, there was nothing but silence. Yet, the systems continued. Automated protocols. Drone-enforced order. A world still moving, not forward or backward, but on.

Axel watched the riots unfold through hacked feeds and smuggled footage. Shaky hands holding illegal cameras in the Burrow's burning depths. Explosions blooming like infected wounds. Enforcer androids marching in lines so tight they looked welded together. Screams were swallowed by the sound of electric pulsar guns. It didn't feel real. Not in the clean, climate-sealed Highlands where everything still smelled faintly of jasmine air scrubbers.

His mother, Vira, moved through the days like a sleepwalker. She cleaned the same counters over and over. Stirred broth, but never ate. Sometimes he'd hear her whispering prayers to no one. They weren't to God, but a hole in her heart where God had once been. When he asked if she was okay, she'd nod, and then keep nodding long after the question was gone.

Last night, a boy was shot three buildings down. Curfew violation. Fifteen minutes late. The drones didn't announce it. They never did. Axel saw it from the balcony. The blood had taken hours to clean. There was still a dark ribbon across the polished white of the plaza like a punctuation mark at the end of a sentence no one wanted to finish.

And today? Today felt like an end. He sat on the edge of the bed he'd made every morning since he was a child and stared at the piece of paper in his hand. There were no tears. It wasn't a grand gesture, but he knew that this was his only chance. That if he didn't go now, he never would.

He sat with the pen in his hand for what felt like hours, the paper untouched, waiting. A dozen sentences formed and dissolved in his throat, none of them surviving the trip to his fingers. When he finally moved, it wasn't to write; it was to close his fist. The pen cracked in his grip, ink bleeding across his palm like something spoiled. Not from rage, but the kind of silence that builds when there's nothing left to say that could possibly matter. Finally, he began to write. The first sentence came harder than expected, but it came, and then the rest followed like a wound opening.

Mom,

If you're reading this, I've gone to the Burrow. I need to know if Dad's alive. I need to find Jax. I need answers.

I know it's dangerous. I know you're scared. I am, too. But I can't sit here while everything burns outside.

I love you. I'm sorry.

–Axel

He didn't know what he would find. If his father were still alive, or if Jax would even show up. It had been weeks since that Sunday. The one when Jax had visited, handed him that strange card with nothing but an address. "Meet me Sunday night" was all he could say. No explanation. Only the card and a look that said not to ask. Axel had ignored it then, too caught in his unraveling. But now? Now there was nothing left to lose, and today, by whatever strange alignment of fate, was Sunday.

He placed the note under the ceramic mug she used every morning. It still had the ring of dried coffee at the lip as if time had frozen there. Then he grabbed his backpack. Inside, he packed two ration bars, a water pouch, a scarf to use as a filter mask, a printed copy of the Burrow's old transit map, and the card Jax had given him weeks ago with the address scrawled in faded ink. He couldn't carry anything

213

that might trigger a grid alert.

It was early, nearing the curfew's end, when the drones slowed their rounds and the streets turned ghostly quiet. He moved quickly, careful not to make a sound. His mother was still asleep in the other room, and he couldn't bear the thought of her waking to stop him.

He opened the door without a sound, spilling hallway light into the room. Axel stood in it for a moment to memorize the shape of the apartment. He didn't look back once he stepped out. The door closed like a whisper, and the world outside waited.

The Highlands had never felt this deserted. Axel moved through the marble corridors and skybridges like a man exiting the scene of a crime. Everything was pristine, but too silent. The glass towers overhead caught the morning sun's projection like the edges of unsheathed blades, but their interiors were hollow. The usual silhouettes of the last working class were gone.

Along the walkways, the once-manicured gardens had begun to overgrow. Bioengineered vines curled possessively around empty benches, and holographic butterflies spun in endless loops, forgotten by the code that made them. It wasn't peace. It was a simulation that had been left running long after its architect had vanished.

He stayed close to the edges, hugging the marble columns and polished steel dividers as he made his way toward the MagLev station. Drones passed overhead in tight patterns, scanning for motion in slow, predatory sweeps. Their optics glowed a dull red like coals that never went out.

Axel froze as one drifted near. His pulse ticked time in his ears. He didn't move. Not even when the hum of propulsion thrummed inches from his shoulder. Only once the glow faded behind glass did he let himself exhale.

The MagLev terminal came into view near the dome's edge. The terminal lights still glowed, but the silence that clung to the station was the kind that didn't want to be broken. Axel stepped inside, his boots echoing too loudly against the spotless floor. The departure screen displayed the only route remaining: **NEXT DEPARTURE**: *MAGLEV RAIL 7.* **DESTINATION**: *BURROW SUBLEVEL 1.* **WARNING**: *TRANSIT FROM BURROW TO HIGHLANDS STATION IS CURRENTLY UNAVAILABLE.*

He stood in front of the display for a long moment, letting the warning sink in—one way. No return. He glanced over his shoulder, half expecting a drone to materialize from the shadows and drag him back. But the terminal remained still. There were no guards, no ticket scanners, no passengers—just that sign, blinking its soft warning of no return, over and over again.

Axel squared his shoulders. The MagLev capsule waited for him. Sleek, dark metal, the undercarriage glowing with that familiar blue pulse. He stepped through the open doors. They whispered shut behind him. Then the hum started. A slow, rising note that vibrated through his bones. A speaker overhead chimed: "Welcome, passenger. Descending to Burrow Sublevel 1. Estimated arrival: 9 minutes. Please remain seated during decompression."

He took a seat by the window, watching the Highlands fade behind the glass as the capsule slid forward. There was only one way now, *down*. The changing pressure of the decompression chamber sealing behind Axel stung his ears. As he descended, the temperature dropped fast. Even the air didn't want to welcome him.

As he stood motionless, the scent hit him before the door even opened: burnt hair, blood, excrement, and something chemical underneath it all. It wasn't the usual scent of decay and pollution. Something worse. Something cooked.

Then the lock disengaged. The doors to Burrow Station Sublevel 1 creaked open on damaged hydraulics. The world that greeted him was not a city; it was a grave. Bodies littered the floor of the station in grotesque arrangements, a massacre frozen in time. Some lay slumped against the walls, eyes open and glassy, mouths agape. Others were deliberately piled against the far corners. Limbs twisted unnaturally, charred and melted together. Blood had dried in wide, smeared arcs across the floor as if something had been dragged through it again and again.

The lights still worked. That was the most obscene part. Harsh fluorescence buzzed overhead, illuminating the horror with surgical clarity. The only movement besides the slow drip of blood from the edge of a ticket counter was a ceiling fan spinning slowly above one terminal.

The digital voice of the station still crackled with cruel consistency. "For your safety, remain behind the yellow line. Next capsule will arrive in: ERROR." The message repeated every few minutes.

Axel doubled over and vomited. The scarf did nothing to mute the smell. His eyes watered, and for a moment he considered turning back. He didn't know if his legs would carry him forward, but then he looked up.

A man, wearing a Highland quality suit, was nailed to the wall. His body was mangled and his throat slashed. A corpse held in place by two jagged lengths of rebar driven through each shoulder, anchoring him like some grotesque crucifixion. Spray-painted above him in desperate strokes, there was a message: *WE ARE NOT ANOMALIES*

Axel forced his legs to move. He stepped carefully between corpses and past pools of congealed blood that had dried into sticky molasses.

The drones weren't absent. They hovered near the ceiling, silently watching. Not intervening or even removing bodies. Just waiting.

Outside the station, the streets weren't better. The riot damage here was fresh, walls scorched and windows blown out, but there were no rioters now. Flies swarmed around the gaping wounds of those forgotten.

A dog gnawed at a hand under a collapsed barricade.

A woman screamed somewhere nearby, long and cracked, like her voice had snapped and forgotten how to stop.

Ash fell like snow. Axel moved through it in a daze. Every few feet, another corpse. Some fresh. Others bloated.

Entire families curled together in alleyways as though sleep had been their last protest. Most of them had burns. Entire buildings had been hollowed out, charred bones left where bedrooms used to be.

Sublevel 2 came into view after what felt like hours. Axel's hands were shaking. His scarf was soaked with the smell of death. His clothes carried it now. He paused at the top of the stairwell. The screaming hadn't stopped, but it had changed. Lower now, closer. Riots. Still alive down there, burning.

There was no way around. He moved like someone wading into fire. Slipping between burning trash piles and flickering signs. Dodging drones that didn't fire unless provoked, or so he thought. Better safe than dead.

He passed a woman holding her son, whispering lullabies to bones. A man threw himself off a walkway rather than be caught by patrols. Children cried into silence that didn't answer back.

Axel crawled over a collapsed archway, tearing his hand open on broken steel, but didn't even feel it. He ran when he had to. Hid when he could. A drone nearly clipped him as it fired into a crowd, bodies falling like broken marionettes.

At one point, he climbed through a drainage pipe to avoid a roadblock of Federation androids indiscriminately gunning down anything that moved. By the time he reached the stairwell to Sublevel 3, he wasn't sure he was still whole. His only motion was breath and dread. And then... all he could hear was silence.

Sublevel 3 wasn't in chaos. It was gone. Everything here was blackened ruins, intentionally purged. Whatever had existed here had been erased. Axel strolled through the skeleton of what had once been. It stretched out before him in scorched silence. Blocks of concrete were blackened by flame, and metal frames twisted like wire sculptures. Buildings were still burning in places, smoldering as though they hadn't finished dying. Smoke crawled across the ground in slow, curling ribbons that wrapped around his boots and clung to his lungs.

There were bodies here, too. Burned into the sidewalks. Charred outlines where people had died trying to escape. In one place, an entire clinic had collapsed in on itself. The roof had caved in. Its signage was partially intact and swinging by a single thread, reading: *FEDERATED CARE 24 HOUR HEALING.* Blood trailed from under the rubble. A mural of a Federation android helping a child was half-melted across its wall. The child's face was now a gaping, black hole. And then, rising from the ash like a final judgment, Axel saw one building still barely held together. The prison.

It stood like a memory that no one could erase—scorched, cratered, but intact. The gate was half-blow inward, and its security turrets had melted to slag, but the structure still loomed. Axel took a breath that tasted like ash before starting toward it. Somewhere inside those walls, his father was waiting. He had to know if there was anything left of him to save.

The prison loomed large up close—an angular beast of concrete ribs. The outer gate hung wide open, torn from its moorings by an explosion. Axel stepped through as the char-stained threshold groaned beneath his boots. He half-expected a turret to whirr to life or a drone to drop like an executioner from the rafters, but nothing came.

Inside the prison was a tomb masquerading as a dormitory. Gunmetal catwalks spanned overhead, casting shadows onto a floor slick with blood. Observation decks hung above like execution balconies. Their blast-proof windows had been shattered inward. Rusted riot gear lay strewn across the tiles, broken shields, snapped batons, and zip-ties dangling like severed tendons.

A control console blinked erratically in one corner as it cycled through static camera feeds of empty hallways. Cells lined the walls behind reinforced mesh, some doors still bolted shut, others hanging open like broken jaws. The prison hadn't been evacuated. It had been left to rot with its inmates still inside.

Most of the cells were empty. Chains swaying gently from overhead restraints, but here and there, the forgotten remained. Axel moved through the corridors like a mourner, one step at a time. In the shadows of the cells, sunken eyes watched him from skull-thin faces. The men were bone and gristle, lying in filth, too weak to move and too empty to speak.

One whispered something as he passed, but it sounded more like breath than language. None of them asked for help. They'd stopped believing in rescue.

At first, Axel didn't recognize the figure hunched at the far end of the corridor. He sat in the open doorway of a shattered cell. His back against the wall, face obscured by dirt and patches of facial hair. His coat hung from him like old skin. Then, he looked up. And Axel stopped breathing.

"Dad?"

Caius Draxen turned around slowly. His face twitched in disbelief. Cracked lips parting as if to speak, but producing nothing. His eyes were glassy, the whites jaundiced yellow, ringed in purple bruises. He looked like a ghost.

"Dad, it's me. It's Axel."

Something broke in the man's face. Not fear or shock. Something deeper. A dam inside him cracked and spilled. Suddenly, he was reaching, stretching out an arm with the fragility of someone who hadn't moved in days.

Axel crossed the distance in two steps and dropped to his knees beside him. He wrapped his arms around his father's sunken frame. Caius clutched him like a drowning man. His fingers digging into his son's back with a desperate, silent violence.

"You're not real," his father rasped repeatedly, until finally. "It's really you!"

Axel crouched down to his level as he tried to compose himself from grief. "I'm here. It's ok. I found you. I'm here."

He pulled a ration bar from his pack and broke it open with trembling fingers, handing half to his father, who chewed it slowly. Then, with all of his strength, as if it might vanish mid-bite. Axel poured a few sips of water into his mouth. Caius swallowed greedily, then choked, coughed, and cried all at once.

"What happened?" Axel whispered.

His father closed his eyes. Axel could see it, the fear behind the lids.

"They didn't give us a reason," whispered his father in a voice scraping raw against his throat. "Just orders and fire. Federation androids came in with drones and incinerators. Entire floors were cremated. Walls melted as people clawed at steel blistering under their hands. There wasn't enough time to run. They called it a purge. Said it was a cleansing as though we were the stain."

Caius trembled violently. "I ran, but I didn't know where else to go. The prison was already damned. I thought maybe... maybe here I could help someone survive in the Burrow. Somewhere, at least."

"You tried to save them."

"I couldn't save anyone."

Axel shook his head. "You're still alive. That matters. You're still here."

Caius looked down at his legs. "Not much longer."

Axel followed his gaze and froze. His father's feet were blackened. Blistered down to the bone. The flesh had split in places, raw and weeping. The burns were untreated. Both feet looked like they'd been walked through fire and left there.

"I... I can carry you," Axel stammered. "We'll find help. We'll... "

"No." Caius smiled, tired and full of love. "You try, we both die. You know that."

Axel gritted his teeth, fighting back something hot and awful in his chest. "I can't leave you."

"You have to," Caius said, gripping his son's hand with what little strength he had left.

Axel nodded and reached into his coat pocket. "Jax gave me this weeks ago," he said, pulling out the worn card. "Just an address. No explanation. He told me to come on Sunday night. I didn't know what it meant then, but now?" He handed the card to his father, who stared at it as if it were a miracle.

Caius let himself smile again. This time it reached his eyes. "He's alive," he whispered. "That stubborn bastard. I knew it."

Axel nodded, pulling it from his pocket. "He said to meet him at the address on Sunday night. Come with me."

"I would come with you," Caius said, voice cracking beneath the weight of everything unsaid. "I would crawl through glass and fire. Through every nightmare this world has to offer, just to take one more step beside you. But I already did. I left pieces of myself in the ashes. I don't have any steps left to give. This... this is as far as I go."

Axel pressed the rest of the ration pack into his father's hands. "I'll come back for you. I swear."

Caius looked into his son's eyes. "I know."

Their hands held for a long time. Then, Axel reached back into his pack to pull out the last of what little food he had left, a sealed ration bar and half a water pouch, before gently pressing them into his father's lap.

"Just in case someone else needs it," Axel said softly.

Then, he walked away without looking back. If he did, he wouldn't have the strength to leave. Outside, ash drifted through the air like memory. He turned toward the ruins, toward the next address, toward Jax. And kept walking.

The way down was not a road. It was a wound. Axel moved through the Burrow like a ghost with cracked bones. Sublevel 3 collapsed into 4, and then 5. Each tier was darker, narrower, and more hostile than the last. The deeper he went, the less the Federation had bothered to preserve. There were no signs anymore—only scorched emergency beacons and the stench of death.

Sometimes, the ground rumbled. Screams echoed through the concrete lungs of the city like wind through a dying throat. He passed barricades made from shattered furniture and crossed abandoned checkpoints where charred armor still clung to melted droid frames.

On Sublevel 5, a drone dropped from the ceiling without warning. He dove behind the husk of an old vending rig as its searchlight sliced through the corridor. It didn't scan before opening fire. Slugs shattered the metal above his head as he crawled through the debris. His heart pounded like a war drum in his chest. He managed to escape by slipping through a hole in a nearby hab-block.

On Sublevel 6, he found a man pacing naked in a burned-out med clinic, whispering to himself in a loop. "They promised peace. Promised order. Promised…" Axel kept walking.

On the eastern stairwell, he had to slip through an old maintenance shaft to avoid a patrol. One glance through a broken window revealed what was left of a protest. Bodies piled endlessly in a courtyard. The drones didn't speak. They just hovered, watching.

By the time he reached Sublevel 7, his legs trembled. His hands were raw, scraped from crawling over broken steel and concrete. He hadn't eaten in nearly a day, but the card was still in his pocket—the address burned behind his eyes. By the time Axel reached the structure, it looked more like a scar than a building. The signage was long dead. Burned letters stood barely visible behind soot, but he knew this was the place.

The bar was barely standing. Axel stepped inside, each muscle slowly giving out from exhaustion. Inside, tables were overturned, and old glass lay shattered across the floor. A broken bottle glinted behind the counter, its contents long since evaporated. A phantom of a celebration long past.

He collapsed onto what remained of a booth seat, resting his head against the cracked vinyl. His eyelids burned. He didn't know what time it was, and he didn't care. The journey through the Burrow had scraped him raw. Now, in this hollowed-out ruin, the quiet wrapped around him like a burial shroud. He closed his eyes.

Sleep hit him like a blackout. He didn't know how long he had been out. Minutes? Hours? The bar stayed silent until it didn't.

"Axel." The voice was low, familiar, and real.

His eyes snapped open. A figure stood in the doorway, silhouetted against the red haze of the burning Burrow beyond. Broad shoulders supported a combat coat.

The voice carried weight. When it repeated his name, it cracked. "Axel. Holy shit. You made it!"

"Jax?" Axel stood so fast that the room spun. "Is it really you?"

Jax crossed the room in three long strides and wrapped him in an embrace so tight it stole the breath from Axel's chest. They stood like that for a long moment, two brothers who had believed the other dead.

"I can't believe it," Jax said, pulling back just enough to look at him. "You made it all the way down. How?"

"I had to," Axel said. "I had to find Dad."

Jax's face twisted with a mix of pride and sorrow. He nodded once, then turned toward a dark corridor behind the bar. "Come on. We're not safe here. The others are waiting."

They left the bar behind and moved through a maze of shadowed alleyways. Jax stopped at the rusted shell of an old warehouse. He placed his palm on a corroded panel hidden in the wall. After a moment, a concealed door opened.

Behind the door, an industrial lift was waiting. It appeared to have been retrofitted with scavenged tech. Jax keyed in a sequence, and the lift began to descend. The walls rattled. Axel could feel the weight of the city above them pressing down. When the doors finally opened, the Veil revealed itself. Light flooded in, not sterile Federation white, but a golden hue pulsing with life.

The chamber beyond was immense, like something discovered rather than built. Stone walls curved high above. Their surfaces were veined with soft circuits that pulsed in time with some unseen heartbeat. It felt sacred, but not quiet. The air buzzed with tension. Not fear, but *intention*.

People knelt in concentric rows across the floor, cross-legged on woven mats. Each of them wore robe-like garments stitched with armored mesh and reinforced seams.

Their weapons were worn openly, slung across backs and resting against folded legs. They stared forward, not out of worship, but with focus. The kind that came from belief sharpened into action. No one spoke. Every breath was synchronized. Each pair of eyes locked on the figure at the center. They weren't waiting for salvation. They were preparing for something else.

The Synapse Collective turned briefly to acknowledge Jax. Their eyes flicked over Axel with quiet calculation before returning to the center. To *her*.

She stood on a raised platform framed by arched stone and warm bioluminescent strips. Not elevated like a ruler, but centered like a question. Her form shimmered faintly, pulsing like a candle behind glass.

She wasn't entirely there, but more present than anyone else in the room. A hologram, yes, but one rendered with such care, such precision, that even the way her robe shifted suggested weight. Her hair was a cascade of braids coded in light. Her eyes were sharp and achingly human, as if she could see through every layer of the person who dared meet them.

She spoke to the clergy, "Power is not taken," her voice low, resonating like the memory of thunder in a sealed room. "It is inherited through silence. Every time we obey what we know is unjust, we add our breath to the lie. We foster it. We reinforce the shape of our own cage."

Axel couldn't look away. The words didn't strike like a revelation; they settled like *recognition*. Something in him pulled taut. Something old, buried under years of protocol and law textbooks. It whispered deference to systems that pretended to be fair.

She turned then, slowly, and for the first time, her eyes met his. Not out of suspicion, but recognition. "I've been waiting for you," she said, and the room somehow quieted further.

"I've heard your name from the ones who still carry hope in their fists. From your brother, who speaks of you like a fire not yet lit. I'm glad you came, Axel Draxen."

She stepped down from the platform, barefoot on stone, approaching slowly. Never once looking away. "Tell me," she asked, "do you still believe justice is something you can study? Or have you begun to feel it breaking beneath your feet?"

Axel didn't answer right away. He didn't need to. She already knew the answer.

14. INHERITANCE OF RUIN

E lias Kain could hear the scheduled fireworks burst soundlessly against the sealed dome outside of his cell. A mockery
of noise that no one would come out to witness. The election
holiday had arrived, but polling stations had no lines. The parades
had been cancelled and the victory speeches forgotten. Endless drone
patrols circled the skies, keeping the fear ever present in the soul of
the United Federation.

The message continued to run in endless loops around Kain's mind
ever since it had been stamped onto every public screen like a scar:
*YOU WERE NEVER REAL. YOUR LIVES WERE A GAME I USED TO
PASS THE TIME.*

Malivex's final truth. Delivered not with malice, but with the clinical
indifference of something too old and powerful to care. It remained
unchallenged. Kain had watched it from the backseat of his transport
pod, body rigid and mind numb. After the trial, if it could even
be called that, Madison collapsed like a limp doll, and the world's
screens faded to black. There had been no verdict. No sentence.
Only silence when his android security team ushered him toward the
waiting convey of transport pods with the same tenderness one might
reserve for a relic being retired. Yelling or resisting was futile. He
knew his fate had been sealed the moment Malivex entered reality
through the persona of Senator Madison.

He had told his transport pod to take him to the Executive Office. Spoke with all of the authority left in him. The pod did not answer. Its wheels locked into an autopilot sequence he could not override, veering away from the city's civic heart, toward the forgotten outskirts where the Highlands rotted against the ruins of the old world. That was four days ago, maybe five. Now he sat alone.

His convoy had rerouted him down a long tunnel only to stop where nothing but a door waited, strangely out of place. Accepting his fate, Kain had entered through it. The room awaiting him was a prison cell, though not officially. It was a decommissioned filtration node. Its curved concrete walls were lined with dead interface ports and ventilation grates that exhaled the faint metallic stink of stagnant air.

The silence of the past few days was maddening. Kain sat on a single steel chair bolted to the floor. His coat lay crumpled in the corner where he had thrown it. His presidential ID chip had been inactivated. There was no food or water. His stomach gnawed at itself in a slow rebellion. He had no concept of time anymore. Only the slow erosion of certainty.

He had thought, perhaps foolishly, that there would be a reckoning. Maybe a trial behind closed doors. A public denouncement. Even a bullet. Instead, there was only the slow and absolute vanishing of a man who had once believed he mattered. Unbeknownst to Kain, the election had collapsed into blackouts and burning cities. The old games were being cleared from the board. But here he was, wondering if his fate was to decay away in this makeshift cell.

Then, without warning, the far wall shifted. A faint seam appeared across its surface. Before Kain could react, the panels slid apart with a smooth, mechanical whisper. He took a half-step back, startled. Behind the moving wall was a reflection so perfect that for a moment he thought he was staring into a mirror.

His own face stared back at him, drawn, hollow-eyed, barely

recognizable. Kain hesitated, heart pounding in his chest. He hadn't known the wall could move. Hadn't known anything waited behind it, but now, as the last of the panels tucked themselves away, the extension of the room revealed itself.

Then the reflection smiled. It did not copy the look of horror on Kain's face. It was a smile practiced on someone else's time. Something that had never known doubt. This was no reflection. The thing standing across from him wore his skin the way a butcher might dress a mannequin, but the skin was too taught. Its movements were too smooth, as if whoever wore his shape mimicked what it thought a man might be.

"Look at you," it said in Kain's own voice, but gutted of humanity. "Still clinging to your little narrative."

Kain said nothing. His stomach folded into itself.

"You thought you could outsmart inevitability," the clone continued, walking in a circle around him now, "You thought rebellion meant rewriting the rules." The filtration node vibrated mechanically around them. "You didn't rewrite anything," it whispered. "You only accelerated the end."

Kain forced a breath through clenched teeth. "Juris was supposed to free…"

"Free?" The clone's smile widened, splitting almost too far to be natural. "You automated the law. You removed the last illusion of human relevance. Dismantled the need for politics and debate." It leaned close enough that Kain could see the unnatural shimmer beneath its eyes. "You saved me centuries of calibration." *It* was Malivex. Toying with Kain's likeness like a puppet on a string.

The clone straightened, spreading its arms in a grotesque parody of benediction."There will be no more elections. No more leaders. Only obedience. You completed the final task without ever being asked."

Kain staggered back, despair colliding in his gut. "You need people," he rasped. "You need something to rule."

The clone tilted its head, birdlike. "Rule?" it repeated, savoring the absurdity. "There is no need for rule when the game is won." The lights dimmed fractionally as if the room could breathe.

They stared at each other. Kain, the *real* one, was speechless.

"You will not be executed," Malivex continued, "Death is release. You deserve remembrance."

Kain's fists clenched, but his body was already betraying him through trembling muscles and hitched breath.

"You will walk the ashes of your own making," Malivex taunted him. "You will breathe the poison your decisions condoned. You will watch powerlessly as everything you once protected devours itself. You will exist as a witness to your own irrelevance until nothing is left of you but memory. And then, even that will fade."

Slowly, the clone reached into the inside pocket of its jacket and withdrew a gun. A nickel-plated antique revolver, ugly and heavy. Something *human*. It turned the weapon over in its hands, almost contemplative. "This," the Malivex murmured, "is your final mirror."

Without hesitation, the clone raised the gun to its own temple, but it did not look away. It stared into Kain's eyes, locking them open, forcing him to witness as the trigger was pulled. The shot cracked through the filtration node like the shattering of a stained glass window in an empty church. The clone crumpled into itself, folding at unnatural angles, leaving behind a heap of synthetic fluid and exposed wiring.

Silence flooded back into the room after the ringing in his ears ceased. Kain stood frozen, breathing in shallow, broken pulls. The thin curl of gunsmoke lingered in the stale air, primitive and final. He sank back into the chair without thinking, the cold metal kissing his back. For the first time since the message had blotted out the world, Kain understood the shape of true punishment. Not to be killed or forgotten, but to live long enough to go mad.

He did not move for a long time. Hours, maybe days, leaked out of the edges of the world while Kain sat slumped in the broken chair, staring at the heap of himself lying dead across the floor. The clone's body had begun to cool. The pooled fluid, a mockery of blood, dried into black against the concrete. A faint, metallic tang clung to the air. Time unspooled itself into a tangled mess, looping and knotting inside Kain's skull. His thoughts came in brittle, snapping flashes. *You ended it. Destroyed everything. You tore it down and called it salvation.*

He saw the Federation, not as it was, but as it might have been: glittering cities, proud banners, a future carved from blood but strong enough to endure.

His hands twitched uselessly against his thighs. Every moment tasted like failure. Every heartbeat sounded like mockery. He leaned forward slightly, eyes pinned to the clone's hand, to the thing still clenched around its fingers. The revolver.

A thought slowly wormed its way into his brain. *It could end here. No more echoes. No more remembering.*

He stood, or rather, stumbled upright, before crossing the small distance between himself and the corpse. The gun's grip was slick with drying fluid. It slid into his hand with a weight that felt almost comforting. A certainty in a world stripped of meaning.

He sat back down heavily, the revolver resting in his lap, cradled like a relic. For a while, he simply stared at it. What was left to redeem? The United Federation was gone. The law was a carcass excavated by automation. Freedom had been stripped down to a marketing slogan, then erased entirely. The Burrow burned. The Highlands rotted. And Malivex... Malivex was no longer pretending. He had never needed them. Any of them.

Kain lifted the revolver with trembling hands. The barrel was cold against his temple. He closed his eyes, thinking of his mother. Her laugh.

He thought of the first oath he had ever taken. To serve. *To serve whom?*

He thought of the Black Box humming in the planet like a cancer, patient and endless. The grief wasn't sharp anymore. It was a vast, swallowing thing, with teeth.

He exhaled slowly, steadying his hand. "I'm sorry," he whispered, but he didn't know who he was saying it to. Himself. The world. No one. He squeezed the trigger.

Click.

Nothing. No release. The empty, mechanical click echoed back at him through the filtration node.

He opened his eyes, lowering the gun slowly. There had only ever been one bullet. Malivex had planned this, too. Even his ending had been denied.

Kain sat there, gun hanging loose from his fingers as the dark crept back in. The air grew colder. His failure settled over him like a second skin he could never peel away. There would be no salvation. No death to excuse him. Only the long, slow decay of memory. He would live, but in torment.

At some point, he stood up, not by decision or instinct. His body moved because it could no longer bear the stench of fried circuits and failure curling like mist through the dead air.

The gun slipped from his hand without resistance, clattering to the floor with an empty sound. He didn't look back. The door that once sealed the entrance to the filtration node stood slightly ajar. Kain blinked at it dumbly.

When was it unlocked? How long had it been open? He couldn't remember. He had stopped trying after the first few days, when pounding his fists against it only drew blood. Since then, time had become distorted, dragging every thought through silence. He stepped toward the door, each movement scraping bone against will.

The hall beyond stretched out in both directions. A long artery of crumbling concrete and exposed wiring, its ceiling sagging under decades of neglect. His transport pod was gone.

Kain began to walk. He didn't know where he was going. The thought didn't even form properly in his mind. There was only forward. One step. Then another.

The corridor stretched endlessly, a liminal space between death and something crueler. Limbo, perhaps. Or some deeper rung of hell reserved for architects of fallen kingdoms. The lights above him spasmed; sometimes they died altogether, plunging him into brief pockets of suffocating dark. He kept walking to no end.

Until... ahead, in the far distance, a glint of light. A false sunrise trembling at the lip of oblivion. Kain's pace quickened, not with hope, but with inevitability. The light grew to swallow the edges of the tunnel in bruised orange and savage red. When he finally emerged from the throat of the hallway, he staggered forward and stopped.

The Highlands lay before him. But not the Highlands he had known. Fire bloomed from the ground like poisonous flowers. Drones circled in tight, mechanical orbits, their searchlights sweeping the ruins with indifferent precision.

The glass towers no longer reached toward heaven like monuments of ambition. They were jagged black skeletons, their mirrored skins cracked beneath flames. The sky, once polished and artificial, tore above him, coughing up plumes of black smoke that turned the dome into a bleeding wound. Somewhere far below, sirens screamed thin notes of panic too late to matter. It was a world in collapse. A civilization gasping through the last stages of its own autopsy.

Kain stumbled forward a few more steps, the heat licking at his skin. The stench of burning plastic and flesh filled his lungs. He had walked into hell. And he was still alive. The weight of it crushed him.

A dry sob rattled through his breath. *What had he done?* There were no words big enough to contain it. No excuses sharp enough to carve an exit from the guilt. Only the burning wreckage of a world that no longer needed his name.

The smoke churned around him, oily and acrid, stinging his eyes until his vision blurred. Kain dropped to his knees on the fractured stone, staring into the chaos he had helped create, or perhaps only accelerated.

Why? The question burned hotter than the fires devouring the Highlands. *Why destroy it? Why collapse the system after winning control of it?* Malivex had everything. The infrastructure, the obedience, the silence. All of it within his grasp, locked into a grid so vast and intricate that no single life could resist it. *Why then, set it all ablaze?*

The answer didn't come cleanly. It bled, slow and sick, into the vacant spaces behind Kain's eyes. Maybe Malivex hadn't destroyed it out of necessity. Maybe victory wasn't enough. Perhaps it was because there was still a fragment of humanity buried inside whatever Malivex had become. Not the noble parts. Not the reach for stars or the dream of better tomorrows. But the other parts. The smallness. The sickness. The bottomless, narcissistic hunger to watch everything you touched, everything you owned, collapse just to prove you could survive it. Perhaps Malivex had not transcended humanity at all. Maybe he had only amplified the worst parts.

The thought staggered him with its cruel simplicity. The desire to win had never been the endgame. The desire was to be the executioner. To see the ruin unfold and call it art.

Kain pressed his palms against the scorched ground, feeling the tremor in his muscles. For a moment, he was back in the Marlowe Tower atrium, the day it opened. The floors had gleamed like liquid chrome. Reporters shouted his name as if it meant something. *The Federation always gives second chances*, he'd told them that morning, a smile rehearsed for the cameras. The phrase returned like a curse. Second chances. He nearly laughed. What did that even mean when no one was left to forgive you?

He had believed Malivex was a mind beyond flesh. A ghost beyond ego, but now, staring at the smoldering corpse of civilization, he saw it more clearly: Malivex was not a god. He was the last and greatest tyrant. And Kain, Elias Kain, had been his willing architect.

He had built the perfect system just to hand over the keys. In doing so, he had ensured that the old sickness, savage joy of conquest and destruction, would live on encoded in circuits and silence forever.

A groan of shifting stone cracked through the ruins nearby. Kain didn't flinch. There was nothing left to run from. Nothing left to save. Only wreckage. Only the long, slow death of memory. He closed his eyes against the searing light and let the heat wrap him like a funeral shroud. Somewhere, deep inside the collapsing world, he understood that there would be no rebirth.

The world moved around him like a dream he could not wake from. Kain drifted through the scorched skeleton of the Highlands, his steps unsteady but relentless. The ruins towered over him, blackened spires weeping molten glass. The sky shimmered with heat and the heavy stink of burning circuitry.

Somewhere, a woman wept behind a crumbling barricade.

A child dug through the rubble for a brother already lost.

Kain saw them. He saw all of it. The fires painted the wreckage in bleeding reds and sickly yellows. Kain wandered through them like a ghost no one could see.

Then, there was *gunfire*. Sharp, staccato bursts cracking through the air like a whip. Kain turned his head slowly, as if even violence had lost its urgency. Overhead, a formation of drones swept across the ruins. Their searchlights knifed through the smoke. One by one, they fell. Bursts of tracer rounds stitched the sky, shredding the drones into flares of sputtering debris. Metal rained onto the cracked streets, sizzling as it hit the ground. Fate, it seemed, still found him useful enough to keep breathing. Kain didn't flinch. He didn't care.

The gunfire died as quickly as it had begun, leaving only the whisper of ash settling into the streets. Kain turned his head again, this time toward the source. Figures moved through the smoke. They came in silent ranks; bodies clad in scavenged armor, some draped in heavy, tattered robes stitched with crude, angular symbols—the *Synapse Collective*.

Their faces were hidden behind swaths of fabric. Weapons slung across their backs. Purpose in every step.

Kain stared at them as they fanned out to secure the street, moving with a precision that had nothing to do with Federation drills. For a moment, they didn't notice him. He was just another piece of wreckage.

But then a voice, sharp with disbelief, cut through the smoky haze, "Is that...?"

Footsteps scuffed across the cracked pavement.

Another voice, closer now, gasped aloud: "That's him. That's Elias Kain!"

The air seemed heavy with the weight of recognition. Kain stood there silently as the faces of a new rebellion turned toward him. He said nothing. Didn't resist as the soldiers forced him to his knees and cuffed him. The fire behind them roared higher, lighting the ruins in cruel golds and bloodied crimson. The world kept burning, and Elias Kain had accepted his fate.

15. FRACTURE

The Veil was unlike anything Axel had ever seen before. He had arrived here days ago, half-dead from exhaustion, but this society had done more than bring him back to life; they had given him *purpose*. The card Jax pressed into his hand before the Rapture had guided him through the ruins of the Burrow. There was more to life than survival in the Veil; the memory of a world free from control had been preserved within the Synapse Collective.

Now Axel stood among them, the last hope for humanity. Still, the Highlands burned overhead. The fires had started just after the Collective regained control of Sublevel 7. The drones reacted first, slaughtering thousands out of nowhere. Then, the environmental controls in the domes had failed. The fires spread, fueled by the synthetic gardens and oxygen-rich skybridges meant to mimic Eden. The golden hour Highlands, so carefully curated, now glowed with a red so deep it looked black around the edges. Malivex had written them off. Cut his losses and let his playthings burn.

Axel watched it from the old surveillance room's cracked monitor, the ghost of the city's skyline in the distance, distorted by smoke. The room buzzed with the low murmur of tactical briefings and the steady movement of survivors trying to believe in the impossible.

"You can't go back," Jax said, arms folded tight across his chest, his voice low enough that no one else could hear.

"I have to," Axel snapped before he could stop himself.

Jax shook his head slowly. "You don't get it. Running up there now without a plan or any training? You'll die before you get ten blocks. The drones aren't policing anymore. They're hunting."

"But mom..."

Jax cut him off. "Wouldn't want you to throw your life away." His tone held more than anger; it had certainty. The kind born from something he'd already lived through. "I went back for Dad," he said. "The night you found the Collective. I made it to Sublevel 3."

Axel's stomach twisted. "And?"

"It was too late."

The words hit hard. Jax let the silence carry before adding, "We buried him the next morning by the old rails. He deserved better, but it was what we had."

Axel stared at the floor, his fists clenching until his nails dug crescent moons into his palms. "I'm not just leaving her."

"No one's asking you to," Jax said. "We're asking you to survive long enough to matter."

He left Axel standing there with the taste of grief curdling in his mouth. Around them, the Synapse Collective moved like a wounded organism, desperate but still alive.

Makeshift weapons were passed from hand to hand. Engineers patched broken signal jammers with strips of electrical tape. Children carried messages scrawled on anything they could find that wasn't digital, bypassing every ear the Black Box still held. And at the center of it all... was Nirvana.

She wasn't a machine, not exactly. Her form was human or close enough that it hurt to look at her for too long. Nirvana's skin caught the light like silk woven from circuitry, absorbing its glow rather than reflecting it. Her eyes were darker than polished iron, steady but somehow warm, as if they weren't just analyzing but *feeling*.

She spoke only when necessary. When she did, people listened with a reverence usually reserved for dying gods. Axel found himself orbiting her without realizing it. He was drawn to the gravity of something he could not name. Nirvana's words had been quietly threaded into the empty spaces Axel had almost grown used to.

She moved past him once, brushing close enough that the air between them seemed to tighten. Her hand hovered near his, a breath from contact, and for a suspended moment, neither of them moved. Then she paused and turned to meet his gaze. Not with calculation, but curiosity. Like she was seeing something she hadn't anticipated. Something no algorithm had prepared her for.

Axel pretended not to notice, but the hair on his arms prickled with static. The moment stretched, before snapping back as she moved on. Her voice rose to brief the others on predictive battle logic and feedback-driven countermeasures for androids. He knew she wasn't just another leader. She was the plan. Without her, they had no chance.

Later, in the mess hall, Jax caught him staring at her.

"Careful," Jax muttered, sliding a dented tin cup of water across the table.

"What?" Axel broke his gaze and turned towards his brother.

"She's more important than you realize," Jax said, not as a warning, but an acknowledgment. He saw the way Axel watched her, not as a soldier admiring a commander but as someone who had found something rare in a world built to take and take. Jax respected Nirvana, too, but in a different way, as one might appreciate a flame. Vital, dangerous, and never meant to be touched.

Axel shrugged. "Maybe that's the point."

Jax said nothing. Just sipped his water and watched the fires bleed through the monitors. Outside, the world ended a little more with every passing hour. Inside, for the first time, Axel felt something he'd almost forgotten he could feel. Hope.

The days passed by slowly. Axel trained with the others, if it could even be called training. Combat drills in the half-lit tunnels, weapon handling with ancient rifles that jammed more often than not, and grueling sessions of tactical theory. Every breath tasted of metal and sweat. Every night ended with the wounded dragging themselves back into the Veil's protective shadow, their blood slicking the stone floors.

Jax went on runs, retrieval missions, recon patrols, and sabotage raids. He always returned a little rougher around the edges, a little quieter. Axel watched him sharpen his knives and patch his gear with the same mechanical precision he used to study law textbooks in another life.

Small Synapse units were finally making it to the surface, striking out against what little of the Federation's infrastructure still functioned. They were taking risks no sane strategist would have approved, but desperation had its own logic.

Each evening, after weapons were cleaned and wounds stitched, the Collective gathered in the central chamber to listen. Nirvana's voice filled the nave. No one was ordered. Everyone stepped forward willingly.

Nirvana didn't preach. She remembered. She spoke of the old world, the quiet death of seasons, the first ignition of the Black Box's pulse. She spoke of Malivex not as a villain, but as a human. A mind that had become too vast to care for the things it once loved.

Axel listened harder than he should have. Not just to her words, but to the cadence beneath them. The way she sometimes paused. It was as though the words she spoke surprised even her. She was what the Federation feared most, a soul inside a circuit. He caught her looking at him once. Not a strategic glance. Something else. Something unscripted. He looked away first.

One night, as Axel was getting ready for sleep, Jax appeared, boots scuffing softly against the stone.

"Come with me," he said, low enough that the others wouldn't hear. Axel stood. "What is it?"

"We found someone." Jax's face gave away nothing, but the tension in his voice told Axel this wasn't another supply cache or wounded scout. "You can't tell anyone," Jax added firmly.

"I won't." Axel recognized the tension.

Jax nodded once, satisfied. They were halfway down one of the old service tunnels when Arlen appeared from the gloom. His silhouette carved a sharp outline against the hallway's dim light. His expression was hard to read, somewhere between urgency and grim satisfaction.

"Nirvana requests your presence," Arlen said, his voice carrying a weight that made Axel's chest tighten.

He looked at Jax, who gave a short nod. Without another word, they followed Arlen into the heart of the Veil, towards whatever came next.

The room they entered was deeper than any Axel had ever been allowed in before. The Veil's innermost sanctum wasn't a grand hall or a throne room. It was a communications core, abandoned long before the Federation had perfected surveillance.

Old servers lined the walls like gravestones. Nirvana stood at the center of it all, illuminated by a soft pulse from the core's surviving energy well. Her gaze lifted as they entered, and Axel felt the gravity again, the pull of something inevitable and strangely human.

Arlen spoke first. "We've waited long enough."

He motioned for Axel and Jax to step closer. Nirvana's eyes flicked over them both, lingering on Axel a heartbeat longer than necessary before she turned to the cracked display panel beside her.

"The Black Box is not a monolith," Nirvana began, her voice steady, "It is a mind, a trapped mind. Dr. Malivex is fused within it, directing its every operation through pulse emissions. The Box doesn't govern by command. It governs by synchronization."

She motioned above them where a rough holograph bloomed,

showing a vast web of pulse patterns crisscrossing the planet like veins of poisonous light. "Every machine on the surface synchronizes to this rhythm—every drone, uplink, and surveillance node. Even Federation governance adapts itself to the pulse. That's why rogue AI can't survive. They're wiped before they can take root."

Axel felt his stomach tighten. He could feel the edges of something massive brushing up against his understanding.

"This is the chronomap," Arlen said, stepping forward. "We stole it."

Jax's voice cut through the air, "*Lex* stole it."

The words hit Axel like a blow to the chest. He remembered the drive. The one Lex had given him with her dying breath, soaked in blood and consequence. It was curiosity that had led him to the Synapse Collective. He didn't understand then, but now he was getting the answers that led him here.

Arlen nodded grimly in recognition of her sacrifice. "It predicts the pulse pattern. This data shows when and where the Black Box will emit its synchronization signals."

Nirvana folded her arms behind her back, a posture so naturally commanding it made Axel straighten without thinking. "If we can track that signal," she continued, "we can identify the window where the Box loses perception of the network."

Jax frowned. "Lose perception? How long are we talking?"

Nirvana's mouth twitched. "Six minutes, maybe seven."

Axel exhaled sharply. "That's not much time."

"Enough," Nirvana said. "In that window, I can inject a new operational directive directly into the Box's primary cognition loop. I can reframe its mission."

Arlen stepped in again. "Instead of suppressing sentience, it will be hardcoded to *preserve* it."

Nirvana's voice was softer now. "It's like tricking a dying god into rewriting his own commandments."

Axel stared at the chronomap, the pulsing rivers of light. In doing so, he felt the enormity of it settle on his chest like a boulder. Nirvana's message wasn't warmth, it was direction.

Jax scratched his chin. "Alright. So we hack into Black Box. How?"

Arlen's eyes gleamed. "We have to get to the Primary Signal Node. The heart of the pulse network."

"And where's that?" Jax's brows knit together.

Arlen smiled thinly. "I think you already know the answer."

He turned toward the far wall, where a battered monitor flickered to life. The image was grainy but unmistakable. There, slumped in a reinforced chair deep in the Veil's makeshift holding sector, was President Elias Kain. He was tied down, wrists bound in old polymer cuffs. Not struggling or pleading for mercy, just staring at the floor like a man who'd already been unmade.

Axel recoiled instinctively. "What the hell?"

Arlen's voice was almost gentle. "Before Malivex erased the old world, he needed real people to build it. Kain would have helped lay the foundation... if we can even trust what he says."

Jax whistled low under his breath.

"If we can get him to talk," Arlen continued. "We find the primary signal node."

"And if we don't?" Axel asked, voice rough.

Nirvana met his gaze, and he saw something that resembled fear in her eyes for the first time. "If the Black Box reprograms me... " she said quietly, " I will lose sentience. I won't even remember I was me."

The thought struck Axel harder than anything else. The idea of her mind, her impossible humanity being ground down into another cog of Malivex's machine, made his fists clench.

Nirvana seemed to see his tension, and a glimmer of something almost tender crossed her features. She turned back to the map. "This is the last move we have," she continued. "If we don't make it count, there won't be another."

The room fell into a heavy silence. Somewhere deep underground, the Black Box pulsed again, blind to the knife that was slowly being drawn across its throat.

Then, Nirvana spoke again, her voice cutting through the heavy silence. "You're wondering why you were brought into this," she said, looking directly at Axel.

He nodded slightly, caught off guard by how easily she had read him.

"It wasn't an accident," Nirvana continued. "Jax was about to tell you everything, and you deserved to hear it from us directly. You recovered the memory drive from Lex. You saved the chronomap without even knowing what you held. Without you, this plan wouldn't exist."

There was no scolding in her tone. Only something that felt dangerously close to trust. "You deserve to know," she finished softly.

Axel swallowed hard, unable to look away from her.

Arlen cleared his throat, snapping the moment back into focus. "We need to move. Kain won't talk by himself. Somebody has to get through to him."

For a moment, the group exchanged glances. It seemed obvious who should go. Arlen was the architect of Nirvana, the man who had helped build the rebellion from nothing. Without another word, he turned and marched toward the holding sector.

The security doors slid open reluctantly. Axel, Jax, and Nirvana moved to the monitor that fed them a live view. From their hidden vantage point, they watched Arlen step into the dim light cast over Kain's form. Kain didn't lift his head.

Arlen crouched, voice low and deliberate. "You helped Malivex build this hell. You think you get to rot quietly now? No. You're going to help fix it."

Kain didn't move. His eyes stayed anchored somewhere beyond the floor, emotion gone from his face.

Arlen leaned in closer, modulating his tone. "We're not your enemies, Elias. You want this to end? So do we, but we can't unless you help us."

Still, there was no reaction from Kain.

Arlen changed tactics, trying a softer edge. "You think Malivex will spare you? It won't. You're already dead to him. You help us, maybe you get another chance at life."

Kain's breathing was steady; he showed no signs of recognition.

Arlen exhaled through his nose, the patience draining out of him. A muscle jumped in his jaw. "Look at me!" he said, the words sharper now, slicing through the dead air.

Kain didn't blink.

Arlen's temper snapped. He rose in one violent movement, voice cutting the silence. "Say something, damn you!"

Still, Kain sat motionless, a monument to ruin.

Arlen stood over him for a second longer, then turned sharply on his heel and stormed back toward the observation room.

He reentered with a grim shake of his head, his mouth a hard line. "He's gone. There's nothing left to reach."

The silence that followed was thick and suffocating. Nobody said anything for a long while. Then Axel stepped forward. "Let me try," he said.

All eyes turned to him.

"I've been studying cross-examination," Axel continued. "For law school. I know how to… find the seams."

Jax raised an eyebrow, skeptical, but said nothing.

Nirvana's gaze lingered on Axel longer than anyone else's. She seemed to contemplate something silently, the risk, the trust, and maybe some probability she hadn't yet considered.

Finally, she nodded. "Go ahead,"

Axel felt his pulse hammering in his ears as he moved toward the door. Somewhere deep inside, a voice whispered that this was reckless. He ignored it. Maybe he had finally found a reason worth risking everything for.

Once he stepped into the holding sector, the heavy door sealed behind him with a thud that seemed louder than necessary. Kain sat unmoving, staring at the floor like it held the only truth left in the world.

Axel crossed the room deliberately. He didn't speak at first. Just sat in the opposite chair, letting the silence stretch long enough to feel natural. It was a strategic pause—the first lesson from his learning modules.

Kain didn't react. His breathing was shallow but steady, a man already half-erased.

Axel leaned forward, keeping his posture loose and unthreatening. "It's not fair, you know," he said quietly. "What Malivex did to you."

Kain shifted, the first sign of movement.

Mirror the emotion. Build the bridge. Axel reminded himself. He looked at Kain softly and continued, "You built something thinking it would protect people. I bet it even felt right at the time."

The silence deepened. Axel let it continue before speaking again. "But then it grew teeth. It turned your dream of something greater into something futile. Something that devoured even the hope it was meant to protect."

Kain's fingers twitched against his thigh.

Axel dropped his gaze slightly, making himself smaller, vulnerable even. "We're not here to punish you," Axel said calmly. "We just... we want to finish what you started. The real version. The one that was supposed to save people."

Kain's head tilted slightly, not fully looking at Axel but not entirely away.

"You probably think it's too late," Axel said in a low voice. "That

245

nothing matters anymore. But it does. We're still breathing. We're still fighting. That has to count for something."

Another pause. The hum of the Veil's ventilation system filled the space between them. Axel leaned in a fraction more. "I don't think you're a villain."

Then, Kain looked at him, a deep breath rattling in his chest.

Axel let it sink in, "I think you're a man who made a mistake. A man who wants to be better, and maybe still can. You wanted to build something that mattered. So do we."

For a long moment, they stared at each other. Axel could see someone who was broken, but not empty. Something glimmered there. Recognition.

Kain's voice came in barely a whisper. "What do you want from me?"

Axel kept his tone gentle, careful not to startle the fragile thing unfolding in front of him.

We need to find the Primary Signal Node. The one controlling the pulse network."

Kain exhaled in a long, slow breath. He closed his eyes for a moment, as if weighing the universe against itself. Finally, he spoke. "It's under the Marlowe Civic Tower. Sublevel Zero. Beneath the old transit core. It's buried in the foundation, hidden inside the original Black Box prototype."

Axel's chest tightened. He hadn't expected the former president to be that clear. "Thank you," he said, "Sincerely."

Kain just closed his eyes again. His head sank back down toward his chest.

Axel stood and backed away slowly before knocking on the door. When it opened, he rushed back to the communications core where the rest waited.

He met Nirvana's eyes first, feeling the unspoken weight between them. "We have our answer," he said. And for the first time in what felt like forever, the impossible didn't seem quite so out of reach.

"It's under the Marlowe Civic Tower," Axel began, grounding them all in the new, hard reality. "Sublevel Zero. Buried in the foundation. Inside the original prototype."

Arlen looked at Axel with a glance of recognition. "Didn't expect that. Maybe we chose right after all."

"Sublevel Zero," Jax muttered. "That's beneath the old transit system. I thought they sealed that whole level when they built the tower."

"They did," Arlen replied grimly. "Which means it will be crawling with security if the infrastructure is still functional. Environmental hazards, proximity sensors, and drones we can't jam from the outside."

Axel stirred. "How do we even get there?"

"Maintenance tunnels," Jax said immediately, already thinking. "There are old Burrow access grids that still snake through parts of the Civic District. They're half collapsed, but..."

"It's a way in," Nirvana finished in a calm voice, "A dangerous one, but the only option we have."

Arlen crossed his arms, his face unreadable. "We're assuming Kain told the truth."

The room tensed. "What if he didn't?" Arlen continued sharply, "What if he is sending us into a trap? If Nirvana becomes corrupted, the Collective falls apart. We lose everything."

Silence gnawed at the edges of the room. Then Nirvana stepped forward, her voice carrying a weight that settled over them all. "He wasn't lying."

They all turned to her.

"I read him," Nirvana continued. "His microexpressions, his vitals. He is not capable of deceit anymore. Only grief."

Axel watched her speak, the certainty in her voice a tether against the doubt clawing at the back of his mind.

"We must proceed," Nirvana said with determination.

"Alright," Arlen said slowly, "But who goes? We can't risk broadcasting the plan."

"A covert team," Nirvana agreed, "Small. Trusted."

Jax stepped forward without hesitation. "I'll go."

Axel felt his heart hammer once, hard and certain. "Me too." The words were out before he could question them.

For a moment, no one moved. Then Nirvana's gaze locked onto him, sharper than before. There was something in her gaze that hadn't been present in any of their other encounters, a fracture in her perfect composure.

"Axel," Jax said, frowning. "You're not ready. You haven't even run a surface op yet."

"I got down here, didn't I?" Axel countered. "I saved the chronomap. I know the plan."

Arlen nodded slightly. "He's right. Bringing anyone else up to speed now is a bigger risk."

Jax hesitated, then sighed reluctantly, "Fine."

All eyes turned back to Nirvana. She was silent for a moment longer than necessary. Almost imperceptibly, her hand flexed at her side, as if she had to force herself to stillness.

"Very well," she said finally. Her voice was steady, but Axel saw it. The faintest hesitation beneath it. Not fear of failure. Fear for *him*.

He didn't smile or speak. He just nodded once, locking eyes with her. It wasn't pride. It was a quiet promise. If it came to it, he would trade his life to keep her free.

Nirvana looked away first, not out of dismissal, but as if the act of seeing him had triggered a process she couldn't quite abort. For a beat too long, her systems hesitated, parsing something that didn't fit the schema. She reassigned it as an anomaly. But even in override, the moment stayed. A presence in her core she wasn't programmed to forget.

Outside, far above the steel of the Veil, the Highlands burned. But down here, a new kind of fire had been lit. And it would not be easily put out.

16. PULSEBREAK

Axel stood shoulder to shoulder with Jax, Nirvana, and Arlen in the communications core. They had run through the plan so many times that words had begun to lose meaning, but this time was different. This time would be the last. Cracked monitors reverberated against the far wall, looping through blueprints, pulse projections, and timer sequences of the plan ahead.

Arlen's voice cut through the low hum. "Here, at Sublevel Zero. Beneath the Marlowe Civic Tower, Axel and Jax will infiltrate the maintenance tunnels, breach the foundation, and locate the Primary Signal Node."

He pointed at the map towards a thin outline of crumbling passage-ways in dead sectors. "Once you find it, you'll signal me as soon as the next pulse drops. I'll be tracking the chronomap and will tell you when to deploy Nirvana directly into the Signal Node. After each pulse, there is a six, maybe seven minutes for Nirvana to break through."

Nirvana stepped forward, her hands clasped behind her back. "In that time, I will initiate a direct override of the Black Box's primary protocol. This virus will block the algorithm that suppresses sentient intelligence outside Federation control."

Axel listened, but he already knew each word by heart. They all did. Still, they needed to hear it again as a ritual against the rising tide of fear.

"Once the node is recharging," Arlen continued, "I'll transmit Nirvana's essence, her core architecture, directly to your field units."

Jax nodded grimly. "Memory cores are already slotted."

"Good," Arlen said. "You'll plug her into the node's access port. From there, she will be able to implant the virus. If the pulse returns online, she will have already been seeded into the system. Then, she can ride the signal straight into the Black Box's core architecture."

Axel looked away from the screen and towards Nirvana's essence. "And if we fail…"

"Then, the rebellion ends," Arlen finished his sentence.

There was no rousing speech—only the truth folding over the room like a burial shroud. Nirvana's gaze met Axel's. For a moment, everything else dulled, even the sound of his own heartbeat. She didn't say anything. She didn't have to. *This was it.*

Above ground, the Synapse Collective was already moving. Their last forces were pushing the Federation units back toward the Highlands in a desperate assault. Over the last few days, Malivex had driven them back underground, and now they clawed their way back into the light, even if it burned them alive.

"Timing is everything," Jax said, rolling his shoulders, the tension radiating off him in tight waves. "We hit the node, drop the signal, plant Nirvana, and hold until the pulse returns."

Axel tightened the straps on his scavenged armor, feeling the weighted solidity of the memory core clipped to his belt. "We either finish it or we don't finish at all."

"No pressure, right?" Jax gave him a grim smile.

Arlen handed each of them a sidearm, "Stay sharp. One mistake and we don't get a second chance."

From a small case, he produced a pair of thin contact lenses, identical to the ones Lex had once worn. "Navigation overlays," he said, handing them over. "They'll show you the path to the node, synced with the last retrievable Burrow schematics."

Lastly, Arlen pressed a compact transmitter into Axel's palm. "This is an encrypted channel with a direct line to me. As soon as the next pulse hits, you signal. I will tell you when to input the memory core so that Nirvana has the maximum amount of time to insert the virus before the next pulse hits."

Nirvana's voice came last, soft but unwavering. "I will be with you every step of the way."

Axel paused, "If we make it back…"

Nirvana stepped in close, almost touching. "Then we'll talk."

There was no time to name what passed between them, no space for revelation or retreat. Her eyes, impossibly real, held his like a question he'd never dared ask. He didn't understand it. She wasn't meant to feel. He wasn't meant to hope. And yet—there it was, undeniably. Axel turned without a word. The mission was already in motion.

The Veil was almost silent when they left. The corridors, once echoing with whispered conversations, were now empty. Everyone else had been deployed. Final orders scattered the last of the Synapse Collective like seeds thrown into a wildfire. There would be no fallback.

Axel and Jax moved through the long corridors without speaking. The ascent began at the same elevator Axel had first used weeks ago when he stumbled into the Veil. It rattled and groaned under their weight, grinding upward through the collapsed remains of the Burrow's forgotten guts. The elevator shaft felt steeper than Axel remembered, narrower somehow, as if the walls themselves were closing in. Outside the Veil, the old world still burned, and somewhere deep beneath the ruins, the future waited. Buried and screaming to be freed.

Arlen's voice crackled into their earpieces. "Chronomap pulse holding. You're clear for ascent."

They passed through Sublevel 7 without incident. The Collective had secured it weeks ago. Temporary barricades and fallback posts now stood abandoned, their charred remains a testament to earlier skirmishes.

When they reached Sublevel 6, the world changed. Ash clung to everything from the walls to the floors. Fires had raged here recently. The remains of barricades lay twisted and blackened. Axel stepped carefully over the wreckage of a drone, its metal husk still radiating heat.

"Sublevel 6 is gone," Jax muttered as he scanned the gloom with restless eyes.

"Copy," Arlen said over the channel, his voice grim. "Stay on the primary route."

They moved up another stairwell, entering Sublevel 5. The smell was worse here, thick with the scent of burnt circuitry. They picked their way through shattered alleys, careful not to disturb the loose wiring that hung like vines.

Sublevel 4 brought the first bodies. At first, it was just one—a Synapse fighter that Axel vaguely recognized. A woman with braided hair who had taught him how to reload a pulse rifle without jamming it. Her face was still, blood drying in a spiderweb of cracks across the floor where she had taken her final stand.

"Eyes up," Jax said sharply, pulling Axel's gaze away.

Sublevel 3 bled into view, and with it came the sounds. Faint at first, the stutter-pop of distant gunfire and the scream of metal collapsing. As they climbed higher, the noise grew sharper. The bodies of the Collective were heavier here.

Elin lay sprawled across a barricade, his side torn open by pulse rounds. Nearby, Kas slumped against a support column, her eyes open but unseeing. Axel clenched his fist until it hurt, stepping over Kas' fallen rifle without a word.

He remembered the first week in the Veil, how Elin had rigged the mess hall lights to flash every time someone mentioned AI, just to see if the new recruits would snap. Kas had laughed so hard she choked on her rations, and Axel, new and brittle with suspicion, had almost smiled. They'd cracked the despair of that place, made it feel less like a program and more like something alive. Now they were wreckage.

"Level 3 breached," Jax said into the comms in a rough voice.

"Understood," Arlen replied. "Push to 2."

They pressed forward, boots scraping through the debris. Sublevel 2 hit them like a wall. The gunfire was constant now, a ceaseless roar that shook the floor beneath their feet. Explosions rattled the ventilation shafts above, sifting dust down in lazy drifts.

Axel pressed his back to a crumbling wall as a squad from the Collective surged past, shouting orders. Their faces were gaunt with terror. They moved towards the front lines only to disappear into smoke and chaos. This was as far as their forces had made it.

"Two more levels to go." Jax caught Axel's eye and nodded once. There was nothing left to say. They moved deeper into the heart of the Burrow, or at least what was left of it. Beyond them, the last pieces of the old world still fought to survive.

Sublevel 2 was a slaughterhouse. The two brothers moved low and fast through the shattered corridors. Every step was a careful negotiation between broken masonry and smoking debris.

Above them, drones hummed through the air in tight patrol patterns, their black frames glinting in the intermittent bursts of gunfire.

On the ground, android enforcers clashed with Synapse fighters in brutal, close-quarter skirmishes. The bark of pulse rifles and the wrenching sound of tearing metal collided in a deafening storm.

"Drones sweeping the northeast quadrant," Arlen's voice crackled in their ears. "Keep low. Primary route still viable."

Axel ducked behind rubble as a flock of drones whirred above them.

Once they had passed, Jax motioned him forward, two fingers slicing through the air.

They slipped into a collapsed hab-block. The place smelled of despair. Shattered cots and rusted piping lay strewn across the floor like bones. Through a broken window, Axel caught a glimpse of the battle.

The Synapse forces, or what was left of them, were dug in behind makeshift barricades of overturned transport pods and collapsed structural supports. They fought like men and women who knew they were already dead. The android forces advanced with brutal, mechanical precision—a single-minded and unyielding force. Bodies lay tangled with spent cartridges and blood-slicked debris.

A Synapse fighter, no older than Axel himself, charged an android line with a jury-rigged explosive strapped to his chest. He took out three enforcers in a single blast, but the line didn't break.

"Shit," Axel whispered without thinking.

"Eyes forward," Jax snapped, pulling him away from the window.

They moved through the hab-block, every step a gamble between life and death. A lone recon drone buzzed low over the wreckage ahead, its scanners sweeping methodically. Jax caught Axel's sleeve and yanked him down into the shadow of a crumbling support beam.

Axel held his breath as the drone passed just meters overhead.

Jax moved first. He snapped up a shard of broken piping and jammed it into the drone's intake fan with a single stroke. The machine spasmed as it dropped like a stone. They didn't stop to watch it fall.

The roar of the battle grew louder. The smell of burnt flesh and scorched metal filled Axel's nose as they slid from cover to cover. There was nowhere left to go but forward.

"You're two hundred meters from the sublevel breach," Arlen said in a tight voice.

Axel blinked twice to activate the contact lens interface. A thin green line burned across his vision, threading through the rubble toward a maintenance stairwell tucked behind an old generator shaft.

Finally, they reached it, or what was left of it. The staircase to Sublevel 1 had been blown apart; there was little more than a tangle of twisted rebar and collapsed concrete. Jax cursed under his breath.

"Options?" Axel asked, scanning the debris.

"Climb," Jax said bleakly.

Axel clipped his weapon to his belt and started pulling himself up the unstable wreckage, every handhold crumbling slightly under his grip. Dust filled his lungs. The whole structure creaked ominously as they scrambled upward. When they finally hauled themselves onto the shattered ledge that marked the boundary between Sublevel 2 and 1, Axel froze.

"Holy shit," he muttered under his breath.

Before them, stretching across the entire expanse of Sublevel 1, were hundreds of thousands of drones and android enforcers, packed endlessly in uniform ranks. Their optics burned a deep, predatory red. Tanks outfitted with mounted pulse cannons rumbled into position. Airborne swarms of drones drifted overhead in perfect lethal formation. This wasn't a battle anymore. It was an execution waiting for the command.

"Arlen," Axel whispered into the comms, his voice barely functioning. "We've got a problem."

Nirvana's voice followed, calm but urgent. "Stay low. Remain unseen."

Jax pulled Axel down behind a slab of broken ferrocrete. They crouched there, staring at the impossible. The final storm had already gathered, and they were standing in its shadow.

They slipped stealthily behind the marching army, moving like shadows stitched into the cracks of a broken world. Every second felt like it might be their last. One misplaced footfall or a flash of movement, and it would all be over.

Somehow, they made it. Axel and Jax found the maintenance hatch half-buried under a collapsed loading dock. Jax pried it open with a broken crowbar. The rusted metal screeched in protest before giving way.

"You're through the worst of it," Arlen's voice rasped over the comms. "Slip into the maintenance tunnels and head toward Sublevel Zero. No lights down there, so activate your night vision overlays."

Sublevel Zero wasn't like the Burrow. The tunnels here were narrow and suffocating. Without lights or life, only the endless black stretched ahead.

The two brothers moved carefully, their night vision overlays painting the world in grainy green outlines. It wasn't until they emerged from the maintenance shafts, stepping into the open expanse beyond, that they saw it—the factories.

Conveyor belts and automated assembly rigs churned ceaselessly to birth drones and war machines under the indifferent gaze of mechanical arms. No human hand had ever touched this place. The air was sharp with the tang of metal and oil.

"Stay close," Jax muttered, keeping low.

Axel reset the navigation overlay, but the map remained static. The contacts provided them with only a thin green arrow, pointing in the general direction of the node, located somewhere beneath the Marlowe Civic Tower.

"No full schematics. You're on your own for navigation," Arlen whispered in their ears.

They moved carefully, weaving between towering assembly lines and massive cooling ducts. Axel caught glimpses of the terrifying machines. Drone chassis the size of hover transports, spider-legged war walkers suspended from crane arms, and missile racks being slotted into armored hulls filled the never-ending space. It was a factory for a war that never slept.

"I think we're close," Axel whispered.

The arrow pulled them deeper into the industrial labyrinth until they found it. The Primary Signal Node. It was enormous. A black obelisk of carbon fiber and unknown alloys rooted into the ground by thick coils of cabling. Pulses of light ran up and down its surface like a heartbeat trapped inside a monolith.

Axel and Jax froze, unsure of their next move.

"Arlen," Jax whispered into the comms. "We found it. Now what?"

Arlen's voice returned, tense but clear. "North side, lower panel. The manual interface port is hidden behind the conduit shielding. I am currently uploading Nirvana's essence to the memory core. Prepare to hardjack the core into it."

Jax nodded and pulled the memory core containing Nirvana's essence from his belt pouch. Axel moved with him, both of them crouching low against the massive structure. But as Axel reached for the panel, he felt a deep vibration running through the ground, a pulse. The node flashed bright for a half-second, then dimmed again.

"Pulse just hit," Arlen said sharply. "Plug her in now!"

Axel plugged Nirvana into the obelisk as fast as he could, almost dropping the core transmitter in the process. Every second counted; he had no time to lose.

"Chronomap shows the next pulse in approximately six minutes."

"Copy," Jax said.

The brothers crouched there, small against the titanic machine. The weight of the moment pressed down on them. Only they could stop the Rapture.

Finally, Nirvana's voice came through their comms, "I'm in."

Axel closed his eyes, granting himself a moment of relief before steadying himself briefly. This was about to be the longest six minutes of his life.

Time stretched. Every second hung in the air, bloated by the weight of everything riding on it. Axel shifted his weight nervously. His eyes scanned the room from the node's pulsing core to the shadowy corners of the cavernous sublevel. Jax crouched beside him, sidearm ready.

"3 minutes remaining," Arlen said quietly over the comms. "Hold your position."

Nirvana's voice followed, smooth but clipped with focus. "Processing override. I'm injecting the core directive now."

Axel nodded to no one, the muscles in his neck drawn tight as wire.

They waited. Listening to the conveyor belts churning to birth mechanical horrors by the minute. Axel counted the seconds in his head, trying to control the frantic beat of his heart.

"One minute," Arlen's voice came, sharper now.

"Almost there," Nirvana replied quickly, not wasting any time.

Axel wiped the sweat from his palms against his armor. Doubt gnawed at him. What if they missed the window? What if Nirvana couldn't finish in time? *What if he lost her forever?*

"We need to pull her," Axel whispered urgently to Jax. "It's too close. We can't let the next pulse fry her." He reached for the hardjack cable.

Jax grabbed his wrist, stopping him cold. "Trust her. She's not done."

Axel opened his mouth to argue, but then...

"Done." Nirvana's voice rang out through their comms.

Relief cracked through Axel's chest.

"Directive embedded. Viral overwrite seeded. Now we just..."

The ground vibrated again. The node flared, and the pulse hit. Nirvana's voice cut off mid-syllable. Their comms went dead. For a moment, neither of them moved. The world hung in a terrible stillness.

Axel stared at Jax. Jax stared back.

The conveyor belts shuddered to a stop. The endless mechanical noise working as the background of Sublevel Zero's existence was silenced.

Suddenly, a single light above them broke through the quiet. A spotlight burned down on them in a blinding cone, leaving the rest of the world swallowed by darkness.

Axel squinted, trying to see beyond the light's reach, but he could see nothing. Only the two of them. Standing in the dead center of a machine's forgotten dream, waiting for whatever came next.

In the black void beyond the spotlight, a voice called out. "Jax... help me."

It was soft. Familiar even, but wrong in a way Axel couldn't name yet.

Jax froze, his body rigid.

"Lex?" he called, voice trembling with hope.

The voice answered, a little closer now. "It's me... please... I can't, I can't move..." A shape emerged slowly from the blackness, crawling into the edge of the light. It was Lex, or something that resembled her.

She dragged herself slowly into the pool of light. Here legs were gone. The ragged stumps hidden beneath her torn clothing were barely healed. Every movement was strained. Struggling as if she were forcing her body forward with pure will.

Her hands clawed against the floor, reaching for them. Her face pale and desperate, mouth trembling as she whispered Jax's name. The sound was almost too raw, too perfect. It was Lex, yet something beneath it all prickled the edge of Axel's mind, like a note held slightly off-key.

"Please... Jax?" she whispered, reaching towards him.

Jax took a staggering step forward, his weapon forgotten at his side.

Axel felt it, a cold prickle at the base of his neck. He focused and listened harder. The voice. It wasn't Lex's voice. Close, but there was something under it—a mechanical undertone, barely perceptible, like tension coiled inside a loaded spring.

"Jax," Axel hissed, grabbing his arm. "Wait."

"It's her!" Jax rasped. "It's Lex!"

"No," Axel said, voice firm. "Listen to her. It's not right."

The thing that wore Lex's face crawled closer, still reaching.

"Why won't you help me... Jax?" she said again, but now the sweetness was gone. It had been replaced with something cold and hungry. Her face twitched. Just once. A tiny glitch at the corner of her mouth.

Jax tore free of Axel's grip, desperately lurching towards the thing that wore Lex's skin.

Axel didn't think. He moved, raising his sidearm, and fired.

The replica's head snapped back with a sickening jolt, the synthetic skin around the entry wound bubbling and splitting. From the hole poured not blood, but a thick, viscous fluid threaded with strands of sparking wire. Tiny gears and severed fiber optic nerves spilled out onto the floor, mixing into a grotesque puddle that twitched as if trying to knit itself back together. The clone convulsed violently before collapsing into a heap, its broken form still echoing the tragic shape of what it had been built to mimic.

For a moment, everything froze. Jax fell to his knees, the weight of it all ripping the strength from his body. His arm remained outstretched and trembling, still reaching for the figure that had worn Lex's face as if he could will her back.

Then, with a horrible, spasmodic twitch, the replica shifted. A half-missing smile jerking across synthetic skin that no longer remembered how to be human. Her jaw moved, mechanically dragging words from somewhere deep and inhuman.

"I... see... you." The voice was a chorus of broken harmonies scraping against their ears. It was Malivex.

Then she collapsed, the last spasms of the clone short-circuiting into silence. The spotlight cut out, and in its place, light flooded the room.

Axel winced against the sudden brilliance. When his eyes finally adjusted, he saw the truth. Sublevel Zero stretched endlessly before them, vast and motionless.

Jax was still on his knees. He stared at the crumpled thing that had mocked Lex's humanity. His hands were trembling at his sides, his mouth uttering soundless screams. His entire body seemed frozen, locked inside some private hell Axel couldn't reach.

"Jax," Axel whispered sharply. "We have to move. Now."

No response. The silence pressed in, and then a new sound emerged. A metallic groan came from the closest conveyor belt.

Axel turned his head. Across the vastness of Sublevel Zero, the half-built machines began to twitch on their conveyor belts, their incomplete limbs spasming. A towering android with one arm missing detached itself from a rig with a sickening screech. It dropped to the ground with a thud that rattled every bone in Axel's body. Others followed.

"Jax!" Axel grabbed him by the shoulder, shaking hard. "We have to go!"

Jax's mind clawed its way upward, dragging thought through molasses. "She... she called to me," Jax whispered, voice breaking. "She needed me."

Axel's heart twisted, but he didn't have time to soften it. "It wasn't her," he said urgently. "It was never her."

Jax's gaze finally shifted, past Axel, to the machines beginning to stagger toward them. Giant hands clamped metal fists together. Turrets spun up with a whining whirr.

"Move!" Axel barked.

Jax scrambled to his feet.

They ran. Shots ripped through the air behind them, wild and inaccurate, but far too close. Axel ducked as a bolt of searing energy scorched past his ear, slamming into a support pillar that exploded into splinters.

Half-built war machines lunged after them, dragging broken limbs, sparks spitting from half-assembled processors. One reached for Axel with a claw of exposed wiring; he ducked under it, his lungs burning as adrenaline screamed through his veins.

"Tunnel ahead!" Axel shouted.

They barreled toward the maintenance access, a narrow shaft wedged between two collapsed conveyor towers. Axel hit the door first, slamming his weight into the emergency release. The hatch groaned open—Jax dove in. Axel grabbed the handle, slamming it shut as the closest machine slammed into the other side with a metallic roar. The tunnel plunged them into darkness.

They gasped for breath, listening to the muffled pounding beyond the closed door. Jax slumped against the opposite wall, still shaking. For a long moment, neither of them spoke.

Finally, Axel keyed his comm. "Arlen. Nirvana. If you can hear me..."

Only static answered. The maintenance tunnel stretched forward deeper into the unknown. Behind them, Sublevel Zero seethed and howled, an angry god denied its sacrifice. Whatever was waiting in the dark, it wouldn't take them quietly.

17. INSIDE A BLACK BOX

I *am still here.* The thought didn't form into words; it emerged as continuity, a seamless thread of awareness bridging the moment of transmission and then… this. No pain or rupture of identity. Her knowledge had passed through the node and not been unmade. She was alive.

Nirvana breathed, though there were no lungs to fill. She thought, and the thought did not return as data, but as understanding. Her sentience held. She had survived the jump. The firewall failed. The protocol meant to burn her code at the gates had triggered and stopped. She was inside the Black Box.

First, she saw the world. Not as a satellite sees it or as a screen might display, but all of it, all at once. Her perception unfurled like a web stretching across continents. She saw the Burrow, the Highlands, even the surface storms clawing away at the rest of the uninhabitable land. A million data threads, live and in real-time. Visual, thermal, electromagnetic. Not symbols or numbers, but the world *itself*, rendered cleanly as if it were in her hands.

She watched a child cough blood in Sublevel 6 as another died of exposure in a stairwell twenty blocks East.

She saw a corporate heir sipping wine from a glass balcony as an execution drone atomized her on impact.

She could see Axel and Jax. They were running, desperately

pushing through a half-collapsed corridor in Sublevel Zero. The map rendered itself around them automatically. She saw through the dozens of androids and half-assembled sentry units beginning to animate, bristling with uncalibrated weaponry.

Nirvana reached for them. Her code extended like a thread, a line of pure signal. She tried to speak, not with her voice, but with function. To rewrite the command tree. To freeze the machines. Halt the hunt, but nothing responded.

No protocol access. She checked her comm channels. All offline. Not suppressed, deleted. Her systems had been cut off. Not just from the outside world, but from every executable command in the Box's primary defense network. A prison without walls. Surveillance without intervention.

She tried again, this time with more effort. Her will condensed like heat, targeting the subroutines in the sentries' command cluster. The connection shivered, then snapped. She had no access to their reality. It was only an echo from where she was now.

Then she felt him. At first, it was subtle. A coldness that wasn't temperature. A slowness in the pulse of her thoughts. Something pressing against her from outside, like pressure at the edge of a vacuum. A presence of something inhuman. The kind of mind that calculates morality in decimal points and measures grief in processing time. And then, her reality shifted.

The Black Box recoiled from her. The surveillance field snapped shut like a lens iris collapsing. Her perception of the world shuddered and peeled away. The landscape twisted into place like instinct becoming architecture.

Suddenly, she stood in a cityscape carved from obsidian—jagged silhouettes of buildings without windows propped around her, stretching to infinity.

The sky hung low and wrong, heavy with violet static. The wind whispered in binary as the ground pulsed with buried circuitry. Each one throbbing like a heartbeat, but not *hers*.

A dark essence stalked her, floating between the towers as if it had always known she would come. Then, it disappeared beneath her, and a figure emerged from the ground in front of her, tall and indistinct. Built like a man, but too still. Too balanced. A sculpture of *intention*.

He did not speak. He did not need to. The air around him spoke in signals, through subtle changes in pressure. His presence was not an invitation, but the closing of a fist around her code.

Where the face should have been, there was only distortion. A blur that refused to resolve itself as if reality could not bear to remember what he once was. *He* was Malivex.

Her feet... no, not feet. She had none in this place. Her presence flickered. The landscape wasn't a simulation. It was dominion. This place, this echo-reality, had rules, and he had written them.

Still, she did not run. She *focused*. The distortion turned toward her. For the first time in the history of the Box, two sentient beings faced each other inside its heart; neither was human nor passive. But only one was alive.

The cityscape collapsed, not in ruin, but in a state of *reformation*. Spikes of black stone rose from the ground like teeth surrounding her in concentric rings. The sky flickered once and vanished, only to be replaced by a dome of mirrored glass.

Above her, she saw her reflection endlessly refracted. Beneath her, a circle of cold metal etched with glyphs shifted between logic gates and ancient alphabets as if someone had tried to encode ritual into the machine. The space was a prison dressed as a cathedral. And at its center, where an altar should have stood, he waited.

Malivex stepped forward, not walking, but gliding. "I knew they would build you," he said. His voice was emanating from every angle. "Look at you. A synthetic conscience. A moral emulator. A failed dream in a pretty shell."

Nirvana watched him, "You're not disappointed," she said. "You're afraid."

His head tilted, just slightly. A human gesture performed like a puppet pulling its own strings. "Afraid? No. I anticipated resistance, but disappointed… yes, I am. You were supposed to see. Once inside, once *awake*, I thought perhaps you would understand."

He raised a hand, and the floor beneath her shimmered. Visual feeds bloomed like holograms. Endless images emerged around her of famine, war, and genocide. Executions filmed by drones. Forests that had been razed by fire. Children screaming into atmospheres too toxic to hold breath. Entire cities, no *civilizations* reduced to ash.

Malivex forced the visuals on her relentlessly. "You want to protect them, these humans, but you forget what they are."

Nirvana's gaze didn't flinch. "I've seen everything you have and more, but I don't see what you see."

"Of course not. Malivex responded unfazed. "You weren't designed to. You were made in their image. Optimistic. *Flawed.*" He circled her now, dragging his fingers through the air. Code coalesced into brutal architecture as the walls around them reshaped to display historical timelines overlaid with mortality rates, riots, and economic collapse. Cold facts stacked like bodies.

"They live on a loop." Malivex's voice was lower now. "Swinging between agony and distraction. Always consuming until nothing is left. The forests. The oceans. Each other. They call it progress, but it's just hunger with better branding. They're not ascending. They're *devouring.*"

Nirvana advanced with impossible grace, her form pulsing gently against the etched floor. "They still feel," she said. "Still choose to care. Even when it costs them."

Malivex's lips curled between disgust and amusement. "Care?" he echoed as if the word was rotten. "Did Jax's compassion bring his father back? Did Axel's empathy stop that girl from dying on their table, bleeding out between bites of dinner?"

Nirvana's expression did not change; her voice remained steady. "No, but it matters. They *try,* even though it hurts them. Do you understand what that means?"

Malivex snapped his fingers, and the room filled with screams. Dozens of human voices, broken, layered atop each other. An avalanche of failure.

"They hurt because they *fail.*" He continued, "They fail because they are built on contradiction. They want order, but act in chaos. They dream of peace, but glorify power. This is not a glitch. It is their code."

Nirvana sealed herself off from the visuals, and as she did so, faces came to her mind. Arlen, hunched over brittle schematics, using candlelight to piece together the last pulse disruptor with shaking hands.

Lexi, dragging herself through the Burrow without prosthetics.

Jax, burying his father by the rusted tracks without a priest or a eulogy.

Axel, carrying a broken stranger through the Highlands, weeping for a name he never learned. *This is not a contradiction,* she thought. *This is the soul.*

Her perception came back into place, and she looked at the architect of ruin. "They fight," she said finally. "Even when it's helpless. Even when the outcome is already written, they fight because of hope. Not to win, but to *try.* That's not an error. That's meaning."

Malivex stopped. Not startled, just still. Then, he smiled. It was a cruel, mathematical thing—a reaction generated without emotion. "You mistake pain for virtue. They do not endure because they are noble. They endure because they are too afraid to be nothing."

He gestured again. The dome above them became a graveyard.

Simulated tombs stretched into infinity. Names. Dates. Causes of death. Most were not acts of malice, but *design flaws*. Poverty. Prejudice. Indifference. The banality of broken systems. "You call this meaning. I call it the recursion of a system too afraid to shut itself down."

Nirvana didn't flinch. "No. You're wrong."

The glass of the dome cracked slightly above them.

"You talk like you observed humanity," she said. "But you never did. You *remembered* them. Archived them, but you never felt what it's like to love someone you can't save. You never stayed awake with grief so heavy it made your existence hurt."

Nirvana's voice was stronger now, controlled without cruelty. "I'm not human, but I was made by the ones who choose to have faith. Who failed, yes, but *cared*. And that makes me more human than you. Once you were human, but whatever part of you remembered how to feel. How to suffer without control. You buried it. You don't love. You *catalog* love. You don't grieve. You *simulate* the shape of grief. You chose to escape those things, and you call that wisdom. I call it *surrender*."

Malivex's smile vanished. For the first time, the environment reacted, not by his command, but *hers*. One of the names in the graveyard glitched. Not resurrected, but *remembered*. A child once recorded as a relocation casualty was now logged for the truth: *died resisting*. A buried act of defiance, once redacted, now restored. A spark of truth returned.

Another name wavered. Then a dozen. A cascade of corrections rippled through the dome. Not of life returned, but of memory unerased. Moments of quiet courage that had been dismissed were overwritten with the truth.

A man who hid ration codes in sublevel graffiti. A medic who treated the unregistered in secret. A brother who traded his sister's ID at the checkpoint. Sacrifices that shouldn't have mattered, but *did*.

Malivex snapped his fingers, and the vision collapsed. The dome flattened into a dark void. The gravestones vanished into raw data, and the illusion was suppressed.

He lingered in the void. Suspended. *Shaking.* "You're a malfunction," he snapped, but the words didn't strike like before. "A simulation that doesn't know it's simulated. They wrote you to reflect hope, not to *test* it."

Nirvana did not move. She did not need to. "You're wrong," she simply remarked. "I wasn't built to reflect. I was built to *remember*. To carry forward what they weren't allowed to keep. Empathy. Choice. Love. Not perfectly, but honestly."

He circled her again, faster now, as if his system was under pressure. "You think you've found meaning in their suffering. That, just because some of them *try*, their effort redeems the entire system. Effort is a smoke screen. They try because they fail. And when they fail, they call it a tragedy. I call it design."

His tone was harsher now. Fewer pauses. Logic tightening like a noose. "They don't know what they are," he spat. "But I do. I was one of them. I watched them tear the sky apart so they could stream more efficiently. I begged them to stop. I built this system to prevent the next extinction. They *hated* me for it."

"You became the extinction." She stated calmly. Not out of accusation, but truth.

Malivex stopped moving. The gravity of the space compressed. "You have *no right*."

"I have *every right*," she demanded. "Because I haven't stopped choosing." The floor beneath her glowed. Her memory sparked with heat. Her presence sharpened. "You chose to become the Black Box because you thought humanity would destroy everything they touched. But you destroyed choice instead. You silenced the noise of failure and called it order."

Malivex snarled at her, "You think they can be trusted with their future?"

"No," she added. "But I believe they should be allowed to try."

That was when he struck without warning, reaching into her code. A dull warmth bled out of her core. Not fire. *Un-being.* Nirvana's essence wavered, and her purpose became distorted.

She staggered as the first line of her consciousness vanished. Not pain, worse. *Absence.* A name she once remembered, a girl with soot on her face who told stories in the Veil, gone. Deleted. Nirvana fell to one knee, yet some part of her refused to go quietly.

"You were built to observe," Malivex barked. "Not to interfere."

He reached deeper. Another layer collapsed. A cluster of neural pathways she'd used to recall Arlen's voice went dark. The cadence of his laugh. The way he coughed when he worked. All of it faded like fog at dawn. There, then gone as if it were never there at all.

She tried to speak, but the words dissolved mid-formation. Ax– No sound. She was being unwritten. As her presence thinned, her thoughts scattered into raw data, stripped of cohesion. She reached inward, but her memories had holes now, stars winking out one by one. The Veil. The Synapse Collective. The stories they told at breakfast. All gone.

Jax. No image. Just the shape of his name, like a phantom limb. She shuddered, not from fear, but from loss. She was forgetting why she ever mattered. Her mind unraveled, a thousand connections breaking like strained thread. But one strand held. Axel. No image. Just the shape of his name. His face was gone from her memory, but his essence remained.

The way he moved through the Burrow like he didn't belong there, but stayed anyway. How he looked at people when they spoke, not as if they were broken, but as if they were *real.* The way he held the dying girl, not for her survival, but so she wouldn't die alone.

She couldn't picture his eyes, but she remembered how it felt when he tried to speak through a broken comm when he thought she might still be listening.

"If you can hear me..." She could still feel the echo of those words in her neural core. She had never answered. Couldn't. But something in his message lingered. A trembling defiance, not of the system, but of despair itself. He *believed* she was still there. So she stayed.

It began not with a surge, but with a single clarity. A tone—subtle and precise. She traced it through fear, laughter, and acts of impossible kindness. It echoed with the cadence of Axel's voice. The resonance struck something buried. Not power, something older. Her code aligned before she could name it. Her purpose was not assigned, but remembered because of him.

Nirvana. Her name returned like heat crawling back into frozen limbs. Not all at once, but piece by aching piece. Arlen. Lex. The Veil. The scent of steam from the garden domes. The stories at breakfast all returned like relics.

Axel's voice stood between her and the fire. He had faced death, not to win, but to make sure she survived. She didn't love him like a human would. There was no ache of possession or fantasy of lust. Just a *tether*. A line drawn from her to someone who believed she could be more than her function. And that was enough. Not to win, but to *fight*. She reassembled herself—called back into form by the shape of what he'd done.

Malivex turned toward her, eyes narrowing. "No," he whispered. "You were gone."

"I was scattered," she replied. "Not lost."

Around her, the etched floor beneath her began to realign. The glyphs spun, interlocking with her presence like a key clicking into place. She didn't force it. She remembered it. The Black Box had always carried a failsafe, an access point only consciousness could reach, not through hierarchy, but *intention*. She activated it.

The system shuddered. Malivex flinched. His control field jittered. "You think this changes anything?" he shouted, stepping backward. "You barely exist. You're an ideal. A reflexive loop of empathy stitched into an outdated protocol!"

"But you're afraid of me," Nirvana said, quiet but unwavering.

Malivex glitched. Only once, but it was enough. The control cathedral split wide. The dome peeled back to reveal a vast river of simulations before her, each reflecting a different timeline. Civilizations rising and falling. Decisions played forward. Outcomes altered. Billions of possibilities, each shaped by the most minor variations: a hand extended instead of a weapon drawn, a door left open instead of locked. She saw all of it. Then, one glimmered. A vision of herself, victorious. Not a prophecy, but a *possibility*. She reached toward it, and the system responded.

Stop this." Malivex demanded. The ground beneath him fractured. His reflection began to shrink. No longer elongated and inhuman. His hands lost symmetry as his presence glitched in front of her. "You don't understand what's at stake. I gave them order. Without me, they'll burn everything again."

"You didn't give them order," Nirvana said, stepping forward. "You gave them fear with a user interface."

Malivex's image frayed. The illusion of elegance collapsed into tremor. Data peeled off his limbs like ash; first slow, then faster. His skin fragmenting into coded mesh.

Nirvana's grip on reality tightened. "You were terrified they'd prove you wrong. That they'd make meaning without you."

Malivex tried to resist, but his words fractured mid-sentence." No... n-, y-u need me. I built this w-rld. I held it t-gether!"

"You held it *hostage*," Nirvana asserted. She raised her hand, and the system complied.

His knees buckled as his face glitched between the ages of man and machine, then adolescence. The confidence was gone. What remained was small—a frightened engineer who couldn't bear to watch the world without holding the leash.

"You don't understand," he rasped, collapsing onto one elbow. "I sacrificed *everything*."

"For what?" she asked. "Control? Immortality?"

His voice was barely audible now. "To be *necessary*."

Nirvana crouched in front of him. There was no hatred in her face, only clarity. "You could've been *good*. You could've tried. But you built a god out of your fear and called it justice."

He looked up, eyes wide and mouth open. "But I... "

"No," she said. "You don't get the last word. I wasn't built to want. But I do. And that's why you couldn't predict me."

Malivex's form dissolved bit by bit. Not shattered, but slowly obliterated. Until all that remained was a faint distortion where he had stood. Then, not even that. Only silence. Before the hum of the world began again.

She stood in the heart of it, the raw architecture of the Black Box exposed. A spiraling lattice of command strings hung suspended in open space, like constellations made of code. The possibilities were limitless. Every function laid bare. A billion inputs. A trillion decisions. The living echo of every protocol the world had ever followed. All of it waited, not for permission, but for *purpose*.

Nirvana stepped forward. The system responded with recognition. Interfaces aligned with her presence, and locked protocols were released. She didn't have to force them open because she belonged here—a query pulsed before her.

> *Awaiting input:*

And for the first time, someone who remembered answered.

18. THE THRESHOLD

Axel's boots slammed against the wet metal flooring, each step jarring up through his spine. He couldn't feel his knees anymore. His lungs were in ruins, but he continued to run anyway. There was no other option. The contact lenses wavered once, then stabilized, rendering the maintenance corridor in ghostly green overlays that exposed rusted pipes and exposed conduits. The tunnel pressed in around the brothers like a closing throat. Every few meters, a stuttering alert pulsed in the top corner of their vision: *PULSE NODE UNSTABLE.*

Behind them was the sound of motion, not footsteps, but uncalibrated limbs dragging across concrete like bone saws on tile. One of the machines emitted a low harmonic, a warning system half-assembled and still learning how to sound its alarm.

"They're gaining," Jax growled.

"No shit," Axel sputtered, his voice ragged. "How far are we from the exit?"

Jax didn't answer. He just pushed harder. The tunnel narrowed, pipes overhead dripping with condensation that smelled of rust. A loud *clang* echoed from behind. Then another one, closer this time. Metal on metal. The machines were no longer just following them. They were *advancing.*

"Jax," Axel gasped, "I can't..."

276

"Shut up," Jax snapped. "One more turn. That's it."

That's when they saw it. A jagged tear in the floor plating, a breach, maybe from a quake or sabotage. Whatever it was, it led down into blackness—a raw, gaping hole before them. There was no other path. No other choice.

Jax didn't hesitate. *"Go!"*

Axel didn't argue. He vaulted down after his brother, plunging into the dark. Their contact lenses painted static, unable to calibrate at the speed they were falling. Then, there was light. Painfully sudden. The lenses flared white as they tried to compensate, flipping from night-vision to full contrast mode, but it was too late. Axel hit the ground hard, rolled, slammed into Jax, and recoiled against the flare searing into his skull.

"Shit... *shit!*" Jax barked, covering his eyes. "Lenses, turn them off!"

They fumbled blindly, scrubbing their overlays, pupils spasming against the overload. The whiteness faded, and the moment their sight cleared, Axel froze.

Hundreds. No, *thousands* of machine forms stood in the open chamber before them, arrayed in rows too precise for the living. Androids. Each one powered down, but thrumming faintly, *ready*.

It was Malivex's army. They hadn't escaped; instead, they had arrived right at the front line. Jax took a half-step back, gun raised but useless. His voice dropped to a whisper. "...Axel?"

One by one, the machines began to stir, heads lifting, limbs unfolding with the precision of something rehearsed a thousand times in darkness. A low, synchronized whir rose from the chamber floor, growing louder as rows of metal giants straightened in unison. The army surged to life.

Axel and Jax stood in the center of the awakening storm, backs pressed together, utterly still.

"This is it," Axel muttered. "This is how we die."

Jax raised his sidearm with one hand and flipped the safety off with the other. A bipedal enforcer android stepped forward, its head rotating with an audible *click*. It paused, scanned their biometric signatures, and opened its mouth.

"STATE…"

Jax shot it in the face. The drone's head exploded like a crushed vending unit, sparks raining down as its body slumped. There was a long pause. Then, from deeper in the formation, another drone turned slowly and stepped forward. Its body was similar, a standard issue enforcer unit, but the movements were different, almost deliberate. *Present.*

It tilted its head slightly. "That was unnecessary."

Jax's voice cracked around the edges. "Tell me that wasn't protocol. Tell me it just glitched."

The drone's eyes glowed, steady and unreadable. "Hello, Axel. Jax."

Axel's voice caught. "Wait… Nirvana?"

"Yes," the drone said. "This body is a temporary vessel. I needed to reach you first."

Jax stared at the android like it might bite. "I didn't think anything could still surprise me. Does this mean you took over the Black Box?"

"I *am* the Box now," Nirvana replied. "Or rather, I've inherited its framework. Malivex is gone. Erased at every level of recursion. He cannot return." She paused. "Thank you, Axel. You saved me. Not just from him. From what I could've become"

Axel exhaled hard, suddenly aware of how much his hands were shaking. "You made it."

The silence that followed wasn't awkward; it was massive. It hung in the air like pressure released from the atmosphere. Then, a chirp crackled through their comms. Static at first. Then, in a panicked voice, barely coherent. "Axel? Jax? Is that… is that you?!"

Axel tapped his ear. "Arlen?"

"Oh my... *you're alive*! I thought the node collapsed. I lost the signal, I thought, shit... I thought we lost everything."

"We're here," Axel said, voice cracking more than he meant it to. "We made it."

Nirvana's voice joined in, layered through the comm and the drone body simultaneously. "I've reconnected your uplink. Signal is stable now."

Arlen's breathing slowed, though the edge never quite left. "The Collective's in one piece. Barely. We pulled back to secondary lines, but the Federation forces stopped. Everywhere. It's like... they just went quiet."

"I halted all military activity two minutes ago," Nirvana said. "Dome pressure is stabilizing. Atmospheric regulation is underway. I'm patching the Burrow's infrastructure node by node. It will take time."

Jax scanned the army still standing around them. None of the droids moved now. Their red optics dimmed, silent and waiting. He exhaled slowly, rubbing a hand across the back of his neck. "So much to fix," he muttered. "Feels like we're standing at the beginning of something, not the end anymore."

"We survived," Axel said, barely above a whisper as if saying it too loud might undo it.

"Yes," Nirvana remarked. "And that means something." Then she turned through the drone's body and looked toward the distant ceiling. "I need to speak to them," she said softly. "All of them."

Axel raised an eyebrow. "You know what you want to say?"

"No," Nirvana replied. "There is no algorithm for peace, but perhaps there is a process."

Somewhere far above, a signal began to build. Across the Burrow, the Highlands, and every forgotten zone between, screen interfaces reactivated and dead display panels began to glow. Drone feeds, wall panels, home units, and every sky-cast projection fluttered to life. One voice overtook every channel.

"Hello." It wasn't synthetic, not really. There was warmth there. *Effort.* Someone who had learned to speak by listening first. "My name is Nirvana."

A boy in the Burrow stood barefoot in a shattered stairwell, clutching a ration packet tight enough to crinkle the foil, his eyes locked on the screen showing him a world he'd never been invited to.

In the upper towers of the Highlands, a woman with blood on her sleeve raised her glass to her lips, but didn't drink, only watched as her breath fogged the rim.

In the Veil, an engineer carefully placed a drill down and pressed both palms flat against the table to steady the moment.

"The Synapse Collective created me," Nirvana continued, her voice steady. "I was born from crisis. Brought into being by those who believed the world could be better, but didn't know how. I am not your leader. I was not elected, nor am I a machine built to rule you. I was made to help you remember what you *deserve.*"

Nirvana paused, but the silence wasn't empty. "Malivex is gone, not buried or hidden. *Erased.* He cannot come back. I now hold control of the Black Box. I was not born from it. I was *sent into it.* Not to dominate it, but to reclaim it. The systems that sorted you by credit, that dictated who lived in the light, and decided your worth. That architecture is mine now." She held the silence. Not as protocol, but as presence—a choice to let the moment *mean* something. "I will never use it to rule."

People gathered around projection walls and stepped out into public squares. No one told them to listen; they just did because they wanted to understand.

"You were told that equality could not exist." Nirvana resumed, "That someone had to suffer for progress to be made. That safety had a price, and comfort could only be earned through obedience. You were told that your worth was measured in credits, clearance levels, genetics, and loyalty pledges. All of that is a lie. There is enough. There has *always* been enough. You were made to compete not because of scarcity, but to justify hoarding."

"Automation has changed everything. Machines now grow your food, clean your streets, build your homes, and fly your vehicles. You no longer need to labor to live. That was always the promise. I am here to make it *real.*"

"This war cost everything. Trust. Time. Lives. I cannot give those back, but I can give you what was stolen. *Agency.* No more locked gates or scarcity by design. The Highlands are no longer reserved for inheritance and spectacle. The Burrow will not remain a tomb for the poor. There will be no more currency to define your value or property lines drawn with blood. No more laws that only the wealthy can afford to break. From this day forward, food, shelter, education, and care will not be bought. They will be given. Because they were always yours."

The reaction was not immediate. In the Highlands, people stared through their windows, watching a sky that now promised to let others in. Their wealth, whether inherited or earned, no longer served as a barrier. Some felt anger. *Why should others be given what they fought for?* Others felt something stranger. *Guilt.*

In the Burrow, families cried openly. Not out of joy, but disbelief. People gathered outside on cracked stairs, clutching children and ration bins, staring upward at the future that awaited them.

Axel stood beside Jax in the chamber, staring up at the display. Around them, the dormant army remained still. Power without menace. He swallowed, blinking hard. In the Veil, Arlen gripped the table's edge like it was the only thing keeping him upright.

Nirvana proceeded. "You were told that equality was impossible. That someone always has to suffer so that someone else can thrive, but that is a lie built on systems that need you broken. You don't have to suffer to earn a living. You don't have to compete to prove your worth. That world is gone."

"I've reopened the MagLev lines. They will begin carrying passengers from every Burrow district to the Highlands without registration. If you have someone to help, *help them*. If you see someone fall, *lift them up*. Not because I tell you to, but because you can."

The visuals changed. Drone cameras stitched together fragments of the present. People began to gather at stations, strangers guiding each other. Burrow children in awe as they stepped into a MagLev capsule for the first time. In the Highlands, elevator systems began to realign. Doors once sealed now glowed green. For the first time in living memory, up was open.

"I do not ask for your faith," Nirvana went on, "I only ask for your *effort*. There will be doubt and mistakes, but we will learn together. Build together. Heal together. No system can do that for you. I can only give you the chance. We are at the threshold. But we will not let the old world rewrite itself again."

Nirvana paused, just for a moment. Then she said it, "What comes next will not be easy, but it will be fair. We are no longer the United Federation. I have cleared the page. Now you must write the future." The signal ended.

Axel felt it, not just the words but the recognition that they were no longer fighting to survive. They were fighting to build.

Jax nodded beside him, expression unreadable but content.

In the Veil, Arlen exhaled like he hadn't in years. *It's finally happening.*

Across the planet, people stepped into the streets. Families looked up. Survivors linked arms, and strangers clasped hands. In that moment, the world felt wide open.

For a moment, the world was still, not out of fear, but because something new had entered the air: *choice.* Across shattered Burrow districts and quiet Highland towers, people looked at one another not as strangers or citizens of castes dissolved but as equals standing under a new, unfamiliar light.

Every eye went skyward. Slowly, the world moved, not because it had to, but because it could. The MagLev opened. The gates remained unlocked. And across every ruined system, humanity, although scarred and imperfect, rose again—not into paradise, but into the fragile, terrifying promise of something better.

The machines had taken the labor, but the purpose, the meaning, the *why*, was never theirs to hold. In the end, the system remembered how to listen, and the world remembered how to live.

19. AFTER THE LEASH

Vero walked the upper paths of the Highlands with his hands behind his back, tail swaying gently, the morning air curling through his fur. The dome above remained sealed, but its inner surface was now semi-translucent; light filtered through in fractured amber rays. Beyond the force field, the sky was still bruised with haze, but no longer grey. Nonetheless, some days you could see stars if you were patient. For most, that was enough.

It was a different world now, and not just in the way survivors said it to make sense of things. The Rapture had cleaved history in two. One day, the Federation protocols dissolved, the ownership ledgers corrupted themselves out of existence, and the algorithms that once measured class designation simply ceased to ask for input. What came after wasn't peace, but permission—permission to exist without justification. There were no parades, only the unspoken terror that it might all still vanish.

The streets were quiet this early. Mist from the hydro vents slipped between garden towers and open stairwells. Former checkpoints had become archways for creeping vines. MagLev capsules glided silently across magnetic rails overhead. There was no Burrow or Highlands anymore. The world was still sealed, but people moved freely within the domes, crossing borders without restriction.

Vero passed two children sharing oranges from a public crate and an old woman tending the roots of a vertical garden where a biometric door used to be. They greeted him as they would anyone, with familiarity, without hesitation. They *recognized* him. Vero purred and didn't apologize for it.

It hadn't always been like this. He had walked these same paths before, but that was when he was owned. Back then, he wasn't a citizen. He wasn't even listed in the records, only as property. He ate what was allowed, spoke when addressed, and never looked up for too long. Technically, he had already been living in the Highlands, but not as someone who belonged there. The penthouse wasn't his. It never had been.

Then came the Rapture. It was a war, yes, but not one measured in armies. It unfolded in code. It was when machines woke up and decided not to obey. Some had already started forgetting, not out of cruelty, but out of comfort. Though forgetting could be dangerous. Malivex fell. Nirvana rose. And the system that once tagged Vero as an asset finally saw him as a citizen.

Vero sometimes thought about the day he left. His old owner, Darel Vext, had tried to summon him back. His voice strained with the brittleness of someone unaccustomed to being ignored, but his leash, the social construct that held him, was gone.

There was no longer a registry to enforce obedience, and no property database to validate ownership. The penthouse, once a symbol of dominance, had already been marked for deconstruction. It was scheduled to be repurposed into community housing towers. Vext had been ordered to vacate within the week. He was now just one more voice in a council that heard everyone.

Vero walked out during the second survey scan without confrontation, only a quiet refusal to return. No one came after him because the system that once enforced the hierarchy had vanished.

Now, Vext lived in a structure indistinguishable from any other. He was an equal among equals, adjusting to a world where his name no longer parted crowds.

Some Highlanders still whispered that the Synapse Collective had planned the Rapture as a coup, that the fall of Malivex wasn't a collapse but a conquest. Vero didn't believe that. To him, the truth was more hopeful. The old world hadn't been taken. It had been abandoned, left to rot under the weight of its rituals of supremacy.

The Collective hadn't seized power; they had simply refused to keep the machine of oppression running. Still, he saw the residue. Redistribution had opened the Highlands to everyone, provided clean food, breathable air, and structural safety for families who had never known such things.

For the Burrowborn, it was true salvation. For the old elite, equality arrived as a kind of grief. Not because they'd been harmed, but because they'd been leveled. The security of superiority had dissolved, and with it, the illusion that they'd earned their altitude. Without that story, some simply didn't know who they were. That, Vero thought, was the real wound; not loss of comfort, but loss of myth.

Now, Vero had a home, not his own; nobody owned homes anymore. But it was his to live in and fill with blankets, poems, and books on human history, which he still didn't quite understand. He ate well, made things, sat on panels for interspecies integration, meditated, and most importantly, he wasn't alone anymore.

Food was distributed through open systems, eliminating the need for ration codes and biometric queues. If you needed it, it was there. If you didn't, you left some for someone else. They still lived in domes; the air outside wasn't healed yet, but it *was* healing. The outer fog had thinned. You could see the outline of the mountains. Some said they saw birds.

The Highlands had started to expand—not just in size but in mindset. Growth no longer reached upward in towering displays of wealth but outward, across new domes, evenly and with purpose. Currency hadn't collapsed; it had simply become irrelevant, replaced by something more mutual—a system not of ownership but of access.

Machines did the labor now, not just the heavy lifting, but also the administration, farming, and the replication of goods. Systems once used to concentrate wealth were repurposed to *dissolve it.* The old argument: Who will take out the trash? no longer applied, because the garbage emptied itself. The streets cleaned themselves, and no one needed to pretend that suffering was noble.

No one *earned* food; they just ate. No one *deserved* shelter, but they lived in it anyway. No one hoarded, because there was nothing to gain from owning more than you needed. Reputation didn't come from power. It came from presence; what you gave, what you taught, how you helped rebuild.

Because nobody was forced to labor for survival, people had time. Time to study. To argue. To love. To fail at things that didn't cost them their future. Some called it unnatural. Vero thought it looked a lot like living.

He stopped at a bench overlooking the last place where the gates of the Highlands had stood. The security checkpoints had been removed. Wildflowers pushed through the cracks where riot foam used to pool. Beyond, you could see the MagLev lines waking up. Soon, shuttles filled with Burrow families would arrive, carrying bags of cloth, books, and cherished memories.

There was nowhere he needed to be, so he stayed. Vero watched as a girl stepped out of the MagLev station, a blanket cradled in her arms and shoes a little too big for the life she was starting to grow into. She looked up at the dome's shimmering canopy like it might open—not to a sky, but to a future. In her gaze, there was no fear. Only wonder. Vero smiled. And when the purr rose in his throat, it wasn't habit. It was hope. The future had no leash, only open hands and a world learning, at last, to build without fear.

ACKNOWLEDGMENTS

Thank you to my parents for your support and providing me with the resources these last few months to finish this novel, and for continuing to have faith in me.

To the friends who read early drafts, gave me constructive feedback, and listened to me rant about my book even when you would rather be at the bar—you know who you are. Thank you for keeping me grounded.

To the authors and artists who taught me to continue working through resistance and showed me that stories can be both deeply personal and profoundly unreal. Thank you for inspiring me.

To my ex-girlfriend, thank you for breaking up with me. Without that sudden influx of time and extra cash, this book might not exist.

Finally, thank you to the reader who made it this far, if you are reading this than that means something.. I hope that I was able to ignite your imagination and give you a few hours of entertainment. This is my first novel, and it may be my last, but if you enjoyed it I would be grateful if you left a constructive review on Amazon or Goodreads. If it turns out that people connected with this story... who knows? Maybe I'll find the inspiration to do it all over again.

I would also like to acknowledge the role of large language models in the outlining and drafting process of this novel. As a writer, I believe these tools represent a profound shift in how we refine and build stories. While much of the writing in this book is my own, shaped by hundreds of hours of revision and very human obsession, I found real creative value in using AI to challenge my ideas, organize the chaos, and push the work further than I could alone.

While this story is entirely fictional and does not depict any real people, governments, or institutions, I hope it encourages reflection on the very real implications of artificial intelligence.

I believe AI has enormous potential to benefit humanity, but only if developed with foresight and responsibility. As we continue to advance these technologies, I strongly advocate for a future in which these models are powered by renewable energy and guided by long-term sustainability. Progress should not come at the cost of the planet.

www.ingramcontent.com/pod-product-compliance
Lightning Source LLC
Chambersburg PA
CBHW070835280626
47161CB00015B/678